Peter Tremayne is the fiction pseudonym of a well-known authority on the ancient Celts, who utilises his knowledge of the Brehon law system and seventh-century Irish society to create a new concept in detective fiction.

This is Sister Fidelma's ninth appearance in novel form: *Absolution by Murder*, *Shroud for the Archbishop*, *Suffer Little Children*, *The Subtle Serpent*, *The Spider's Web*, *Valley of the Shadow*, *The Monk Who Vanished* and *Act of Mercy* are also available from Headline.

'This collection is an essential canonical text for Sister Fidelma acolytes' *Publisher's Weekly*

'Fidelma's fans will welcome this first-ever collection, many stories of which are appearing here for the first time' *Kirkus Reviews*

'A treasure trove of small gems for historical mystery fans' *Booklist*

'The Sister Fidelma books give the readers a rattling good yarn. But more than that, they bring vividly and viscerally to life the fascinating lost world of the Celtic Irish. I put down *The Spider's Web* with a sense of satisfaction at a good story well told, but also speculating on what modern life might have been like had that civilisation survived' Ronan Bennett

To discover more about the world of Sister Fidelma, visit her own website at
http://www.sisterfidelma.hypermart.net

Hemlock At Vespers

A Collection of Sister Fidelma Mysteries

Peter Tremayne

HEADLINE

First published in Great Britain in 2000 by
HEADLINE BOOK PUBLISHING

First published in paperback in 2000
by HEADLINE BOOK PUBLISHING

10 9 8 7 6 5 4 3 2 1

ISBN 0 7472 6432 5

Typeset by Letterpart Ltd
Reigate, Surrey

Printed and bound in Great Britain by
Clays Ltd, St Ives plc.

HEADLINE BOOK PUBLISHING
A division of Hodder Headline
338 Euston Road
London NW1 3BH

www.headline.co.uk
www.hodderheadline.com

For John Carson,
Fan and collector *extraordinaire*!
To celebrate twenty-one years of friendship.
May your shadow never grow less.

Table of Contents

Introduction

❧

The Sister Fidelma mysteries are set during the seventh century AD, mainly in her native Ireland.

Sister Fidelma is not simply a religieuse, a member of what we now call the Celtic Church, whose conflicts with Rome on matters of theology and social governance are well known; as well as differences in rituals, the dating of Easter and the wearing of a dissimilar tonsure, celibacy was not widely practised and many religious houses contained individuals of both sexes who raised their children to the continued service of God. Fidelma is also a qualified *dálaigh*, or advocate of the law courts of Ireland, using the ancient Brehon Law system, for in those days a woman could be equal with men in the professions, and many women were lawyers and judges. There is even a record of a female judge, Brig, correcting on appeal a judgement given by a male judge, Sencha, on women's rights.

Those who have followed Sister Fidelma's adventures in the series of novels, might be unaware that she made her debut in short story form. Four different stories featuring Fidelma appeared in separate publications in October, 1993, and it was the gratifying response to these stories which precipitated Fidelma into the series of novels but also created a demand for even more short stories. The fifteen stories in this volume comprise the complete set of those published at the time of writing this introduction.

To let you into a secret, there might not have been a Fidelma. Under my other hat, as a Celtic scholar, I decided to create the concept of an Irish female religieuse who was a lawyer, and who solved crimes under the ancient Brehon law system of Ireland, primarily to demonstrate to a wider audience both the fascinating system of law and the prominent role that women could and did play in that period. I drafted the first story back in 1993 and named her Sister Buan. It was an ancient Irish name meaning 'enduring'. Buan occurs in myth as a tutor to the hero Cúchulainn. When I showed the draft to my good friend Peter Haining, the anthologist and writer, he loved the story but threw up his hands in dismay at the name. He felt it did not trip easily off the tongue, in spite of its shortness.

As I reflected on this, suddenly, Fidelma was born. It was as if she had been waiting to catch my attention. The name is also ancient and means 'of the smooth hair'. Once Fidelma 'introduced herself' to me, everything fell into place. The name gave her an instant background and a family! The masculine and feminine forms of the name were popular among the royal dynasty of the Eóghanachta who ruled the kingdom of Munster from their capital of Cashel (Co. Tipperary). And it was an area that I knew very well, for my father's family had been settled sixty kilometres from Cashel for seven hundred years, so the records show. Cashel was always a special place, of magic, mystery and history for me.

Fidelma immediately identified herself as the daughter of the Cashel King Failbe Fland, who died c. AD 637–639 within months of Fidelma's birth. So before she became a religieuse and a lawyer, Fidelma was raised as an Eóghanachta princess.

Sharp-eyed readers will have realised that a strict chronology is followed in the novels. The stories have so far taken place between the spring of AD 664 and autumn of AD 666. In fact, AD 666 was a rather busy time for Fidelma, for it was the year in which four full-length mystery adventures occurred between January and October.

The adherence to a set chronology also applies to the short stories. Fidelma first appears at around the age of twenty-seven, having trained not only at an Irish ecclesiastic centre but at the secular college of the Brehon (Judge) Morann at Tara; there was, incidentally, a real Brehon Morann whose dictums still survive in ancient Irish literature. Fidelma achieved her qualifications in law to the level of *Anruth*, one degree below the highest that the ecclesiastical and secular colleges could bestow. While she was a student, she had an unhappy *affaire do coeur* with a warrior who was not her intellectual equal. She subsequently joined the community which had been founded by St Brigid at Kildare, and while there started to achieve a reputation by solving difficult legal mysteries, and her talents as a lawyer, a *dálaigh* in Old Irish, became much in demand.

Readers may be surprised that Brother Eadulf plays no part in any of the short stories. In the first novel, *Absolution By Murder* (1994), Fidelma, already with a reputation as an incisive inquirer and legal expert, was sent to advise the Irish delegation at the Synod of Whitby in AD 664. This Synod was the location of the famous historical debate between representatives of the Celtic and the Roman Church. It was there that Fidelma met the young Saxon monk named Brother Eadulf. He had been trained in Ireland but now wore the tonsure of Rome. He became her 'Doctor Watson' and has featured in every novel except one – *Suffer Little Children* (1995).

In the following stories, Fidelma solves the mysteries without Eadulf's good-intentioned but often critical assistance. This is because several of the stories, such as 'Murder in Repose' and 'Murder by Miracle', are set prior to Fidelma's meeting with Eadulf. Other early adventures include 'Tarnished Halo', 'Abbey Sinister' and 'Our Lady of Death'.

In the early stories Fidelma announces herself as 'Fidelma of Kildare'. A reader once wrote and asked me why she decided to leave that community, for after the events of *Suffer Little Children* (1995) she takes on the mantle of 'Fidelma of Cashel'. The reason why she began her break with Kildare is explained in 'Hemlock at Vespers'. At that point Fidelma set off to discuss her problems with her mentor, the chubby faced and kindly Abbot Laisran of the great abbey of Durrow where, in the mid-seventh century, young men and women from no fewer than eighteen nations were recorded as students. 'A Canticle for Wulfstan' is located at Durrow. While there Fidelma receives a cry for help from a close friend of her childhood, a girl she has grown up with, who has been accused of murdering her husband and her own child. The resultant adventure is told in 'At the Tent of Holofernes'. On her continued journey to the High King's court at Tara, she finds that the Yellow Plague, which devastated much of Europe at this time, had been instrumental in causing the death of the joint High Kings, Diarmuid and Blathmac. The new High King, Sechnasach, is about to be installed, but part of the ceremonial regalia has gone missing. Civil war and anarchy could result if Sechnasach cannot prove his right to the kingship by showing the sacred artefacts. The mystery is recounted in 'The High King's Sword'.

From there Fidelma is off to Whitby to attend the Synod, as previously mentioned. From Whitby she travels to Rome with a party which includes Brother Eadulf. In the autumn of that year, the newly appointed Archbishop of Canterbury is found murdered in the papal palace – an actual historical event – and Fidelma and Eadulf join forces to solve the mystery in *Shroud for the Archbishop* (1995). The short story, 'The Poisoned Chalice' is also set in Rome in this same period but, again, Eadulf is not in attendance. Fidelma and Eadulf part company in Rome, Fidelma to return home while Eadulf is to instruct the new Archbishop of Canterbury, Theodore of Tarsus, before accompanying him to England to assume his duties. Fidelma makes her journey home via the Abbey of Nivelles, an Irish foundation in the forest of Seneffe, in what is now Belgium, where 'Holy Blood' takes place.

Back in Ireland in AD 665 she returns to Tara, the setting for 'A Scream from the Sepulchre'. She then goes back to Kildare where she solves a race course mystery in 'The Horse that Died for Shame'. She is uncomfortable at Kildare, and when her brother, Colgú, sends her a message to return to Cashel because her help is urgently needed, she sets off eagerly.

It is still AD 665 and the King of Cashel, Fidelma's cousin, Cathal Cú Cen Máthair, is dying. His last request sends Fidelma into a harrowing adventure in an out-of-the-way Irish monastery featured in *Suffer Little Children* (1995). By the end of the story King Cathal has died and Fidelma's brother, Colgú, the heir-apparent, is now King of Munster. Indeed, Colgú was a great historical Munster King who ruled between AD 665–678/701.

Fidelma is reunited with Eadulf in extraordinary circumstances in the midwinter setting of a remote abbey in south-west Ireland featuring in the next book *The Subtle Serpent* (1996). The adventure culminates in January AD 666. From then on Fidelma and Eadulf join forces and Munster's capital, Cashel, becomes their base. They remain in partnership in *The Spider's Web* (1997), *Valley of the Shadow* (1998) and *The Monk Who Vanished* (1999). Only now and then does Fidelma find herself without Eadulf's assistance, for example in the short stories 'Invitation to a Poisoning' and 'Those That Trespass'.

Welcome, then, to a period which we mistakenly call 'The Dark Ages'. For Ireland, it was an 'Age of Golden Enlightenment', when law, order, literacy and the recording of knowledge created one of the most fascinating European civilisations; a time when missionaries from Ireland, singly and in groups, set off to spread learning and literacy as far east as Kiev in the Ukraine, north to Iceland and the Faroes, and south to Spain and across the Alps into Italy, to Taranto where an Irish monk named Cathal became St Cataldus, patron saint of the city. It was a time of high artistic achievement, the production of the great illuminated Gospel books, of breath-taking metal-working, the fabulous reliquaries, book shrines, chalices and crosses; of a native literature that is second to none and, of course, a fascinating law system and social order that in many ways, was as advanced in its philosophy and application as our own.

But, and there is always a 'but', in the affairs of mankind, it was a very human age, encompassing all the virtues and vices that humans are prey to; virtues and vices that we can recognise and understand today. The motives for crime have remained unaltered over the centuries, and in seventh-century Ireland there was still a need for a keen-eyed examiner with an analytical mind, yet often with a humane interpretation of the law for, as Fidelma herself once remarked, 'law is not always justice'. So we can now follow the good Sister into a world which may be one in which the superficial surroundings are unfamiliar to us but in which we still recognise the same fears, envies, loves and hates that have and do exist in all ages and in all civilisations.

Peter Tremayne

Hemlock at Vespers

∾

S ister Fidelma was late. The vesper-bell had already
ceased proclaiming the arrival of the sixth canonical
hour, the times set aside for prayers, long before she reached
the dusk-shrouded gates of the grey stone abbey building.
The services were over and the community had already filed
into the refectory for the evening meal as she, having
cursorily brushed the dust of travel from her, entered and
hurried towards her place with arms folded into her habit,
her head bent in submissive attitude.

While her head was lowered, the keen observer might have
noticed that there was little else that was submissive about
Sister Fidelma's bearing. Her tall, well-proportioned figure,
scarcely disguised by her flowing robe, carried the attitude of
a joy in living, a worship of activity, rather than being cowed
by the sombre dignity associated with a religieuse. As if to
add to this impression, rebellious strands of red hair broke
from beneath her head-dress adding to the youthful colouring
of her pale, fresh face and piercing green eyes which hardly
concealed a bubbling vitality and sense of humour.

The refectory hall was lit by numerous spluttering oil
lamps whose pungent smell mingled with the heavy aroma
of the smoky turf fire which smouldered in the great hearth
set at the head of the chamber. Lamps and fire combined to
generate a poor heat against the cold early spring evening.

1

The abbess had already started the *Gratias* as Sister Fidelma, ignoring the scandalised or amused glances from the lines of Sisters – each expression fitting their individual characters – slipped into her place at the end of one of the long tables and genuflected, slightly breathlessly, and with more than seemly haste.

'*Benedic nobis, Domine Deus, et omnibus donis Tuis quae ex lorgia liberalitate Tua sumnus per . . .*'

The sudden cry of agony was followed by several seconds of shocked silence. Then the cry, a harsh male howl, came again, followed by a crash of someone falling and the sound of breaking pottery. Sister Fidelma, eyes wide at the unexpectedness of the interruption, raised her head. Indeed, all those in the great refectory hall of the abbey had done so, peering around with excited whispers.

All eyes came to stare towards the end of the hall, to the table which was usually occupied by the visitors to the House of Blessed Brigid in Kildare. There was a commotion near the table and then Sister Fidelma saw one of the community hurry forward to where the abbess, and the other leading members of the House of Brigid, stood behind their table which was placed on a slightly raised platform to dominate the hall.

She saw Sister Poitigéir, whom she recognised as the sister-apothecary, lean forward and whisper excitedly into the abbess's ear. The abbess's placidity of features did not alter. She simply inclined her head in dismissal of her informant.

By this time a babble of sound had erupted from the hundred or so members of the community gathered to partake of their evening meal following the celebration of vespers.

The abbess banged her earthenware mug on the table for silence, determined to finish the formula of the *Gratias*.

'. . . *sumnus per Jesum Christum Dominum nostrum. Amen.*'

Across the hall, Sister Fidelma could see two members of

the community labouring to carry what appeared to be a man's body from the refectory. She saw Follaman, a large, ruddy-faced man, who looked after the male guests at the community's hostel, enter the refectory and help the sisters with their burden.

'*Amen.*' The word echoed raggedly but there was scarcely another sound as the hundred members of the community slid into their seats. This was the moment when the meal usually began with the handing round of bread, but the abbess held up her hand to prevent the monitors from commencing to dispense the meal.

There was an expectant silence. She cleared her throat.

'My children, we must delay our repast a moment. Our guest has been taken ill and we must await the report of our sister-apothecary who believes that our guest may have eaten something which has disagreed with him.'

She stilled another eruption of excited murmuring with a sharp gesture of her thin white hand.

'While we wait, Sister Mugain shall lead you in the devotion . . .'

Without further explanation, the abbess swept from the platform while Sister Mugian began intoning a mixture of Latin and Irish in her shrill voice:

> *Regem regum rogamus*
> *In nostris sermonibus*
> *anacht Nóe a luchtlach*
> *diluui temporibus*

> King of Kings
> We pray to you
> Who protected Noah
> In the day of the Flood

Sister Fidelma leant close to Sister Luan, a gawky girl, beside whom she sat.

3

'Who was the person who was carried out?' she asked softly.

Sister Fidelma had only just rejoined her community after a two week journey to Tara, the royal capital of the five kingdoms of Ireland, seat of the High King.

Sister Luan paused until the strident tones of Sister Mugain paused in her chant:

> *Regis regum rectissimi*
> *prope est dies Domini . . .*

'It was a guest lodging in the *tech-óired*. A man named Sillán from Kilmantan.'

Each religious house throughout the country had a quarter named the *tech-óired*, a hostel where travellers lodged, or where important guests were given hospitality.

'Who was this man, Sillán?' demanded Sister Fidelma.

An imperious hand fell on her shoulder. She started nervously and glanced up, firmly expecting a rebuke for talking during the devotions.

The hawk-like features of Sister Ethne gazed disapprovingly down at her, her thin lips compressed. Sister Ethne, elderly and pinched faced, was feared by the younger members of the community. Her pale, dead eyes seemed to gaze through anyone she looked upon. It was whispered that she was so old that she had been in the service of Christ when the Blessed Brigid had come to this spot a century before, to establish the first religious house for women in the country under the great oak tree from which her church took the name Kildare, the Church of the Oak. Sister Ethne was the *bean-tigh*, the house steward of the community, whose job it was to oversee the internal affairs and running of the community.

'The abbess requires your presence in her chamber immediately,' Sister Ethne sniffed. It was a habit with her. She could speak in no other way except to punctuate her sentences with disapproving sniffs.

Wondering, Sister Fidelma rose and followed the elderly religieuse from the hall, knowing that the eyes of all the sisters were following her in curiosity, in spite of their bent heads as they continued their pious chanting.

The Abbess Ita of Kildare sat before a long oak table in the chamber which she used as her study. Her face was set and determined. In her fifties, Ita was still a handsome, commanding woman, whose amber eyes usually shone with a quiet jocularity. Now it was hard to see their expression for they sparkled unnaturally in the flickering reflective light of the two tall beeswax candles which lit the shadowy room. The sweet scent of wild hyacinth and narcissus blended to give a pleasant aroma to the chamber.

'Come in, Sister Fidelma. Was your trip to Tara successful?'

'It was, Mother Abbess,' replied the girl as she moved into the chamber, aware that Sister Ethne had followed her in and closed the door, standing in front of it with arms folded into her habit.

Sister Fidelma waited quietly while the abbess seemed to gather her thoughts. The abbess's gaze suddenly seemed to become preoccupied with a pile of half a dozen small rocks which lay on the table. She rose, with an apologetic gesture, and gathered them up, dropping them into a receptacle. She turned, reseating herself with a contrite smile.

'Some stones I was gathering to create a small rock garden,' she felt urged to explain. 'I dislike clutter.' Abbess Ita bit her lip, hesitated and then shrugged, coming abruptly to the point.

'Were you in the refectory?'

'I was. I had just arrived at Kildare.'

'A problem has arisen which is of great concern to our community. Our guest, Sillán of Kilmantan, is dead. Our sister-apothecary says he was poisoned.'

Sister Fidelma tried to conceal her astonishment.

'Poisoned? By accident?'

'That we do not know. The sister-apothecary is now examining the food in the refectory hall. That was why I forbade our community to eat.'

Sister Fidelma frowned.

'Do I take it that this Sillán began to eat before you had finished the *Gratias*, Mother Abbess?' she asked. 'You will recall that he cried in agony and collapsed while you were not yet finished.'

The abbess's eyes widened a little and then she nodded, agreeing with the point.

'Your perception justifies your reputation as a solver of mysteries, Fidelma. It is good that our community is served by one skilled in such matters and in the laws of the Brehons. Indeed, this is why I asked Sister Ethne to bring you here. I know you have just returned from your journey and that you are fatigued. But this is a matter of importance. I would like you to undertake the immediate inquiry into Sillán's death. It is imperative that the matter be cleared up as quickly as possible.'

'Why so quickly, Mother Abbess?'

'Sillán was an important man. He was in this territory at the request of the Uí Failgi of Ráith Imgain.'

Sister Fidelma realised what this meant.

Kildare stood in the territory of the petty kingdom of the Uí Failgi. The royal residence of the kings of the Uí Failgi was situated at the fortress of Ráith Imgain, to the north-west of Kildare on the edge of the wasteland known as the Bog of Aillín. Several questions sprang into her mind but she bit her lip. They could be asked later. It was clear that the abbess had no wish to incur the enmity of Congall, the petty king of the territory, who was known simply as the Uí Failgi, for, under the Brehon Law, the petty king and his assembly granted the land to the community of Kildare and they could just as easily drive the community out if displeased. All ecclesiastical lands were granted by the clan assemblies for there was no such thing as private property within the

6

kingdom of Ireland. Land was apportioned and allotted at the decision of the assemblies which governed the tribes and kingdoms.

'Who was this man Sillán, Mother Abbess?' asked Sister Fidelma. 'Was he a representative of the Uí Failgi?'

It was Sister Ethne who volunteered the information, punctuating the sentences with sniffs.

'He was an *uchadan*, an artificer who worked in the mines of Kilmantan; so Follaman, who looks after our hostel, told me.'

'But what was he doing here?'

Did the abbess cast a warning glance at Sister Ethne? Sister Fidelma caught only an involuntary movement of Sister Ethne's eyes towards the abbess and by the time Fidelma glanced in her direction the abbess's features were calm and without expression. Fidelma exhaled softly.

'Very well, Mother Abbess. I will undertake the inquiry. Do I have your complete authority to question all whom I would wish to?'

'My child, you are a *dálaigh* of the Brehon Court,' the abbess smiled thinly. 'You are an advocate qualified to the level of *Anruth*. You do not need my authority under law. You have the authority of the Brehons.'

'But I need your permission and blessing as head of my community.'

'Then you have it. You may use the *tech-screpta*, the library chamber, to work in. Let me know when you have something to report. Go with God. *Benedictus sit Deus in Donis Suis.*'

Sister Fidelma genuflected.

'*Et sanctus in omnis operibus Suis*,' she responded automatically.

Sister Ethne had placed two rough, unglazed earthenware lamps, their snouts fashioned to support a wick, to light the dark shadowy vault which was the *tech-screpta*, the great library of the community which housed all the books and treasures of the House of the Blessed Brigid. Sister Fidelma sat at the library table, in the chair usually occupied by the *leabhar-coimdaech*, the librarian who guarded the great works contained in the chamber. The treasure trove of manuscript books hung in rows in the finely worked leather book satchels around the great chamber. The *tech-screpta* of Kildare even boasted many ancient 'rods of the *fili*', wands of hazel and aspen on which Ogham script was carved from an age long before the scribes of Ireland had decided to adopt the Latin alphabet with which to record their learning.

The *tech-screpta* was chilly in spite of the permanent fire which was maintained there to stop dampness corroding the rows of books.

Sister Ethne, as steward of the community, had volunteered to aid Sister Fidelma, by finding and bringing to her anyone she wished to examine. She sniffed as she endeavoured to adjust the lamps to stop abrasive smoke and reeking tallow odour from permeating the library chamber.

'We will start by confirming the cause of Sillán's death,' Sister Fidelma announced, once she had noticed that Sister Ethne had finished her self-appointed task. After a moment's reflection she went on: 'Ask the sister-apothecary to join me here.'

Sister Potigéir was nervous and bird-like in her movements, reminding Sister Fidelma of a crane, moving with a waddling apprehensiveness, now and then thrusting her head forward on her long neck in an abrupt jerking motion which seemed to threaten to throw the head forward off the neck altogether. But Sister Fidelma had known the sister-apothecary since she had joined the community at Kildare and knew, too, that her anxious idiosyncrasy disguised a keen and analytical mind when it came to the science of botany and chemistry.

'What killed Sillán of Kilmantan?'

Sister Poitigéir pursed her lips a moment, thrusting her head forward quickly and then drawing it back.

'*Conium maculatum*,' she pronounced breathlessly.

'Poison hemlock?' Sister Fidelma drew her brows together.

'There was no questioning the convulsions and paralysis. He expired even as we carried him from the refectory hall. Also . . .' she hesitated.

'Also?' encouraged Sister Fidelma.

Sister Poitigéir bit her lower lip for a moment and then shrugged.

'I had noticed earlier this afternoon that a jar containing powdered leaves of the plant had been removed from my apothecary. It was there this morning but I noticed it was missing two hours before vespers. I meant to report the matter to the Mother Abbess after the service.'

'Why do you keep such a poison in your apothecary?'

'Properly administered, it can have good medicinal use as a sedative and anodyne. It serves all spasmodic affections. We not only have it in our apothecary but we grow it in our gardens which are tended by myself and Follaman. We grow many herbs. Hemlock can heal many ailments.'

'And yet it can kill. In ancient Greece we are told that it was given to criminals as a means of execution and among the Jews it was given to deaden the pain of those being stoned to death. I have heard it argued that when Our Lord hung upon the Cross He was given vinegar, myrrh and hemlock to ease His pain.'

Sister Poitigéir nodded several times in swift, jerky motions.

Sister Fidelma paused a moment or two.

'Was the poison administered in the food served in the refectory?'

'No.'

'You seem positive,' Sister Fidelma observed with some interest.

'I am. The effect of the poison is not instantaneous. Additionally, I have checked the food taken to the refectory for the evening meal. There is no sign of it having been contaminated.'

'So are you saying that the poison was administered before Sillán entered the refectory?'

'I am.'

'And was it self-administered?'

Sister Poitigéir contrived to shrug.

'Of that, I have no knowledge. Though I would say it is most unlikely.'

'Why?'

'Because taking poison hemlock results in an agonising death. Why drink hemlock and then enter into the refectory for an evening meal if one knows one is about to die in convulsions?'

It was a point that seemed reasonable to Sister Fidelma.

'Have you searched Sillán's chamber and the guest quarters for the missing jar of powdered hemlock leaves?'

Sister Poitigéir gave a quick, nervous shake of her head.

'Then I suggest that is your next and immediate task. Let me know if you find it.'

Sister Fidelma asked to see Follaman next. He was a big burly man, not a religieux but a layman hired by the community to take care of the guest quarters. Each community employed a *timthirig*, or servant, to look after its *tech-óired*. It was Follaman's job to look after the wants of the male guests and to undertake the work that was too heavy for the female members of the community and assist the Sisters in the harder chores of the community's gardens.

Follaman was a broad shouldered, foxy haired man, with ruddy complexion and watery blue eyes. His face was dashed with freckles as if a passing cart had sprayed mud upon him. He was in his mid-forties, a man without guile rather like a large boy, still with the innocent wonder of youth. In all, a simple man.

'Have you been told what has transpired here, Follaman?'

Follaman opened his mouth, showing blackened teeth. Sister Fidelma noticed, with some distaste, that he obviously did not regard his personal cleanliness as a priority.

He nodded silently.

'Tell me what you know about Sillán.'

Follaman scratched his head in a bemused fashion.

'He was a guest here.'

'Yes?' she encouraged. 'When did he arrive at Kildare?'

Follaman's face lightened with relief. Sister Fidelma realised that she had best put direct questions to the man for he was not the quickest wit she had encountered. She assessed him as slow in thought, without perceptive subtleness.

'He came here eight nights ago, Cailech.' Follaman addressed all the Sisters formally by the title 'Cailech', the term given by the lay people to all religieuses meaning 'one who had taken the veil' from the term *caille*, signifying a veil.

'Do you know who he was? What brought him here?'

'Everyone knows that, Cailech.'

'Tell me. For I have been away from Kildare these last two weeks.'

'Ah, yes. That is so,' agreed the big man, having paused a moment to examine what Sister Fidelma said. 'Well, Cailech, Sillán told me that he was a *bruithneóir*, a smelter, from the mines in the Kilmantan mountains.'

'What mines would those be, Follaman?'

'Why, the gold-mines, Cailech. He worked in the gold-mines.'

Sister Fidelma successfully prevented her eyes from widening.

'So why was he in Kildare? Surely, there are no gold-mines here?'

'It is said that the Uí Failgi asked him to come here.'

'Indeed? But do you know why?'

Follaman shook his head of reddish hair.

11

'No, Cailech, that I do not. He spent but little time in the guest-house, sleeping there and then leaving at daybreak only to return for the evening meal.'

'To your knowledge, where was Sillán during this afternoon?'

The big man scratched his chin thoughtfully.

'It was today that he came back early and stayed in his chamber in the guest-house.'

'Was he there all afternoon?'

Follaman hesitated. 'He went to see the abbess soon after he returned. He was with her a while and then he emerged from her chamber with anger on his face. Then he returned to his own chamber.'

'Did he say what had angered him?'

'No, Cailech. I asked him whether he required anything. That being my duty.'

'And did he call for refreshment?'

'Only for water . . . no, he asked for mead. Nothing else.'

'Did you take the mead to him?'

'I did. In a stone jar from the kitchens.'

'Where is it now?'

'I have not tidied the guest-house. I think it must still be there.'

'Do you know what poison hemlock is?'

'It is a bad thing. That I know.'

'Do you know what it looks like? The shape and colour of the plant?'

'I am only a poor servant, Cailech. I would not know. Sister Poitigéir would know such things.'

'So Sillán called for mead. And you took it to him. Did he drink it straight away, or did you leave the jar with him?'

'I left it with him.'

'Could anyone have tampered with the jar?'

Follaman's brown creased with a concentration of effort.

'I would not know, Cailech. They could, I suppose.'

Sister Fidelma smiled. 'Never mind, Follaman. Tell me,

are you sure that Sillán stayed in the *tech-óired* all afternoon until vespers?'

Follaman frowned and then shook his head slowly.

'That I would not be sure of. It seemed so to me. And he began preparing to leave the abbey at first light. He packed his bags and told me to ensure that I had saddled his chestnut mare in readiness.' Follaman hesitated and continued sheepishly. 'That was when he had to accompany me to the stables, Cailech. So, yes, he did leave the hostel after all.'

'For what purpose did he go to the stables with you?' frowned Sister Fidelma, puzzled.

'Why, to show me his horse. We have several whose shades are the same to me. You see, I lack the ability to tell one colour from another.'

Sister Fidelma compressed her lips. Of course, she had forgotten that Follaman was colour-blind. She nodded and smiled encouragingly at the big man.

'I see. But Sillán made no mention of what had angered him, or why he had decided to depart?'

'No, Cailech. He just said that he was bound for Ráith Imgain, that is all.'

The door opened and Sister Poitigéir returned. Sister Fidelma glanced towards her and the sister-apothecary nodded swiftly in her bird-like manner.

Follaman looked from one to the other, puzzled.

'Is that all, Cailech?'

Sister Fidelma smiled reassuringly.

'For the time being, Follaman.'

The big man left the library room. Sister Fidelma sat back and studied the closed oak door with a frown. There was a discordant bell ringing distantly in her mind. She rubbed the bridge of her nose for a moment, exhaling in annoyance as her thoughts became no clearer. Then she turned to the anxious Sister Poitigéir with an inquiring gaze.

'I found a jug of mead in the chamber occupied by Sillán. While the mead disguises the unpleasant odour of the hemlock, nevertheless I was able to discern its traces. A draught of such a mixture would be enough to kill a strong man. But there was no sign of the jar of crushed leaves taken from the apothecary.'

'Thank you, Sister Poitigéir,' Fidelma nodded. She waited until the sister-apothecary had left before she stretched back into her chair and sighed deeply.

Sister Ethne regarded her with perplexity.

'What now, Sister? Is your inquiry over?'

Sister Fidelma shook her head.

'No it is not over, yet, Sister Ethne. Far from it. There is, indeed, a mystery here. Sillán was murdered. I am sure of it. But why?'

There came a sudden sound of commotion from the gates of the abbey which were usually shut just after vespers and not opened until dawn. Sister Ethne frowned and strode as rapidly as dignity allowed to the window of the *tech-screpta*.

'There are a dozen horsemen arriving,' she sniffed in disapproval. 'But they bear a royal standard. I must go down to receive them.'

Sister Fidelma nodded in preoccupation. It was only when Sister Ethne went hurrying off to fulfil her duties as the steward of the community that a thought crossed her mind and she went to the window and gazed down at the courtyard below.

In the light of the flickering torches she saw that several riders had dismounted. Follaman had gone forward to help them. There was light enough for Fidelma to see that they were warriors and one carried the royal standard of the Uí Failgi of Ráith Imgain while another held the traditional *ríchaindell*, the royal light which, during the hours of darkness, was always carried to light the way of a great chieftain or his heir-elect. The new arrivals were no ordinary visitors. Sister Fidelma forgot her training, pursing her lips together in a soundless whistle.

★ ★ ★

It was only after the passing of a few minutes that the door of the *tech-screpta* flew unceremoniously open and a stocky young man entered, followed by another man, with a worried-looking Sister Ethne trailing behind. Sister Fidelma turned from the window and regarded the intruders calmly.

The stocky young man took a pace forward. His richly decorated clothes were still covered in the dust of travel. His eyes were steel-grey, piercing as if they missed nothing. He was handsome, haughty and his demeanour announced his rank.

'This is Sister Fidelma,' Sister Ethne's voice almost quavered, even forgetting to sniff, as she nervously pushed her way through the door to stand to one side of the young man.

Sister Fidelma did not move but stood regarding the young man quizzically.

'I am told that Sillán of Kilmantan is dead. Poisoned. I am told that you are conducting an inquiry into this matter.' The phrases were statements and not questions.

Sister Fidelma felt no urge to reply to the young man's brusque manner.

She let her restless green eyes travel over his features, which gathered into a frown at her lack of response. She paused a moment and then moved her gaze to the muscular warrior at his side, before allowing her eyes to move to the clearly nervous Sister Ethne. Fidelma's raised eyebrows asked a question.

'This is Tírechán, Tanist of the Uí Failgi,' Sister Ethne's voice was breathless.

The *tanist* was the heir-elect to the kingship or chieftaincy; an heir was elected during the reign of a king or clan chieftain which prevented any successional squabbles after his death or abdication.

Sister Fidelma moved back to her chair and sat down, motioning Tírechán to be seated on the opposite side of the table to her.

The young prince's face showed his astonishment at her behaviour. Angry blood tinged his cheeks.

'I am Sister Fidelma,' she announced, quietly, before he spoke, for she saw the words forming to burst from his lips. 'I am a *dálaigh* of the Brehon Court, qualified to the level of *Anruth*.'

Tírechán swallowed the words that had gathered on his lips and a look of understanding, mingled with respect, spread over his features. A *dálaigh*, an advocate of the Brehon Court, especially one qualified to the level of *Anruth*, could meet and be accorded equality with any provincial king or chieftain and could even speak at ease before the High King himself. An *Anruth* was only one degree below the highest professorship of *Ollamh* whose words even a High King would have to obey. He regarded Sister Fidelma with a slightly awed air of surprise at her attractive youthfulness for one who held such authority. Then he moved forward and seated himself before her.

'I apologise, Sister. No one had informed me of your rank, only that you were investigating the death of Sillán.'

Sister Fidelma decided to ignore the apology. The *tanist's* bodyguard now drew the door shut and stood before it, arms folded. Sister Ethne, a worried expression still on her features, realising that she had neglected to introduce Sister Fidelma in proper form, stood where she had halted, her lips compressed.

'I presume that you knew the man Sillán?'

'I knew *of* him,' corrected the *tanist* of the Uí Failgi.

'You came here to meet him?'

'I did.'

'For what purpose?'

The *tanist* hesitated and dropped his eyes.

'On the business of my chieftain, the Uí Failgi . . .'

Sister Fidelma smiled thinly as the man hesitated again. He obviously had difficulty speaking of the private business of his chieftain.

'Perhaps I can help?' Fidelma encouraged, as the thought suddenly took shape in her mind. Indeed, the logic of the idea was unquestionable. 'Sillán was from Kilmantan whose hills are full of gold-mines, for do we not speak of that area as Kilmantan of the gold? Sillán was a *bruithneóir*, a qualified artificer. Why would the king of Ráith Imgain ask such a man to come to Kildare?'

The *tanist* stirred uncomfortably beneath her amused but penetrating gaze. Then he responded with almost surly defiance.

'I take it that what I say shall be treated in confidence?'

Sister Fidelma showed her annoyance at such an impudent question.

'I am a *dálaigh* of the Brehon Court.' She spoke quietly. The rebuke needed no further embellishment.

The cheeks of the young prince reddened. But he spoke again as though he had need to defend something.

'Since the twenty-sixth High King of Milesian descent, the noble Tigernmas, first had gold dug and smelted in Ireland, gold has been searched for throughout the country. From Derry and Antrim in the north, south to the mountains of Kilmantan and the shores of Carman, gold-mines have been worked. Yet our need for gold to enhance our courts and to increase our trade is not diminished. We look for new mines.'

'So the Uí Failgi asked Sillán to come to Kildare to search for gold?' Fidelma interpreted.

'The production of gold has not kept pace with the demand, Sister Fidelma. We have to import it from Iberia and other far off places. Our need is keen. Are not the Eóghanacht of Glendamnách at war with the Uí Fidgente over possession of the gold-mines of Cuillen in the land of holly trees?'

'But why would the Uí Failgi think that there was gold at Kildare?' demanded Sister Fidelma abruptly.

'Because an aged man recalled that once the lands of Kildare held such a mine, knowledge of which has long passed from the minds of men. Seizing on this old man's recollection, the Uí Failgi sought out Sillán whose fame for seeking the veins of gold was legend among the mountain people of Kilmantan. He asked Sillán to come to Kildare and seek out this lost mine.'

'And did he find it?'

An angry spasm passed the face of the *tanist*.

'That is what I came to discover. Now I am told that Sillán is dead. Dead from poison. How came this to be?'

Sister Fidelma wrinkled her nose.

'That is what my investigation shall discover, *Tanist* of the Uí Failgi.'

She sat back in her chair and gazed meditatively at the young chieftain.

'Who knows of Sillán's mission here?'

'It was known only to Sillán; to the Uí Failgi; to myself as *tanist* and to our chief Ollamh. No one else knew. A knowledge of the whereabouts of gold does harm to the minds of men and drives them mad. It was better not to tempt them by spreading such knowledge abroad.'

Fidelma nodded absently in agreement.

'So if gold had been discovered, it would have been of benefit to the Uí Failgi?'

'And to his people. It would bring prestige and prosperity to our trade with other kingdoms.'

'Sillán came from the territory of the Uí Máil, might he not have spoken of this enterprise to his own chieftain?'

'He was paid well enough,' frowned the *Tanist* of the Uí Failgi, his features showing that the thought had already occurred to him.

'But if the Uí Máil, or even the Uí Faeláin to the north-east, knew that there was gold in Kildare, surely this might lead to territorial dispute and warfare for possession of the gold? As you correctly state, there is a war between the Uí Fidgente and Eóghanacht of Glendamnách over the mines of Cuillin.'

The *tanist* sighed impatiently.

'Kildare is in the territory of the Uí Failgi. If the neighbouring chieftains invaded Kildare then the wrong would be theirs and our duty to prevent them.'

'But that is not what I asked. Might this discovery not lead to enmity and warfare?'

'That was why the mission was so secret; why none but Sillán was to know the reason for his being in Kildare.'

'Now Sillán is dead,' mused Sister Fidelma. 'Did you know he was leaving here to return to Ráith Imgain tomorrow?'

The *tanist's* face showed his surprise. Then a new look replaced the expression, one of scarcely concealed excitement.

'Which means that he must have found the gold-mine!'

Sister Fidelma smiled a little as she sought to follow his reasoning.

'How do you arrive at that conclusion, Tírechán?'

'Because he had only been here eight days and no other reason would cause Sillán to return to the Uí Failgi other than to report his success.'

'That is a broad assumption. Perhaps he was returning because he realised that this search for a legendary goldmine in Kildare was a hopeless task.'

The *tanist* ignored her observation.

'Are you sure that he was leaving Kildare tomorrow?'

'He told our *timthirig*, Follaman, that he would be leaving,' Fidelma assured him.

The *tanist* snapped his fingers, his face agitated.

'No, no. The mine must have been found. Sillán would not have given up the search so soon. But where, where did he find it? Where is the mine?'

Sister Fidelma shook her head slowly.

'The more important question to be resolved is how Sillán came by his death.'

'By the grace of God, Sister Fidelma, that is not my task,' the young man replied in a thankful tone. 'But my chieftain, the Uí Failgi, will need to know the location of the gold-mine which Sillán must have discovered.'

She rose, inviting the *tanist* to do so.

'You and your men are doubtless staying the night at our *tech-óired*. I suggest, Tírechán, that you now go and cleanse the dust of travel from yourself. I will keep you informed of anything that you should know.'

Reluctantly, the *tanist* rose and motioned to his bodyguard to open the door of the *tech-screpta*. On the threshold he turned hesitantly as if he would press her further.

'*Benedictus benedicat*,' Sister Fidelma dismissed him firmly. He sighed, grimaced and withdrew.

When he had gone, she resumed her seat and spread her hands, palms downward, on the table. For a moment or so she was completely wrapped in her thoughts, forgetting the presence of Sister Ethne. Finally, the *bean-tigh's* rasping cough, as the steward tried to attract her attention, stirred her from her contemplations.

'Is that all now, Sister?' asked the *bean-tigh* hopefully.

Sister Fidelma rose again with a shake of her head.

'Far from it, Sister Ethne. I should now like to see Sillán's chamber in the *tech-óired*. Bring one of the lamps.'

The chamber in the *tech-óired*, or guests' hostel, was not dissimilar to the cells occupied by the members of the community. It was a small, dark, grey stone room with a tiny slit of a window over which hung a heavy woven cloth to keep out the chill night air. A small cot of pine wood, with a straw palliasse and blankets, stood in one corner. A stool and a table were the only other furnishings. On the table stood a single candle. The hostel was provided with only poor lights. The candle was simply a single rush peeled and soaked in animal grease. It gave scant light and burned down very quickly which was why Fidelma had had the foresight to bring one of the oil lamps with her.

Sister Fidelma paused on the threshold of the room and

examined it very carefully as Sister Ethne set down the lamp on the table.

Sillán had apparently already packed for his journey, for a heavy satchel was dumped on the foot of the bed. It was placed next to a smaller work-bag of leather.

Sister Fidelma crossed to the bed and picked up the leather work-bag. It was heavy. She peered inside and saw a collection of tools which, she supposed, were the tools of Sillán's profession. She laid the bag aside and peered into the satchel. These were Sillán's personal effects.

Finally, she turned to Sister Ethne.

'I will not be long here. Would you go to the Mother Abbess and tell her that I would like to see her in her chamber within the hour? And I would like to see her alone.'

Sister Ethne sniffed, opened her mouth to speak, thought better of it, bobbed her head and left the room.

Fidelma turned back to the satchel of personal belongings and took them out one by one, examining them minutely. When she had done so, she explored the interior of the satchel with her fingertips, raising the lamp in one hand and examining the dust on the tips of her fingers with a frown.

She then repeated her careful examination with the tools and implements in Sillán's work-bag. Once again she ran her hand over the dust in the bottom of the bag and examined it carefully in the light.

Only after a careful examination did she replace everything as she had found it.

Then she lowered herself to her knees and began a microscopic examination of the floor, slowly, inch by inch.

It was when she was peering under the wooden cot that what seemed a small lump of rock came in contact with her hand. Her fingers closed around it and she scrambled backwards into the room and held it up to the light of the lamp.

At first sight it seemed, indeed, just a piece of rough-hewn rock. Then she rubbed it on the stone flagged floor and held it once again to the light.

Part of it, where she had abraded it, gleamed a bright yellow.

A satisfied smile spread over her features.

Abbess Ita sat upright in her chair, her calm, composed features just a little too set to be an entirely natural expression. It was as if she had not stirred from the chair since last Fidelma had seen her. Abbess Ita regarded Sister Fidelma with her amber eyes wary as a pine-marten might watch a circling hawk.

'You may be seated, Sister,' the abbess said. It was an unusual invitation, one showing deference to Sister Fidelma's legal status rather than her religious one.

'Thank you, Mother Abbess,' Fidelma replied, as she lowered herself into a chair facing Abbess Ita.

'The hour grows late. How does your inquiry progress?'

Sister Fidelma smiled gently.

'It draws towards its conclusion,' she answered. 'But I am in need of further information.'

Abbess Ita gestured with one hand, a motion from the wrist only, as if in invitation.

'When Sillán came to see you this afternoon, what was said which caused him anger?'

Abbess Ita blinked; the only reaction which expressed her surprise at the directness of the question.

'Did he come to see me?' she asked slowly, parrying as if playing for time.

Sister Fidelma nodded firmly.

'He did, as you know.'

Abbess Ita let out a long sigh.

'It would be foolish to attempt to conceal the truth from you. I have known you too long, Fidelma. It always surprised me that you chose the life of a religieuse rather than pursuing a more worldly existence. You have a perception and a reasoning that is not given to everyone.'

Sister Fidelma ignored the praise. She waited quietly for

the abbess to reply to her question.

'Sillán came to apprise me of certain things which he had discovered . . .'

'He had discovered the lost gold-mine of Kildare.'

This time Abbess Ita could not conceal the faint ripple of muscle as she sought to control the astonishment on her face. She struggled to compose herself for some moments and then her lips became thin in an almost bitter smile.

'Yes. I suppose that you learnt this much from the *Tanist* of the Uí Failgi, whom I am told has just arrived seeking hospitality here. You doubtless know that Sillán was a man skilled in the profession of mining; that he had been sent here by the Uí Failgi to find an ancient gold-mine and explore its potential.'

'I do. But his mission was a secret known only to Sillán, the Uí Failgi and his *tanist*, Tírechán. How did you come to learn about it?'

'Sillán himself came to tell me about it this very afternoon.'

'Not before?'

'Not before,' agreed the abbess with emphasis.

'Then tell me what transpired.'

'It was after noon, well after the noon Angelus, that Sillán came to see me. He told me what he was doing in Kildare. In truth, I had suspected it. He had arrived here eight days ago and carried credentials from the Uí Failgi. What could a man from Kilmantan be doing here with approval of the Uí Failgi? Oh, I had heard the ancient legends of the lost gold-mine of Kildare. So I had suspected.'

She paused for a moment.

'And?' encouraged Sister Fidelma.

'He came to tell me that he had found it, had found the old gold-mine which had been worked centuries ago and had explored some of its passageways. Furthermore, he declared that the gold-seams were still in evidence and were still workable. He was leaving Kildare tomorrow to report his find to the Uí Failgi.'

'Why, then, Mother Abbess, did he break secrecy with the Uí Failgi and tell you this?'

Abbess Ita grimaced.

'Sillán of Kilmantan respected our community and wanted to warn us. It was as simple as that. You see, our abbey lies directly above the mine workings. Once this was known, then there is little doubt that the Uí Failgi would have ordered our eviction from this spot, this blessed spot where the Holy Brigid gathered her disciples and preached under the great oak, founding her community. Even should our community be simply ordered to move a short distance, we would have to give up the holy soil where Brigid and her descendants are buried, their clay mingling with the earth to make it sanctified.'

Sister Fidelma gazed thoughtfully at the troubled face of the abbess, listening to the suppressed emotion in her voice.

'So the only purpose he had in telling you this, Mother Abbess, was to warn the community?'

'Sillán, in his piety, thought it only fair to warn me what he had discovered. He merely wanted to give our community time to prepare for the inevitable.'

'Then what angered him?'

Abbess Ita compressed her lips a moment. When she spoke, her voice was firm and controlled.

'I tried to reason with him. I asked him to keep the secret of the lost mine. At first I appealed to him by virtue of our common faith, by the memory of the Blessed Brigid, by the faith and future of our community. He refused, politely but firmly, saying he was bound by honour to report his discovery to the Uí Failgi.

'Then I tried to point out the greater implications. Should news of the gold-mine be broadcast, then war might follow as it has done at Cuillin.'

Sister Fidelma nodded slowly as Abbess Ita confirmed her own thoughts.

'I am aware of the conflict over the mines at Cuillin, Mother Abbess.'

'Then you will realise that Kildare, while in the territory of the Uí Failgi, is but a short distance from the territories of the Uí Faeláin to the north east and the Uí Máil to the south east with only the desolate plain of the Bog of Aillín to protect us. The word "gold" will cause a fire to be lit in the hearts of chieftains avaricious for the power it will bring. This dear, green spot, now so peaceful and so pleasant, would be stained red with the blood of warriors, and of the people that once lived here in harmony with the green plains and hills of Kildare. Our community of Kildare will be swept away like chaff from the wheat.'

'Yet why did Sillán become angry?' pressed Sister Fidelma.

The Abbess Ita's expression was painful.

'When I had told him this, and when he still insisted that his duty lay in telling the Uí Failgi, I told him that his would then be the responsibility for what followed. I told him that God's curse would pursue him for destroying the peace of this land. That he would be damned in the next world as well as this one. The name Sillán would become the synonym for the destruction of the holy shrine of Brigid of Kildare.'

'What then?'

'His face reddened in anger and he flung himself from the room, averring that he would depart at first light.'

'When did you see him again?'

'Not until vespers.'

Sister Fidelma gazed thoughtfully into the eyes of the Abbess Ita.

The amber orbs smouldered as they reflected back Sister Fidelma's scrutiny.

'You dare think . . .?' whispered the Abbess Ita, her face pale, reading the suspicion in the younger face before her.

Sister Fidelma did not drop her gaze.

'I am here as a *dálaigh*, Abbess Ita, not as a member of your community. My concern is truth, not etiquette. A man lies dead in this abbey. He was poisoned. From the circumstances, it was a poison that was not self-administered. Then by whom and for what reason? To keep Sillán from revealing the secret of the lost mine to the Uí Failgi? That seems a logical deduction. And who stands to gain by the suppression of that knowledge? Why, none but the community of this abbey, Mother Abbess.'

'And the people of the surrounding countryside!' snapped Abbess Ita, angrily. 'Do not forget that in your equation, Sister Fidelma. Do not forget all the blood that will be saved during the forthcoming years.'

'Right cannot be served by wrong, it is the law. And I must judge what is lawful. Knowing that it was the law that I must serve as a *dálaigh* of the Brehon Court, separate from my role as a member of this community, why did you ask me to investigate this matter? You yourself could have conducted the inquiry. Why me?'

'In such a matter of importance, a report from a *dálaigh* of the Brehon Court would carry much weight with the Uí Failgi.'

'So you had hoped that I would not discover the existence of the gold-mine?' frowned Sister Fidelma.

Abbess Ita had risen in agitation from her chair. Fidelma rose so that her eyes were on a level with the Abbess's own agitated gaze.

'Tell me directly, Mother Abbess: did you poison, or arrange to have poisoned, Sillán to prevent him speaking with the Uí Failgi?'

For several moments there was an icy silence. The sort of silence which precedes an eruption of the earth. Then the Abbess Ita's anger faded and a sad expression crossed her face. She dropped her gaze before the younger woman.

'Mine was not the hand that administered poison to Sillán though I confess that the heaviness of my heart lifted when I heard of the deed.'

In the quietude of her cell, Sister Fidelma lay on her cot, fully clothed, hands behind her head, staring into the darkness. She had extinguished the light of her candle and lay merely contemplating the shadows without really registering them as she turned over in her mind the facts of the mysterious death of Sillán.

There was something staring her in the face about this matter, a clue which was so obvious that she was missing it. She felt it in her being. It was there, in her mind, if only she could draw it out.

She had no doubt in her mind that Sillán had been killed because of the knowledge he possessed.

And Sister Fidelma found herself in sympathy with the suppression of that knowledge.

Yet that was not the law, the law that she was sworn to uphold as a *dálaigh* of the Brehon Court. Yet the law was simply a compact between men. Rigid law could be the greater injustice. While the law was blind, in an ideal world justice should be able to remove the bandage from its eyes long enough to distinguish between the unfortunate and the vicious.

Her mind spinning in moral dilemma, Sister Fidelma drifted unknowingly into a sleep.

Sister Fidelma became aware firstly of someone pulling at her arm and then of the dim tolling of the Angelus bell.

Sister Ethne's pale, hawk-like features cleared out of the blurred vision as Fidelma blinked and focused her eyes.

'Quickly, Sister, quickly. There has been another death.'

Fidelma sat up abruptly and stared at Sister Ethne in incredulity. It lacked an hour before dawn but the *bean-tigh* had already lit the candle in her cell.

'Another death? Who?'

'Follaman.'

'How?' demanded Fidelma, scrambling from her cot.

'In the same manner, Sister. By poison. Come quickly to the *tech-óired*.'

Follaman, the *timthirig* of the community, lay on his back, his face contorted in pain. One arm was flung out in a careless gesture and from the still fingers, Sister Fidelma followed the line to the broken pottery on the floor. It had once been an earthenware goblet. There was a dark stain of liquid which had seeped into the flagstone below.

The sister-apothecary was already in the room, having been summoned earlier, and had examined the corpse.

'The goblet contained hemlock, Sister Fidelma,' bobbed Sister Poitigéir quickly as Fidelma turned to her. 'It was drunk in the same manner as Sillán drank his poison. But Follaman drank the liquid in the night and no one heard his final cries.'

Sister Fidelma surveyed the scene grimly then she turned to Sister Ethne.

'I will be with the Mother Abbess for a while. See that no one disturbs us.'

Abbess Ita stood at the window of her chamber, watching the reds, golds and oranges of the rising dawn.

She half-turned as Sister Fidelma entered, then, ascertaining who it was, she turned back to the open window. The sharp colours of dawn were flooding the room with a pleasant, golden aura.

'No, Fidelma,' she said before Fidelma spoke. 'I did not poison Follaman.'

Fidelma's lips thinned.

'I know that you did not, Mother Abbess.'

With a surprised frown, Abbess Ita turned and stared at Fidelma for a moment. Then she motioned her to be seated and slid herself into her chair. Her face was pale and strained. She seemed to have slept little.

'Then you already know who the culprit is? You know how Sillán and Follaman died?'

Sister Fidelma nodded.

'Last night, Mother Abbess, I was struggling to decide

28

whether I, as a *dálaigh*, should serve the law or serve justice.'

'Is that not the same thing, Fidelma?'

Sister Fidelma smiled softly.

'Sometimes it is; sometimes not. This matter, for example, is a case where the two things diverge.'

'Yes?'

'It is obvious that Sillán was killed unlawfully. He was killed to prevent him revealing his knowledge that a gold-mine is situated under these venerable buildings. Was the person who slaughtered him right or wrong to kill him? By what standards do we judge? The taking of a life is wrong by our laws. But if Sillán had disclosed his knowledge, and that knowledge had led to the driving forth of this community from its lands, or had led to warfare between those who would then covet these lands, would that have been justice? Perhaps there is a natural justice which rules above all things?'

'I understand what you are saying, Fidelma,' replied the abbess. 'The death of one innocent may prevent the deaths of countless others.'

'Yet do we have the right to make their choice? Is that not something which we should leave in the hands of God?'

'It can be argued that sometimes God places in our hands the tools by which His will is carried out.'

Sister Fidelma studied the abbess's face closely.

'Only two people now know of Sillán's discovery.'

Abbess Ita raised an eyebrow.

'Two?'

'I know, Mother Abbess and you know.'

The abbess frowned.

'But surely the poisoner of Follaman knows?'

'*Knew*,' corrected Sister Fidelma softly.

'Explain.'

'It was Follaman who administered the hemlock which killed Sillán.'

The abbess bit her lip.

'But why would Follaman do that?'

'For the very reason that we have discussed, to prevent Sillán telling the Uí Failgi about the gold.'

'Yes, but Follaman . . .? He was a simple man.'

'Simple and loyal. Had he not worked here at the abbey as the keeper of the hostel since he was a boy? He loved this place as much as any of our community. He was not a religieux but he was as much a member of the community as anyone else.'

'How did Follaman know?'

'He overheard you and Sillán arguing. I suspect that he purposely eavesdropped on you. Follaman knew, or surmised, what profession Sillán practised. He might well have followed Sillán on his explorations. Whether he did or not is beside the point. When Sillán came back yesterday afternoon, Follaman certainly deduced that he had made some find, for Sillán told Follaman that he would be leaving for Ráith Imgain the next morning. He probably followed Sillán to your room and overheard what passed between you.

'Since you could not act against the laws of man and God, he would serve a natural justice in his own way. He took the jar of poison hemlock from the apothecary and when Sillán asked for a drink, he supplied it. Follaman did not know the precise quantity needed and so Sillán did not suffer the full effects until after the bell called the community into the refectory for the evening meal following vespers.'

Abbess Ita was following Sister Fidelma closely.

'And then?'

'Then I began my investigation, then the *tanist* of the Uí Failgi arrived seeking Sillán or an explanation for his death.'

'But who killed Follaman?'

'Follaman knew that sooner or later he would be discovered. But more importantly in his guileless mind there was also the guilt of having taken a man's life to be considered. Follaman was a simple man. He decided that he should accept punishment. The honour-price of a life. What greater honour-price for the life of Sillán could he offer than his own? He also took a draught of the poison hemlock.'

There was a pause.

'It is a plausible story, Sister Fidelma. But how do you substantiate it?'

'Firstly, when I questioned Follaman, he knew all about Sillán's profession. Secondly, he made two slips. He told me that he had seen Sillán coming from your chamber with anger on his face. Your chamber is on the far side of the abbey to the hostel. Therefore Follaman must have been near your chamber door. But, most importantly, when I asked Follaman if he knew what hemlock looked like, he denied any knowledge.'

'Why is that damning?'

'Because one of Follaman's duties is to help in the herb garden of the community and Sister Poitigéir had just informed me that she grew hemlock in the garden for medicinal purposes; the very plant used in the apothecary came from the garden. And Sister Poitigéir said she was helped in this task by Follaman. He knew what hemlock looked like. So why did he lie to me?'

Abbess Ita sighed deeply.

'I see. What you are saying is that Follaman tried to protect us, protect our community here at Kildare?'

'I am. He was a simple man and saw no other way.'

The abbess smiled painfully.

'In truth, Sister, with all my knowledge, I saw no other path that would have led me to the same result. So what do you propose?'

'There are times when the law brings injustice with it and the triumph of justice is mankind's only peace. So the question is between justice or the stricture of the law.' Fidelma hesitated and grimaced. 'Let it be natural justice. I shall officially report that the result of my inquiry is that Sillán met his death by accident, so did Follaman. A contaminated jug of water, which had been made up by

Follaman to destroy the vermin in the abbey vaults, became inadvertently used to mix with the mead in the hostel. The contaminated jug was not discovered until Follaman had also died.'

Abbess Ita gazed speculatively at Sister Fidelma.

'And what do we tell the *Tanist* of the Uí Failgi about the gold-mine?'

'That Sillán had decided to return to Ráith Imgain because the legend of the gold-mine of Kildare was simply a legend and nothing more.'

'Very well,' the abbess had a smile of contentment on her face. 'If this is what you are prepared to report then I endorse your report with my authority as the head of this community. In such a manner may our community be saved for future generations. For the falsehood of the report, I absolve you from all responsibility and sin.'

It was the smile of the abbess which troubled Fidelma in her decision. She would, for the sake of natural justice, have held her tongue. But the relieved complacency of Abbess Ita suddenly irritated her. And, if she carefully analysed herself, was it not that her pride in her reputation as a solver of mysteries had been pricked?

Sister Fidelma slowly reached into her robe and pulled out the small piece of rock which she had picked up in the chamber that Sillán had occupied. She tossed it on the table. The abbess gazed down at it.

'It was part of Sillán's proof of his discovery. You'd better keep that safe with the other pieces of gold which Follaman gave you after he had poisoned Sillán . . . at your instruction.'

Abbess Ita's face was suddenly ashen and the whites showed around her amber eyes.

'How . . .?' she stuttered.

Sister Fidelma smiled bitterly.

'Do not fear, Mother Abbess. All will be as I have said it was. Your secret is safe with me. What I do is for the good of our community, for the future of the House of the Blessed Brigid of Kildare, and those people who live within the peace of the shadows of these walls. It is not for me to judge you. For that you will have to answer to God and the shades of Sillán and Follaman.'

Abbess Ita's lips trembled.

'But how . . .' she whispered again.

'I have stressed that Follaman was a simple man. Even if he had the wit to understand the implications of Sillán's find for the abbey and the community around it, could he really have taken the poison hemlock and administered it?'

'But you, yourself, have demonstrated he could. Sister Poitigéir told you that Follaman helped her attend the plants in the herb garden and would know what hemlock looked like.'

'Follaman knew what the plant looked like; yes. But he would have to be told what the crushed leaves of hemlock were. You need to discern colours for that. Follaman could not pick out a jar of crushed hemlock leaves by their purple spots and white tips once the distinctive shape had been destroyed. You see, what was staring me in the face the whole while was a simple fact. Follaman was colour-blind. He could not discern colours. Someone would have had to have given Follaman the poison to administer.'

Abbess Ita's lips were compressed into a thin, hard line.

'But I did not kill Follaman,' she said fiercely. 'Even if I admit that I suggested to Follaman that our community would best be served by the demise of Sillán, even if I admit I showed Follaman a method to do that deed, who killed Follaman? I did not do it!'

'No,' replied Fidelma. 'It was as I have said. At your suggestion, Follaman administered the poison to Sillán because you told him it was God's will. You used him as a tool. But he, being a simple man, could not live with the guilt he felt in taking a life. He took his own life in self-retribution. He had not given all the hemlock to Sillán but kept some aside in his room. Last night he drank it as a penance for the deed. His was the penance, Mother Abbess, but yours is the guilt.'

Abbess Ita stared at her blankly.

'What am I to do?' she demanded but her voice broke a little.

Sister Fidelma gave a slight smile of cynicism.

'With your permission, Mother Abbess, I shall be leaving Kildare this morning. I will make my report to the Tanist of the Uí Failgi first. Do not worry. The good of the community is uppermost in my mind. That good outweighs the law. But I shall make a pilgrimage to the shrine of the Blessed Patrick at Armagh to pay penance for the falsehood of my report.'

Sister Fidelma paused and gazed into the troubled amber eyes of the Abbess Ita.

'I cannot help relieve your guilt. I suggest, Mother Abbess, that you acquire the services of a sympathetic confessor.'

The High King's Sword

❧

'God's curse is upon this land,' sighed the Abbot Colmán, spiritual adviser to the Great Assembly of the chieftains of the five kingdoms of Ireland.

Walking at his side through the grounds of the resplendent palace of Tara, the seat of the High Kings of Ireland, was a tall woman, clad in the robes of a religieuse, her hands folded demurely before her. Even at a distance one could see that her costume did not seem to suit her for it scarcely hid the attractiveness of her youthful, well-proportioned figure. Unruly strands of red hair crept from beneath her habit adding to the allure of her pale fresh face and piercing green eyes. Her cheeks dimpled and there was a scarcely concealed humour behind her enforced solemnity.

'When man blames God for cursing him, it is often to disguise the fact that he is responsible for his own problems,' Sister Fidelma replied softly.

The abbot, a thick-set and ruddy faced man in his mid-fifties, frowned and glanced at the young woman at his side. Was she rebuking him?

'Man is hardly responsible for the terrible Yellow Plague that has swept through this land,' replied Colmán, his voice heavy with irritation. 'Why, it is reported that one third of our population has been carried off by its venomousness. It has spared neither abbot, bishop nor lowly priest.'

35

'Nor even High Kings,' added Sister Fidelma, pointedly.

The official mourning for the brothers Blathmac and Diarmuid, joint High Kings of Ireland, who had died within days of each other from the terrors of the Yellow Plague, had ended only one week before.

'Surely, then, a curse of God?' repeated the abbot, his jaw set firmly, waiting for Sister Fidelma to contradict him.

Wisely, she decided to keep silent. The abbot was obviously in no mood to discuss the semantics of theology.

'It is because of these events that I have asked you to come to Tara,' the abbot went on, as he preceded her into the chapel of the Blessed Patrick, which had been built next to the High King's palace. Sister Fidelma followed the abbot into the gloomy, incense-sweetened atmosphere of the chapel, dropping to one knee and genuflecting to the altar before she followed him to the sacristy. He settled his stocky figure into a leather chair and motioned for her to be seated.

She settled herself and waited expectantly.

'I have sent for you, Sister Fidelma, because you are an advocate, a *dálaigh*, of the Brehon courts, and therefore knowledgeable in law.'

Sister Fidelma contrived to shrug modestly while holding herself in repose.

'It is true that I have studied eight years with the Brehon Morann, may his soul rest in peace, and I am qualified to the level of *Anruth*.'

The abbot pursed his lips. He had not yet recovered from his astonishment at his first meeting with this young woman who was so highly qualified in law, and held a degree which demanded respect from the highest in the land. She was only one step below an *ollamh* who could even sit in the presence of the High King himself. The abbot felt awkward as he faced Sister Fidelma of Kildare. While he was her superior in religious matters, he, too, had to defer to the social standing and legal authority which she possessed as a *dálaigh* of the Brehon Court of Ireland.

'I have been told of your qualifications and standing, Sister Fidelma. But, apart from your knowledge and authority, I have also been told that you possess an unusual talent for solving puzzles.'

'Whoever has told you that flatters me. I have helped to clarify some problems. And what little talent I have in that direction is at your service.' Sister Fidelma gazed with anticipation at the abbot as he rubbed his chin thoughtfully.

'For many years our country has enjoyed prosperity under the joint High Kingship of Blathmac and Diarmuid. Therefore their deaths, coming within days of one another, must be viewed as a tragedy.'

Sister Fidelma raised an eyebrow.

'Is there anything suspicious about their deaths? Is that why you have asked me here?'

The abbot shook his head hurriedly.

'No. Their deaths were but human submission to the fearsome Yellow Plague which all dread and none can avoid once it has marked them. It is God's will.'

The abbot seemed to pause waiting for some comment but, when Sister Fidelma made none, he continued.

'No, Sister, there is nothing suspicious about the deaths of Blathmac and Diarmuid. The problem arises with their successor to the kingship.'

Sister Fidelma frowned.

'But I thought that the Great Assembly had decided that Sechnasach, the son of Blathmac, would become High King?'

'That was the decision of the provincial kings and chieftains of Ireland,' agreed the abbot. 'But Sechnasach has not yet been inaugurated on the sacred Stone of Destiny.' He hesitated. 'Do you know your Law of Kings?'

'In what respect?' Sister Fidelma countered, wondering where the question was leading.

'That part relating to the seven proofs of a righteous king.'

'The Law of the Brehons states that there are seven proofs of the righteous king,' recited Sister Fidelma dutifully. 'That he be approved by the Great Assembly. That he accept the Faith of the One True God. That he hold sacred the symbols of his office and swear fealty on them. That he rule by the Law of the Brehons and his judgement be firm and just and beyond reproach. That he promote the commonwealth of the people. That he must never command his warriors in an unjust war . . .'

The abbot held up his hand and interrupted.

'Yes, yes. You know the law. The point is that Sechnasach cannot be inaugurated because the great sword of the Uí Néill, the "Caladchalog", which was said to have been fashioned in the time of the ancient mist by the smith-god Gobhainn, has been stolen.'

Sister Fidelma raised her head, lips slightly parted in surprise.

The ancient sword of the Uí Néill was one of the potent symbols of the High Kingship. Legend had it that it had been given by the smith-god to the hero Fergus Mac Roth in the time of the ancient ones, and then passed down to Niall of the Nine Hostages, whose descendants had become the Uí Néill kings of Ireland. For centuries now the High Kings had been chosen from either the sept of the northern Uí Néill or from the southern Uí Néill. The 'Caladchalog', 'the hard dinter', was a magical, mystical sword, by which the people recognised their righteous ruler. All High Kings had to swear fealty on it at their inauguration and carry it on all state occasions as the visible symbol of their authority and kingship.

The abbot stuck out his lower lip.

'In these days, when our people go in fear from the ravages of the plague, they need comfort and distraction. If it was known throughout the land that the new High King could not produce his sword of office on which to swear his sacred oath of kingship then apprehension and terror would seize the people. It would be seen as an evil omen at the start of Sechnasach's rule. There would be chaos and panic. Our people cling fiercely to the ancient ways and traditions but, particularly at this time, they need solace and stability.'

Sister Fidelma compressed her lips thoughtfully. What the abbot said was certainly true. The people firmly believed in the symbolism which had been handed down to them from the mists of ancient times.

'If only people relied on their own abilities and not on symbols,' the abbot was continuing. 'It is time for reform, both in secular as well as religious matters. We cling to too many of the pagan beliefs of our ancestors from the time before the Light of Our Saviour was brought to these shores.'

'I see that you yourself believe in the reforms of Rome,' Sister Fidelma observed shrewdly.

The abbot did not conceal his momentary surprise.

'How so?'

Sister Fidelma smiled.

'I have done nothing clever, Abbot Colmán. It was an elementary observation. You wear the tonsure of St Peter, the badge of Rome, and not that of St John from whom our own Church takes its rule.'

The corner of the abbot's mouth drooped.

'I make no secret that I was in Rome for five years and came to respect Rome's reasons for the reforms. I feel it is my duty to advocate the usages of the Church of Rome among our people to replace our old rituals, symbolisms and traditions.'

'We have to deal with people as they are and not as we would like them to be,' observed Sister Fidelma.

'But we must endeavour to change them as well,' replied the abbot unctuously, 'setting their feet on the true path to God's grace.'

'We will not quarrel over the reforms of Rome,' replied Sister Fidelma quietly. 'I will continue to be guided by the

rule of the Holy Brigid of Kildare, where I took my vows.
But tell me, for what purpose have I been summoned to
Tara?'

The abbot hesitated, as if wondering whether to pursue
his theme of Rome's reforms. Then he sniffed to hide his
irritation.

'We must find the missing sword before the High King's
inauguration, which is tomorrow, if we wish to avoid civil
strife in the five kingdoms of Ireland.'

'From where was it stolen?'

'Here, from this very chapel. The sacred sword was
placed with the *Lia Fáil*, the Stone of Destiny, under the
altar. It was locked in a metal and wood chest. The only key
was kept on the altar in full view. No one, so it was thought,
would ever dare violate the sanctuary of the altar and chapel
to steal its sacred treasures.'

'Yet someone did?'

'Indeed they did. We have the culprit locked in a cell.'

'And the culprit is . . .?'

'Ailill Flann Esa. He is the son of Donal, who was High
King twenty years ago. Ailill sought the High Kingship in
rivalry to his cousin, Sechnasach. It is obvious that, out of
malice caused by the rejection of the Great Assembly, he
seeks to discredit his cousin.'

'What witnesses were there to his theft of the sword?'

'Three. He was found in the chapel alone at night by two
guards of the royal palace, Congal and Erc. And I, myself,
came to the chapel a few moments later.'

Sister Fidelma regarded the abbot with bewilderment.

'If he were found in the chapel in the act of stealing the
sword, why was the sword not found with him?'

The abbot sniffed impatiently.

'He had obviously hidden it just before he was discovered. Maybe he heard the guards coming and hid it.'

'Has the chapel been searched?'

'Yes. Nothing has been found.'

'So, from what you say, there were no witnesses to see Ailill Flann Esa actually take the sword?'

The abbot smiled paternally.

'My dear Sister, the chapel is secured at night. The deacon made a check last thing and saw everything was in order. The guards passing outside observed that the door was secure just after midnight, but twenty minutes later they passed it again and found it open. They saw the bolt had been smashed. The chapel door is usually bolted on the inside. That was when they saw Ailill at the altar. The altar table had been pushed aside, the chest was open and the sword gone. The facts seem obvious.'

'Not yet so obvious, Abbot Colmán,' Sister Fidelma replied thoughtfully.

'Obvious enough for Sechnasach to agree with me to have Ailill Flann Esa incarcerated immediately.'

'And the motive, you would say, is simply one of malice?'

'Obvious again. Ailill wants to disrupt the inauguration of Sechnasach as High King. Perhaps he even imagines that he can promote civil war in the confusion and chaos, and, using the people's fears, on the production of the sacred sword from the place where he has hidden it, he thinks to overthrow Sechnasach and make himself High King. The people, in their dread of the Yellow Plague, are in the mood to be manipulated by their anxieties.'

'If you have your culprit and motive, why send for me?' Sister Fidelma asked, a trace of irony in her voice. 'And there are better qualified *dálaigh* and Brehons at the court of Tara, surely?'

'Yet none who have your reputation for solving such conundrums, Sister Fidelma.'

'But the sword must still be in the chapel or within its vicinity.'

'We have searched and it cannot be found. Time presses. I have been told that you have the talent to solve the mystery of where the sword has been hidden. I have heard how skilful you are in questioning suspects and extracting the truth from them. Ailill has, assuredly, hidden the sword nearby and we must find out where before the High King's inauguration.'

Sister Fidelma pursed her lips and then shrugged.

'Show me where the sword was kept and then I will question Ailill Flann Esa.'

Ailill Flann Esa was in his mid-thirties; tall, brown-haired and full-bearded. He carried himself with the pride of the son of a former High King. His father had been Donal Mac Aed of the northern Uí Néill, who had once ruled from Tara twenty years before.

'I did not steal the sacred sword,' he replied immediately Sister Fidelma identified her purpose.

'Then explain how you came to be in the chapel at such a time,' she said, seating herself on the wooden bench that ran alongside the wall of the tenebrous grey stone cell in which he was imprisoned. Ailill hesitated and then seated himself on a stool before her. A wooden bed and a table comprised the other furnishings of the cell. Sister Fidelma knew that only Ailill's status gave him the luxury of these comforts and alleviated the dankness of the granite jail in which he was confined.

'I was passing the chapel . . .' began Ailill.

'Why?' interrupted Sister Fidelma. 'It was after midnight, I believe?'

The man hesitated, frowning. He was apparently not used to people interrupting. Sister Fidelma hid a smile as she saw the struggle on his haughty features. It was clear he wished to respond in annoyance but realised that she was an *Anruth* who had the power of the Brehon Court behind her. Yet he hesitated for a moment or two.

'I was on my way somewhere . . . to see someone.'

'Where? Who?'

'That I cannot say.'

She saw firmness in his pinched mouth, in the compressed lips. He would obviously say nothing further on that matter. She let it pass.

'Continue,' she invited after a moment's pause.

'Well, I was passing the chapel, as I said, and I saw the door open. Usually, at that time of night, the door is closed and the bolt in place. I thought this strange, so I went in. Then I noticed that the altar had been pushed aside. I went forward. I could see that the chest, in which the sword of office was kept, had been opened . . .'

He faltered and ended with a shrug.

'And then?' prompted Sister Fidelma.

'That is all. The guards came in at that moment. Then the abbot appeared. I found myself accused of stealing the sword. Yet I did not.'

'Are you saying that this is all you know about the matter?'

'That is all I know. I am accused but innocent. My only misdemeanour is that I am my father's son and presented a claim before the Great Assembly to succeed Blathmac and Diarmuid as High King. Although Sechnasach won the support of the Great Assembly for his claim, he has never forgiven me for challenging his succession. He is all the more ready to believe my guilt because of his hatred of me.'

'And have you forgiven Sechnasach for his success before the Great Assembly?' Sister Fidelma asked sharply.

Ailill grimaced in suppressed annoyance.

'Do you think me a mean person, Sister? I abide by the law. But, in honesty, I will tell you that I think the Great Assembly has made a wrong choice. Sechnasach is a traditionalist at a time when our country needs reforms. We need reforms in our secular law and in our Church.'

Sister Fidelma's eyes narrowed.

'You would support the reforms being urged upon us by the Roman Church? To change our dating of Easter, our ritual and manner of land-holding?'

'I would. I have never disguised it. And there are many who would support me. My cousin Cernach, the son of Diarmuid, for example. He is a more vehement advocate of Rome than I am.'

'But you would admit that you have a strong motive in attempting to stop Sechnasach's inauguration?'

'Yes. I admit that my policies would be different to those of Sechnasach. But above all things I believe that once the Great Assembly chooses a High King, then all must abide by their decision. Unless the High King fails to abide by the law and fulfil its obligations, he is still High King. No one can challenge the choice of the Great Assembly.'

Sister Fidelma gazed directly into Ailill's smouldering brown eyes.

'And did you steal the sword?'

Ailill sought to control the rage which the question apparently aroused.

'By the powers, I did not! I have told you all I know.'

The warrior named Erc scuffed at the ground with his heel, and stirred uneasily.

'I am sure I cannot help you, Sister. I am a simple guardsman and there is little to add beyond the fact that I, with my companion Congal, found Ailill Flann Esa in the chapel standing before the chest from which the sacred sword had been stolen. There is nothing further I can add.'

Sister Fidelma compressed her lips. She gazed around at the curious faces of the other warriors who shared the dormitory of the High King's bodyguard. The murky chamber, used by a hundred warriors when they were resting from their guard duties, stank of spirits and body sweat which mixed into a bitter scent.

'Let me be the judge of that.' She turned towards the door. 'Come, walk with me for a while in the fresh air, Erc. I would have you answer some questions.'

Reluctantly the burly warrior laid aside his shield and

javelin and followed the religieuse from the dormitory, accompanied by a chorus of whispered comments and a few lewd jests from his comrades.

'I am told that you were guarding the chapel on the night the theft occurred,' Sister Fidelma said as soon as they were outside, walking in the crystal early morning sunlight. 'Is that correct?'

'Congal and I were the guards that night, but our duties were merely to patrol the buildings of which the chapel is part. Usually from midnight until dawn the doors of the chapel of the Blessed Patrick are shut. The chapel contains many treasures and the abbot has ordered that the door be bolted at night.'

'And what time did you arrive at your posts?'

'At midnight exactly, Sister. Our duties took us from the royal stables, fifty yards from the chapel to the great refectory, a route which passes the chapel door.'

'Tell me what happened that night.'

'Congal and I took up our positions. We walked by the chapel door. It seemed shut as usual. We turned at the door of the great refectory from which point we followed a path which circumvents the buildings, so that our patrol follows a circular path.'

'How long does it take to circumnavigate the buildings?'

'No more than half-an-hour.'

'And how long would you be out of sight of the door of the chapel?'

'Perhaps twenty minutes.'

'Go on.'

'It was on our second patrol, as I say, a half-hour later, that we passed the door of the chapel. It was Congal who spotted that the door was opened. We moved forward and then I saw that the door had been forced. The wood was splintered around the bolt on the inside. We entered and saw Ailill Flann Esa standing before the altar. The altar had been pushed back from the position where it covered the Stone of

Destiny and the chest in which the sacred sword was kept had been opened.'

'What was Ailill doing? Did he look flustered or short of breath?'

'No. He was calm enough. Just staring down at the open chest.'

'Wasn't it dark in the chapel? How did you see so clearly?'

'Some candles were lit within the chapel and provided light enough.'

'And then?'

'He saw our shadows and started turning on us. At that point the abbot came up behind us. He saw the sacrilege at once and pointed to the fact that the sword was gone.'

'Did he question Ailill?'

'Oh, surely he did. He said the sword had gone and asked what Ailill had to say.'

'And what did Ailill say?'

'He said that he had just arrived there.'

'And what did you say?'

'I said that was impossible because we were patrolling outside and had the chapel door in sight for at least ten minutes from the royal stable doorway. Ailill must have been inside for that ten minutes at least.'

'But it was night time. It must have been dark outside. How could you be sure that Ailill had not just entered the chapel before you, covered by the darkness?'

'Because the torches are lit in the grounds of the royal palace every night. It is the law of Tara. Where there is light, there is no treachery. Ailill must have been in the chapel, as I have said, for at least ten minutes. That is a long time.'

'Yet even ten minutes does not seem time enough to open the chest, hide the sword, and repose oneself before you entered.'

'Time enough, I'd say. For what else could be done with the sword but hide it?'

'And where is your companion, Congal? I would question him.'

Erc looked troubled and genuflected with a degree of haste.

'God between me and evil, Sister. He has fallen sick with the Yellow Plague. He lies close to death now and maybe I will be next to succumb to the scourge.'

Sister Fidelma bit her lip, then she shook her head and smiled reassuringly at Erc.

'Not necessarily so, Erc. Go to the apothecary. Ask that you be given an infusion of the leaves and flowers of the *centaurium vulgare*. It has a reputation for keeping the Yellow Plague at bay.'

'What is that?' demanded the warrior, frowning at the unfamiliar Latin words.

'*Dréimire buí*,' she translated to the Irish name of the herb. 'The apothecary will know it. To drink of the mixture is supposedly a good preventative tonic. By drinking each day, you may avoid the scourge. Now go in peace, Erc. I have done with you for the meanwhile.'

Sechnasach, lord of Midhe, and High King of Ireland, was a thin man, aged in his mid-thirties, with scowling features and dark hair. He sat slightly hunched forward on his chair, the epitome of gloom.

'Abbot Colmán reports that you have not yet discovered where Ailill has hidden the sword of state, Sister,' he greeted brusquely as he gestured for Sister Fidelma to be seated. 'May I remind you that the inauguration ceremony commences at noon tomorrow?'

The High King had agreed to meet her, at her own request, in one of the small audience chambers of the palace of Tara. It was a chamber with a high vaulted ceiling and hung with colourful tapestries. There was a crackling log fire in the great hearth at one end before which the High King sat in his ornate carved oak chair. Pieces of exquisite furniture, brought as gifts to the court from many parts of the world, were placed around the chamber with decorative ornaments in gold and silver and semi-precious jewels.

'That presupposes Ailill stole the sword,' observed Sister Fidelma calmly as she sat before him. She observed strict protocol. Had she been trained to the degree of *ollamh* she could have sat in the High King's presence without waiting for permission. Indeed, the chief *ollamh* of Ireland, at the court of the High King, was so influential that even the High King was not allowed to speak at the Great Assembly before the chief *ollamh*. Sister Fidelma had never been in the presence of a High King before and her mind raced hastily over the correct rituals to be observed.

Sechnasach drew his brows together at her observation.

'You doubt it? But the facts given by Abbot Colmán are surely plain enough? If Ailill did not steal it, who then?'

Sister Fidelma raised a shoulder and let it fall.

'Before I comment further I would ask you some questions, Sechnasach of Tara.'

The High King made a motion of his hand as though to invite her questions.

'Who would gain if you were prevented from assuming the High Kingship?'

Sechnasach grimaced with bitter amusement.

'Ailill, of course. For he stands as *tánaiste* by choice of the Great Assembly.'

Whenever the Great Assembly elected a High King, they also elected a *tánaiste* or 'second'; an heir presumptive who would assume office should the High King become indisposed. Should the High King be killed or die suddenly then the Great Assembly would meet to confirm the *tánaiste* as High King but at no time were the five kingdoms left without a supreme potentate. Under the ancient Brehon Law of Ireland, only the most worthy were elected to kingship and there was no such concept of hereditary right by primogeniture such as practised in the lands of the Saxons or Franks.

'And no one else? There are no other claimants?'

'There are many claimants. My uncle Diarmuid's son, Cernach, for example, and Ailill's own brothers, Conall and Colcu. You must know of the conflict between the southern and northern Uí Néill? I am of the southern Uí Néill. Many of the northern Uí Néill would be glad to see me deposed.'

'But none but Ailill stand as the obvious choice to gain by your fall?' pressed Sister Fidelma.

'None.'

Compressing her lips, Sister Fidelma rose.

'That is all at this time, Sechnasach,' she said.

The High King glanced at her in surprise at the abruptness of her questioning.

'You would give me no hope of finding the sacred sword before tomorrow?'

Sister Fidelma detected a pleading tone to his voice.

'There is always hope, Sechnasach. But if I have not solved this mystery by noon tomorrow, at the time of your inauguration, then we will see the resolution in the development of events. Events will solve the puzzle.'

'Little hope of averting strife, then?'

'I do not know,' Sister Fidelma admitted candidly.

She left the audience chamber and was moving down the corridor when a low soprano voice called to her by name from a darkened doorway. Sister Fidelma paused, turned and gazed at the dark figure of a girl.

'Come inside for a moment, Sister.'

Sister Fidelma followed the figure through heavy drapes into a brightly lit chamber.

A young, dark-haired girl in an exquisitely sewn gown of blue, bedecked in jewels, ushered her inside and pulled the drape across the door.

'I am Ornait, sister of Sechnasach,' the girl said breathlessly.

Sister Fidelma bowed her head to the High King's sister.

'I am at your service, Ornait.'

'I was listening behind the tapestries, just now,' the girl

said, blushing a little. 'I heard what you were saying to my brother. You don't believe Ailill stole the sacred sword, do you?'

Sister Fidelma gazed into the girl's eager, pleading eyes, and smiled softly.

'And you do not want to believe it?' she asked with gentle emphasis.

The girl lowered her gaze, the redness of her cheeks, if anything, increasing.

'I know he could not have done this deed. He would not.' She seized Sister Fidelma's hand. 'I know that if anyone can prove him innocent of this sacrilege it will be you.'

'Then you know that I am an advocate in the Brehon Court?' asked Sister Fidelma, slightly embarrassed at the girl's emphatic belief in her ability.

'I have heard of your reputation from a sister of your order at Kildare.'

'And the night Ailill was arrested in the chapel, he was on his way to see you? It was foolish of him not to tell me.'

Ornait raised her small chin defiantly.

'We love each other!'

'But keep it a secret, even from your brother?'

'Until after my brother's inauguration as High King, it will remain a secret; when he feels more kindly disposed towards Ailill. Now he does not forgive him for standing against him before the Great Assembly. We shall tell him afterwards.'

'You do not think Ailill feels any resentment towards your brother, a resentment which might have motivated him to hide the sacred sword to discredit Sechnasach?'

'Ailill may not agree with my brother on many things but he agrees that the decision of the Great Assembly, under the Brehon Law, is sacred and binding,' replied Ornait, firmly. 'And he is not alone in that. My cousin, Cernach Mac Diarmuid, believes that he has a greater right to the High Kingship than Sechnasach. He dislikes my brother's attitude against any reform suggested by Rome. But Cernach does not come to the "age of choice" for a month yet when he can legally challenge my brother to the High Kingship. Being too young to challenge for office, Cernach supported Ailill in his claim. It is no crime to be unsuccessful in the challenge for the High Kingship. Once the Great Assembly make the decision, there is an end to it. No, a thousand times – no! Ailill would not do this thing.'

'Well, Sister?' The abbot stared at Sister Fidelma with narrowed eyes.

'I have nothing to report at the moment, just another question to ask.'

She had gone to see Abbot Colmán in his study in the abbey building behind the palace of Tara. The abbot was seated behind a wooden table where he had been examining a colourful illuminated manuscript. He saw her eyes fall on the book and smiled complacently.

'This is the Gospel of John produced by our brothers at Clonmacnoise. A beautiful work which will be sent to our brothers at the Holy Island of Colmcille.'

Sister Fidelma glanced briefly at the magnificently wrought handiwork. It was, indeed, beautiful but her thoughts were occupied elsewhere. She paused a moment before asking:

'If there were civil strife in the kingdom, and from it Ailill was made High King, would he depart from the traditional policies propounded by Sechnasach?'

The abbot was taken off guard, his jaw dropping and his eyes rounding in surprise. Then he frowned and appeared to ponder the question for a moment.

'I would think the answer is in the affirmative,' he answered at last.

'Particularly,' went on Sister Fidelma, 'would Ailill press the abbots and bishops to reform the Church?'

The abbot scratched an ear.

'It is no secret that Ailill favours a rapprochement with the Church of Rome, believing its reforms to be correct. There are many of the Uí Néill house who do. Cernach Mac Diarmuid, for instance. He is a leading advocate among the laymen for such reforms. A bit of a hothead but influential. A youth who stands near the throne of Tara but doesn't reach the "age of choice" for a month or so when he may take his place in the assemblies of the five kingdoms.'

'But Sechnasach does not believe in reforms and would adhere strongly to the traditional rites and liturgy of our Church?'

'Undoubtedly.'

'And, as one of the pro-Roman faction, you would favour Ailill's policies?'

The abbot flushed with indignation.

'I would. But I make no secret of my position. And I hold my beliefs under the law. My allegiance is to the High King as designated by that law. And while you have a special privilege as an advocate of the Brehon Court, may I remind you that I am Abbot of Tara, father and superior to your order?'

Sister Fidelma made a gesture with her hand as if in apology.

'I am merely seeking facts, Abbot Colmán. And it is as *dálaigh* of the Brehon Court that I ask these questions, not as a Sister of Kildare.'

'Then here is a fact. I denounced Ailill Flann Esa. If I had supported what he has done in order to overthrow Sechnasach simply because Ailill would bring the Church in Ireland in agreement with Rome, then I would not have been willing to point so quickly to Ailill's guilt. I could have persuaded the guards that someone else had carried out the deed.'

'Indeed,' affirmed Sister Fidelma. 'If Ailill Flann Esa were guilty of this sacrilege then you would not profit.'

'Exactly so,' snapped the abbot. 'And Ailill is guilty.'

'So it might seem.'

Sister Fidelma turned to the door, paused and glanced back.

'One tiny point, to clarify matters. How is it that you came to be in the chapel at that exact time?'

The abbot drew his brows together.

'I had left my *Psalter* in the sacristy,' he replied irritably. 'I went to retrieve it.'

'Surely it would have been safe until morning? Why go out into the cold of night to the chapel?'

'I needed to look up a reference; besides I did not have to go out into the night . . .'

'No? How then did you get into the chapel?'

The abbot sighed, in annoyance.

'There is a passage which leads from the abbey here into the chapel sacristy.'

Sister Fidelma's eyes widened. She suddenly realised that she had been a fool. The fact had been staring her in the face all the time.

'Please show me this passage.'

'I will get one of the brethren to show you. I am busy with the preparations for the inauguration.'

Abbot Colmán reached forward and rang a silver bell which stood upon the table.

A moon-faced man clad in the brown robes of the order of the abbey entered almost immediately, arms folded in the copious sleeves of his habit. Even from a distance of a few feet, Sister Fidelma could smell the wild garlic on his breath, a pungent odour which caused her to wrinkle her nose in distaste.

'This is Brother Rogallach,' the abbot motioned with his hand. 'Rogallach, I wish you to show Sister Fidelma the passage to the chapel.' Then, turning to her, he raised his eyebrows in query. 'Unless there is anything else . . .?'

'Nothing else, Colmán,' Sister Fidelma replied quietly. 'For the time being.'

★ ★ ★

Brother Rogallach took a candle and lit it. He and Sister Fidelma were standing in one of the corridors of the abbey building. Rogallach moved towards a tapestry and drew it aside to reveal an entrance from which stone steps led downwards.

'This is the only entrance to the passage which leads to the chapel?' asked Sister Fidelma, trying to steel her features against his bad breath.

Brother Rogallach nodded. He stood slightly in awe of the young woman for it was already common gossip around the abbey as to her status and role.

'Who knows about it?' she pressed.

'Why, everyone in the abbey. When the weather is intemperate we use this method to attend worship in the chapel.' The monk opened his mouth in an ingenuous smile, displaying broken and blackened teeth.

'Would anyone outside the abbey know about it?'

The monk grimaced eloquently.

'It is no secret, Sister. Anyone who has lived at Tara would know of it.'

'So Ailill would know of its existence?'

Brother Rogallach gestured as if the answer were obvious.

'Lead on then, Brother Rogallach,' Sister Fidelma instructed, thankful to push the monk ahead of her so that she was not bathed by the foul stench of his breathing.

The moon-faced monk turned and preceded her down the steps and through a musty but dry passage whose floor was laid with stone flags. It was a winding passage along which several small alcoves stood, most of them containing items of furniture. Sister Fidelma stopped at the first of them and asked Rogallach to light the alcove with his candle. She repeated this performance at each of the alcoves.

'They are deep enough for a person to hide in let alone to conceal a sword,' she mused aloud. 'Were they searched for the missing sword?'

The monk nodded eagerly, drawing close so that Sister

Fidelma took an involuntary step backward. 'Of course, I was one of those called to assist in the search. Once the chapel was searched, it was obvious that the next likely hiding place would be this passageway.'

Nevertheless, Sister Fidelma caused Rogallach to halt at each alcove until she had examined it thoroughly by the light of his candle. At one alcove she frowned and reached for a piece of frayed cloth caught on a projecting section of wood. It was brightly coloured cloth, certainly not from the cheerless brown robes of a religieux, but more like the fragment of a richly woven cloak. It was the sort of cloth that a person in the position of wealth and power would have.

It took a little time to traverse the passage and to come up some steps behind a tapestry into the sacristy. From there Sister Fidelma moved into the chapel and across to the chapel door.

Something had been irritating her for some time about the affair. Now that she realised the existence of the passage, she knew what had been puzzling her.

'The chapel door is always bolted from the inside?' she asked.

'Yes,' replied Rogallach.

'So if you wanted to enter the chapel, how would you do it?'

Rogallach smiled, emitting another unseen cloud of bitter scent to engulf her.

'Why, I would merely use the passage.'

'Indeed, if you knew it was there,' affirmed Sister Fidelma, thoughtfully.

'Well, only a stranger to Tara, such as yourself, would not know that.'

'So if someone attempted to break into the chapel from the outside, they would obviously not know of the existence of the passage?'

Rogallach moved his head in an affirmative gesture.

Sister Fidelma stood at the door of the chapel and gazed down at the bolt, especially to where it had splintered from the wood and her eyes narrowed as she examined the scuff marks on the metal where it had obviously been hit with a piece of stone. Abruptly, she smiled broadly as she realised the significance of its breaking. She turned to Rogallach.

'Send the guard Erc to me.'

Sechnasach, the High King, stared at Sister Fidelma with suspicion.

'I am told that you have summoned the Abbot Colmán, Ailill Flann Esa, my sister Ornait and Cernach Mac Diarmuid to appear here. Why is this?'

Sister Fidelma stood, hands demurely folded before her, as she confronted Sechnasach.

'I did so because I have that right as a *dálaigh* of the Brehon Courts and with the authority that I can now solve the mystery of the theft of your sword of state.'

Sechnasach leaned forward in his chair excitedly. 'You have found where Ailill has hidden it?'

'My eyes were blind for I should have seen the answer long ago,' Sister Fidelma replied.

'Tell me where the sword is,' demanded Sechnasach.

'In good time,' Sister Fidelma answered calmly. 'I need a further answer from you before I can reveal the answer to this puzzle. I have summoned Cernach, the son of your uncle Diarmuid, who was, with your father, joint High King?'

'What has Cernach to do with this matter?'

'It is said that Cernach is a most vehement supporter of the reforms of the Church of Rome.'

Sechnasach frowned, slightly puzzled.

'He has often argued with me that I should change my attitudes and support those abbots and bishops of Ireland who would alter our ways and adopt the rituals of Rome. But he is still a youth. Why, he does not achieve the "age of choice" for a month or so and cannot even sit in council. He has no authority though he has some influence on the young members of our court.'

Sister Fidelma nodded reflectively.

'This agrees with what I have heard. But I needed some confirmation. Now let the guards bring in Ailill and the others and I will tell you what has happened.'

She stood silently before the High King while Ailill Flann Esa was brought in under guard, followed by the Abbot Colmán. Behind came a worried-looking Ornait, glancing with ill-concealed anxiety at her lover. After her came a puzzled-looking, dark-haired young man who was obviously Cernach Mac Diarmuid.

They stood in a semi-circle before the High King's chair. Sechnasach glanced towards Sister Fidelma, inclining his head to her as indication that she should start.

'We will firstly agree on one thing,' began Sister Fidelma. 'The sacred sword of the Uí Néill kings of Tara was stolen from the chapel of the Blessed Patrick. We will now also agree on the apparent motive. It was stolen to prevent the inauguration of Sechnasach as High King tomorrow . . . or to discredit him in the eyes of the people, to foment civil disorder in the five kingdoms which might lead to Sechnasach being overthrown and someone else taking the throne.'

She smiled briefly at Sechnasach.

'Are we agreed on that?'

'That much is obvious.' It was Abbot Colmán who interrupted in annoyance. 'In these dark times, it would only need such an omen as the loss of the sacred sword to create chaos and alarm within the kingdoms of Ireland. I have already said as much.'

'And what purpose would this chaos and alarm, with the overthrow of Sechnasach, be put to?' queried Sister Fidelma. Before anyone could reply she went on. 'It seems easy to see. Sechnasach is sworn to uphold the traditions of the kingdoms and of our Church. Rome claims authority over all the Churches but this claim had been disputed by the Churches of Ireland, Britain and Armorica as well as the Churches of the East. Rome wishes to change our rituals, our liturgy and the computations whereby we celebrate the *Cáisc* in remembrance of our Lord's death in Jerusalem. And there are some among us, even abbots and bishops, who support Rome and seek the abandoning of our traditions and a union with the Roman Church. So even among us we do not all speak with one voice. Is that not so, Ailill Flann Esa?'

Ailill scowled.

'As I have told you, I have never denied my views.'

'Then let us agree entirely on the apparent inner motive for the theft of the sword. Destabilisation of the High King and his replacement by someone who would reject the traditionalist ways and throw his support behind the reforms in line with Rome.'

There was a silence. She had their full attention.

'Very well,' went on Sister Fidelma. 'This seems an obvious motive. But let us examine the facts of the theft. Two guards passed the door of the chapel in which the sword was kept shortly after midnight. The door was secured. But when they passed the chapel door twenty minutes later, they saw it ajar with the bolt having been forced. Entering, they saw Ailill standing at the altar staring at the empty chest where the sword had been kept. Then the abbot entered. He came into the chapel from the sacristy to which he had gained entrance from the passage which leads there from the abbey. He accused Ailill of stealing the sword and hiding it. The sword was not found in the chapel. If Ailill had stolen the sword, how had he time to hide it so well and cleverly? Even the ten minutes allowed him by the guards was not time enough. This is the first problem that struck my thoughts.'

She paused and glanced towards Ornait, the sister of the High King.

'According to Ailill Flann Esa, he was walking by the chapel. He saw the door ajar and the bolt forced. He went inside out of curiosity and perceived the empty chest. That is his version of events.'

'We know this is what he claims,' snapped Sechnasach. 'Have you something new to add?'

'Only to clarify,' replied Fidelma, unperturbed by the High King's agitation, 'Ailill's reason to be passing the chapel at that hour was because he was on his way to meet with Ornait.'

Ornait flushed. Sechnasach turned to stare at his sister, mouth slightly open.

'I regret that I cannot keep your secret, Ornait,' Sister Fidelma said with a grimace. 'But the truth must be told for much is in the balance.'

Ornait raised her chin defiantly towards her brother.

'Well, Ornait? Why would Ailill meet with you in dead of night?' demanded the High King.

The girl pushed back her head defiantly.

'I love Ailill and he loves me. We wanted to tell you, but thought we would do so after your inauguration when you might look on us with more charity.'

Sister Fidelma held up her hand as Sechnasach opened his mouth to respond in anger.

'Time enough to sort that matter later. Let us continue. If Ailill speaks the truth, then we must consider this. Someone knew of Ailill's appointment with Ornait. That person was waiting inside the chapel. Being a stranger to Tara, I had not realised that the chapel could be entered from within by means of a passageway. In this matter I was stupid. I should have known at once by the fact that the chapel doors bolted from *within*. The fact was staring me in the face. I should have realised that if the chapel was left bolted at night, then there must obviously be another means for the person who secured the bolt to make their exit.'

'But everyone at Tara knows about that passage,' pointed out Sechnasach.

'Indeed,' smiled Sister Fidelma. 'And it would be obvious that at some stage I would come to share that knowledge.'

'The point is that the bolt on the door was forced,' Abbot Colmán pointed out in a testy tone.

'Indeed. But not from the outside,' replied Sister Fidelma. 'Again my wits were not swift, otherwise I would have seen it immediately. When you force a bolted door, it is the metal on the door jamb, which secures the bolt, that gets torn from its fixtures. But the bolt itself, on the chapel door, was the section which had been splintered away from its holdings.'

She stood looking at their puzzled expressions for a moment.

'What happened was simple enough. The culprit had entered the chapel from the passage within. They had taken the key, pushed back the altar, opened the chest. The sword had been removed and taken to a place of safety. Then the culprit had returned to arrange the scene. Ensuring that the guards were well beyond the door, the perpetrator opened it, took up a stone and smashed at the bolt. Instead of smashing away the metal catch on the door jamb, the bolt on the door was smashed. It was so obvious a clue that I nearly overlooked it. All I saw at first was a smashed bolt.'

Ornait was smiling through her tears.

'I knew Ailill could not have done this deed. The real perpetrator did this deed for the purpose of making Ailill seem the guilty one. Your reputation as a solver of puzzles is well justified, Sister Fidelma.'

Sister Fidelma responded with a slightly wan smile.

'It needed no act of genius to deduce that the evidence could only point to the fact that Ailill Flann Esa could not have stolen the sword in the manner claimed.'

Ailill was frowning at Sister Fidelma.

'Then who is the guilty person?'

'Certain things seemed obvious. Who benefited from the deed?' Sister Fidelma continued, ignoring his question. 'Abbot Colmán is a fierce adherent of Rome. He might benefit in this cause if Sechnasach was removed. And Abbot Colmán was in the right place at the right time. He had the opportunity to do this deed.'

'This is outrageous!' snarled the abbot. 'I am accused

unjustly. I am your superior, Fidelma of Kildare. I am the Abbot of Tara and . . .'

Sister Fidelma grimaced. 'I need not be reminded of your position in the Church, Abbot Colmán,' she replied softly. 'I also remind you that I speak here as an advocate of the Brehon Court and was invited here to act in this position by yourself.'

Colmán, flushed and angry, hesitated and then said slowly: 'I make no secret of my adherence to the Rome order but to suggest that I would be party to such a plot . . .'

Sister Fidelma held up a hand and motioned him to silence.

'This is true enough. After all, Ailill would be Colmán's natural ally. If Colmán stole the sword, why would he attempt to put the blame onto Ailill and perhaps discredit those who advocated the cause of Rome? Surely, he would do his best to support Ailill so that when civil strife arose over the non-production of the sacred sword, Ailill, as *tanaiste*, the heir-presumptive, would be in a position to immediately claim the throne of Sechnasach?'

'What are you saying?' asked Sechnasach, trying to keep track of Sister Fidelma's reasoning.

Sister Fidelma turned to him, her blue eyes level, her tone unhurried.

'There is another factor in this tale of political intrigue. Cernach Mac Diarmuid. His name was mentioned to me several times as a fierce adherent of Rome.'

The young man who had so far stood aloof and frowning, now started, his cheeks reddening. A hand dropped to his side as if seeking a weapon. But no one, save the High King's bodyguard, was allowed to carry a weapon in Tara's halls.

'What do you mean by this?'

'Cernach desired the throne of Tara. As son of one of the joint High Kings, he felt that it was his due. But moreover, he would benefit most if both Sechnasach and Ailill were discredited.'

'Why . . .!' Cernach started forward, anger on his face. One of the warriors gripped the young man's arm so tightly that he winced. He turned and tried to shake off the grip but made no further aggressive move.

Sister Fidelma spoke to one of the guards.

'Is the warrior, Erc, outside?'

The guard moved to the door and called.

The burly warrior entered holding something wrapped in cloth. He glanced at Sister Fidelma and nodded briefly.

Sister Fidelma turned back to the High King.

'Sechnasach, I ordered this man, Erc, to search the chamber of Cernach.'

Cernach's face was suddenly bloodless. His eyes were bright, staring at the object in Erc's hand.

'What did you find there, Erc?' asked Sister Fidelma quietly.

The warrior moved forward to the High King's seat, unwrapping the cloth as he did so. He held out the uncovered object. In his hands there was revealed a sword of rich gold and silver mountings, encrusted with a colourful display of jewels.

'The "Caladchalog"!' gasped the High King. 'The sword of state!'

'It's a lie! A lie!' cried Cernach, his lips trembling. 'It was planted there. She must have planted it there!'

He threw out an accusing finger towards Sister Fidelma. Sister Fidelma simply ignored him.

'Where did you find this, Erc?'

The burly warrior licked his lips. It was clear he felt awkward in the presence of the High King.

'It was lying wrapped in cloth under the bed of Cernach, the son of Diarmuid,' he replied, brusquely.

Everyone's eyes had fallen on the trembling young man.

'Was it easy to find, Erc?' asked Sister Fidelma.

The burly warrior managed a smile.

'Almost too easy.'

'Almost too easy,' repeated Sister Fidelma with a soft emphasis.

'Why did you do this deed, Cernach Mac Diarmuid?' thundered Sechnasach. 'How could you behave so treacherously?'

'But Cernach did not do it.'

Fidelma's quiet voice caused everyone to turn back to stare at her in astonishment.

'Who then, if not Cernach?' demanded the High King in bewilderment.

'The art of deduction is a science as intricate as any of the mysteries of the ancients,' Sister Fidelma commented with a sigh. 'In this matter I found myself dealing with a mind as complicated in thinking and as ruthless in its goal as any I have encountered. But then the stake was the High Kingship of Ireland.'

She paused and gazed around at the people in the chamber, letting her eyes finally rest on Sechnasach.

'There has been one thing which has been troubling me from the start. Why I was called to Tara to investigate this matter? My poor reputation in law is scarcely known out of the boundaries of Holy Brigid's house at Kildare. In Tara, at the seat of the High Kings, there are many better qualified in law, many more able *dálaigh* of the Brehon Courts, many more renowned Brehons. The Abbot Colmán admitted that someone had told him about me for he did not know me. I have had a growing feeling that I was being somehow used. But why? For what purpose? By whom? It seemed so obvious that Ailill was demonstrably innocent of the crime. Why was it obvious?'

Ailill started, his eyes narrowing as he stared at her. Sister Fidelma continued oblivious of the tension in the chamber.

'Abbot Colmán summoned me hither. He had much to gain from this affair, as we have discussed. He also had the opportunity to carry out the crime.'

'That's not true!' cried the abbot.

Sister Fidelma turned and smiled at the ruddy-faced cleric.

'You are right, Colmán. And I have already conceded that fact. You did not do it.'

'But the sword was found in Cernach's chamber,' Sechnasach pointed out. 'He must surely be guilty.'

'Several times I was pointed towards Cernach as a vehement advocate of Roman reforms. A youthful hothead, was one description. Several times I was encouraged to think that the motive lay in replacing Sechnasach, a traditionalist, with someone who would encourage those reforms. And, obligingly, the sword was placed in Cernach's chamber by the real culprit, for us to find. To Cernach my footsteps were carefully pointed . . . But why Cernach? He was not even of the "age of choice", so what could he gain?'

There was a silence as they waited tensely for her to continue.

'Abbot Colmán told me that Cernach was a supporter of Rome. So did Ailill and so did Ornait. But Ornait was the only one who told me that Cernach desired the throne, even though unable to do so by his age. Ornait also told me that he would be of age within a month.'

Sister Fidelma suddenly wheeled round on the girl.

'Ornait was also the only person who knew of my reputation as a solver of mysteries. Ornait told the abbot and encouraged him to send for me. Is this not so?'

She glanced back to Abbot Colmán who nodded in confusion.

Ornait had gone white, staring at Sister Fidelma.

'Are you saying that I stole the sword?' she whispered with ice in her voice.

'That's ridiculous!' cried Sechnasach. 'Ornait is my sister.'

'Nevertheless, the guilty ones are Ailill and Ornait,' replied Sister Fidelma.

'But you have just demonstrated that Ailill was innocent of the crime,' Sechnasach said in total bewilderment.

'No. I demonstrated that evidence was left for me in order that I would believe Ailill was innocent; that he could not have carried out the deed as it was claimed he had. When things are obvious, beware of them.'

'But why would Ornait take part in this theft?' demanded the High King.

'Ornait conceived the plan. Its cunning was her own. It was carried out by Ailill and herself and no others.'

'Explain.'

'Ailill and Ornait entered the chapel that night in the normal way through the passage. They proceeded to carry out the plan. Ornait took the sword while Ailill broke the bolt, making sure of the obvious mistake. They relied on discovery by the two guards and Ailill waited for them. But, as always in such carefully laid plans, there comes the unexpected. As Ornait was proceeding back through the passage she saw the abbot coming along it. He had left his *Psalter* in the sacristy and needed it. She pressed into an alcove and hid until he had gone by. When she left the alcove she tore her gown on some obstruction.'

Sister Fidelma held out the small piece of frayed colourful cloth.

'But the rest of the plan worked perfectly. Ailill was imprisoned. The second part of the plan was now put into place. Ornait had been informed by a sister from my house at Kildare that I was a solver of mysteries. In fact, without undue modesty, I may say that Ornait's entire plan had been built around me. When the sword could not be found, she was able to persuade Abbot Colmán to send for me to investigate its mysterious disappearance. Colmán himself had never heard of me before Ornait dropped my name in his ear. He has just admitted this.'

The abbot was nodding in agreement as he strove to follow her argument.

'When I arrived, the contrived evidence led me immediately to believe Ailill Flann Esa was innocent, as it was supposed to do. It also led me to the chosen scapegoat, Cernach Mac Diarmuid. And in his chamber, scarcely concealed, was the sacred sword. It was all too easy for me. That ease made me suspicious. Both Ailill and Ornait were too free with Cernach's name. Then I saw the frayed cloth in the passage and I began to think.'

'But if it was a simple plot to discredit me by the non-production of the sword,' observed Sechnasach, 'why such an elaborate plot? Why not simply steal the sword and hide it where it could not be so easily recovered?'

'That was the matter which caused the greatest puzzle. However, it became clear to me as I considered it. Ornait and Ailill had to be sure of your downfall. The loss of the sword would create alarm and dissension among the people. But it was not simply chaos that they wanted. They wanted your immediate downfall. They had to ensure that the Great Assembly would come to regret their decision and immediately proclaim for Ailill at the inauguration.'

'How could they ensure that?' demanded Abbot Colmán. 'The Great Assembly had already made their decision.'

'A decision which could be overturned any time before the inauguration. After aspersions had been cast on Sechnasach's judgement, his ability to treat people fairly, the Great Assembly could change its support. By showing the Great Assembly that Sechnasach was capable of unjustly accusing one who had been his rival, this could be done. I am also sure that Sechnasach would be accused of personal enmity because of Ornait's love of Ailill. I was part of Ornait's plan to depose her brother and replace him with Ailill. I was to be invited to Tara for no other purpose but to demonstrate Ailill's innocence and Cernach's guilt. Doubt on Sechnasach's judgement would be a blemish on his ability for the High Kingship. Remember the Law of Kings, the law of the seven proofs of a righteous King? That his judgement be firm and just and beyond reproach. Once Sechnasach's decision to imprison Ailill was shown to have been unjust, Ailill, as *tánaiste*, would be acclaimed in his place with Ornait as his queen.'

Sechnasach sat staring at his sister, reading the truth in

her scowling features. If the veracity of Sister Fidelma's argument needed support, it could be found in the anger and hate written on the girl's features and that humiliation on Ailill's face.

'And this was done for no other reason than to seize the throne, for no other motive than power?' asked the High King incredulously. 'It was not done because they wanted to reform the Church in line with Rome?'

'Not for Rome. Merely for power,' Fidelma agreed. 'For power most people would do anything.'

Murder in Repose

❧

'There is no question of Brother Fergal's guilt in this crime,' said the Brehon with assurance. 'He clearly murdered the girl.'

He was a stocky man, this chief judge of the clan of the Eóghanacht of Cashel. His round, lugubrious face was betrayed by a pair of bright, sharp eyes. His slow-speaking meticulous manner disguised a mind that was sharp and decisive. Here was a man who, as his profession demanded, looked at life carefully and weighed the evidence before making a decision. And he was no one's fool.

Sister Fidelma, tall, green-eyed, stood before the Brehon with hands folded demurely in front of her. Her robes and hood, from under which wisps of red hair stuck out, scarcely disguised her youthfulness nor her feminine attractiveness. The Brehon had placed her age in the mid-twenties. He noticed that her stance was one of controlled agitation, of someone used to movement and action. The habit of a religieuse did not suit her at all.

'The abbess has assured me that Brother Fergal is no more capable of taking a life than a rabbit is capable of flying through the air.'

The Brehon of the Eóghanacht of Cashel sighed. He made little effort to conceal his irritation at the young woman's contradiction.

'Nevertheless, Sister, the evidence is plain. The man Fergal was found in his *bothán*, the cabin he had rebuilt, on the slopes of Cnoc-gorm. He was asleep. By his side was the body of the girl, Barrdub. She had been stabbed to death. There was blood on Fergal's hands and on his robes. When he was awakened, he claimed that he had no knowledge of anything. That is a weak defence.'

Sister Fidelma bowed her head, as if acknowledging the logic of the Brehon's statement.

'What were the circumstances of the finding of the body of the girl Barrdub?'

'Barrdub's brother, Congal, had been worried. The girl, it seems, had been smitten with a passion for this Brother Fergal. He is a handsome young man, it must be admitted. That night, according to Congal, his sister went out and did not return. Early in the morning, Congal came to me and asked me to accompany him to Fergal's *bothán* to confront them. Barrdub is not yet at the age of choice, you understand, and Congal stands as her guardian in law for they have no other relatives living. Together we found Fergal and the body of Barrdub as I have described.'

Sister Fidelma compressed her lips. The evidence was, indeed, damning.

'The hearing will be at noon tomorrow,' the Brehon went on. 'Brother Fergal must give account to the law for no one can stand above the jurisdiction of the Brehons, either priest or druid.'

Sister Fidelma smiled thinly.

'Thanks be to the holy Patrick that it is two centuries since the druids of Ireland accepted the teachings of the Saviour of this world.'

The Brehon returned her smile.

'Yet they say that many who live in the mountains or in remote fastnesses still practise the old ways; that there are many whom the teachings of Christ have not won from the worship of The Dagda and the ancient gods of Ireland. We

70

have such a one even here, in our territory. Erca is a hermit who also lives on the slopes of Cnoc-gorm and claims to practise the old ways.'

Sister Fidelma shrugged indifferently.

'I am not here to proselytise.'

The Brehon was examining her carefully now.

'What precisely is your role in this affair, Sister? Do you simply represent the Abbey which, I understand, now stands in place of Brother Fergal's *fine* or family? Remember, in law, the *fine* must ensure that the penalties are provided when judgement is given by the court.'

'I am aware of the law, Brehon of the Eóghanacht,' replied Sister Fidelma. 'The abbess has sent me to this place in the capacity of a *dálaigh*; an advocate to plead before the court on behalf of Brother Fergal.'

The Brehon raised an eyebrow, slightly surprised. When the girl had come to him, he had assumed that she was simply one of Brother Fergal's religious community who had come to find out why he had been arrested and charged with murder.

'The law requires that all advocates must be qualified to plead before the *Dál*.'

Sister Fidelma drew herself up, a little annoyed at the patronage in the man's voice, at his arrogant assumption.

'I am qualified. I studied law under the great Brehon Morann of Tara.'

Once again the Brehon barely concealed his surprise. That the young girl before him could be qualified in the law of Éireann was astonishing in his eyes. He was about to open his mouth when the girl pre-empted his question by reaching within her robes and passing him an inscribed vellum. The Brehon read quickly, eyes rounded, hesitated and passed it back. His glance was now respectful, his voice slightly awed.

'It states that you are a qualified *Anruth*.'

To have qualified to the level of *Anruth* one had to have

studied at a monastic or bardic school for between seven to nine years. The *Anruth* was only one degree below the highest qualification, the *Ollamh*, or professor, who could sit as an equal with kings. The *Anruth* had to be knowledgeable in poetry, literature, law and medicine, speaking and writing with authority on all things and being eloquent in debate.

'I was with the Brehon Morann for eight years,' Fidelma replied.

'Your right to act as advocate before the court is recognised, Sister Fidelma.'

The young religieuse smiled.

'In that case, I call upon my right to speak with the accused and then with the witnesses.'

'Very well. But there can be only one plea before the court. The evidence is too damning to say other than that Brother Fergal is guilty of the murder of Barrdub.'

Brother Fergal was, as the Brehon said, a handsome young man no more than five and twenty years of age. He wore a bewildered expression on his pale features. The brown eyes were wide, the auburn hair was tousled. He looked like a young man awakened from sleep to find himself in a world he did not recognise. He rose awkwardly as Sister Fidelma entered the cell, coughing nervously.

The burly jailer closed the door behind her but stood outside.

'The grace of God to you, Brother Fergal,' she greeted.

'And of God and Mary to you, Sister,' responded the young religieux automatically. His voice was slightly breathless and wheezy.

'I am Fidelma sent from the abbey to act as your advocate.'

A bitter expression passed over the face of the young man.

'What good will that do? The Brehon has already judged me guilty.'

'And are you?'

Fidelma seated herself on a stool which, apart from the

rough straw palliasse, was the only furniture in the cell, and gazed up at the young monk.

'By the Holy Virgin, I am not!' The cry was immediate, angry and despairing at the same time. The young man punctuated his response with a paroxysm of coughing.

'Be seated, Brother,' said Fidelma solicitously. 'The cell is cold and you must take care of your cough.'

The young man contrived to shrug indifferently.

'I have suffered from asthma for several years now, Sister. I ease it by inhaling the odours of the burning leaves of *stramóiniam* or taking a little herbal drink before I retire at night. Alas, such a luxury is denied me here.'

'I will speak to the Brehon about it,' Fidelma assured him. 'He is not a harsh man. Perhaps we can find some leaves and seeds of the *stramóiniam* and have them sent in to you.'

'I would be grateful.'

After a little while, Fidelma reminded the young man that she awaited his story.

Reluctantly, he squatted on the palliasse and coughed again.

'Little to tell. The abbess sent me to the clan of Eóghanacht of Cashel, to preach and administer to them, four weeks ago. I came here and rebuilt a deserted cell on the blue hill of Cnoc-gorm. For a while all went well. True that in this part of Éireann, two hundred years after the blessed saint Patrick converted our people, I have found some whose hearts and souls have not been won over for Christ. That was a great sadness to me . . .'

'I have heard that there is one here who still follows the old ways of the druids,' Fidelma commented encouragingly when the young man paused and faltered in his thoughts.

'The hermit Erca? Yes. He dwells on Cnoc-gorm, too. He hates all Christians.'

'Does he now?' mused Fidelma. 'But tell me, what of the events of the night of the murder?'

Brother Fergal grimaced expressively.

'All I remember is that I returned to my cell at dusk. I was exhausted for I had walked sixteen miles that day, taking the Word of Christ to the shepherds in the mountains. I felt a soreness on my chest and so I heated and drank my herbal potion. It did me good for I slept soundly. The next thing I knew was being shaken awake to find the Brehon standing over me and Congal with him. Congal was screaming that I had killed his sister. There was blood on my hands and clothes. Then I saw, in my cell, the poor, blooded body of the girl, Barrdub.'

He started coughing again. Fidelma watched the face of the young religieux intently. There was no guile there. The eyes were puzzled yet honest.

'That is all?' she pressed when he had drawn breath.

'You asked me what I knew of the events of the night of the murder. That is all.'

Fidelma bit her lip. It sounded an implausible story.

'You were not disturbed at all? You heard nothing? You went to sleep and knew nothing until the Brehon and Congal woke you, when you saw blood on your clothes and the body of the dead girl in your cabin?'

The young man moaned softly, placing his face in his hands.

'I know nothing else,' he insisted. 'It is fantastic, I know, but it is the truth.'

'Do you admit that you knew the girl, Barrdub?'

'Of course. In the time I was here, I knew everyone of the clan of Eóghanacht.'

'And what of Barrdub? How well did you know her?'

'She came to religious service regularly and once or twice came to help me when I was rebuilding my *bothán*. But so did many others from the village here.'

'You had no special relationship with Barrdub?'

Priests, monks and nuns of the Celtic Church could enter into marriage provided such unions were blessed by a bishop or the congregation of the abbey.

'I had no relationship with Barrdub other than as pastor to one of his flock. Besides, the girl is not yet of the age of choice.'

'You know that Congal is claiming that Barrdub was in love with you and that you had encouraged this? The argument of the prosecution will be that she came to you that night and for some reason you rejected her and when she would not leave you, you killed her. It will be argued that her love became an embarrassment to you.'

The young monk looked outraged.

'But I did not! I only knew the girl slightly and nothing passed between us. Why . . . why, the girl is also betrothed, as I recall, to someone in the village. I can't remember his name. I can assure you that there was nothing between the girl and me.'

Fidelma nodded slowly and rose.

'Very well, Brother Fergal. If you have nothing else to tell me . . .?'

The young man looked up at her with large, pleading eyes.

'What will become of me?'

'I will plead for you,' she consented. 'But I have little so far to present to the court in your defence.'

'Then if I am found guilty?'

'You know the law of the land. If you are adjudged guilty of homicide then you must pay the honour-price of the girl, the *eric*, to her next of kin. The girl, I understand, was a free person, the daughter of a member of the clan assembly. The *eric* fine stands at forty-five milch cows plus four milch cows as the fee to the Brehon.'

'But I have no wealth. It was given up when I decided to serve Christ and took a vow of poverty.'

'You will also know that your family becomes responsible for the fine.'

'But my only family is the abbey, our order of brothers and sisters in Christ.'

Fidelma grimaced.

'Exactly so. The abbess has to decide whether she will pay your *eric* fine on behalf of our order. And the greater trial for your immortal soul will be heard under her jurisdiction. If you are judged guilty of killing Barrdub then not only must you make atonement to the civil court but, as a member of the religieux, you must make atonement to Christ.'

'What if the abbess refuses to pay the *eric* fine . . .?' whispered Fergal, his breath becoming laboured again.

'It would be unusual for her to refuse,' Fidelma assured him. 'In some exceptional circumstances she can do so. It is the right of the abbess to renounce you if your crime is so heinous. You can be expelled from the abbey. If so, you can be handed over by the Brehon to the victim's family to be disposed of, to treat as a slave or punish in any way thought fitting to compensate them. That is the law. But it will not come to that. The abbess cannot believe that you killed this girl.'

'Before God, I am innocent!' sobbed the young man.

Fidelma strode with the Brehon up the winding path to the tree-sheltered nook on Cnoc-gorm where Fergal had refurbished an old *bothán* for use as his cell. The Brehon led the way to the building which was constructed of inter-laid stones without mortar.

'This is where you found Brother Fergal and the dead girl, Barrdub?' asked Fidelma, as they paused outside the door.

'It is,' acknowledged the Brehon. 'Though the girl's body has been removed. I cannot see what use it will be to your advocacy to view this place.'

Fidelma simply smiled and went in under the lintel.

The room was small and dark, almost like the cell in which she had left Fergal, except that the *bothán* was dry whereas the cell was damp. There was a wooden cot, a table and chair, a crucifix and some other items of furnishing.

Fidelma sniffed, catching a bitter-sweet aromatic smell which permeated from the small hearth. The smell was of burnt leaves of *stramóiniam*.

The Brehon had entered behind her.

'Has anything been removed apart from the girl's body and the person of Brother Fergal?' Fidelma asked as her eye travelled to a wooden vessel on the table.

'As you see, nothing has been touched. Brother Fergal was in the bed, there, and the girl lay by the hearth. Only the girl's body and the person of Brother Fergal have been removed. Nothing else has been removed as nothing else was of consequence.'

'No other objects?'

'None.'

Fidelma went to the table, took up the wooden vessel and sniffed at it. There was a trace of liquid left and she dipped her finger in it and placed it, sniffing as she did so, against her lips. She grimaced at the taste and frowned.

'As Brehon, how do you account for the fact that, if Brother Fergal is guilty, it would follow he killed Barrdub and then went to bed, leaving her body here, and slept peacefully until morning? Surely a person who killed would have first done their best to hide the body and remove all trace of the crime lest anyone arrive and discover it?'

The round-faced Brehon nodded and smiled.

'That had already occurred to me, Sister Fidelma. But I am a simple judge. I have to deal with the facts. My concern is the evidence. It is not in my training to consider why a man should behave in the way he does. My interest is only to know that he does behave in such a manner.'

Fidelma sighed, set down the vessel and looked round again before leaving the cell.

Outside she paused, noticing a dark smear on one of the upright stone pillars framing the doorway. It was a little over shoulder height.

'Barrdub's blood, I presume?'

'Perhaps made as my men were carrying the body out,' agreed the Brehon uninterestedly.

Fidelma gazed at the smear a moment more before turning to examine the surroundings of the *bothán* which was protected by a bank of trees to one side, bending before the winds which whipped across the hill, while bracken grew thickly all around. The main path to the *bothán*, which led down to the village, was narrow and well-trodden. An even narrower path ascended farther up the hill behind the building while a third track meandered away to the right across the hillside. The paths were certainly used more than occasionally.

'Where do they lead?'

The Brehon frowned, slightly surprised at her question.

'The way up the hill will eventually bring you to the dwelling of the hermit, Erca. The path across the hillside is one of many that goes wherever you will. It is even an alternative route to the village.'

'I would see this Erca,' Fidelma decided.

The Brehon frowned, went to say something and then shrugged.

Erca was everything Fidelma had expected.

A thin, dirty man, clad in a single threadbare woollen cloak; he had wild, matted hair and staring eyes, and he showered abuse on them as they approached his smoking fire.

'Christians!' he spat. 'Out of my sight with your foreign god. Would you profane the sacred territory of The Dagda, father of all gods?'

The Brehon frowned angrily but Fidelma smiled gently and continued to approach.

'Peace to you, brother.'

'I am not your brother!' snarled the man.

'We are all brothers and sisters, Erca, under the one God who is above us all, whichever name we call Him by. I mean you no harm.'

'Harm, is it? I would see the gods of the Dé Danaan rise

up from the *sidhe* and drive all followers of the foreign god out of this land as they did with the evil Fomorii in the times of the great mists.'

'So you hate Christians?'

'I hate Christians.'

'You hate Brother Fergal?'

'This land could not set boundaries to my hatred of all Christians.'

'You would harm Brother Fergal, if you could?'

The man cracked his thumb at her.

'That to Fergal and all his kind!'

Fidelma seemed unperturbed. She nodded towards the cooking pot which sat atop the man's smoking fire.

'You are boiling herbs. You must be knowledgeable of the local herbs.'

Erca sneered.

'I am trained in the ancient ways. When your mad Patrick drove our priests from the Hill of Slane and forced our people to turn to his Christ, he could not destroy our knowledge.'

'I see you have a pile of pale brown roots, there. What herb is that?'

Erca frowned curiously at her a moment.

'That is *lus mór na coille*.'

'Ah, deadly nightshade,' Fidelma acknowledged. 'And those leaves with the white points next to them?'

'Those of the leaves of the *muing*, or poison hemlock.'

'And they grow on this hill?'

Erca made an impatient gesture of affirmation.

'Peace to you, then, Brother Erca,' Fidelma ended the conversation abruptly, and she turned away down the hill leaving the bewildered Erca behind. The perplexed Brehon trotted after her.

'No peace to you, Christian,' came Erca's wild call behind them as the hermit collected his thoughts. 'No peace until all worshippers of foreign gods are driven from the land of Éireann!'

Fidelma said nothing as she made her way down the hillside back to Fergal's *bothán*. As she reached it, she darted inside and then re-emerged a moment or two later carrying the wooden vessel.

'I shall need this in my presentation. Will you take it into your custody?'

'What line are you following, Sister?' frowned the Brehon as he accepted the vessel and they continued on to the village. 'For a moment I thought you might be suggesting that Erca is somehow involved in this matter.'

Fidelma smiled but did not answer the question.

'I would now like to see the brother of Barrdub. What was his name? Congal?'

They found the brother of Barrdub in a poor dwelling by the river bank, a *bothán* of rotting wood. The Brehon had made some preparation as they walked to Congal's cabin.

'Congal's father was once the hostel keeper for the Eóghanacht of Cashel, a man held in high honour, and a spokesman at the clan assembly. Congal was not the man his father was. Congal was always a dreamer. When his father died, he squandered away what could have been his so that he and his sister were reduced to living in this *bothán* and Congal forced to hire himself to work for other members of the clan rather than run his own cattle.'

Congal was a dark, brooding person with fathomless grey eyes as deep and angry as the sea on a stormy winter's day.

'If you have come to defend the murderer of my sister, I will answer no questions!' he told Fidelma belligerently, his thin, bloodless lips set firm.

The Brehon sighed in annoyance.

'Congal, you will obey the law. It is the right of the *dálaigh*, the advocate, to ask you questions and your duty to reply truthfully.'

Sister Fidelma motioned the man to be seated but he would not.

'Did you ever take *stramóiniam* to Brother Fergal?' she opened.

Congal blinked at the unexpectedness of her question.

'No,' he replied. 'He purchased his asthma medication from Iland the herbalist.'

'Good. Now I have heard how you discovered the body of your sister. Before you confirm the Brehon's account of that discovery, I want you to tell me what made you seek your sister in Brother Fergal's *bothán* when you knew her to be missing?'

Congal grimaced.

'Because Barrdub was enamoured of the man. He mesmerised her and used her.'

'Mesmerised? Why do you say this?'

Congal's voice was harsh.

'I knew my sister, did I not? Since Fergal came to this village, Barrdub mooned after the man like a sick cow after a farmer, always making excuses to go to visit him and help him rebuild the priest's *bothán*. It was disgusting.'

'Why disgusting?' the Brehon chimed in, suddenly interested. 'If she would have Fergal, or he would have her, there was nothing to prevent her save she have your consent or had reached the age of choice. You know as well as I do that all servants of Christ have the ancient right to marry the partner of their choice, even to an abbot or abbess?'

'It was disgusting because she was betrothed to Rimid,' Congal insisted.

'Yet before Fergal arrived here,' the Brehon observed wryly, 'you objected to Rimid as husband for Barrdub.'

Congal flushed.

'Why did you object to Rimid?' interposed Fidelma.

'Because . . .'

'Because he could not afford the full bride-price,' offered the Brehon before the man could reply. 'Isn't that so?'

'The *tinnscra* is as old as Éireann. No one marries without an offering of dowry to compensate the family of the bride,' Congal said stubbornly.

'And you were Barrdub's only family?' asked Fidelma.

'She kept my house. With her gone, I have no one else. It is right that I be compensated according to our ancient law.'

'Presumably, you raised this same objection over her liaison with Fergal? As a religieux he was not able to supply a *tinnscra*.'

Congal said sullenly: 'There was no question of that. He had no thought of marriage. He was using my sister and when she went to him seeking marriage, he killed her.'

'That remains to be proved,' Fidelma responded. 'Who else knew about the affair between your sister and Fergal?'

'No one,' Congal said promptly. 'My sister only admitted it to me with great unwillingness.'

'So you kept it to yourself? Are you sure no one else knew? What of Rimid?'

Congal hesitated, his eyes downcast.

'Yes,' he answered reluctantly. 'Rimid knew.'

'I will see this Rimid next,' Fidelma told the Brehon. She turned to leave and then hesitated, pausing to examine bunches of dried flowers and plants hung on the wall by the fireplace.

'What herb is this?'

Congal frowned at her for a moment.

'I have no knowledge of such things. Barrdub gathered all our herbs for cooking.'

Outside the Brehon cast a long puzzled look at Fidelma.

'You are greatly interested in herbs, sister,' he observed.

Fidelma nodded. 'Did you know that Brother Fergal suffers from asthma and that he is in the habit of inhaling the fumes of the burning leaves of *stramóiniam* or drinking an infusion of similar herbs each night to ease his chest?'

The Brehon shrugged. 'Some people are so afflicted,' he conceded, perplexed at her comment. 'Is it important?'

'Where will we find Rimid?'

'He may be at his work at this hour,' the Brehon sighed.

Fidelma raised an eyebrow. 'I was under the impression that Rimid did not work because Congal intimated that he was in no position to pay the *tinnscra*.'

The Brehon smiled broadly.

'Congal objected to the fact that Rimid could not pay the *full* bride-price. Rimid is not a man of wealth but he is a freeman of the clan and, unlike Congal, can sit in the clan assembly.'

'Congal cannot? He is so poor?'

'As you saw. A self-inflicted poverty. He has great schemes but they all come to nothing for he dreams of marvellous ways to gain respect and advancement in the clan but his expectations always exceed his means. He often has to rely on the generosity of the clan to feed himself. It makes him bitter.'

'And Barrdub? Was she bitter also?'

'No. Her hope was to escape her brother's poverty through marriage.'

'She must have been disappointed when Congal refused Rimid's offer of marriage.'

'This was so. I thought she might wait until she reached the *aimsir togu*, the age of consent, when she would be a woman and with full right of choice. Then I thought she would marry with Rimid. When she reached the age where she could decide, there would be no question of Congal being able to demand a bride-price. I think Rimid shared that belief. He was bitter when he learnt that Barrdub was throwing herself at Brother Fergal.'

'Was he now?' mused Fidelma. 'Well, let us go and speak with this Rimid. You say he might be at his work? Where would that be?'

The Brehon sighed.

'He might be at the *bothán* of Iland, the herbalist.'

Fidelma halted and stared at the Brehon in astonishment.

'Is Rimid a herbalist?'

The Brehon shook his head.

'No, no. He is not a professional man. He is employed by the herbalist to go abroad each day and gather the herbs and flowers wanted for the preparations.'

Rimid's face was full of bitter hatred. He was a flushed-faced, excitable youth, scarcely beyond the age of choice.

'Yes. I loved Barrdub. I loved her and she betrayed me. I might have won her back, but for this man, Fergal. I will kill him.'

The Brehon sniffed disdainfully.

'It is not your right, Rimid. The law will punish and seek compensation.'

'Yet if I meet him on the highway, I will slay him with as little compunction as I will a vermin.'

'Your hatred is great, Rimid, because you feel that he stole Barrdub from you,' interposed Fidelma. 'That is understandable. Did you also hate Barrdub?'

Rimid's eyes widened.

'Hate? No! I loved her.'

'Yet you say that she betrayed you, deserted your love for Brother Fergal. You must have been angry with her . . . angry enough . . .'

Fidelma let her voice trail off purposely.

Rimid blinked.

'Never! I would never harm her.'

'In spite of your hate? And did you also hate Congal?'

'Why hate Congal?' Rimid seemed puzzled.

'But he also denied you Barrdub by refusing your offer of a *tinnscra* which he thought was not sufficient.'

Rimid shrugged.

'I disliked Congal, yes. But Barrdub was only six months away from the *aimsir togu*, the age of choice, and she promised that when that time came we would marry without her brother's approval.'

'Did Congal know this?'

Rimid shrugged. 'I do not know. It is likely that Barrdub told him.'

'How did he accept it?'

'There was nothing he could do . . . but then Brother Fergal came along.'

'But Fergal did not have a *tinnscra* to offer. He is one of our order and took a vow of poverty.'

'Congal says there was no question of marriage. Fergal just mesmerised and played with the affections of Barrdub until she became too troublesome to him.'

'Mesmerised?' Fidelma frowned. 'An interesting choice of word, Rimid.'

'It is true.'

'Did you rebuke Barrdub about her relationship?'

Rimid hesitated and shook his head.

'I was blind. I did not know what was going on behind my back until the day before the murder.'

'How did you find out?'

'Congal told me. I met him on the road that evening with anger in his face. Barrdub had told him that day.'

'And when did you know about her death?'

'I was going to Fergal's *bothán* that morning to have it out with him when I met the Brehon and Congal on the path and they told me of Barrdub's death. Two men were carrying Barrdub's body on a litter and Fergal had been arrested for the crime.'

Fidelma glanced quickly to the Brehon for confirmation and he nodded.

'How long have you been a herb gatherer, Rimid?' Fidelma suddenly asked.

'Since I was a boy,' the man replied, hesitating slightly at her abrupt turn of tack.

'Did you, or Iland the herbalist, supply herbs to Brother Fergal?'

'I did not, but I knew that Iland did. I gather herbs for

Iland. Fergal suffered from want of breath and took herbs for the condition.'

'Was that well known?'

'Many knew,' replied Rimid.

'Barrdub knew?'

'Yes. She mentioned it to me once when we were at religious service.'

'Congal. Did he know?'

Rimid shrugged. 'Many knew. I do not know who specifically did or who did not.'

Fidelma paused and then smiled.

'I am finished.' She turned to the Brehon. 'I am now prepared to plead before the court tomorrow.'

Most of the clan of the Eóghanacht of Cashel were assembled in the great hall of the chieftain. The chieftain, Eóghan himself, sat on the right-hand side of the Brehon, who would sit in judgement. It was law and courtesy to consult with the chieftain of the clan when judgement was made.

Brother Fergal stood before the Brehon and the chieftain, a thickset and muscular clansman at his shoulder, with sword and shield, to keep order. Fergal was placed before a small waist-high wooden bar which was known as the *cos-na-dála*, the foot of the court, from which all accused before the *Dál*, or court, had to plead.

To the right of this was a small platform which had been erected for the prosecution's advocate or *dálaigh*; a thin, sharp-faced man. To the left, on a similar platform, sat Sister Fidelma, hands demurely folded in her lap, yet her clear green eyes missing nothing. The witnesses had been summoned and the *Dál* was crowded with the men and women of the clan, for never in the memory of the village had a member of the religieux been charged with the heinous crime of murder.

The Brehon, calling for silence, asked Brother Fergal if he accepted Sister Fidelma as his advocate for it was, according to ancient law, Fergal's right to conduct his own defence. Brother Fergal shook his head and indicated that Sister Fidelma would speak for him.

The prosecution then delivered his case in the manner which the Brehon had already advised Sister Fidelma.

There was a murmur of expectation as Sister Fidelma finally rose to address the Brehon.

'Brother Fergal is innocent of this crime,' she began in a loud compelling tone.

There was silence among the people.

'Do you dispute the evidence?' asked the Brehon, smiling slightly now. 'Remember, I went with Congal and discovered Barrdub's body lying in Brother Fergal's *bothán* with Fergal asleep on his bed. I saw the blood on his clothes.'

'I do not dispute that,' Fidelma assured him. 'But that in itself is no proof of the act of murder. The events as the prosecution describes them are not in contention, only the manner of their interpretation.'

Rimid let out an angry protest from the well of the court.

'Fergal is a murderer! She only seeks to protect one of her own!'

The Brehon gestured him to silence.

'Continue with your defence, Sister Fidelma.'

'Brother Fergal suffers from asthma. He is known to take herbal remedies to relieve his condition. This was known to several people. That night he returned to his *bothán* exhausted. He usually lit a fire of *stramóiniam* leaves and inhaled them before bed. But sometimes, when he was too exhausted, he took a drink of an infusion of similar herbs.'

Brother Fergal was staring at her.

'Fergal, did you inhale or drink the herbs that night?'

'I was too tired to sit up and prepare the inhalation. I always kept a kettle with an infusion of herbs ready. So I merely heated and drank a measure.'

'And you knew nothing more until the morning?'

'Nothing until I was awakened by the Brehon and Congal,' agreed the monk.

'You slept soundly. Is that usual?'

Brother Fergal hesitated, frowning as if he had not considered the matter before.

'Unusual. My chest often troubles me so that I wake in the early hours and must ease it with more of the infusion.'

'Quite so. You slept unusually soundly. So soundly that someone could enter your *bothán* without disturbing you? As, indeed, did the Brehon and Congal. You had to be shaken awake by both of them or you would not have known of their presence.'

The court was quiet and the Brehon was looking at her with curiosity.

'What are you suggesting, Sister Fidelma?'

'I suggest nothing. I present evidence. I took a wooden vessel from Brother Fergal's *bothán* in your presence and gave it to you as evidence.'

The Brehon nodded and indicated the wooden vessel on the table before him.

'This is so. There is the bowl.'

'Is this the vessel from which you drank, Fergal?'

The monk examined the vessel and nodded.

'It is mine. There is my name scratched on its surface. It is the vessel from which I drank.'

'There remains some liquid at the bottom of the vessel and I tasted it. It was not an infusion of *stramóiniam*.'

'What then?' demanded the Brehon.

'To please the court, we could call Iland, the herbalist, to examine it and give his opinion. But the court knows that I am an *Anruth* and qualified in the knowledge of herbs.'

'The court accepts your knowledge, Sister Fidelma,' replied the Brehon impatiently.

Fidelma bowed her head.

'It contains the remains of an infusion of *lus mór na coille* together with *muing*.'

'For those not acquainted with herbs, explain what these are,' instructed the Brehon, frowning.

'Certainly. The *lus mór na coille*, which we call deadly nightshade, is a powerful sedative inducing sleep, while *muing*, or poison hemlock, if taken in large doses can produce paralysis. Any person knowledgeable about herbs will tell you this. By drinking this infusion, Brother Fergal was effectively drugged. He slept the sleep of one dead and was oblivious to everything. It was lucky that he was aroused at all. It may well be that whoever provided him with the potion did not expect him to ever awake. Brother Fergal would simply have been found dead, next to Barrdub. The conclusion would have been that he killed her and then took this poisonous mixture in an act of remorse.'

She paused at the disturbance which her words provoked. Brother Fergal stood staring at her with a shocked, pale face.

The Brehon, calling for silence, then addressed himself to Fidelma.

'Are you saying that Barrdub was killed in Fergal's *bothán* while he slept and he did not know it?'

'No. I am saying that the person who drugged Fergal, killed Barrdub elsewhere and carried her body to the *bothán*, leaving it inside. That person then rubbed some of her blood on Fergal's hands and clothes while he lay in his drugged slumber. Having created the scene, that person then departed. The murderer made several errors. He left the tell-tale evidence of the drinking vessel in which were the remains of the drugs. And he left Barrdub's blood smeared on the side of the door when he carried her body into the bothán.'

'I recall you showing me that stain,' the Brehon intervened. 'At the time I pointed out that it was probably caused when we removed the body.'

'Not so. The stain was at shoulder height. When you removed the body, it is reported that your men placed it on a litter. Two men would have carried the litter.'

The Brehon nodded confirmation.

'The highest the litter, with the body, could be carried in comfort would be at waist height. But the stain was at shoulder height. Therefore, the stain was not caused when the body was removed from the *bothán* but when it was carried in. The murderer, being one person, had to carry the body on his own. The easiest method to carry such a dead weight is on the shoulders. The stain was made at shoulder height when the body was carried inside by the murderer.'

'Your argument is plausible,' conceded the Brehon. 'But not conclusive.'

'Then let me put this before the court. Your argument is that brother Fergal stabbed Barrdub to death in a mad frenzy. Then, exhausted, too exhausted to take the body out of his *bothán* to conceal the murder, he fell asleep on his bed and was found the next morning.'

'That is as the prosecution contends.'

'Where then is the weapon?'

'What?' The word came slowly from the mouth of the Brehon, a growing doubt appearing in his eyes.

'You made no mention of a weapon, the knife by which Barrdub was stabbed to death. If you did not take it when you found Fergal that morning, it must have still been there. I searched the *bothán*. I found no weapon. Brother Fergal carries no such knife.'

The Brehon bit his lip.

'It is true, no weapon was found.'

'Yet a weapon must exist with Barrdub's blood upon it.'

'Fergal could have hidden it,' countered the Brehon, realising his fault for not instigating the search before.

'Why? Why hide the weapon when he was too exhausted to hide the body?'

'Your arguments are possible explanations. Yet if Fergal did not murder Barrdub, who did?' Before she could answer, the Brehon's eyes lit up. 'Ah, so that is why you were interested in the hermit Erca's herbs? Do you contend that

he did this? That he did it to harm Fergal? We all know that
he hates every Christian.'

Fidelma shook her head emphatically.

'Erca hates all Christians, but he did not do this. He
simply confirmed my suspicion that I had tasted two powerful drugs which could be easily obtained in the vicinity. A
deeper motive lies behind this murder than simply a hatred
of Christians.'

She turned and caught Rimid's pale face. The man's lips
were trembling.

'She is trying to lay the blame on me!' he cried.

The Brehon also was looking at Rimid with deep suspicion. He demanded: 'Was not your hatred of Fergal great?
You said as much to us yesterday.'

'I did not do it. I loved Barrdub . . . I . . .' Rimid sprang to
his feet and began to fight his way out of the great hall.

'Seize him!' cried the Brehon. Two clansmen moved
forward.

But Fidelma had turned to the Brehon with shaking head.

'No, let him go. It was not Rimid.'

The Brehon frowned. Rimid, caught between the two clansmen, halted his struggles and glanced back in bewilderment.

'Who then?' the Brehon demanded in exasperation.

'Barrdub was murdered by Congal.'

There was a gasp.

'A lie! The bitch lies!' Congal had leapt to his feet in the
great hall, his face pale, his hands clasped into fists.

'Congal murdered his own sister?' The Brehon was
incredulous. 'But why?'

'For one of the oldest motives of all. For gain.'

'But, Barrdub has no property. What gain is in this deed?'

Sister Fidelma sighed sadly.

'Congal was an impecunious man. His father had held a
good position within the clan and Congal, if all went well,
could have expected no less. But things were never well for
Congal. He was capricious, undependable. He preferred to

dream and make great plans which always went awry. He was reduced, with his sister, to living in a poor wood and mud *bothán*, hiring out his labour to his neighbours who were better off than he was. They pitied him. That made him bitter. All this was common knowledge. You, Brehon, told me as much.

'Rimid and Barrdub were in love with each other. Rimid was not possessed of great wealth. He survived as most of us do, content to earn his living. But when Rimid went to ask Congal's approval to marry Barrdub, who was not yet at the age of consent, Congal refused. Why? Because Congal did not care for his sister's happiness. He cared for wealth. He demanded the full bride-price or *tinnscra* due for the daughter of a free hostel keeper of the tribe, even though both his sister and he had long fallen from that social position.'

'Yet that was his right in law,' interposed the Brehon.

'A right, truly. But sometimes rights can be a form of injustice,' replied Fidelma.

'Carry on.'

'Rimid could not afford the full *tinnscra*. Barrdub was indignant and made it clear to her brother that when she reached the age of consent, when she had free and equal choice, she would go with Rimid anyway. Her brother would not profit from any *tinnscra* then.'

Sister Fidelma paused a moment to gather her thoughts.

'Congal had conceived the idea that his only hope to alleviate his poverty and become respectable in the tribe was to get his hands on twenty milch cows which a prospective husband would pay for the full *tinnscra* or bride-price. Then a new idea came into his mind. A fantastic idea. Why settle for twenty milch cows for the bride-price? If his sister was slain, the murderer or his family would have to pay compensation and that compensation was set in law at no less than forty-five milch cows, the foundation of a respectable herd and one which would make him a person of position in the tribe. But he would have to ensure that the person charged with the crime could pay such a sum.

'Then Brother Fergal appears. It is true that an individual monk is not wealthy. However, it is the law that members of the *fine* or family of a person unable to pay the *eric* or compensation become responsible for the payment to the victim's family. It is well known that the abbey stands in place of a family. If a member of the abbey is found guilty of a crime, then the abbey would be expected to pay the *eric*. Congal reasoned that the abbey could well afford the forty-five milch cows that would be the compensation. Poor Barrdub's fate was then sealed.

'Congal knew of Fergal's ailment and means of medica-tion. He prepared the potion, threw out Fergal's usual mixture and substituted his own drugged brew. He reasoned that Fergal would not check the contents of his kettle before he heated the herbal drink. Then Congal saw Rimid and prepared the way further by telling him that Barrdub was smitten by Fergal, that they were in love. Finally, Congal went to find Barrdub and the rest we already know.

'He killed her, carried her into Fergal's *bothán* as soon as the monk had dropped into his deep sleep, and left her there, smearing Fergal's hands and clothes with her blood. His two major mistakes were not leaving the murder weapon at the scene and not destroying the traces of the herbs in Fergal's bowl.'

She turned to where Congal was standing, his face white, his mouth working.

'There stands your contemptible killer. He murdered his own sister for a herd of cows.'

With a shriek, Congal drew a knife and leapt towards Sister Fidelma. People scattered left and right before his frenzied figure.

Just before he reached her, the dark figure of a man intercepted him and struck him full in the face. It was Rimid. Congal collapsed senseless to the ground. As Rimid made to move forward, Fidelma reached forward and laid her slender hand on his shoulder.

'Revenge is no justice, Rimid. If we demand vengeance for every evil done against us, we will be guilty of greater evil. Let the court deal with him.'

Rimid hesitated.

'He has no means of paying adequate compensation to those he has wronged,' he protested.

Fidelma smiled softly.

'He has a soul, Rimid. He attempted to wrong a member of the family of the abbey. The abbey will demand compensation; the compensation will be his soul which will be given to God for disposal.'

'You will have him killed? Dispatched to God in the Otherworld?'

She shook her head gently.

'God will take him when the time is ordained. No, he will come to serve at the abbey and, hopefully, find repentance in the service.'

After Brother Fergal had been absolved and Congal taken to be held for his trial, Fidelma walked to the door of the great hall with the Brehon.

'How did you suspect Congal?' asked the man.

'A man who lies once, will lie again.'

'In what lie did you discover him?'

'He claimed he knew nothing about herbs but he knew soon enough what the herb *stramóiniam* is used for and that Brother Fergal took it regularly. The rest was a mixture of elementary deduction and bluff for it might have been hard to prove conclusively without Congal's admittance of guilt.'

'You are an excellent advocate, Sister Fidelma,' observed the Brehon.

'To present a clever and polished argument is no great art. To perceive and understand the truth is a better gift.'

She paused at the door and smiled at the judge. 'Peace with you, Brehon of the Eóghanacht of Cashel.' Then she was gone, striding away along the dusty road towards the distant abbey.

Murder by Miracle

෨

As the boat rocked its way gently against the natural granite quay, Sister Fidelma could see her welcome committee standing waiting. The committee consisted of one young, very young, man; fresh-faced and youthful, certainly no more than twenty-one summers in age. He wore a noticeable expression of petulance, coupled with resolution, on his features.

At the boatman's gesture, Sister Fidelma eased herself into position by the side of the vessel and grabbed for the rope ladder, hauling herself quickly up on to the grey granite quay. She moved with a youthful agility which seemed at odds with her demure posture and religious habit. To the young man watching her perilous ascent, her tall but well-proportioned figure, strands of red hair escaping from under her head-dress, the young, attractive features and bright green eyes, had not been what he was expecting when he had been informed that a *dálaigh*, an advocate of the Brehon Court, was coming to the island. This young woman was not his idea of a religieuse let alone a respected member of the law courts of Éireann.

'Sister Fidelma? Did you have a good trip over?' The young man's voice was slow, his tone measured, not really friendly but 'correct'. The phrase 'coldly polite' came into Fidelma's mind and she grimaced wryly before allowing her features to break into an amused grin. The grin disconcerted the young man for a moment. It was also at odds with her status. It was an urchin grin of frivolity. Fidelma gestured wordlessly to the seas breaking behind her.

With the late autumnal seas running dirty grey and heavy with yellow-cream foamed caps, the trip from the mainland had not been one that she had enjoyed. The wind was cold and blustery and whistling against this serrated crag of an island which poked into the wild, angry Atlantic like the top of an isolated hill that had been severed from its fellows by a flood of brooding water. Approaching the island, the dark rocks seemed like the comb of a fighting cock. She had marvelled how anyone could survive and scratch a living on its seemingly inhospitable wasteland.

On her way out the boatman had told her that only one hundred and sixty people lived on the island, which, in winter, could sometimes be cut off for months with not even a deftly rowed currach being able to make a landing. The island's population were close-knit, introspective, mainly fisherfolk, and there had been no suspicious deaths there since time immemorial.

That was, until now.

The young man frowned slightly and when she made no reply he spoke again.

'There was no need to bother you with this matter, Sister Fidelma. It is quite straightforward. There was no need to bring you out from the mainland.'

Sister Fidelma regarded the young man with a soft smile.

There was no disguising the fact that he felt put out. Sister Fidelma was an outsider interfering with his jurisdiction.

'Are you the *bó-aire* of the island?' she asked.

The young man drew himself up with a posture of dignity in spite of his youth.

'I am,' he replied with a thinly disguised air of pride. *The bó-aire* was a local magistrate, a chieftain without land whose wealth was judged by the number of cows he owned, hence he was called a 'cow chief'. Small communities, such as those on the tiny islands off the coast, were usually ruled by a *bó-aire* who owed allegiance to greater chieftains on the mainland.

'I was visiting Fathan of the Corca Dhuibhne when news of this death reached him,' Fidelma said softly.

Fathan of the Corca Dhuibhne was the chieftain over all these islands. The young *bó-aire* stirred uncomfortably. Sister Fidelma continued:

'Fathan requested me to visit and aid you in your inquiry.' She decided that this formula was a more diplomatic way of approaching the proud young magistrate than by recounting the truth of what Fathan had said. Fathan knew that the *bó-aire* had only just been appointed and knew, too, that the matter needed a more experienced judgement. 'I have some expertise in inquiry into suspicious deaths,' Fidelma added.

The young man bit his lip sullenly.

'But there is nothing suspicious about this death. The woman simply slipped and fell down the cliff. It's three hundred feet at that spot. She didn't have a chance.'

'So? You are sure it was an accident?'

Sister Fidelma became aware that they had both been standing on the quay with the wind whipping at them and the salt sea spray dampening their clothing. She was wet in spite of the heavy wool cloak she had put on for the crossing from An Chúis on the mainland.

'Is there somewhere we can go for shelter? Somewhere more comfortable to talk this over?' She posed the second question before the young man could reply to her first.

The young *bó-aire* reddened at the implied rebuke.

'My *bothán* is up the road here, Sister. Come with me.'

He turned to lead the way.

There were one or two people about to acknowledge the *bó-aire* as he passed and to cast curious glances at Sister Fidelma. The news of her arrival would soon be all over the island, she thought. Fidelma sighed. Island life seemed all very romantic in the summer but even then she preferred life on the mainland, away from the continually howling winds and whipping sea spray.

In the snug, grey stone cabin of the *bó-aire*, a smouldering turf fire supplied a degree of warmth but the atmosphere was still damp. A young woman of the *bó-aire's* household provided an earthenware vessel of mead, heated with a hot iron bar from the fire. The drink put warmth and vigour into Fidelma.

'What's your name?' she asked as she sipped the drink.

'Fogartach,' replied the *bó-aire* stiffly, realising that he had trespassed by neglecting to introduce himself properly to his guest.

Sister Fidelma felt the time had come to ensure the proud young man knew his place.

'Well, Fogartach, as local magistrate, what qualification in law do you hold?'

The young man's head rose a little in vanity.

'I studied at Daingean Chúis for four years. I am qualified to the level of *dos* and know the *Bretha Nemed* or Law of privileges as well as any.'

Sister Fidelma smiled softly at his arrogance.

'I am qualified in law to the level of *Anruth*,' she said quietly, 'having studied eight years with the Brehon Morann of Tara.'

The *bó-aire* coloured, perhaps a little embarrassed that he had sounded boastful before someone who held a degree that was only one step below the highest qualification in the five kingdoms of Éireann. Little more needed to be said. Sister Fidelma had, as gently as she could, established her authority over the *bó-aire*.

'The matter is straightforward enough,' Fogartach said, a little sulky. 'It was an accident. The woman slipped and fell down the cliff.'

'Then the investigation should not take us long,' replied Sister Fidelma with a bright smile.

'Investigation? I have my report here.'

The young man turned with a frown to a sheaf of paper.

'Fogartach,' Fidelma said slowly and deliberately, 'Fathan of the Corco Dhuibhne is anxious that everything is, as you say, straightforward. Do you realise who the woman was?'

'She was a religieuse, such as yourself.'

'A religieuse? Not just any religieuse, Fogartach. The woman was Cuimne, daughter of the High King.'

The young man frowned.

'I knew her name was Cuimne and that she carried herself with some authority. I did not realise she was related to the High King.'

Sister Fidelma grimaced helplessly.

'Did you also not realise that she was the Abbess Cuimne from Ard Macha, personal representative of the most powerful churchman in Éireann?'

The young *bó-aire's* face was red with mortification. He shook his head silently.

'So you now see, Fogartach,' went on Fidelma, 'that the chieftain of the Corco Dhuibhne cannot allow any question to arise over the manner of her death. Abbess Cuimne was an important person whose death may have ramifications at Tara as well as Ard Macha.'

The young *bó-aire* bit his lip, seeking a way to justify himself.

'Position and privilege do not count for much on this little windswept rock, Sister,' he replied in surly fashion.

Fidelma's eyes widened.

'But they count with Fathan of the Corco Dhuibhne, for he is answerable to the King of Cashel and the King of Cashel is answerable to the High King and to the Archbishop of Ard Macha. That is why Fathan has sent me here,' she added, now deciding the time had come to be completely brutal with the truth.

She paused to let the young man consider what she was saying before continuing.

'Well, take me through what you know of this matter, Fogartach.'

The *bó-aire* sat back uneasily, bit his lip for a moment and then resigned himself to her authority.

'The woman . . . er, the Abbess Cuimne arrived on the island four days ago. She was staying at the island's *bruighean*, the hostel run by Bé Bail, the wife of Súilleabháin, the hawk-eyed, a local fisherman. Bé Bail has charge of our island hostel. Not that we have much use for it, few people ever bother to visit our island.'

'What was Abbess Cuimne doing here?'

The *bó-aire* shrugged.

'She did not say. I did not even know she was an abbess but simply thought her to be a member of some community come here to find isolation for a while. You know how it is with some religious? They often seek an isolated place to meditate. Why else should she be here?'

'Why indeed?' Fidelma echoed softly and motioned the young man to continue.

'She told Bé Bail that she was leaving the island yesterday. Ciardha's boat from An Chúis would have arrived about noon. She packed her satchel after breakfast and went off to walk alone. When she didn't return at noon, and Ciardha's boat had left, Bé Bail asked me to keep a lookout for her. The island is not so large that you can get lost.

'Well, a little after lunch, Buachalla came running to me . . .'

'Who is Buachalla?'

'A young boy. A son of one of the islanders.'

'Go on.'

'The boy had spotted Abbess Cuimne's body below Aill Tuatha, that's the cliffs on the north of the island. I organised a couple of men together with the apothecary . . .'

'An apothecary? Do you have a resident apothecary on the island?' Fidelma interposed in surprise.

'Corcrain. He was once personal physician to the *Eóghanacht* of Locha Léin. He had a desire to withdraw to the island a year ago. He sought solitude after his wife's death but has become part of our community, practising his art for the good of the islanders.'

'So, a couple of islanders, the apothecary and yourself, all followed the young boy, Buachalla?'

'We found the body of Abbess Cuimne at the foot of the cliffs.'

'How did you get down to it?'

'Easy enough. There's a stony beach under the cliffs at that point. There is an easy path leading down to it. The path descends to the stretch of rocks about a half-mile from where she fell. At the point she fell, incidentally, cliffs rise to their highest point. It was just under the highest point that we found the body.'

'Did Corcrain examine her?'

'He did so. She was dead so we carried her back to his *bothán* where he made a further examination and found . . .'

Sister Fidelma held up her hand.

'I'll speak to the apothecary shortly. He will tell me what he found. Tell me, did you make a search of the area?'

The *bó-aire* frowned and hesitated.

'Search?'

Sister Fidelma sighed inwardly.

'After you found the body, what then?'

'It was obvious what had happened. Abbess Cuimne had been walking on the edge of the cliffs, slipped and fell. As I said, it is three hundred feet at that point.'

'So you did not search the top of the cliff or the spot where she fell?'

Fogartach smiled faintly.

'Oh, her belongings, such as she carried, were with Bé Bail at the hostel. She carried little else save a small satchel. You must know that religious carry but little with them when they travel. There was no need to look further. I have her belongings here, Sister. The body has already been buried.'

Sister Fidelma bit her tongue in exasperation at the ignorant conceit of the young man.

'Where do I find Corcrain, the apothecary?'

'I'll show you,' said the *bó-aire*, rising.

'Just point me in the right direction,' Fidelma replied sarcastically. 'I promise not to get lost.'

The young *bó-aire* was unable to prevent an expression of irritation from crossing his face. Fidelma smiled maliciously to herself. She suspected that the young *bó-aire's* arrogance was due to the fact that he considered her unworthy of her office because of her sex. Some of the island people, she knew, adhered to curious notions.

Corcrain's *bothán*, or cabin, stood only two hundred yards away across the rising ground, one of many well-spaced stone buildings strung out across the slopes of the island like rosary beads. The slopes rose from the sea to stretch towards the comb-like rocks forming the back of the island which sheltered the populated area from the fierce north winds.

The apothecary was nearly sixty, a swarthy man, whose slight frame still seemed to exude energy. His grey eyes twinkled.

'Ah, so you are the female Brehon that we have all been hearing about?'

Fidelma found herself returning the warm guileless smile.

'I am no Brehon, merely an advocate of the Brehon Court, apothecary. I have just a few questions to ask you. Abbess Cuimne was no ordinary religieuse. She was sister of the High King and representative of the Archbishop of Ard Macha. This is why Fathan, chieftain of the Corco Dhuibhne, wants to assure himself that everything is as straightforward as it should be. Unless a proper report is sent to Tara and to Ard Macha, Abbess Cuimne's relatives and colleagues might be prone to all sorts of imaginings, if you see what I mean.'

Corcrain nodded, obviously trying to disguise his surprise.

'Are you a qualified apothecary?'

'I was apothecary and chief physician to the Eóghanacht kings of Locha Léin,' replied Corcrain. It was just a matter-of-fact statement without arrogance or vanity.

'What was the cause of Abbess Cuimne's death?'

The old apothecary sighed. 'Take your pick. Any one of a number of the multiple fractures and lacerations whose cause seems consistent with a fall down a three-hundred-foot granite cliff on to rocks below.'

'I see. In your opinion she slipped and fell down the cliff?'

'She fell down the cliff,' the apothecary replied.

Sister Fidelma frowned at his choice of words.

'What does that mean?'

'I am no seer, Sister. I cannot say that she slipped nor how she came to go over the cliff. All I can say is that her injuries are consistent with such a fall.'

Fidelma watched the apothecary's face closely. Here was a man who knew his job and was careful not to intrude his own interpretation on the facts.

'Anything else?' she prompted.

Corcrain bit his lip. He dropped his gaze for a moment.

'I chose to withdraw to a quiet island, Sister. After my wife died, I resigned as physician at the court of the Eóghanacht and came here to live in a small rural community to forget what was going on in the outside world.'

Fidelma waited patiently.

'It has taken me a full year to become accepted here. I don't want to create enmity with the islanders.'

'Are you saying that there was something which makes you unhappy about the circumstances of Abbess Cuimne's death? Did you tell this to the *bó-aire*?'

'Fogartach? By the living God, no. He's a local man. Besides, I wasn't aware of the "something", as you put it, until after they had brought the body back here and I had begun my examination.'

'What was this "something"?'

'Well, there were two "somethings" in reality and nothing from which you can deduce anything definite.'

Fidelma waited while the apothecary seemed to gather his thoughts together.

'The first curiosity was in the deceased's right hand, which was firmly clenched. A section of silver chain.'

'Chain?' Fidelma queried.

'Yes, a small silver chain.' The apothecary turned, brought out a small wooden box and opened it.

Fidelma could see in it that there was a section of chain which had obviously been torn away from something, a piece no more than two inches in length. She picked it up and examined it. She could see no artisan's marks on the silver. It had been worked by a poor, provincial craftsman, not overly proud of his profession.

'Did Abbess Cuimne wear any jewellery like that? What of her crucifix, for example?'

'Her own crucifix, which I gave to the *bó-aire*, is much richer, and worked in gold and ivory. It looked as if it were fashioned under the patronage of princes.'

'But you would say that when she fell she was clutching a broken piece of silver chain of poor quality?'

'Yes. That is a fact.'

'You said there were two "somethings". What else?'

The apothecary bit his lip as if making up his mind before revealing it to Sister Fidelma.

'When a person falls in the manner she did, you have to expect a lot of bruising, contusions . . .'

'I've been involved in falls before,' Sister Fidelma observed dryly.

'Well, while I was examining the body I found some bruising to the neck and shoulders, the fleshy part around the nape of the neck. The bruising was slightly uniformed, not what one would expect from contact with rocks during a fall.'

'How would you decipher those marks?'

'It was as if Abbess Cuimne had, at some time, been gripped by someone with powerful hands from behind.'

Fidelma's green eyes widened.

'What are you suggesting?'

'Nothing. It's not my place to. I can't even say how the bruising around the neck and shoulders occurred. I just report what I see. It could be consistent with her general injuries but I am not entirely satisfied it is.'

Fidelma put the piece of silver chain in the leather purse at her waist.

'Very well, Corcrain. Have you prepared your official report for the *bó-aire* yet?'

'When I heard that a Brehon from the mainland was coming, I thought that I'd wait and speak with him . . . with her, that is.'

She ignored his hasty correction.

'I'd like to see the spot where Abbess Cuimne went over.'

'I'll take you up there. It's not a long walk.'

The apothecary reached for a blackthorn walking stick, paused and frowned at Sister Fidelma's sandals.

'Do you not have anything better to wear? The mud on the path would destroy those frail things.'

Fidelma shook her head.

'You have a good-sized foot,' observed the apothecary, meditatively. He went to a chest and returned with a stouter pair of leather round-top shoes of untanned hide with three layers of hide for the sole, such as the islanders wore. 'Here, put these on. They will save your dainty slippers from the mud on the island.'

A short time later, Fidelma, feeling clumsy but at least dry in the heavy untanned leather island shoes, was following Corcrain along the pathway.

'Had you seen Abbess Cuimne before the accident?' Fidelma asked as she panted slightly behind her guide's wiry, energetic form as Corcrain strode the ascending track.

'It's a small island. Yes, I saw and spoke to her on more than one occasion.'

'Do you know why she was here? The *bó-aire* did not even know that she was an abbess. But he seems to think she was simply a religieuse here in retreat, to meditate in this lonely spot away from distraction.'

'I didn't get that impression. In fact, she told me that she was engaged in the exploration of some matter connected with the island. And once she said something odd . . .'

He frowned as he dredged his memory.

'It was about the bishop of An Chúis. She said she was hoping to win a wager with Artagán, the bishop.'

Sister Fidelma's eyes widened in surprise.

'A wager. Did she explain what?'

'I gathered that it was connected with her search.'

'But you don't know what that search was for?'

Corcrain shook his head.

'She was not generally forthcoming, so I can understand why the *bó-aire* did not even learn of her rank; even I did not know that, though I suspected she was no ordinary religieuse.'

'Exploration?' Sister Fidelma returned to Corcrain's observation.

Corcrain nodded. 'Though what there is to explore here, I don't know.'

'Well, did she make a point of speaking to anyone in particular on the island?'

The apothecary frowned, considering for a moment.

'She sought out Congal.'

'Congal. And who is he?'

'A fisherman by trade. But he is also the local *seanchaí*, the traditional historian and storyteller of the island.'

'Anyone else?'

'She went to see Father Patrick.'

'Who?'

'Father Patrick, the priest on the island.'

They had reached the edge of the cliffs now. Sister Fidelma steeled herself a little, hating the idea of standing close to the edge of the wild, blustery, open space.

'We found her directly below this spot,' Corcrain pointed.

'How can you be so sure?'

'That outcrop of rock is a good enough marker.' The apothecary indicated with the tip of his blackthorn.

Fidelma bent and examined the ground carefully.

'What are you looking for?'

'Perhaps for the rest of that chain. I'm not sure.'

She paused and examined a patch of broken gorse and trodden grass with areas of soft muddy ground. There were deep imprints of shoes, which the faint drizzle had not yet washed away. There was nothing identifiable, just enough remaining to show that more than one person had stood in this spot.

'So this area is consistent with the spot she must have gone over from?'

The apothecary nodded.

Fidelma bit her lip. The marks could well indicate that more than one person had left the path, two yards away from the edge at this point, and stood near to the edge of the cliff. But the most important thing about the cliff edge here was the fact that, as it was at least two yards away from the worn track, there was surely no way that the Abbess Cuimne could go over the cliff by accident while walking along the path. To fall over, she would have had already deliberately to leave the pathway, scramble across some shrub and gorse and balance on that dangerous edge. But if not an accident . . . what then?

There was something else, too, about the cliff edge. But she did not wish to move too close, for Fidelma hated high, unprotected places.

'Is there a means of climbing down here?' she suddenly asked Corcrain.

'Only if you are a mountain goat, I reckon. No, it's too

dangerous. Not that I am saying it is totally impossible to get down. Those with knowledge of climbing such inaccessible spots might well attempt it. There are a few caves set into the face of the cliff along here and once some people from the mainland wanted to go down to examine them.'

'At this spot?'

'No. About three hundred yards along. But the *bó-aire* saw them off, declaring it was too dangerous. That was last year.'

Fidelma took off her short woollen cloak, which she wore to protect her from the almost continuous drizzle of the island's grey skies, and put it down near the cliff edge. Then she knelt down before stretching full-length on it and easing forward to peer over the edge. It was as the apothecary said, only someone skilled in the art of climbing or a mountain goat would even attempt to climb down. She shivered for a moment as she stared at the rocky beach three hundred feet below.

When she had stood up and brushed down her cloak she asked Corcrain, 'Where do I find this man Congal?'

Congal was a big man. He sat before a plate piled with fish and a boiled duck's egg. Though he sat at table, he still wore his fisherman's clothes, as if he could not be bothered to change on entering his *bothán*. Yet the clothes simply emphasised his large, muscular torso. His hands, too, were large and calloused.

'Sad, it is,' he growled across the scrubbed pine table to where Sister Fidelma sat with a bowl of sweet mead which he had offered in hospitality. 'The woman had a good life before her but it is a dangerous place to be walking if you don't know the ground.'

'I'm told that she was exploring here.'

The big man frowned.

'Exploring?'

'I'm told that she spoke with you a few times.'

'Not surprising that she would do so. I am the local *seanchaí*. I know all the legends and tales of the island.' There was more than a hint of pride in his voice. Sister Fidelma realised that pride went with the islanders. They had little enough but were proud of what they did have.

'Is that what she was interested in? Ancient tales?'

'It was.'

'Any subject or tale in particular?'

Congal shifted as if defensively.

'None as I recall.'

'What then?'

'Oh, just tales about the ancient times, when the druids of Iarmuma used to hunt down the priests of Christ and kill them. That was a long time ago, even before the Blessed Patrick came to our shores.'

'You provided her with some of these tales?'

Congal nodded.

'I did so. Many priests of Christ found a refuge on this island during the pagan times. They fled from the mainland while the king of Iarmuma's men were burning down the churches and communities.'

Sister Fidelma sighed. It did not sound the sort of subject Abbess Cuimne would be interested in pursuing. As representative of the Archbishop, she had, as Sister Fidelma knew, special responsibility for the uniform observances of the faith in Ireland.

'But no story in particular interested her?' she pressed.

'None.'

Was Congal's voice too emphatic? Sister Fidelma felt an uneasy pricking at the back of her neck, that odd sensation she always felt when something was wrong, or someone was not telling the full truth.

Back at the cabin of the *bó-aire*, Sister Fidelma sorted through the leather satchel which contained the belongings of the dead Abbess. She steeled herself to sorting through the items which became objects of pathetic sentiment. The items proclaimed the Abbess to have some vanity, the few cosmetics and a jar of perfume, her rosary and crucifix, a splendidly worked piece of ivory and gold, which proclaimed her rank, as sister to the High King, rather than her role as a humble religieuse. The rosary beads were of imported ivory. There were items of clothes for her journey. All were contained in the leather shoulder satchel which travelling monks and nuns carried on their journeys and pilgrimages.

Sister Fidelma sorted through the satchel twice before she realised what was worrying her. She turned to the impatient *bó-aire*.

'Fogartach, are you sure these are all the Abbess Cuimne's possessions?'

The young magistrate nodded vehemently.

Sister Fidelma sighed. If Abbess Cuimne was on the island to carry out some search or investigation, surely she would have had a means of recording notes? Indeed, where was the pocket missal that most religious of rank carried? Over a century before, when Irish monks and nuns had set out on their missions to the far corners of the world, they had to carry with them liturgical and religious tracts. It was necessary, therefore, that such works were small enough for missionaries to carry with them in special leather satchels called *tiag liubhar*. Therefore the monks engaged in the task of copying such books began to reduce their size. Such small books were now carried by almost all learned members of the church. It would be odd if the Abbess had not carried even a missal with her.

She drummed her fingers on the table-top for a while. If the answer to the conundrum was not forthcoming on the island, perhaps it might be found in the wager with Artagán, the bishop of An Chúis on the mainland. She made her decision and turned to the expectant *bó-aire*.

'I need a currach to take me to An Chúis on the mainland at once.'

The young man gaped at her in surprise.

'Have you finished here, Sister?'

'No. But there is someone I must consult at An Chúis immediately. The boat must wait for me so that I can return here by this afternoon.'

Bishop Artagán rose in surprise when Sister Fidelma strode into his study at the abbey of An Chúis, after being ceremoniously announced by a member of his order. It was from here that Artagán presided over the priesthood of the Corco Dhuibhne.

'There are some questions I would ask you, Bishop,' she announced as soon as the introductions were over.

'As a *dálaigh* of the Brehon Court, you have but to ask,' agreed the bishop, a flaccid-faced, though nervous, man of indeterminable age. He had led her to a seat before his fire and offered hospitality in the form of heated mead.

'The Abbess Cuimne . . .' began Fidelma.

'I have heard the sad news,' interrupted the bishop. 'She fell to her death.'

'Indeed. But before she went to the island, she stayed here in the abbey, did she not?'

'Two nights while waiting for a calm sea in order to travel to the island,' confirmed Artagán.

'The island is under your jurisdiction?'

'It is.'

'Why did the Abbess Cuimne go to the island? There is talk that she had a wager with you on the result of her visit and what she would find there.'

Artagán grimaced tiredly.

'She was going on a wild goose chase,' he said disarmingly. 'My wager was a safe one.'

Fidelma drew her brows together in perplexity.

'I would like an explanation.'

'The Abbess Cuimne was of a strong personality. This was natural as she is . . . was . . . sister to the High King. She had great talents. This, too, is natural, for the Archbishop at

Armagh appointed her as his personal representative to ensure the uniformity of holy office among the monasteries and churches of Éireann. I have met her only twice. Once at a synod at Cashel and then when she came to stay before going to the island. She entertained views that were sometimes difficult to debate with her.'

'In what way do you mean?'

'Have you heard the legend of the reliquary of the Blessed Palladius?'

'Tell me it,' invited Fidelma in order to cover her bewilderment.

'Well, as you know, two and a half centuries ago, the Christian community in Éireann was very small but, God willing, increasing as people turned to the word of Christ. By that time they had reached such a size that they sent to the holy city of Rome to ask the Pope, Celestine, the first of his name to sit on the throne of Peter, the disciple of Christ, to send them a bishop. They wanted a man who would teach and help them follow the ways of the living God. Celestine appointed a man named Palladius as the first bishop to the Irish believing in Christ.'

Artagán paused before continuing.

'There are two versions of the story. Firstly, that Palladius, *en route* to Éireann, took sick in Gaul and died there. Secondly, that Palladius did reach our shores and administer to the Irish, eventually being foully murdered by an enraged druid in the pay of the king of Iarmuma.'

'I have heard these stories,' confirmed Sister Fidelma. 'It was after Palladius's death that the Blessed Patrick, who was then studying in Gaul, was appointed bishop to Ireland and returned to this land, where once he had been held as a hostage.'

'Indeed,' agreed Artagán. 'A legend then arose in the years after Palladius's death: that relics of this holy saint were placed in a reliquary; a box with a roof-shaped lid, about twelve centimetres wide by six in length by five deep. They are usually made of wood, often yew; lined inside in lead and on the outside ornate with gilt, copper alloy, gold foil, with amber and glass decoration. Beautiful things.'

Sister Fidelma nodded impatiently. She had seen many such reliquaries among the great abbeys of Éireann.

'The legend had it that Palladius's relics were once kept at Cashel, seat of the Eóghanacht kings of Munster. Then about two hundred years ago there was a revival of the beliefs of the druids in Iarmuma. The king of Iarmuma resumed the old religion and a great persecution of Christian communities began. Cashel was stormed. But the relics were taken into the country for safe-keeping; taken from one spot to another until the relics of our first bishop were taken to the islands, away from the ravages of man. There they disappeared.'

'Go on,' prompted Sister Fidelma when the bishop paused.

'Well, just think of it. What a find it would be if we could discover the relics of the first bishop of Éireann after all this time! What a centre of pilgrimage their resting place would make, what a great abbey could be built there which would attract attention from the four corners of the world . . .'

Sister Fidelma grimaced wryly.

'Are you saying that the Abbess Cuimne had gone to the island searching for the reliquary of Palladius?'

Bishop Artagán nodded.

'She informed me that in Ard Macha, in the great library there, she had come across some old manuscripts which indicated that the reliquary was taken to an island off the mainland of the Corco Dhuibhne. The manuscripts, which she refused to show me, were claimed to contain notes of its location written at the time. The notes had been kept in an old book in the library of the monastery of Ard Macha. There were legends of priests fleeing to these islands during the persecutions of the king of Iarmuma, but surely we would have known had the sacred reliquary been taken there.'

The bishop sniffed disparagingly.

'So you did not agree with Abbess Cuimne that the reliquary was on the island?' queried Sister Fidelma.

'I did not. I am something of a scholar of the period myself. Palladius died in Gaul. That much is obvious, for most records recount that fact.'

'So this is why you thought that the abbess was on a wild goose chase?'

'Indeed, I did so. The relics of Palladius have not survived the ravages of time. If they have, then they would be in Gaul, not here. It was hard to dissuade Abbess Cuimne. A strong-willed woman, as I have told you.'

The bishop suddenly frowned.

'But what has this to do with your investigation into her death?'

Sister Fidelma smiled gently and rose from her seat.

'I only needed to assure myself of the purpose of her visit to the island.'

On the bouncing trip back, over the harsh, choppy grey seas, Sister Fidelma sat in the currach and reflected with wrinkled forehead. So it was logical that the Abbess Cuimne had talked about the reliquary of Palladius to Congal, the *seanchaí* of the island; why then had the man not been forthcoming about that fact? What was the big fisherman trying to hide? She decided to leave Congal for the time being and go straight away on landing to talk with the island's priest, Father Patrick. He had been the second person whom the Abbess Cuimne had made a special effort to talk with on the island.

Father Patrick was an old man, certainly into his mid- or even late eighties. A thin wisp of a man, who, Sister Fidelma thought, would be blown away by the winds that buffeted the island. A man of more bone than flesh, with large knuckles, a taut parchment-like skin and a few strands of white hair.

From under overhanging brows, pale eyes of indiscernible colour stared at Fidelma.

Father Patrick sat in a chair by his fireside, a thick wool shawl wrapped around his frail frame and held close by a brooch around his scrawny neck.

Yet withal the frailty and age, Fidelma felt she was in the presence of a strong and dynamic personality.

'Tell me about the reliquary of Palladius,' Sister Fidelma opened abruptly. It was a shot in the dark but she saw that it paid off.

The aged face was immobile. Only the eyes blinked once as a token of surprise. But Fidelma's quiet eyes picked up the involuntary action.

'What have you heard about the old legend?'

The rasping voice was so pitched that Fidelma was hard pressed to hear any emotion, but there was something there . . . something defensive.

'*Is* it a legend, Father?' asked Fidelma with emphasis.

'There are many old legends here, my daughter.'

'Well, Abbess Cuimne thought she knew this one to be true. She told the Bishop of the Corco Dhuibhne that she was going to see the reliquary before she left the island.'

'And now she is dead,' the old priest observed almost with a sigh. Again the watery pale eyes blinked. 'May she rest in peace.'

Sister Fidelma waited a moment. The priest was silent.

'About the reliquary . . .' she found herself prompting.

'So far as people are concerned it is only a legend and will remain so.'

Sister Fidelma frowned, trying to interpret this statement.

'So it is not on the island?'

'No islander has seen it.'

Fidelma pursed her lips in an effort to suppress her annoyance. She had the distinct feeling that Father Patrick was playing semantic games with her. She tried another tack.

'Abbess Cuimne came to talk with you on a couple of occasions, didn't she? What did you talk about?'

'We talked about the folklore of the island.'

'About the reliquary?'

The priest paused. 'About the legend of the reliquary,' he corrected.

'And she believed it was here, on the island, isn't that so?'

'She believed so.'

'And it is not?'

'You may ask any islander if they have seen it or know of its whereabouts.'

Fidelma sighed impatiently. Again there had come the semantic avoidance of her question. Father Patrick would have made a good advocate, skilful in debate.

'Very well, Father. Thank you for your time.'

She was leaving the priest's cell when she met Corcrain, the apothecary, at the step.

'How ill is Father Patrick?' Fidelma asked him directly.

'Father Patrick is a frail old man,' the apothecary replied. 'I fear he will not be with us beyond this winter. He has already had two problems with his heart, which grows continually weaker.'

'How weak?'

'Twice it has misbeat. The third time may prove fatal.'

Sister Fidelma pursed her lips.

'Surely the bishop could retire an old man like that? He could go to rest in some comfortable abbey on the mainland.'

'Surely; if anyone could persuade Father Patrick to leave the island. He came here as a young man sixty years ago and has never left. He's a stubborn old fellow. He thinks of the island as his fiefdom. He feels responsible, personally, for every islander.'

Sister Fidelma sought out Congal again. This time the *seanchaí* met her with suspicion.

'What did the Abbess Cuimne want to know about the

reliquary of Palladius?' demanded Sister Fidelma without preamble.

The big man's jaw dropped a little at the unexpectedness of her question.

'She knew it was on the island, didn't she?' pressed Fidelma, not giving the man a chance to reflect on the question.

Congal compressed his lips.

'She thought it was so,' he replied at last.

'Why the secret?'

'Secret?'

'If it is on the island, why has it been kept secret?'

The big man shifted awkwardly.

'Have you spoken with Father Patrick?' he asked sullenly.

'I have.'

Congal was clearly unhappy. He hesitated again and then squared his shoulders.

'If Father Patrick has spoken with you, then you will know.'

Fidelma decided not to enlighten the storyteller that Father Patrick had told her virtually nothing.

'Why keep the fact that the reliquary is on the island a secret?' she pressed again.

'Because it is the reliquary of Palladius; the very bones of the first bishop appointed to the Irish believing in Christ, the blessed saint who brought us out of the darkness into Christian light. Think, Sister Fidelma, what would happen if it were generally known that the relics were here on this island. Think of the pilgrims who would come streaming in, think of the great religious foundations that would be raised on this island, and everything that would follow that. Soon people from all over the world would be coming here and destroying our peace. Soon our community would be swamped or dispersed. Better that no one knows about the relics. Why, not even I have seen them nor know where they are hidden. Only Father Patrick . . .'

Congal caught sight of Sister Fidelma's face and must have read its amazed expression.

'Did Father Patrick tell you . . .? What did Father Patrick tell you?' he suddenly demanded, his face full of suspicion.

There was an abrupt knocking at the *bothán* door and before Congal could call out the young *bó-aire* put his head around the door. His face was troubled.

'Ah, Sister, Corcrain the apothecary asks if you could return at once to Father Patrick's cell. Father Patrick has been taken ill but is demanding to see you.'

Corcrain met her at Father Patrick's door.

'I doubt if he has long, Sister,' he said quietly. 'Not long after you left he had that third shock to the heart that I was warning against. However, he insists on seeing you alone. I'll be outside if you need me.'

The old priest was lying in bed, his face was wan with a curiously bluish texture to the skin.

The eyes flickered open, the same colourless pale eyes.

'You know, don't you, my daughter?'

Sister Fidelma decided to be truthful.

'I suspect,' she corrected.

'Well, I must make my peace with God and better that you should know the truth rather than let me depart with only suspicion to shroud my name.'

There was a long pause.

'The reliquary is here. It was brought by priests fleeing from the king of Iarmumua's warriors over two hundred and fifty years ago. They hid it in a cave for safe-keeping. For generations, the priest officiating on this island would tell only his successor of its whereabouts. Sometimes when a priest wasn't available, an islander would be told so that the knowledge would pass on to each new generation. I came here as a young priest some sixty years ago and learnt the secret from the old priest I was to replace.'

The old man paused to take some deep breaths.

'Then the Abbess Cuimne came. A very intelligent woman. She had found evidence. She checked the legends with Congal, who knows a lot save only where the relics are hidden. He tried to stop her going further by telling her nothing, little short of lying to her. Then she came to me. To my horror, she had a piece of parchment, a series of jumbled notes written in the hand of no less a person than the Blessed Patrick himself. When Palladius died, Patrick had been sent by the Pope to succeed him as bishop to the Irish. The parchment contained a map, directions which were meaningless unless one knew what it was that one was looking for, and the place one had to look in.

'Abbess Cuimne was clever. She had heard of the legends and found this paper tucked into an ancient book belonging to the Blessed Patrick in Ard Macha's great library. She made some educated guesses, my daughter.'

'And you tried to dissuade her from continuing her search?'

'I did everything to persuade her that legends are not necessarily reality. But she was determined.'

'And then?'

'Then I was honest with her. I pleaded with her to spare this island the consequence of the revelation of the news that it was the hiding place of the reliquary. I pointed out the consequences to this community if such a thing was made public. You are a woman with some imagination, Sister Fidelma. I can tell. Imagine what would happen to this peaceful little island, to this happy little community.'

'Could the relics not be taken off the island?' asked Fidelma. 'Perhaps they could be sent to Cashel or even to Ard Macha?'

'And then this island would lose the holy protection given to it by being the repository of the sacred relics. No. The relics were brought here for a purpose and here they must remain.'

The old priest's voice had suddenly become sharp. Then he fell silent for a while before continuing.

'I tried my best to make her see what a disaster it would be. We have seen what disasters have happened to other communities where relics have been found, or miracles have been witnessed, and great abbeys have been built and shrines erected. Small communities were devastated. Places of simple pious pilgrimage have been made into places of crass commercial enterprise. Devastation beyond imagining, all the things which so repelled our Saviour. Did He not chase the moneylenders and merchants from the temple grounds? How much more would He turn on those who made His religion a subject of commercialism today? No, I did not want that for our tiny island. It would destroy our way of life and our very soul!'

The old priest's voice was vehement now.

'And when Abbess Cuimne refused to accept your arguments, what did you do?' prompted Sister Fidelma, quietly.

'At first, I hoped that the abbess would not be able to decipher properly the figures which would lead her to the reliquary. But she did. It was the morning that she was due to leave the island . . .'

He paused and an expression of pain crossed his face. He fought to catch his breath but shook his head when Fidelma suggested that she call the apothecary.

Sister Fidelma waited patiently. The priest finally continued.

'As chance would have it I saw the Abbess Cuimne on the path to Aill Tuatha, the north cliff. I followed her, hoping against hope. But she knew where she was going.'

'Is that where the reliquary is hidden,' asked Fidelma. 'In one of the cliff-top caves at Aill Tuatha?'

The priest nodded in resignation.

'The abbess started to climb down. She thought the descent was easy. I tried to stop her. To warn of her of the danger.'

The priest paused, his watery eyes now stirring in emotion.

'I am soon going to meet my God, my daughter. There is no priest on the island. I must make my peace with you. This is by nature of my confession. Do you understand?'

Fidelma paused; a conflict between her role as an advocate of the Brehon Court and that as a member of a religious order with respect for the confessional caused her to hesitate. Then she finally nodded.

'I understand, Father. What happened?'

'The abbess started to descend the cliff towards the cave entrance. I cried out and told her if she must go down to be careful. I moved forward to the edge of the cliff and bent down even as she slipped. Her hand reached out and grabbed at my crucifix, which I wore on a silver chain around my neck. The links of the chain snapped. In that moment I grabbed for her, holding on momentarily to her shoulders and even her neck.

'Alas, I am old and frail; she slid from my grip and went hurtling down to the rocks.'

The priest paused, panting for breath.

Sister Fidelma bit her lip.

'And then?' she prompted.

'Peering down, I could see that she was dead. I knelt a while in prayer, seeking to absolve her for her sins, of which audacity and arrogance were the only ones I knew. Then a thought struck me, which grew in my mind and gave me comfort. We are all in God's hands. It occurred to me that it was His intervention. He might have saved the abbess. Instead, perhaps it was His will that had been wrought, a miracle which prevented the reliquary being discovered. One death to prevent a great evil, the destruction of our community. The thought has given me comfort, my daughter. So I simply picked up my broken crucifix, though some of the chain was missing. Then I forced myself to walk back to the path, walk down to the beach and search her. I found her missal and inside the piece of paper that had given her the clue, the one written by the Blessed Patrick. I took them both and I returned here. I was silly, for I should have simply taken the paper and left her missal. I realised how odd it must have looked to the trained eye that it was missing. But I was exhausted. My health was none too good. But the reliquary was safe . . . or so I thought.'

Sister Fidelma gave a deep, troubled sigh.

'What did you do with the paper?'

'God forgive me, though it was written in the hand of the Blessed Patrick, I destroyed it. I burnt it in my hearth.'

'And the missal?'

'It is there on the table. You may send it to her kinsmen.'

'And that is all?'

'It is all, my daughter. Yet my conscience has troubled me. Am I, in turn, arrogant enough to think that God would enact a murder . . . even for such a pious purpose? My grievous sin is not coming forward to the *bó-aire* with my story. But my main purpose was to keep the secret of the reliquary. Now I am dying. I must tell someone of the secret. Perhaps God has willed that you, a total stranger to this island, should know the truth as you had learnt part of that truth already. What is the old Latin hexameter? – *quis*, *quid*, *ubi*, *quibus*, *auxilius*, *cur*, *quomodo*, *quando*?'

Sister Fidelma smiled softly at the old man.

'Who is the criminal? What is the crime? Where was it committed? By what means? With what accomplices? Why? In what way? When?'

'Exactly so, my daughter. And now you know these things. You suspected either Congal or myself of some dark crime. There was no crime. If it was, the cause was a miracle. I felt I had no choice but to tell you and place the fate of this island and its community in your hands. Do you understand what this means, my daughter?'

Sister Fidelma slowly nodded.

'I do, Father.'

'Then I have done what I should have done before.'

★　★　★

Outside the priest's cell a number of islanders had gathered, gazing at Sister Fidelma with expressions varying between curiosity and hostility. Corcrain looked quizzically at her but Fidelma did not respond to his unspoken questions. Instead she went to find Congal to tell him about the cave at Aill Tuatha. That was Congal's responsibility, not her burden.

The gulls swooped and cried across the grey granite quay of the island. The blustery winds caught them, causing it to seem as if they had stopped momentarily in their flight, and then they beat their wings at the air and swooped again. The sea was choppy and through its dim grey mist Sister Fidelma could see Ciardha's boat from An Chúis, heaving up and down over the short waves as it edged in towards the harbour. It was not going to be a pleasant voyage back to the mainland. She sighed.

The boat would be bringing a young priest to the island to take over from Father Patrick. He had fallen into a peaceful sleep and died a few hours after Sister Fidelma had spoken with him.

Fidelma's choice had been a hard one. She had returned to the *bó-aire's* cabin and pondered all night over the young magistrate's official report in the light of what she now knew.

Now she stood waiting for the boat to arrive to take her away from the island. At her side the fresh-faced young magistrate stood nervously.

The boat edged in towards the quay. Lines were thrown and caught, and the few travellers climbed their way to the quay up the ancient rope ladder. The first was a young man, clean-featured and looking appallingly youthful, wearing his habit like a brand-new badge of office. Congal and Corcrain were standing at the head of the quay to greet him.

Sister Fidelma shook her head wonderingly. The priest did not look as if he had learnt yet to shave and already he was 'father' to one hundred and sixty souls. She turned and impulsively held out her hand to the young *bó-aire*, smiling.

'Well, many thanks for your hospitality and assistance, Fogartach. I'll be speaking to the Chief Brehon and to Fathan of the Corco Dhuibhne. Then I'll be glad to get back to my interrupted journey back to my Abbey of Kildare.'

The young man held on to Sister Fidelma's hand a fraction of a second longer than necessary, his worried eyes searching her face.

'And my report, Sister?'

Sister Fidelma broke away and began her descent, halting a moment on the top rung of the ladder. In spite of the young man's arrogance, it was wrong to continue to play the cat and mouse with him.

'As you said, Fogartach, it was a straightforward case. The Abbess Cuimne slipped and fell to her death. A tragic accident.'

The young *bó-aire's* face relaxed and, for the first time, he smiled and raised a hand in salute.

'I have learnt a little wisdom from you, *Anruth* of the Brehon Court,' he said stiffly. 'God keep you safe on your journey until you reach your destination!'

Sister Fidelma smiled back and raised a hand.

'Every destination is but a gateway to another, Fogartach,' she answered. Then she grinned her urchin grin before dropping into the stern of the gently rocking currach as it waited for her below.

A Canticle for Wulfstan

❧

Abbot Laisran smiled broadly. He was a short, rotund, red-faced man. His face proclaimed a permanent state of jollity, for he had been born with that rare gift of humour and a sense that the world was there to provide enjoyment to those who inhabited it. When he smiled, it was no faint-hearted parting of the lips but an expression that welled from the depths of his being, bright and all encompassing. And when he laughed it was as though the whole earth trembled in accompaniment.

'It is so good to see you again, Sister Fidelma,' Laisran boomed, and his voice implied it was no mere formula but a genuine expression of his joy in the meeting.

Sister Fidelma answered his smile with an almost urchin grin, quite at odds with her habit and calling. Indeed, those who examined the young woman closely, observing the red hair thrusting from beneath her head-dress, seeing the bubbling laughter in her green eyes, and the natural expression of merriment on her fresh, attractive face, would wonder why such an alluring young woman had taken up the life of a religieuse. Her tall, yet well-proportioned figure seemed to express a desire for a more active life than that in the cloistered confines of a religious community.

'And it is good to see you again, Laisran. It is always a pleasure to come to Durrow.'

Abbot Laisran reached out both his hands to take Fidelma's extended one, for they were old friends. Laisran had known Fidelma since she had reached the age of choice, and he, it was, who had persuaded her to take up the study of law under the Brehon Morann of Tara. Further, he had persuaded her to continue her studies until she had reached the qualification of *Anruth*, one degree below that of *Ollamh*, the highest rank of learning. It had been Laisran who had advised her to join the community of Brigid at Kildare when she had become accepted as a *dálaigh*, an advocate of the Brehon Court. In the old days, before the Light of Christ reached the shores of Éireann, all those who held professional office were of the caste of druids. When the druids gave up their power to the priests and communities of Christ, the professional classes, in turn, enlisted in the new holy orders as they had done in the old.

'Shall you be long among us?' inquired Laisran.

Fidelma shook her head.

'I am on a journey to the shrine of the Blessed Patrick at Ard Macha.'

'Well, you must stay and dine with us this night. It is a long time since I have had a stimulating talk.'

Fidelma grimaced with humour.

'You are abbot of one of the great teaching monasteries of Ireland. Professors of all manner of subjects reside here with students from the four corners of Ireland. How can you be lacking stimulating discourse?'

Laisran chuckled.

'These professors tend to lecture, there is little dialogue. How boring monologues can be. Sometimes I find more intelligence among our students.'

The great monastery on the plain of the oaks, which gave it the name Durrow, was scarcely a century old but already its fame as a university had spread to many peoples of Europe. Students flocked to the scholastic island, in the middle of the Bog of Aillin, from numerous lands. The Blessed Colmcille had founded the community at Durrow before he had been exiled by the High King and left the shores of Éireann to form his more famous community on Iona in the land of the Dàl Riada.

Sister Fidelma fell in step beside the abbot as he led the way along the great vaulted corridors of the monastery towards his chamber. Brothers and laymen scurried quietly hither and thither through the corridors, heads bowed, intent on their respective classes or devotions. There were four faculties of learning at Durrow: theology, medicine, law and the liberal arts.

It was mid-morning, halfway between the first Angelus bell and the summons of the noonday Angelus. Fidelma had been up before dawn and had travelled fifteen miles to reach Durrow on horseback, the ownership of a horse being a privilege accorded only to her rank as a representative of the Brehon Court.

A solemn-faced monk strode across their path, hesitated and inclined his head. He was a thin, dark-eyed man of swarthy skin who wore a scowl with the same ease that Abbot Laisran wore a smile. Laisran made a curious gesture of acknowledgement with his hand, more as one of dismissal than recognition, and the man moved off into a side room.

'Brother Finan, our professor of law,' explained Laisran, almost apologetically. 'A good man, but with no sense of humour at all. I often think he missed his vocation and that he was designed in life to be a professional mourner.'

He cast a mischievous grin at her.

'Finan of Durrow is well respected among the Brehons,' replied Fidelma, trying to keep her face solemn. It was hard to keep a straight face in the company of Laisran.

'Ah,' sighed Laisran, 'it would lighten our world if you came to teach here, Fidelma. Finan teaches the letter of the law, whereas you would explain to our pupils that often the law can be for the guidance of the wise and the obedience of fools, that justice can sometimes transcend law.'

Sister Fidelma bit her lip.

'There is sometimes a moral question which has to be resolved above the law,' she agreed. 'Indeed, I have had to face decisions between law and justice.'

'Exactly so. Finan's students leave here with a good knowledge of the law but often little knowledge of justice. Perhaps you will think on this?'

Sister Fidelma hesitated.

'Perhaps,' she said guardedly.

Laisran smiled and nodded.

'Look around you, Fidelma. Our fame as a centre of learning is even known in Rome. Do you know, no fewer than eighteen languages are spoken among our students? We resort to Latin and sometimes Greek as our lingua franca. Among the students that we have here are not just the children of the Gael. We have a young Frankish prince, Dagobert, and his entourage. There are Saxon princes, Wulfstan, Eadred, and Raedwald. Indeed, we have a score of Saxons. There is Talorgen, a prince of Rheged in the land of Britain . . .'

'I hear that the Saxons are making war on Rheged and attempting to destroy it so they can expand their borders,' observed Fidelma. 'That cannot make for easy relationships among the students.'

'Ah, that is so. Our Irish monks in Northumbria attempt to teach these Saxons the ways of Christ, and of learning and piety but they remain a fierce warrior race intent on conquest, plunder, and land. Rheged may well fall like the other kingdoms of the Britons before them. Elmet fell when I was a child. Where the Britons of Elmet once dwelt, now there are Saxon farmers and Saxon thanes.'

They halted before Laisran's chamber door. The bishop opened it to usher Fidelma inside.

Fidelma frowned. 'There has been perpetual warfare between the Britons and the Saxons for the last two and a half centuries. Surely it is hard to contain both Briton and Saxon within the same hall of learning?'

They moved into Laisran's official chamber, which he used for administering the affairs of the great monastery. He motioned Fidelma to be seated before a smouldering turf fire and went to pour wine from an earthenware jug on the table, handing a goblet to her and raising the other in salute.

'*Agimus tibi gratia, Omnipotens Deus*,' he intoned solemnly but with a sparkle of humour in his eyes.

'Amen,' echoed Sister Fidelma, raising the goblet to her lips and tasting the rich red wine of Gaul.

Abbot Laisran settled himself in a chair and stretched out his feet towards the fire.

'Difficult to contain Briton and Saxon?' he mused, after a while. In fact, Sister Fidelma had almost forgotten that she had asked the question. 'Yes. We have had several fights among the Britons and the Saxons here. Only the prohibition of weapons on our sacred ground has so far prevented injury.'

'Why don't you send one group or the other to another centre of learning?'

Laisran sniffed.

'That has already been suggested by Finan, no less. A neat, practical, and logical suggestion. The question is . . . which group? Both Britons and Saxons refuse to go, each group demanding that if anyone leave Durrow then it should be the other.'

'Then you have difficulties,' observed Fidelma.

'Yes. Each is quick to anger and slow to forget an insult, real or imaginary. One Saxon princeling, Wulfstan, is very arrogant. He has ten in his retinue. He comes from the land of the South Saxons, one of the smaller Saxon kingdoms, but to hear him speak you would think that his kingdom encompassed the world. The sin of pride greatly afflicts him. After his first clash with the Britons he demanded that he be given a chamber whose window was barred from ingress and whose door could be bolted from the inside.'

'A curious request in a house of God,' agreed Sister Fidelma.

'That is what I told him. But he told me that he feared for his life. In fact, so apprehensive was his manner, so genuine did his fear appear, that I decided to appease his anxiety and provide him with such a chamber. I gave him a room with a barred window in which we used to keep transgressors but had our carpenter fix the lock so that the door could be barred from the inside. Wulfstan is a strange young man. He never moves without a guard of five of his retinue. And after Vespers he retires to his room but has his retinue search it before he enters and only then will he enter alone and bar the door. There he remains until the morning Angelus.'

Sister Fidelma pursed her lips and shook her head in wonder.

'Truly one would think him greatly oppressed and frightened. Have you spoken to the Britons?'

'I have, indeed. Talorgen, for example, openly admits that all Saxons are enemies of his blood but that he would not deign to spill Saxon blood in a house of God. In fact, the young Briton rebuked me, saying that his people had been Christian for centuries and had made no war on sacred ground, unlike the Saxons. He reminded me that within the memory of living man, scarcely half a century ago, the Saxon warriors of Aethelfrith of Northumbria had defeated Selyf map Cynan of Powys in battle at a place called Caer Legion, but they profaned their victory by slaughtering a thousand British monks from Bangor-is-Coed. He averred that the Saxons were scarcely Christian in thought and barely so in word and deed.'

'In other words . . .?' prompted Fidelma when Laisran paused to sip his wine.

'In other words, Talorgen would not harm a Saxon protected by the sacred soil of a Christian house, but he left no doubt that he would not hesitate to slay Wulfstan outside these walls.'

'So much for Christian charity, love, and forgiveness,' sighed Fidelma.

Laisran grimaced. 'One must remember that the Britons have suffered greatly at the hands of the Saxons during these last centuries. After all, the Saxons have invaded and conquered much of their land. Ireland has received great communities of refugees fleeing from the Saxon conquests in Britain.'

Fidelma smiled whimsically. 'Do I detect that you approve of Talorgen's attitude?

Laisran grinned.

'If you ask me as a Christian, no, no, of course not. If you ask me as a member of a race who once shared a common origin, belief, and law with our cousins, the Britons, then I must say to you that I have a sneaking sympathy for Talorgen's anger.'

There came a sudden banging at the door of the chamber, so loud and abrupt that both Laisran and Fidelma started in surprise. Before the abbot had time to call out, the door burst open and a middle-aged monk, his face red, his clothes awry from running, burst breathlessly into the room.

He halted a few paces inside the door, his shoulders heaving, his breath panting from exertion.

Laisran rose, his brows drawing together in an unnatural expression of annoyance.

'What does this mean, Brother Ultan? Have you lost your senses?'

The man shook his head, eyes wide. He gulped air, trying to recover his breath.

'God between us and all evil,' he got out at last. 'There has been a murder committed.'

Laisran's composure was severely shaken.

'Murder, you say?'

'Wulfstan, the Saxon, your Grace! He has been stabbed to death in his chamber.'

The blood drained from Laisran's face and he cast a

startled glance towards Sister Fidelma. Then he turned back to Brother Ultan, his face now set in stern lines.

'Compose yourself, Brother,' he said kindly, 'and tell me slowly and carefully. What has occurred?'

Brother Ultan swallowed nervously and sought to collect his thoughts.

'Eadred, the companion of Wulfstan, came to me during the mid-morning hour. He was troubled. Wulfstan had not attended the morning prayers nor had he been at his classes. No one had seen him since he retired into his chamber following Vespers last night. Eadred had gone to his chamber and found the door closed. There was no response to his summons at the door. So, as I am master of the household, he came to see me. I accompanied him to Wulfstan's chamber. Sure enough, the door was closed and clearly barred on the inside.'

He paused a moment and then continued.

'Having knocked awhile, I then, with Eadred's help, forced the door. It took a while to do, and I had to summon the aid of two other Brothers to eventually smash the wooden bars that secured it. Inside the chamber . . .' He bit his lip, his face white with the memory.

'Go on,' ordered Laisran.

'Inside the chamber was the body of Wulfstan. He lay back on the bed. He was in his night attire, which was stained red with congealed blood. There were many wounds in his chest and stomach. He had been stabbed several times. It was clear that he had been slain.'

'What then?'

Brother Ultan was now more firmly in control. He contrived to shrug at Laisran's question.

'I left the two Brothers to guard the chamber. I told Eadred to return to his room and not to tell anyone until I sent for him. Then I came immediately to inform you, your Grace.'

'Wulfstan killed?' Laisran whispered as he considered the implications. 'Then God protect us, indeed. The land of the

South Saxons may be a small kingdom, but these Saxons band together against all foreigners. This could lead to some incident between the Saxons and the land of Éireann.'

Sister Fidelma came forward from her seat, frowning at the master of the household.

'Let me get this clear, Brother Ultan, did you say that the chamber door was locked from the inside?'

Brother Ultan examined her with a frown of annoyance, turning back to Abbot Laisran as though to ignore her.

'Sister Fidelma is a *dálaigh* of the Brehon Court, Brother,' Laisran rebuked softly.

The Brother's eyes widened and he turned hurriedly back to Sister Fidelma with a look of respect.

'Yes, the door of Wulfstan's chamber was barred from the inside.'

'And the window was barred?'

A look of understanding crossed Ultan's face.

'No one could have entered or left the chamber through the window, Sister,' he said slowly, swallowing hard, as the thought crystallised in his mind.

'And yet no one could have left by the door?' pressed Sister Fidelma remorselessly.

Ultan shook his head.

'Are you sure that the wounds of Wulfstan were not self-inflicted?'

'No!' whispered Ultan, swiftly genuflecting.

'Then how could someone have entered his chamber, slaughtered him, and left it, ensuring that the door was bolted from the inside?

'God help us, Sister!' cried Ultan. 'Whoever did this deed was a sorcerer! An evil demon able to move through walls of stone!'

Abbot Laisran halted uneasily at the end of the corridor in which two of his brethren stood to bar the way against any inquisitive members of the brethren or students. Already, in spite of Brother Ultan's attempt to stop the spread of the news, word of Wulfstan's death was being whispered among the cloisters. Laisran turned to Sister Fidelma, who had followed at his heels, calm and composed, her hands now folded demurely in the folds of her gown.

'Are you sure that you wish to undertake this task, Sister?'

Sister Fidelma wrinkled her nose.

'Am I not an advocate of the Brehon Court? Who else should conduct this investigation if not I, Laisran?'

'But the manner of his death . . .'

She grimaced and cut him short.

'I have seen many bodies and only few have died peacefully. This is the task that I was trained for.'

Laisran sighed and motioned the two brothers to stand aside.

'This is Sister Fidelma, a *dálaigh* of the Brehon Court who is investigating the death of Wulfstan on my behalf. Make sure that she has every assistance.'

Laisran hesitated, raised his shoulder almost in a gesture of bewilderment, then turned and left.

The two Brothers stood aside respectfully as Sister Fidelma hesitated at the door.

The chamber of Wulfstan was one which led off a corridor of dark granite stone on the ground floor of the monastery. The door, which now hung splintered on its hinges, was thick – perhaps about two inches thick – and had been attached to the door frame with heavy iron hinges. Unlike most doors she was accustomed to, there was no iron handle on the outside. She paused awhile, her keen green eyes searching the timber of the door which showed the scuffing of Ultan's attempts to force it.

Then she took a step forward but stayed at the threshold, letting her keen eyes travel over the room.

Beyond was a bed, a body laid sprawled on its back, arms flung out, head with wild staring eyes directed towards the ceiling in a last painful gape preceding death. The body was clad in a white shirt which was splattered with blood. The wounds were certainly not self-inflicted.

From her position, she saw a small wooden chair, on which was flung a pile of clothes. There was also a small table with an oil lamp and some writing materials on it. There was little else in the room.

The light entered the gloomy chamber from a small window which stood at a height of eight feet from the floor and was criss-crossed with iron bars through which one might thrust an arm to shoulder length, but certainly no more than that could pass beyond. All four walls of the chamber were of stone blocks, while the floor as well was flagged in great granite slabs. The ceiling of the room was of dark oak beams. There was little light to observe detail in the chamber, even though it was approaching the noonday. The only light that entered was from the tiny, barred window.

'Bring me a strong lamp, Brothers,' Fidelma called to the two monks in the corridor.

'There is a lamp already in the room, Sister,' replied one of them. Sister Fidelma hid her annoyance.

'I want nothing in this room touched until I have examined it carefully. Now fetch me the lamp.'

She waited, without moving, until one of the Brothers hurried away and returned with an oil lamp.

'Light it,' instructed Fidelma.

The monk did so.

Fidelma took it from his hand with a nod of thanks.

'Wait outside and let no one into the room until I say so.'

Holding the lamp, she stepped forward into the curious chamber of death.

Wulfstan's throat had been slashed with a knife or sword and there were several great stab wounds in his chest around his heart. His night attire was torn by the weapon and bloodied as were the sheets around him.

On the floor beside the bed was a piece of fine cloth which was bloodstained. The blood had dried. She picked it up and examined it. It was an elegantly woven piece of linen which was embroidered. It carried a Latin motto. She examined the bloodstains on it. It appeared as if whoever had killed Wulfstan had taken the kerchief from his pocket and wiped his weapon clean, letting the kerchief drop to the floor beside the body in a fit of absent-mindedness. Sister Fidelma placed the kerchief in the pocket within the folds of her robe.

She examined the window next. Although it was too high to reach up to it, the bars seemed secure enough. Then she gazed up at the heavy wooden planking and beams which formed the ceiling. It was a high chamber, some eleven feet from floor to ceiling. The floor too, seemed solid enough.

Near the bed she suddenly noticed a pile of ashes. She dropped to one knee beside the ashes and examined them, trying not to disperse them with her breath, for they appeared to be the remnants of some piece of paper, or vellum, perhaps. Not a very big piece either, but it was burnt beyond recognition.

She rose and examined the door next.

There were two wooden bars which had secured it. Each bar, when in place, slotted into iron rests. The first was at a height of three feet from the bottom of the door while the second was five feet from the bottom. She saw that one of the iron rests had been splintered from the wooden door jamb, obviously when Ultan had broken in. The pressure against the bar had wrenched the rest from its fastenings. But the bottom set of rests were in place and there was no sign of damage to the second bar, which was lying just behind the door. Both bars were solid enough. The ends were wrapped with twine, she presumed to stop the wood wearing against the iron rests in which they lodged. On one of the bars the pieces of twine had become unwound, blackened, and frayed at the end.

Here, indeed, was a problem to be solved, unless the owner of the kerchief could supply an answer.

She moved to the door and suddenly found herself slipping. She reached out a hand to steady herself. There was a small pool of blackened grease just inside the door. Her sharp eyes caught sight of a similar pool on the other side of the door. Bending to examine them, she frowned as she noticed two nails attached on the door frame, either side of the door. A short length of twine, blackened and frayed at the end, was attached to each nail.

Sister Fidelma compressed her lips thoughtfully and stood staring at the door for a long while before turning to leave the death chamber.

In Abbot Laisran's chamber, Sister Fidelma seated herself at the long table. She had arranged with the abbot to interview any she felt able to help her in arriving at a solution to the problem. Laisran himself offered to sit in on her encounters but she had felt it unnecessary. Laisran had taken himself to a side room, having presented her with a bell to summon him if she needed any help.

Brother Ultan was recruited to fetch those whom she wanted to see and was straightaway dispatched to bring Wulfstan's fellow Saxon prince, Eadred, who had helped Ultan discover the body, as well as his cousin Raedwald.

Eadred was a haughty youth with flaxen hair and cold blue eyes that seemed to have little expression. His features seemed fixed with a mixture of disdain and boredom. He entered the chamber, eyes narrowing as he beheld Sister Fidelma. A tall, muscular young man in his late twenties accompanied Eadred. Although he carried no arms, he acted as if he were the prince's bodyguard.

'Are you Eadred?' Fidelma asked the youth.

The young man scowled.

'I do not answer questions from a woman.' His voice was harsh, and that combined with his guttural accent made his stilted Irish sound raucous.

Sister Fidelma sighed. She had heard that Saxons could be

arrogant and that they treated their womenfolk more as chattels than as human beings.

'I am investigating the death of your countryman, Wulfstan. I need my questions to be answered,' she replied firmly.

Eadred merely ignored her.

'Lady.' It was the tall muscular Saxon who spoke and his knowledge of Irish was better than that of his prince. 'I am Raedwald, thane of Staeningum, cousin to the thane of Andredswald. It is not the custom of princes of our race to discourse with women if they be not of equal royal rank.'

'Then I am obliged for your courtesy in explaining your customs, Raedwald. Eadred, your cousin, seems to lack a knowledge of the law and customs of the country in which he is now a guest.'

Ignoring the angry frown on Eadred's features, she reached forward and rang the silver bell on the table before her. The Abbot Laisran entered from a side room.

'As you warned me, your Grace, the Saxons seem to think that they are above the law of this land. Perhaps they will accept the explanation from your lips.'

Laisran nodded and turned to the young men. He bluntly told them of Fidelma's rank and position in law, that even the High King had to take note of her wisdom and learning. Eadred continued to scowl but he inclined his head stiffly when Laisran told him that he was under legal obligation to answer Fidelma's questions. Raedwald seemed to accept the explanation as a matter of course.

'As your countryman considers you of royal rank, I will deign to answer your questions,' Eadred said, moving forward and seating himself without waiting for Fidelma's permission. Raedwald continued to stand.

Fidelma exchanged a glance with Laisran, who shrugged.

'The customs of the Saxons are not our customs, Sister Fidelma,' Laisran said apologetically. 'You will ignore their tendency to boorish behaviour.'

Eadred flushed angrily.

'I am a prince of the blood royal of the South Saxons, descended through the blood of Aelle from the great god Woden!'

Raedwald, who stood silently with arms folded behind him, looking unhappy, opened his mouth and then closed it firmly.

Abbot Laisran genuflected. Sister Fidelma merely stared at the young man in amusement.

'So you are not yet truly Christian, believing only in the One True God?'

Eadred bit his lip.

'All Saxon royal houses trace their bloodline to Woden, whether god, man, or hero,' he responded, with a slightly defensive tone.

'Tell me something of yourself then. I understand that you were cousin to Wulfstan? If you find speaking in our language difficult, you may speak in Latin or Greek. I am fluent in their usage.'

'I am not,' rasped Eadred. 'I speak your language from my study here but I speak no other tongue fluently, though I have some knowledge of Latin.'

Sister Fidelma hid her surprise and gestured for him to continue. Most Irish princes and chieftains she knew spoke several languages fluently besides their own, especially Latin and some Greek.

'Very well. Wulfstan was your cousin, wasn't he?'

'Wulfstan's father, Cissa, king of the South Saxons, was brother to my father, Cymen. I am thane of Andredswald, as my father was before me.'

'Tell me how Wulfstan and yourself came to be here, in Durrow.'

Eadred sniffed.

'Some years ago, one of your race, a man called Diciul, arrived in our country and began to preach of his god, a god with no name who had a son named Christ. Cissa, the king, was converted to this new god and turned away from Woden.

The man of Éireann was allowed to form a community, a monastery, at Bosa's Ham, in our land, and many went to hear him teach. Cissa decided that Wulfstan, who was heir apparent to the kingship, should come to the land of Éireann for education.'

Sister Fidelma nodded, wondering whether it was the young man's poor usage of Irish that made him seem so disapproving of Cissa's conversion to Christ.

'Then Wulfstan is the *tanist* in your land?'

Abbot Laisran intervened with a smile.

'The Saxons have a different system of law from us, Sister Fidelma,' he interrupted. 'They hold that the eldest son inherits all. There is no election by the *derbhfine* such as we have.'

'I see,' nodded Fidelma. 'Go on, Eadred. Cissa decided to send Wulfstan here.'

The young man grimaced sourly.

'I was ordered to accompany him and learn with him. We came together with our cousin Raedwald, thane of Staeningum, and ten churls and five slaves to attend our needs, and here we have been now for six moons.'

'And not the best of our students,' muttered Laisran.

'That's as may be,' snapped Eadred. 'We did not ask to come, but were ordered by Cissa. I shall be pleased to depart now and take the body of my kinsman back to my country.'

'Does the Latin inscription *cave quid dicis* mean anything to you?'

Eadred sniffed.

'It is the motto of the young Frankish prince, Dagobert.'

Sister Fidelma gazed thoughtfully at the young man before turning to Raedwald. The muscular young man's face was flushed and confused.

'And you, Raedwald? Does it mean anything to you?'

'Alas, I have no Latin, lady,' he mumbled.

'So? And when did you last see Wulfstan?'

'Just after Vespers.'

'What happened exactly?'

'As usual, Wulfstan was accompanied by myself and Eadred, with two of our churls and two slaves, to his chamber for the night. We searched the chamber as usual and then Wulfstan entered and dismissed us.'

Eadred nodded in agreement.

'I talked awhile with Raedwald in the corridor. We both heard Wulfstan secure the wooden bars. Then I went off to my chamber.'

Sister Fidelma glanced again towards Raedwald.

'And you can confirm this, Raedwald?'

Eadred flushed.

'You doubt my word?' His voice was brittle.

'This investigation will be conducted under our law, Eadred,' retorted Fidelma in annoyance.

Raedwald looked awkward.

'I can confirm what Eadred says, lady,' he replied. 'The thane of Andredswald speaks the truth. As soon as we heard the bars slide shut we both knew that the prince, Wulfstan, had secured himself in for the night and so we both departed for our sleeping chambers.'

Sister Fidelma nodded thoughtfully.

'You can also confirm, Eadred, that Wulfstan was afraid of being attacked? Why was that?'

Eadred sniffed.

'There are too many mad *welisc* in this place and one in particular had made several threats against him . . . that barbarian Talorgen!'

'*Welisc*? Who are they?' frowned Fidelma, puzzled.

Laisran gave a tired smile.

'The Saxons call all Britons *welisc*. It is a name which signifies that they are foreigners.'

'I see. So you left Wulfstan safely secured in his room? You did not seem to be as afraid of the Britons as your cousin. Why was that?'

Eadred laughed bitterly.

'I would not be thane of Andredswald if I could not defend myself against a pack of *welisc* cowards. No, I fear no barbarian's whelp nor his sire, either.'

'And the rest of your Saxon entourage? Did they fear the Britons?'

'Whether they feared or not, it is of no significance. I command them and they will do as I tell them.'

Sister Fidelma exhaled in exasperation. It would be difficult to live in a Saxon country if one was not a king or a thane, she thought.

'When did you realise that Wulfstan was missing?' she prompted.

'At prayers following the first bell . . .'

'He means the Angelus,' explained Laisran.

'He did not come to prayers and, thinking he had slept late, I went to classes.'

'What classes were these?'

'That weasel-faced Finan's class on the conduct of law between kingdoms.'

'Go on.'

'During the mid-morning break, having realised that Wulfstan was missing, I went to his room. The door was shut, signifying he was still inside. I banged upon the door. There was no response. I then went to look for Brother Ultan, the house-churl . . .'

'The steward of our community,' corrected Laisran softly.

'We went to Wulfstan's chamber and Ultan had to call upon two other Brothers to help us break in the door. Wulfstan had been feloniously slain. One doesn't have to search far for the culprit.'

'And who might that be?' invited Sister Fidelma.

'Why, it is obvious. The *welisc*-man, Talorgen, who calls himself a prince of Rheged. He had threatened Wulfstan's life. And it is well known the *welisc* practise sorcery . . .'

'What do you mean?' Fidelma asked sharply.

'Why, the fact that Wulfstan had been slaughtered in his

bed chamber while the window was barred and the door shut and secured from the inside. Who else but a *welisc* would be able to shape change and perpetrate such a monstrous deed?'

Sister Fidelma hid her cynical smile.

'Eadred, I think you have much to learn, for you seem to be wallowing in the superstition of your old religion.'

Eadred sprang up, his hand going to his belt where a knife might be worn.

'I am thane of Andredswald! I consented to be questioned by a mere woman because it is the custom of this land. However, I will not be insulted by one.'

'I am sorry that you think that I insult you,' Sister Fidelma replied, with a dangerous glint in her eyes. 'You may go.'

Eadred's face was working in a rage but Laisran moved forward and opened the door.

The young Saxon prince turned and stormed out. Raedwald hesitated a moment, made a gesture almost of apology, and then followed the prince out of the room.

'Did I not tell you that these Saxons are strange, haughty people, Fidelma?' smiled Laisran almost sadly.

Sister Fidelma shook her head.

'They probably have their good and bad like all peoples. Raedwald seems filled more with the courtesy of princes than his cousin Eadred.'

'Well, if Eadred and his followers are to be judged, then we have had their bad. As for Raedwald, although a thane and older than either Wulfstan or Eadred, he seems quiet and was dominated by them both. He is more of a servant than a master. I gather this is because his cousins both stand in closer relationship to their king than he does.' Laisran paused and cast her a curious glance. 'Why did you ask them about the Latin motto – *cave avid dicis*?'

'It was a motto found on a piece of linen which wiped the weapon that killed Wulfstan. It could have been dropped by the killer or it could have been Wulfstan's.'

Laisran shook his head.

'No. Eadred was right. That belligerent motto, Fidelma, "beware what you say", is the motto of the Frankish prince – Dagobert; I have recently remarked on its pugnacity to the young man.'

Sister Fidelma stretched reflectively. 'It seems things do not look good for Dagobert of the Franks. He now stands as the most likely suspect.'

'Not necessarily. Anyone could have taken and dropped the cloth and there are many here who have come to hate the arrogance of the Saxons. Why, I have even heard the dour Finan declare that he would like to drown the lot of them!'

Fidelma raised her eyebrows.

'Are you telling me that we must suspect Finan, the professor of your law faculty?'

Abbot Laisran suddenly laughed.

'Oh, the idea of Finan being able to shape-change to enter a locked room, commit murder, and sneak out without disturbing the locks, is an idea I find amusing but hardly worthy of consideration.'

Sister Fidelma gazed thoughtfully at Laisran.

'Do you believe that this murder could only be carried out by sorcery, then?'

Laisran's rotund face clouded and he genuflected quickly.

'God between me and all evil, Fidelma, but is there any other explanation? We come from a culture which accepted shape-changing as a normal occurrence. Move among our people and they will tell you that druids still exist and have such capabilities. Wasn't Diarmuid's foster brother changed into a boar, and wasn't Caer, the beloved of Aengus Og, condemned to change her form every alternate year?'

'These are ancient legends, Laisran,' admonished Sister Fidelma. 'We live in reality, in the here and now. And it is among the people of this community that we will find the person who slew Wulfstan. Before I question Dagobert, however, I would like to see Wulfstan's chamber once more.'

Abbot Laisran pulled at his lower lip. His usually jovial

face was creased in a frown of perplexity.

'I do not understand, Sister Fidelma. Everyone in our community here, at Durrow, had cause to kill Wulfstan and everyone is suspect. Is that what you are saying? At the same time that everyone is suspect, no one could have done the deed, for its implementation was beyond the hand of any human agency.'

'Now that I did not say,' Sister Fidelma admonished the abbot firmly, as she led the way along the corridor to halt at the open door of what had been Wulfstan's chamber.

The body of Wulfstan had been removed to the chapel of St Benignus, where preparations were being made to transport its sarcophagus to the coast, from where Eadred and his entourage would accompany it, by sea, to the land of the South Saxons which lay on the southern shore of Britain.

Sister Fidelma stared once again at the grey stone-flagged floor. She walked over the slabs, pressing each with her foot. Then she stared upwards towards the ceiling, which rose about eleven feet above the chamber floor. Her eyes eventually turned back to the bars on the window.

'Give me a hand,' she suddenly demanded.

Abbot Laisran stared at her in surprise as she began pushing the wooden table towards the window.

Hastily, he joined her in the effort, grinning sheepishly.

'If the young novitiates of my order could see their abbot heaving furniture about . . .' he began.

'They would realise that their abbot was merely human,' replied Fidelma, smiling.

They pushed the table under the barred window and, to Abbot Laisran's astonishment, Sister Fidelma suddenly scrambled on top of the table. It rose three feet above the ground and, by standing on it, Sister Fidelma, being tall, could reach easily to the bars of the solitary window whose bottom level was eight feet above the floor. She reached up with both her hands and tested each inch thick iron bar carefully.

The lowering of her shoulders showed her disappointment.

Slowly she clambered down, helped by the arm of Laisran.

Her lips were compressed. 'I thought the bars might have been loose.'

'It was a good idea,' smiled Laisran, encouragingly.

'Come, show me the floor above this,' Sister Fidelma said abruptly.

With a sigh, Laisran hastened after her as she strode swiftly away.

The floor above turned out to be equally disappointing. Over Wulfstan's chamber stretched a long wooden floor which was the floor of one of the long dormitories for the novitiates of the community. There were over a dozen beds in the dormitory. Even had she not examined the boards of the floor carefully, to see whether any had been prised up in order that a person could be lowered into the chamber below, and realised that none of the floorboards had been moved in many years, Sister Fidelma would still have recognised the fact that such an exercise would have necessitated the participation of everyone in the dormitory.

She turned away with disappointment on her features.

'Tell me, Laisran, what lies below Wulfstan's chamber?'

Laisran shook his head.

'I have had that thought also, Fidelma,' he confided. 'Nothing but solid earth lies below. There is no cellar, nor tunnel. The stone flags are laid on solid ground, so no person could enter the chamber by removing one of the floor stones. Besides,' he smiled wryly, 'what would Wulfstan have been doing during the commotion required to enter his chamber by the removing of the ceiling planks or floor slabs, or the removal of the bars of the window?'

Sister Fidelma smiled.

'The pursuit of truth is paved by the consideration and rejection of all the alternatives, no matter how unlikely they may be, Laisran.'

'The truth,' replied the abbot, looking troubled, 'is that it was impossible for the hand of man to strike down Wulfstan while he was locked alone in his chamber.'

'Now that I *can* agree with.'

Abbot Laisran looked puzzled.

'I thought you said that no sorcery was employed. Do you mean that he was not killed by the hand of a man?'

'No,' grinned Sister Fidelma. 'I mean that he was not alone in his chamber. It is a syllogism. Wulfstan was stabbed to death. Wulfstan was in his bedchamber. Therefore he was not alone in his bedchamber when he was killed.'

'But . . .'

'We have ruled out the argument that our murderer could have come through the window. Do you agree?'

Laisran frowned, trying hard to follow the logic.

'We have ruled out the possibility that our murderer could have entered the chamber through the roof.'

'Agreed.'

'We have concluded that it would be impossible for the murderer to enter via the stone-flagged floor.'

Abbot Laisran nodded emphatically.

'Then that leaves one obvious method of entry and exit.'

'I do not see . . .' he began.

'The chamber door. That is how our murderer gained entry and how he left.'

'Impossible!' Laisran shook his head. 'The door was secured from the inside.'

'Nevertheless, that was how it was done. And whoever did it hoped that we would be so bemused by this curiosity that we would not inquire too deeply of the motive, for he hoped the motive was one that was obvious to all: the hatred of Wulfstan and the Saxons. Ideas of sorcery, of evil spirits, of Wulfstan being slain by no human hand, might cloud our judgement, or so our killer desired it to do.'

'Then you know who the killer is?'

Fidelma shook her head.

'I have not questioned all the suspects. I think it is now time that we spoke with the Frankish prince, Dagobert.'

★　★　★

Dagobert was a young man who had been brought from the land of the Franks when he was a child. It was claimed that he was heir to the Frankish empire, but his father had been deposed and the young prince had been taken into exile in Ireland until the time came when he could return. He was tall, dark, rather attractive, and spoke Irish almost as fluently as a native prince. Laisran had warned Sister Fidelma that the young man was well connected and betrothed to a princess of the kings of Cashel. There would be repercussions if Dagobert was not accorded the full letter of the Brehon Law.

'You know why you are here?' began Sister Fidelma.

'That I do,' the young man smiled. 'The Saxon pig, Wulfstan, has been slain. Outside the band of Saxons who followed the young whelp, there is a smile on the face of every student in Durrow. Does that surprise you, Sister Fidelma?'

'Perhaps not. I am told that you were known to have had an argument with him?'

Dagobert nodded.

'What about?'

'He was an arrogant pig. He insulted my ancestry and so I punched him on the nose.'

'Wasn't that difficult to do, with his bodyguard? I am also told that Raedwald was never far away and he is a muscular young man.'

Dagobert chuckled.

'Raedwald knew when to defend his prince and when not. He diplomatically left the room when the argument started. A man with a sense of honour is Raedwald of the South Saxons. Wulfstan treated him like dirt beneath his feet even though he was a thane and blood cousin.'

Sister Fidelma reached into her robes and drew out the bloodstained embroidered linen kerchief and laid it on the table.

'Do you recognise this?'

Dagobert frowned and picked it up, turning it over in his hands with a puzzled expression.

'It is certainly mine. There is my motto. But the blood-stains . . .?'

'It was found by the side of Wulfstan's body. I found it. It was obviously used to wipe the blood off the weapon that killed him.'

Dagobert's face whitened.

'I did not kill Wulfstan. He was a pig but he simply needed a sound thrashing to teach him manners.'

'Then how came this kerchief to be by his side in his chamber?'

'I . . . I loaned it to someone.'

'Who?'

Dagobert bit his lip, shrugging.

'Unless you wish to be blamed for this crime, Dagobert, you must tell me,' insisted Fidelma.

'Two days ago I loaned the kerchief to Talorgen, the prince of Rheged.'

Finan inclined his head to Sister Fidelma.

'Your reputation as an advocate of the Brehon Court precedes you, Sister,' the dark, lean man greeted her. 'Already it is whispered from Tara how you solved a plot to overthrow the High King.'

Fidelma gestured Finan to be seated.

'People sometimes exaggerate another's prowess, for they love to create heroes and heroines to worship. You are a professor of law here?'

'That is so. I am qualified to the level of six years of *Sai*, being a professor of law only.'

The *Sai* was a qualification of six years of study and the degree below that of *Anruth* held by Fidelma.

'And you taught Wulfstan?'

'Each of us has a cross to bear, as did Christ. Mine was the teaching of the Saxon thanes.'

'Not all the Saxons?'

Finan shook his head.

'No. Only the three thanes, as they refused to sit at lessons with churls, and only the express order of the Abbot Laisran made them attend class with the other students. They were not humble before the altar of Christ. In fact, I formed the opinion that they secretly mocked Christ and clung to the worship of their outlandish god Woden.'

'You disliked the Saxons?'

'I hated them!'

The vehemence in the man's voice made Sister Fidelma raise her eyebrows.

'Isn't hate an emotion unknown to a Brother of the order, especially one qualified as a *Sai*?'

'My sister and brother took up the robes of the religious and decided to accept a mission to preach the word of Christ in the lands of the East Saxons. A few years ago I encountered one of the missionaries who had gone in that band. They had arrived in the land of the East Saxons and sought to preach the word of Christ. The heathen Saxons stoned them to death, only two of the band escaping. Among those who met a martyr's fate were my own sister and brother. I have hated all Saxons ever since.'

Sister Fidelma gazed into the dark eyes of Finan.

'Did you kill Wulfstan?'

Finan returned her scrutiny squarely.

'I could have done so at another time, in another place. I have the hatred in me. But no, Sister Fidelma, I did not kill him. Neither do I have the means to enter a barred room and leave it as though no one had entered.'

Fidelma nodded slowly.

'You may go, Finan.'

The professor of law rose reluctantly. He paused and said reflectively, 'Wulfstan and Eadred were not liked by any in this monastery. Many young men with hot tempers have challenged them in combat since they have been here.

Dagobert the Frank, for one. Only the fact that such challenges are forbidden on sacred soil has prevented bloodshed thus far.'

Fidelma nodded absently.

'Is it true that the Saxons are leaving tomorrow?' Finan demanded.

She raised her head to look at him.

'They are returning with the body of Wulfstan to their own land,' she affirmed.

A contented smile crossed Finan's face.

'I cannot pretend that I regret that, even if it has cost one of their lives to prompt the move. I had hoped that they would have left Durrow yesterday.'

She glanced up at the law professor, interested.

'Why would they leave?'

'Some Saxon messenger arrived at the monastery yesterday afternoon seeking Wulfstan and Eadred. I half-hoped that it was a summons to return to their country. However, praise be that they are departing now.'

Fidelma frowned in annoyance.

'Let me remind you, Finan, that unless we find the culprit, not only this centre of learning, but all the five kingdoms of Éireann will be at risk, for the Saxons will surely want to take compensation for the death of their prince.'

Talorgen of Rheged was a youth of average stature, fresh-faced and sandy of hair. He already wore a wispy moustache, but his cheeks and chin were clean shaven.

'Yes. It is no secret that I challenged Wulfstan and Eadred to combat.'

His Irish, though accented, was fluent and he seemed at ease as he sat in the chair Sister Fidelma had indicated.

'Why?'

Talorgen grinned impishly.

'I hear that you have questioned Eadred. From his manner you may judge Wulfstan's arrogance. It is not hard to be provoked by them, even if they were not Saxons.'

'You do not like Saxons?'

'They are not likeable.'

'But you are a prince of Rheged, and it is reported that the Saxons are attacking your land.'

Talorgen nodded, his mouth pinched. 'Oswy calls himself Christian king of Northumbria, but he still sends his barbaric hordes against the kingdoms of the Britons. For generations now the people of my land have fought to hold back the Saxons, for their thirst for land and power is great. Owain, my father, sent me here, but I would, by the living Christ, rather be at his side, wielding my sword against the Saxon foemen. My blade should drink the blood of the enemies of my blood.'

Sister Fidelma regarded the flush-faced young man with curiosity.

'Has your blade already drunk the blood of your people's enemies?'

Talorgen frowned abruptly, hesitating, and then his face relaxed. He chuckled.

'You mean, did I kill Wulfstan? That I did not. I swear by the living God! But hear me, Sister Fidelma, it is not that I did not want to. Truly, sometimes the faith of Christ is a hard taskmaster. Wulfstan and his cousin Eadred were so dislikeable that I scarcely believe there is anyone in this community who regrets the death of Wulfstan.'

She took out the bloodstained kerchief and laid it on the table.

'This was found by the body of Wulfstan. It was used to wipe the blood from the weapon that killed him. It belongs to Dagobert.'

'You mean Dagobert . . .?' The prince of Rheged's eyes opened wide as he stared from the kerchief to Sister Fidelma.

'Dagobert tells me that he gave you this kerchief in loan two days ago.'

Talorgen examined the kerchief carefully and then slowly nodded.

'He is right. It is the same one, I can tell from the embroidery.'

'How then did it get into Wulfstan's chamber?'

Talorgen shrugged.

'That I do not know. I remember having it in my chamber yesterday morning. I saw it was gone and thought Dagobert had collected it.'

Sister Fidelma regarded Talorgen steadily for a moment or two.

'I swear, Sister,' said the prince of Rheged earnestly. 'I would not have hesitated to kill Wulfstan outside these walls, but I did not kill him within them.'

'You are forthright, Talorgen.'

The young man shrugged.

'I am sprung of the house of Urien of Rheged, whose praise was sung by our great bard Taliesin. Urien was the Golden King of the North, slain in stealth by a traitor. Our house is even-handed, just and forthright. We believe in honesty. We meet our enemies in daylight on the plain of battle, not at night in the darkened recesses of some bedchamber.'

'You say that there are many others in this community who held enmity against Wulfstan? Was there anyone in particular that you had in mind?'

Talorgen pursed his lips.

'Our teacher Finan often told us that he hated the Saxons.'

Sister Fidelma nodded.

'I have spoken with Finan.'

'As you already know, Dagobert quarrelled with Wulfstan in the refectory and bloodied his mouth two nights ago. Then there was Riderch of Dumnonia, Fergna of Midhe, and . . .'

Sister Fidelma held up her hand.

'I think that you have made your point, Talorgen. Everyone in Durrow is a suspect.'

★ ★ ★

Sister Fidelma found Raedwald in the stables making preparations for the journey back to the land of the South Saxons.

'There is a question I would ask you on your own, Raedwald. Need I remind you of my authority?'

The Saxon warrior shook his head.

'I have learnt much of your law and customs since I have been in your country, Sister. I am not as Eadred.'

'And you have learnt some fluency in our tongue,' observed Fidelma. 'More fluency and understanding than your cousin.'

'It is not my place to criticise the heir apparent to the kingship of the South Saxons.'

'But I think that you did not like your cousin Wulfstan?'

Raedwald blinked in surprise at her directness and then he shrugged.

'I am merely a thane in the house of Cissa, I cannot like or dislike my appointed king.'

'Why were you not on guard outside the chamber of Wulfstan last night?'

'It was not the custom. Once Wulfstan had secured himself inside, he was well guarded. You have seen the chamber he asked Abbot Laisran to devise for him. Once he was locked inside, there was, apparently, no danger for him. I slept in the next chamber and at his call should he need help.'

'But he did not call?'

'His killer slashed his throat with his first blow. That much was obvious from his body.'

'It becomes obvious that he willingly let the killer into his chamber. Therefore, he knew the killer and trusted him.'

Raedwald's eyes narrowed.

Fidelma continued.

'Tell me, the messenger who arrived from your country yesterday, what message did he bring Wulfstan?'

Raedwald shook his head.

'That message was for Wulfstan only.'

'Is the messenger still here?'

'Yes.'

'Then I would question him.'

'You may question but he will not answer you.' Raedwald smiled grimly.

Sister Fidelma compressed her lips in annoyance.

'Another Saxon custom? Not even your messengers will speak with women?'

'Another Saxon custom, yes. But this is a custom of kings. The royal messenger has his tongue cut out so that he can never verbally betray the message that he carries from kings and princes to those who might be their enemies.'

Abbot Laisran gestured to those he had summoned to his study chamber, at Sister Fidelma's request, to be seated. They had entered the room with expressions either of curiosity or defiance, according to their different personalities, as they saw Sister Fidelma standing before the high-mantled hearth. She seemed absorbed in her own thoughts as she stood, hands folded demurely before her, not apparently noticing them as they seated themselves around. Brother Ultan, as steward of the community, took his stand before the door with hands folded into his habit.

Abbot Laisran gave Fidelma an anxious glance and then he, too, took his seat.

'Why are we here?' demanded Talorgen abruptly.

Fidelma raised her head to return his gaze.

'You are here to learn how Wulfstan died and by whose hand,' she replied sharply.

There was a brief pause before Eadred turned to her with a sneer.

'We already know how my kinsman Wulfstan died, woman. He died by the sorcery of a barbarian. Who that barbarian is, it is not hard to deduce. It was one of the *welisc* savages, Talorgen.'

Talorgen was on his feet, fists clenched.

'Repeat your charges outside the walls of this abbey and I will meet your steel with mine, Saxon cur!'

Dagobert came to his feet to intervene as Eadred launched forward from his chair towards Talorgen.

'Stop this!' The usually genial features of Laisran were dark with anger. His voice cut the air like a lash.

The students of the ecclesiastical school of Durrow seemed to freeze at the sound. Then Eadred relaxed and dropped back in his seat with a smile that was more a sneer than amusement. Dagobert tugged at Talorgen's arm and the prince of Rheged sighed and reseated himself, as did the Frankish prince.

Abbot Laisran growled like an angry bear.

'Sister Fidelma is an official of the Brehon Court of Éireann. Whatever the customs in your own lands, in this land she has supreme authority in conducting this investigation and the full backing of the law of this kingdom. Do I make myself clear?'

There was a silence.

'I shall continue,' said Fidelma quietly. 'Yet what Eadred says is partially true.'

Eadred stared at her with bewilderment clouding his eyes.

'Oh yes,' smiled Fidelma. '*One* of you at least knows how Wulfstan died and who is responsible.'

She paused to let her words sink in.

'Let me first tell you how he died.'

'He was stabbed to death in his bed,' Finan, the dark-faced professor of law, pointed out.

'That is true,' agreed Sister Fidelma, 'but without the aid of sorcery.'

'How else did the assassin enter a locked room and leave it, still locked from the inside?' demanded Eadred. 'How else but sorcery?'

'The killer wanted us to think that it was sorcery. Indeed, the killer prepared an elaborate plan to confuse us and lay the blame away from him. In fact, so elaborate was the plan that it had several layers. One layer was merely to confuse and frighten us by causing us to think the murder was done by a supernatural agency; another was to indicate an obvious suspect, while a third object was to implicate another person.'

'Well,' Laisran sighed, 'at the moment I have yet to see through the first layer.'

Sister Fidelma smiled briefly at the rotund abbot.

'I will leave that to later. Let us firstly consider the method of the killing.'

She had their complete attention now.

'The assassin entered the room by the door. In fact, Wulfstan let his assassin into the bedchamber himself.'

There was an intake of breath from the usually taciturn Dagobert.

Unperturbed, she continued.

'Wulfstan knew his killer. Indeed, he had no suspicions, no fear of this man.'

Abbot Laisran regarded her with open-mouthed astonishment.

'Wulfstan let the killer in,' she continued. 'The assassin struck. He killed Wulfstan and left his body on the bed. It was an act of swiftness. To spread suspicion, the killer wiped his knife on a linen kerchief which he mistakenly thought belonged to Talorgen, prince of Rheged. As I said, if we managed to see beyond the charade of sorcery, then the assassin sought to put the blame for the murder on Talorgen. He failed to realise that the kerchief was borrowed two days ago from Dagobert. He did not realise that the kerchief prominently carried Dagobert's motto on it. It was a Latin motto which exhorts "Beware what you say"!'

She paused to let them digest this information.

'How then did the killer now leave the bedchamber and manage to bar the door from the inside?' asked Dagobert.

'The bedchamber door was barred with two wooden bars. They were usually placed on iron rests which are attached to the frame of the door. When I examined the first wooden bar I observed that at either end there were two pieces of twine wrapped around it as if to protect the wood when it is placed in the iron rests. Yet on the second wooden bar, the curiosity was that the twine had two lengths of four feet still loose. Each end of the twine had been frayed and charred.'

She grimaced and repeated herself.

'A curiosity. Then I noticed that there was a rail at the top of the door on which a heavy woollen curtain could be drawn across the door when closed in order to prevent a draught. It was, of course, impossible to see whether the curtain had been drawn or not once the room was broken into, for the inward movement of the door would have swept the curtain aside on its rail.'

Eadred made a gesture of impatience.

'Where is this explanation leading?'

'Patience, and I will tell you. I noticed two small spots of grease on the ground on either side of the door. As I bent to examine these spots of grease I saw two nails fixed into the wood about three inches from the ground. There were two short pieces of twine still tied on these nails and the ends were frayed and blackened. It was then I realised just how the assassin had left the room and left one of the bars in place.'

'One?' demanded Abbot Laisran, leaning forward on his seat, his face eager.

Fidelma nodded.

'Only one was really needed to secure the door from the inside. The first bar, that at three feet from the bottom of the door, had not been set in place. There were no marks on the bar and its twine protection was intact, nor had the iron rests been wrenched away from the door jamb when Ultan forced the door. Therefore, the conclusion was that this bar was not in place. Only the second bar, that which rested across the top of the door, about two feet from the top, had been in place.'

'Go on,' instructed Laisran when she paused again.

'Having killed Wulfstan, the assassin was already pre-pared. He undid the twine on both ends of the wooden bar and threaded it around the wooden curtain rail across the top of the door. He set in place, or had already placed them during the day, when the chamber was open, two nails. Then he raised the wooden bar to the level of the curtain rail. He secured it there by tying the ends of the twine to the nails at ground level. This construction allowed him to leave the room.'

Laisran gestured with impatience.

'Yes, but how could he have manipulated the twine to lower the bar in place?'

'Simply. He took two reed candles and as he went to leave he placed a candle under either piece of the string near the ground. He took a piece of the paper and lit it from his tinder box – I found the ashes of the paper on the floor of the chamber, where he had to drop it. He lit the two reed candles on either side of the door under the twine. Then he left quickly. The twine eventually burned through, releasing the bar, which dropped neatly into place in the iron rests. It had, remember, only two feet to drop. The candles continued to burn until they became mere spots of grease, almost unno-ticeable, except I slipped on one. But the result was that we were left with a mystery. A room locked on the inside with a corpse. Sorcery? No. Planning by a devious mind.'

'So what happened then?' Talorgen encouraged, breaking the spellbound silence.

'The assassin left the room, as I have described. He wanted to create this illusion of mystery because the person he wished to implicate was one he felt his countrymen would believe to be a barbaric sorcerer. As I indicated, he wished to place suspicion on you, Talorgen. He left the room and talked to someone outside Wulfstan's bedcham-ber for a while. Then they heard the bar drop into place and that was the assassin's alibi, because it was clear that they had heard Wulfstan, still alive, slide the bar to lock his chamber door.'

Raedwald was frowning as it seemed he struggled to follow her reasoning.

'You have given an excellent reconstruction,' he said slowly. 'But it is only a hypothesis. It remains only a hypothesis unless you name the assassin and his motive.'

Sister Fidelma smiled softly.

'Very well. I was, of course, coming to that.'

She turned and let her gaze pass over their upraised faces as they watched her. Then she let her gaze rest on the haughty features of the thane of Andredswald.

Eadred interpreted her gaze as accusation and was on his feet before she had said a word, his face scowling in anger.

Ultan, the steward, moved swiftly across the room to stand before Sister Fidelma, in anticipation lest Eadred let his emotions, which were clearly visible on his angry features, overcome him.

'You haven't told us the motive.' Dagobert the Frank said softly. 'Why would the thane of Andredswald murder his own cousin and prince?'

Sister Fidelma continued to stare at the arrogant Saxon.

'I have not yet said that the thane of Andredswald is the assassin,' she said softly. 'But as for motive, the motive is the very laws of the Saxon society, which, thanks be to God, are not our laws.'

Abbot Laisran was frowning.

'Explain, Fidelma. I do not understand.'

'A Saxon prince succeeds to the kingship by primogeniture. The eldest son inherits.'

Dagobert nodded impatiently.

'That is also so with our Frankish succession. But how does this provide the motive for Wulfstan's murder?'

'Two days ago a messenger from the kingdom of the South Saxons arrived here. His message was for Wulfstan. I discovered what his message was.'

'How?' demanded Raedwald. 'Royal messengers have their tongues cut out to prevent them revealing such secrets.'

Fidelma grinned.

'So you told me. Fortunately this poor man was taught to write by Diciul, the missionary of Éireann who brought Christianity and learning to your country of the South Saxons.'

'What was the message?' asked Laisran.

'Wulfstan's father had died, another victim of the Yellow Plague. Wulfstan was now king of the South Saxons and urged to return home at once.'

She glanced at Raedwald.

The big Saxon nodded silently in agreement.

'You admitted that much to me when I questioned you, Raedwald,' went on Fidelma. 'When I asked you if you liked Wulfstan you answered that it was not up to you to like or dislike your appointed king. A slip of the tongue, but it alerted me to the possible motive.'

Raedwald said nothing.

'In such a barbaric system of succession, where the order of birth is the only criterion for claiming an inheritance or kingdom, there are no safeguards. In Éireann, as among our cousins in Britain, a chieftain or king not only has to be of a bloodline but has to be elected by the *derbhfine* of his family. Without such a safeguard it becomes obvious to me that only the death of a predecessor removes the obstacles of the aspirant to the throne.'

Raedwald pursed his lips and said softly: 'This is so.'

'And, with Wulfstan's death, Eadred will now succeed to the kingship?'

'Yes.'

Eadred's face was livid with anger.

'I did not kill Wulfstan!'

Sister Fidelma turned and stared deeply into his eyes.

'I believe you, for Raedwald is the assassin,' she said calmly.

Finan made a grab at Raedwald as the muscular Saxon thane sought desperately to escape from the room. Dagobert leapt forward together with Ultan, the steward, to help restrain the struggling man. When the thane of Staeningum had been overpowered, Sister Fidelma turned to the others.

'I said that the assassin had a devious mind. Yet in the attempt to lead false trails, Raedwald overexcelled himself and brought suspicion down on him. In trying to implicate Talorgen, Raedwald made a mistake and caused confusion by thinking the kerchief to be Talorgen's. It bore Dagobert's motto in Latin. Raedwald has no Latin and so did not spot his mistake. This also ruled out Eadred from suspicion, as Eadred knew Latin to the degree that he could recognise Dagobert's motto.'

She settled her gaze on Eadred.

'If you had also been slain, then Raedwald was next in line to the kingship, was he not?'

Eadred made an affirmative gesture.

'But . . .'

'Raedwald was going to implicate you as the assassin and then show how you tried to put the blame on Talorgen. He would have either had you tried for murder under our law or, if all else failed . . . I doubt whether you would have returned safely to the land of the South Saxons. Perhaps you might have fallen overboard on the sea voyage. Whichever way, both Wulfstan and you would have been removed from the succession, leaving it clear for Raedwald to claim the throne.'

Eadred shook his head wonderingly. His voice was tinged with reluctant admiration.

'Never would I have suspected that a woman possessed such a meticulous mind to unravel the deviousness of this treachery in the way that you have done. I shall look upon your office with a new perspective.'

Eadred turned abruptly to the Abbot Laisran.

'I and my men will depart now, for we must return to my

country. With your permission, Abbot, I shall take Raedwald with me as my prisoner. He will stand trial according to our laws and his punishment will be prescribed by them.'

Abbot Laisran inclined his head in agreement.

Eadred moved to the door, and as he did so, his eyes caught sight of Talorgen of Rheged.

'Well, *welisc*. It seems I owe you an apology for wrongly accusing you of the murder of Wulfstan. I so apologise.'

Talorgen slowly stood up, his face trying to control his surprise.

'Your apology is accepted, Saxon.'

Eadred paused and then he frowned.

'The apology notwithstanding, there can never be peace between us, *welisc*!'

Talorgen sniffed.

'The day such a peace will come is when you and your Saxon hordes will depart from the shores of Britain and return to the land whence you came.'

Eadred stiffened, his hand going to his waist then he paused and relaxed and almost smiled.

'Well said, *welisc*. It will never be peace!'

He strode from the room with Ultan and Dagobert leading Raedwald after him.

Talorgen turned and smiled briefly towards Sister Fidelma.

'Truly, there are wise judges among the Brehons of Ireland.'

Then he, too, was gone. Finan, the professor of law, hesitated a moment.

'Truly, now I know why your reputation is great, Fidelma of Kildare.'

Sister Fidelma gave a small sigh as he left.

'Well, Fidelma,' Abbot Laisran smiled in satisfaction, reaching for a jug of wine, 'it seems that I have provided you with some diversion on your pilgrimage to the shrine of the Blessed Patrick at Ard Macha.'

Sister Fidelma responded to the rotund abbot's wry expression.

'A diversion, yes. Though I would have preferred something of a more pleasant nature to have occupied my time.'

Abbey Sinister

◆◇◆

The black guillemot, with its distinctive orange legs and mournful, warning cry, swooped and darted above the currach. It was an isolated traveller among a crowd of more hardy, sooty, white-rumped storm petrels and large, dark coloured cormorants, wheeling, diving and flitting against the soft blue May sky.

Sister Fidelma sat relaxed in the stern of the boat and let the tangy odour of the salt water spray gently caress her senses as the two oarsmen, seated facing her, bent their backs to their task. Their oars, dipping in unison, caused the light craft to dance over the waves of the great bay which seemed so deceptively calm. The clawing waters of the hungry Atlantic were not usually so good natured as now and often the islands, through which the currach was weaving, could be cut off for weeks or months at a time.

They had left the mainland, with its rocky terrain and scrawny vegetation, to cross the waters of the large estuary known as Roaring Water Bay, off the south-west coast of Ireland. Here the fabled Cairbre's 'hundred islands' had been randomly tossed like lumps of earth and rock into the sea as if by some giant's hand. At the moment the day was soft, the waters passive and the sun producing some warmth, making the scene one of tranquil beauty.

As the oarsmen stroked the vessel through the numerous

islands, the heads of inquisitive seals popped out of the water to stare briefly at them, surprised at their aquatic intrusion, before darting away.

Sister Fidelma was accompanied by a young novitiate, a frightened young girl, who huddled beside her in the stern seat of the currach. Fidelma had felt obliged to take the girl under her protection on the journey to the abbey of St Ciaran of Saigher, which stood on the island of Chléire, the farthest island of this extensive group. But the escort of the novitiate was purely incidental for Fidelma's main purpose was to carry letters from Ultan, the archbishop of Armagh, to the abbot at Chléire and also to the abbot of Inis Chloichreán, a tiny religious house on one of the remoter rocky islands within the group.

The lead rower, a man made old before his time by a lifetime exposed to the coastal weather, eased his oar. He smiled, a disjointed, gap-toothed smile at Fidelma. His sea-coloured eyes, set deep in his leather-brown face, gazed appreciatively at the tall young woman with the red hair. He had seen few religious who had such feminine poise as this one; few who seemed to be so effortlessly in command.

'There's Inis Cloichreán to our right, Sister.' He thrust out a gnarled hand to indicate the direction, realising that, as he was facing the religieuse, the island actually lay to her left. 'We are twenty minutes from it. Do you wish to land there first or go on to Chléire?'

'I have no need to be long on Chloichreán,' Fidelma replied after a moment of thought. 'We'll land there first as it is on our way.'

The rower grunted in acknowledgement and nodded to the second rower. As if at a signal, they dipped their oars together and the currach sped swiftly over the waves towards the island.

It was a hilly, rocky island. From the sea, it appeared that its shores were nothing more than steep, inaccessible cliffs whose grey granite was broken into coloured relief by sea pinks and honeysuckle chambers which filled the rocky outcrops.

Lorcán, the chief rower, expertly directed the currach through offshore jagged peaks of rock, thrusting from the sea. The boat danced this way and that in the foam waters that hissed and gurgled around the jagged points of granite, creating tiny but dangerous whirlpools. He carefully manoeuvred a zig-zag path into a small, sheltered cove where a natural harbour awaited them.

Fidelma was amazed at his skill.

'None but a person with knowledge could land in such a place,' she observed.

Lorcán grinned appreciatively.

'I am one of the few who know exactly where to land on this island, Sister.'

'But the members of the abbey, surely they must have some seamanship among them to be here?'

'Abbey is a grandiose name for Selbach's settlement,' grunted the second oarsman, speaking for the first time since they had left the mainland.

'Maenach is right,' confirmed Lorcán. 'Abbot Selbach came here two years ago with about twelve Brothers; he called them his apostles. But they are no more than young boys, the youngest fourteen and the eldest scarcely nineteen. They chose this island because it was inaccessible and few knew how to land on it. It is true that they have a currach but they never use it. It is only for emergencies. Four or five times a year I land here with any supplies that they might want from the mainland.'

'Ah, so it is a hermitage,' Fidelma said. There were many of the religious in Ireland who had become solitary hermits or, taking a few followers, had found some out of the way place to set up a community where they could live together in isolated contemplation of the faith. Fidelma did not really trust hermits, or isolated communities. It was not, in her estimation, the way to serve God by shutting oneself off from His greatest Creation – the society of men and women.

'A hermitage, indeed,' agreed Maenach mournfully.

Fidelma gazed around curiously.

'It is not a large island. Surely one of the Brothers must have seen our landing yet no one has come to greet us.'

Lorcán had secured the currach to a rock by a rope and now bent forward to assist Fidelma out of the craft while Maenach used his balance to steady it.

'We'd better all get out,' Fidelma said, more for the attention of the frightened young novitiate, Sister Sárnat, than Maenach. The young girl, no more than sixteen, dutifully scrambled after Fidelma, keeping close like a chick to a mother hen.

Maenach followed, pausing to stretch languidly once he stood on dry land.

Lorcán was pointing up some steps carved in the granite slope which led from the small cove up to the top of the cliff.

'If you take those steps, Sister, you'll come to Selbach's community,' he said. 'We'll await you here.'

Fidelma nodded, turning to Sister Sárnat.

'Will you wait here or do you want to come with me?'

The young sister shivered as if touched by a cold wind and looked unhappy.

'I'll come with you, Sister,' she sniffed anxiously.

Fidelma sighed softly. The girl was long past 'the age of choice' yet she was more like a ten-year-old, frightened with life and clutching at the nearest adult to protect her from potential lurking terrors. The girl intrigued Fidelma. She wondered what had possessed her to join a religious house while so young, without experience of life or people.

'Very well, follow me then,' she instructed.

Lorcán called softly after her.

'I'd advise you not to be long, Sister.' He pointed to the western sky. 'There's a backing wind coming and we'll have a storm before nightfall. The sooner we reach Chléire, the sooner we shall be in shelter.'

'I'll not be long,' Fidelma assured him and began to lead the way up the steps with Sárnat following quickly behind.

'How can he know that there'll be a storm,' the young novitiate demanded breathlessly as she stumbled to keep up with Fidelma. 'It's such a lovely day.'

Fidelma grimaced.

'A seaman will know these things, Sárnat. The signs are there to be read in the sky. Did you observe the moon last night?'

Sárnat looked puzzled.

'The moon was bright,' she conceded.

'But if you had truly examined it then you would have seen a red glow to it. The air was still and comparatively dry. It is almost a guarantee of stormy winds from the west.'

Fidelma suddenly paused and pointed to some plants growing along the edge of the pathway.

'Here's another sign. See the trefoil? Look at the way its stem is swollen. And those dandelions nearby, their petals are contracting and closing. Both those signs mean it will be raining soon.'

'How do you know these things?' asked the girl wonderingly.

'By observation and listening to the old ones, those who are wise in the ancient knowledge.'

They had climbed above the rocky cliffs and stood overlooking a sheltered depression in the centre of the island where a few gaunt, bent trees grew amidst several stone, beehive-shaped huts and a small oratory.

'So this is Abbot Selbach's community?' Fidelma mused. She stood frowning at the collection of buildings. She could see no movement nor signs of life. She raised her voice. 'Hello there!'

The only answer that came back was an angry chorus of disturbed seabirds; of newly arrived auks seeking their summer nesting places who suddenly rose, black and white or dark brown with brilliantly coloured bills and webbed feet. The black guillemots, gulls and storm petrels followed, swirling around the island in an angry, chiding crowd.

Fidelma was puzzled. Someone must have heard her yet there was no response.

She made her way slowly down the grassy path into the shallow depression in which the collection of stone buildings stood. Sárnat trotted dutifully at her side.

Fidelma paused before the buildings and called again. And again there was no reply.

She moved on through the complex of buildings, turning round a corner into a quadrangle. The shriek came from Sister Sárnat.

There was a tree in the centre of the quadrangle; a small tree no more than twelve feet high, bent before the cold Atlantic winds, gaunt and gnarled. To the thin trunk of this tree, secured by the wrists with leather thongs, which prevented it from slumping to the ground, the body of a man was tied. Although the body was secured with its face towards the tree trunk, there was no need to ask if the man was dead.

Sister Sárnat stood shaking in terror at her side.

Fidelma ignored her and moved forward a pace to examine the body. It was clad in bloodstained robes, clearly the robes of a religieux. The head was shaven at the front, back to a line stretching from ear to ear. At the rear of his head, the hair was worn long. It was the tonsure of the Irish church, the *airbacc giunnae* which had been an inheritance from the druids. The dead man was in his sixties; a thin, sharp featured individual with sallow skin and a pinched mouth. She noticed that, hanging from a thong round his neck, he wore a crucifix of some value; a carefully worked silver cross. The bloodstains covered the back of the robe which actually hung in ribbons from the body.

Fidelma saw that the shoulders of the robe were torn and bloodied and beneath it was lacerated flesh. There were several small stab wounds in the back but the numerous ripping wounds showed that the man had clearly been scourged by a whip before he had met his death.

Fidelma's eyes widened in surprise as she noticed a piece of wood fixed to the tree. There was some writing on it. It was in Greek: 'As the whirlwind passes, so is the wicked no more . . .' She tried to remember why it sounded so familiar. Then she realised that it was out of the 'Book of Proverbs'.

It was obvious to her eye that the man had been beaten and killed while tied to the tree.

She became distracted by the moaning of the girl and turned, suppressing her annoyance.

'Sárnat, go back to the cove and fetch Lorcán here.' And when the girl hesitated, she snapped, 'Now!'

Sárnat turned and scurried away.

Fidelma took another step towards the hanged religieux and let her eyes wander over the body, seeking more information. She could gather nothing further other than that the man was elderly and a religieux of rank, if the wealth of the crucifix was anything to go by. Then she stepped back and gazed around her. There was a small oratory, no larger than to accommodate half-a-dozen people at most behind its dry stone walls. It was placed in the centre of the six stone cells which served as accommodation for the community.

Fidelma crossed to the oratory and peered inside.

She thought, at first in the gloom, that it was a bundle of rags lying on the small altar. Then, as her eyes grew accustomed to the dim light, she saw that it was the body of a young religieux. It was a boy not even reached manhood. She noticed that his robes were dank and sodden. The fair brown hair dried flat against his temples. The features were not calm in death's repose but contorted in an odd manner, as if the boy had died in pain. She was about to move forward to make a closer investigation, when she nearly tripped over what seemed to be another bundle.

Another religieux lay face downwards, arms outstretched, almost like a supplicant praying towards the altar. His hair was dark. He was clad in the robes of a brother. This religieux was older than the youth.

She moved forward and knelt down, seeking a pulse in his neck with her two fingers. It was faint but it was there right enough though the body was unnaturally cold. She bent further to examine the face. The man was about forty. Even unconscious the features were placid and quite handsome. A pleasant face, Fidelma conceded. But dried blood caked one side of the broad forehead where it had congealed around a wound.

She shook the man by the shoulder but he was deeply unconscious.

Checking her exhalation of breath, Fidelma stood up and, moving swiftly, she went from stone cell to stone cell but each one told the same story. There was no one hiding from her within the buildings. The cells of the community were deserted.

Lorcán came running along the path from the cove.

'I left the girl behind with Maenach,' he grunted as he came up to Fidelma. 'She was upset. She says that someone is dead and . . .'

He paused and stared around him. From this position, the tree with its gruesome corpse was hidden to him.

'Where is everyone?'

'There is a man still alive here,' Fidelma said, ignoring the question. 'He needs our immediate attention.'

She led the way to the small oratory, stooping down to enter and then standing to one side so that Lorcán could follow.

Lorcán gasped and genuflected as he saw the young boy.

'I know this boy. His name is Sacán from Inis Beag. Why, I brought him here to join the community only six months ago.'

Fidelma pointed to the figure of the dark-haired man on the floor which Lorcán had not observed.

'Do you recognise that Brother?' she asked.

'The saints defend us!' exclaimed the boatman as he bent down. 'This is Brother Spelán.'

Fidelma pursed her lips.

'Brother Spelán?' she repeated unnecessarily.

Lorcán nodded unhappily.

'He served as Abbot Selbach's *dominus*, the administrator of this community. Who did this deed? Where is everyone?'

'Questions can be answered later. We need to take him to a more comfortable place and restore him to consciousness. The boy – Sacán, you called him? – well, he is certainly beyond our help.'

'Sister,' replied Lorcán, 'my friend Maenach knows a little of the physician's art. Let me summon him so that he might assist us with Spelán.'

'It will take too long.'

'It will take but a moment,' Lorcán assured her, taking a conch shell from a rough leather pouch at his side. He went to the door and blew on it long and loudly. It was echoed by a tremendous chorus of frightened birds. Lorcán paused a moment before turning with a smile to Fidelma. 'I see Maenach on the cliff top with the young Sister. They are coming this way.'

'Then help me carry this Brother to one of the nearby cells so that we may put him on a better bed than this rough floor,' instructed Fidelma.

As she knelt down to help lift the man she suddenly noticed a small wooden cup lying nearby. She reached forward and placed it in her *marsupium*, her large purse-like bag, slung from her waist. There would be time to examine it later.

Between them, they carried Brother Spelán, who was quite heavy, to the nearest cell and laid him on one of two wooden cots which were within.

Maenach came hurrying in with Sister Sárnat almost clutching at his sleeve. Lorcán pointed to the unconscious religieux.

'Can you revive him?' he asked.

Maenach bent over the man, raising his unconscious eyelids and then testing his pulse.

'He is in a deep coma. Almost as if he is asleep.' He examined the wound. 'It is curious that he has been rendered so deeply unconscious from the blow that made this wound. The wound seems superficial enough. The brother's breathing is regular and untroubled. I am sure he will regain consciousness after a while.'

'Then do what you can, Maenach,' Fidelma said. 'Sister Sárnat, you will help him,' she instructed the pale, shivering young girl who still hovered uncertainly at the door of the cell.

She then took the boatman, Lorcán, by the arm and led him from the cell, turning him towards the quadrangle, and pointing silently to the figure bound to the tree.

Lorcán took a step forward and then let out a startled exhalation of breath. It was the first time he had observed the body.

'God look down upon us!' he said slowly as he genuflected. 'Now there are two deaths among the religious of Selbach!'

'Do you know this person?' Fidelma asked.

'Know him?' Lorcán sounded startled at the question. 'Of course. It is the Abbot Selbach!'

'Abbot Selbach?'

Fidelma pursed her lips with astonishment as she re-examined the body of the dead abbot. Then she gazed around her towards the empty landscape.

'And did you not say that Selbach had a community of twelve Brothers here with him?'

Lorcán followed her gaze uncertainly.

'Yes. Yet the island seems deserted,' he muttered. 'What terrible mystery is here?'

'That is something we must discover,' Fidelma replied confidently.

'We must leave for the mainland at once,' Lorcán advised. 'We must get back to Dún na Séad and inform The Ó hEidersceoil.'

The Ó hEidersceoil was the chieftain of the territory.

Fidelma raised a hand to stay the man even as he was turning back to the cell where they had left Brother Spelán.

'Wait, Lorcán. I am a *dálaigh*, an advocate of the Law of the *Fenechus*, holding the degree of *Anruth*. It is my task to stay and discover how Abbot Selbach and little Sacán met their deaths and why Brother Spelán was wounded. Also we must discover where the rest of the community has disappeared to.'

Lorcán gazed at the young religieuse in surprise.

'That same danger may yet attend us,' he protested. 'What manner of magic is it that makes a community disappear and leaves their abbot dead like a common criminal bound to a tree, the boy dead and their *dominus* assaulted and unconscious?'

'Human magic, if magic you want to call it,' Fidelma replied irritably. 'As an advocate of the law courts of the five kingdoms of Ireland, I call upon you for assistance, I have this right by the laws of the *Fenechus*, under the authority of the Chief Brehon. Do you deny my right?'

Lorcán gazed at the religieuse a moment in surprise and then slowly shook his head.

'You have that right, Sister. But, look, Abbot Selbach is not long dead. What if his killers are hiding nearby?'

Fidelma ignored his question and turned back to regard the hanging body, her head to one side in reflection.

'What makes you say that he is not long dead, Lorcán?'

The sailor shrugged impatiently.

'The body is cold but not very stiff. Also it is untouched by the scavengers . . .'

He gestured towards the wheeling birds. She followed his gaze and could see among the seabirds, the large forms of black-backed gulls, one of the most vicious of coastal scavengers. And here and there she saw the jet black of carrion crows. It was the season when the eggs of these harsh-voiced predators would be hatching along the cliff top nests and the young birds would be demanding to be fed by the omnivorous parents, feeding off eggs of other birds, even small mammals and often rotting carcasses. She realised that the wheeling gulls and crows would sooner or later descend on a corpse but there was no sign that they had done so already.

'Excellently observed, Lorcán,' she commented. 'And presumably Brother Spelán could not have been unconscious long. But do you observe any other peculiar thing about the abbot's body?'

The boatman frowned at her and glanced at the slumped corpse. He stared a moment and shook his head.

'Selbach was flogged and then stabbed three times in the back. I would imagine that the thrust of the knife was upwards, between the ribs, so that he died instantly. What strange ritual would so punish a man before killing him?'

Lorcán stared more closely and sighed deeply.

'I don't understand.'

'Just observe for the moment,' Fidelma replied. 'I may need you later to be a witness to these facts. I think we may cut down the body and place it out of reach of the birds within the oratory.'

Lorcán took his sharp sailor's knife and quickly severed the ropes. Then he dragged the body into the oratory at Fidelma's direction.

Fidelma now had time to make a more careful examination of the young boy's body.

'He has clearly been immersed for a while in the sea. Not very long but several hours at least,' she observed. 'There are no immediate causes of death. He has not been stabbed nor has he been hit by any blunt instrument.'

She turned the body and gave a quick sudden intake of breath.

'But he has been scourged. See, Lorcán?'

The boatman saw that the upper part of the boy's robe had been torn revealing that his back was covered in old and new welts and scars made by a whip.

'I knew the boy's family well on Inis Beag,' he whispered. 'He was a happy, dutiful boy. His body was without blemish when I brought him here.'

Fidelma made a search of the boy's sodden clothing; the salt water drying out was already making white lines and patches on it. Her eyes narrowed as she examined the prayer cord which fastened the habit. A small metal hook was hanging from it on which a tiny leather sheath was fastened containing a small knife, a knife typical of those used by some rural orders to cut their meat or help them in their daily tasks. Caught on the projecting metal hook was a torn piece of woollen cloth. Carefully, Fidelma removed it and held it up.

'What is it, Sister?' asked Lorcán.

'I don't know. A piece of cloth caught on the hook.' She made a quick examination. 'It is not from the boy's clothing.' She placed it in her *marsupium*, along with the wooden cup. Then she cast one final look at the youthful body before covering it. 'Come, let us see what else we can find.'

'But what, sister?' Lorcán asked. 'What can we do? There is a storm coming soon and if it catches us here then here we shall have to remain until it passes.'

'I am aware of the coming storm,' she replied imperturbably. 'But first we must be sure of one thing. You say there were twelve brothers here as well as Selbach? Then we have accounted for only two of them, Spelán and Sacán. Our next step is clear – we must search the island to assure ourselves that they are not hidden from us.'

Lorcán bit his lip nervously.

'What if it were pirates who did this deed? I have heard tales of Saxon raiders with their longboats, devastating villages further along the coast.'

'A possibility,' agreed Fidelma. 'But it is not a likely one.'

'Why so?' demanded Lorcán. 'The Saxons have raided along the coasts of Gaul, Britain and Ireland for many years, looting and killing . . .'

'Just so,' Fidelma smiled grimly. 'Looting and burning communities; driving off livestock and taking the people to be slaves.'

She gestured to the deserted but tranquil buildings.

Lorcán suddenly realised what she was driving at. There was no sign of any destruction nor of any looting or violence enacted against the property. On the slope behind the oratory, three or four goats munched at the heather while a fat sow snorted and grunted among her piglets. And if that were not enough, he recalled that the silver crucifix still hung around the neck of the dead abbot. There had been no theft here. Clearly, then, there had been no pirate raid on the defenceless community. Lorcán was even more puzzled.

'Come with me, Lorcán, and we will examine the cells of the Brothers,' instructed Fidelma.

The stone cell next to the one in which they had left Spelán had words inscribed on the lintel.

Ora et labora. Work and pray. A laudable exhortation thought Fidelma and she paused underneath. The cell was almost bare and its few items of furniture were simple. On a beaten earthen floor, covered with rushes strewn as a mat, there were two wooden cots, a cupboard, a few leather *tiag leabhair* or book satchels, hung from hooks, containing several small gospel books. A large ornately carved wooden cross hung on a wall.

There was another maxim inscribed on a wall to one side of this cell.

Animi indices sunt eculi.
The eyes are the betrayer of the mind.

Fidelma found it a curious adage to exhort a Christian community to faith. Then her eyes fell on a piece of written vellum by the side of one of the cots. She picked it up. It was a verse from one of the Psalms. 'Break thou the arm of the wicked and the evil man; seek out his wickedness till thou find none . . .' She shivered slightly for this was not a dictum of a God of love.

Her eyes fell on a box at the foot of the bed. On the top box was an inscription in Greek.

Pathémata mathémata. Sufferings are lessons.

She bent forward and opened the box. Her eyes rounded in astonishment. Contained within were a set of scourges, of whips and canes. There were some words carved on the underside of the lid. They were in plain Irish.

> God give me a wall of tears
> my sins to hide;
> for I remain, while no tears fall, unsanctified.

She looked across to Lorcán in surprise.

'Do you know whose cell this was?' she demanded.

'Assuredly,' came the prompt reply. 'Selbach shared this cell with his *dominus* – Spelán. The cell we placed Spelán in, the one nearest the oratory, belongs to two other members of the community.'

'Do you know what sort of man Selbach was? Was he a man who was authoritarian, who liked to inflict punishment? Was the Rule of his community a harsh one?'

Lorcán shrugged.

'That I would not know. I did not know the community that well.'

'There is evidence of pain and punishment in this place,' Fidelma sensed a cold tingle against her spine. 'I do not understand it.'

She paused, noticing a shelf on which stood several jars and bottles. She moved to them and began to examine the contents of each jar, sniffing its odours or wetting the tip of her finger from the concoctions before cautiously tasting it.

Then she reached into her *marsupium* and took the wooden cup she had retrieved from the floor of the oratory. It had recently been used for the wood still showed the dampness of its contents. She sniffed at it. A curious mixture of pungent odours came to her nostrils. Then she turned back to the shelf and examined the jars and bottles of herbs again. She could identify the dried heads of red clover, dried horse-chestnut leaves and mullein among the jars of herbs.

Lorcán stood watching her impatiently.

'Spelán uses this as the community's apothecary,' he said. 'On one of my trips here I cut my hand and it was Spelán who gave me a poultice of herbs to heal it.'

Fidelma sighed a little as she gave a final look around.

Finally she left the cell, followed by an unhappy Lorcán, and began to examine the other cells again but this time more carefully. There was evidence in one or two of them that some personal items and articles of clothing had been hurriedly removed, but not enough to support the idea of the community being attacked and robbed by an outside force.

Fidelma emerged into the quadrangle feeling confused.

Lorcán, at her side, was gazing up at the sky, a worried expression on his face.

Fidelma knew that he was still concerned about the approaching weather but it was no time to retreat from this mystery. Someone had killed the abbot of the community and a young brother, knocked the *dominus* unconscious and made ten further members of the brotherhood disappear.

'Didn't you say that the community had their own boat?' she asked abruptly.

Lorcán nodded unhappily.

'It was not in the cove when we landed,' Fidelma pointed out.

'No, it wouldn't be,' replied the boatman. 'They kept their boat further along the shore in a sheltered spot. There is a small shingled strand around the headland where a boat can be beached.'

'Show me,' Fidelma instructed. 'There is nothing else to do until Spelán recovers consciousness and we may learn his story.'

Somewhat reluctantly, with another glance at the western sky, Lorcán led the way along the pathway towards the cove but then broke away along another path which led down on the other side of a great rocky outcrop which served as a headland separating them from the cove in which they had landed.

Fidelma knew something was wrong when they reached a knoll before the path twisted and turned through granite pillars towards the distant pounding sea. Her eyes caught the flash of black in the sky circling over something on the shore below.

They were black-backed gulls. Of all gulls, these were birds to be respected. They frequently nested on rocky islands such as Inis Chloichreán. It was a carrion eater, a fierce predator given to taking mammals even as large as cats. They had obviously found something down on the beach. Fidelma could see that even the crows could not compete with their larger brethren. There were several pairs of crows above the mêlée, circling and waiting their chance.

Fidelma compressed her lips firmly.

Lorcán continued to lead the way down between the rocks. The area was full of nesting birds. May was a month in which the black-backed gulls, along with many other species, laid their eggs. The rocky cliffs of the island were ideal sites for birds. The females screamed furiously as they entered the area but Lorcán ignored their threatening displays. Fidelma did not pretend that she was unconcerned.

'The brothers kept their boat just here . . .' began Lorcán, reaching a large platform of rocky land about twelve feet above a short pebbly beach. He halted and stared.

Fidelma saw the wooden trestles, on which the boat had apparently been set. There was no vessel resting on them now.

'They used to store the boat here,' explained Lorcán, 'placed upside down to protect it against the weather.'

It was the gathering further down on the pebbly strand, an area of beach no more than three yards in width and perhaps ten yards long, that caused Fidelma to exclaim sharply. She realised what the confusion of birds was about. A dozen or more large gulls were gathered, screaming and fighting each other, while forming an outer circle were several other birds who seemed to be interested spectators to the affair. Here and there a jet black carrion crow perched, black eyes watching intently for its chance, while others circled over-head. They were clustering around something which lay on the pebbles. Fidelma suspected what it was.

'Come on!' she cried, and climbed hastily down to the pebbly strand. Then she halted and picked up several large pebbles and began to hurl them at the host of carrion eaters. The scavengers let forth screaming cries of anger and flapped their great wings. Lorcán joined her, picking up stones and throwing them with all his strength.

It was not long before the wheeling mass of birds had dispersed from the object over which they had been fighting. But Fidelma saw that they had not retreated far. They swirled high in the air above them or strutted nearby, beady eyes watching and waiting.

Nonetheless, she strode purposefully across the shingle.

The religieux had been young, very young with fair hair.

He lay on his back, his robes in an unseemly mess of torn and frayed wool covered in blood.

Fidelma swallowed hard. The gulls had been allowed an hour or so of uninterrupted work. The face was pitted and bloody, an eye was missing. Part of the skull had been smashed, a pulpy mess of blood and bone. It was obvious that no bird had perpetrated that damage.

'Can you tell who this was, Lorcán?' Fidelma asked softly.

The boatman came over, one wary eye on the gulls. They were standing well back but with their eyes malignantly on the humans who had dared drive them from their unholy feasting. Lorcán glanced down. He pulled a face at the sight.

'I have seen him here in the community, Sister. Alas, I do not know his name. Sister, I am fearful. This is the third dead member of the community.'

Fidelma did not reply but steeled herself to bend beside the corpse. The leather *crumena* or purse was still fastened at his belt. She forced herself to avoid the lacerated features of the youth and his one remaining bright, accusing eye, and put her hand into the purse. It was empty.

She drew back and shook her head.

Then a thought occurred to her.

'Help me push the body over face down,' she instructed.

Keeping his curiosity to himself, Lorcán did so.

The robe was almost torn from the youth's back by the ravages of the birds. Fidelma did not have to remove the material further to see a patch of scars, some old, some new, some which showed signs of recent bleeding, criss-cross over his back.

'What do you make of that, Lorcán?' Fidelma invited.

The boatman thrust out his lower lip and raised one shoulder before letting it fall in an exaggerated shrug.

'Only that the boy has been whipped. Not once either but many times over a long period.'

Fidelma nodded in agreement.

'That's another fact I want you to witness, Lorcán.'

She stood up, picking up a few stones as she did so and shying them at two or three large gulls who were slowly closing the distance between them. They screamed in annoyance but removed themselves to a safer position.

'How big was the community's currach?' she asked abruptly.

Lorcán understood what she meant.

'It was big enough to carry the rest of the brethren,' he replied. 'They must be long gone, by now. They could be anywhere on the islands or have even reached the mainland.'

He paused and looked at her. 'But did they go willingly or were they forced to go? Who could have done this?'

Fidelma did not reply. She motioned Lorcán to help her return the body to its original position and stared at the crushed skull.

'That was done with a heavy and deliberate blow,' she observed. 'This young religieux was murdered and left here on the strand.'

Lorcán shook his head in utter bewilderment.

'There is much evil here, Sister.'

'With that I can agree,' Fidelma replied. 'Come, let us build a cairn over his body with stones so that the gulls do not feast further on him – whoever he was. We cannot carry him back to the settlement.'

When they arrived back at the community, having completed their task, Maenach greeted them in the quadrangle with a look of relief.

'Brother Spelán is coming round. The young Sister is nursing him.'

Fidelma answered with a grim smile.

'Now perhaps we may learn some answers to this mystery.'

Inside the cell, the Brother was lying against a pillow. He looked very drowsy and blinked several times as his dark, black eyes tried to focus on Fidelma.

She motioned Sister Sárnat to move aside and sat on the edge of the cot by Spelán.

'I have given him water only, Sister,' the girl said eagerly, as if expecting her approval. 'The boatman,' she gestured towards Maenach, who stood at the doorway with Lorcán, 'bathed and dressed the wound.'

Fidelma smiled encouragingly at the Brother.

'Are you Brother Spelán?'

The man closed his eyes for a moment, his voice sounded weak.

'I am Spelán. Who are you and what are you doing here?'

'I am Fidelma of Kildare. I am come here to bring the

Abbot Selbach a letter from Ultan of Armagh.'

Spelán stared at her.

'A letter from Ultan?' He sounded confused.

'Yes. That is why we landed on the island. What has happened here? Who hit you on the head?'

Spelán groaned and raised a hand to his forehead.

'I recall.' His voice grew strong and commanding. 'The abbot is dead, Sister. Return to Dún na Séad and ask that a Brehon be sent here for there has been a great crime committed.'

'I will take charge of the matter, Spelán,' Fidelma said confidently.

'You?' Spelán stared at her in bewilderment. 'You don't understand. It is a Brehon that is needed.'

'I am a *dálaigh* of the court qualified to the level of *Anruth*.'

Spelán's eyes widened a fraction for he realised that the qualification of *Anruth* allowed the young religieuse to sit in judgement with kings and even with the High King himself.

'Tell me what took place here?' Fidelma prompted.

Spelán's dark eyes found Sister Sárnat and motioned for her to hand him the cup of water from which he took several gulps.

'There was evil here, Sister. An evil which grew unnoticed by me until it burst forth and enveloped us all in its maw.'

Fidelma waited without saying anything.

Spelán seemed to gather his thoughts for a moment or two.

'I will start from the beginning.'

'Always a good place for starting a tale,' Fidelma affirmed solemnly.

'Two years ago I met Selbach who persuaded me to join him here in order to build a community which would be dedicated to isolation and meditative contemplation of the works of the Creator. I was the apothecary at an abbey on the mainland which was a sinful place – pride, gluttony and other vices were freely practised there. In Selbach I believed that I had found a kindred spirit who shared my own views. We searched together for a while and eventually came across eleven young souls who wanted to devote themselves to our purpose.'

'Why so young?' demanded Fidelma.

Spelán blinked.

'We needed youth to help our community flourish for in youth lies strength against the hardships of this place.'

'Go on,' pressed Fidelma when the man paused.

'With the blessing of Ultan of Armagh and the permission of the local chieftain, The Ó hEidersceoil, we came to this isolated place.'

He paused to take another sip of water.

'And what of this evil that grew in your midst?' encouraged Fidelma.

'I am coming to that. There is a philosophy among some of the ascetics of the faith that physical pain, even as the Son of the Living God had to endure, pain such as the tortures of the flesh, is the way to man's redemption, a way to salvation. Mortification and suffering are seen as the paths to spiritual salvation.'

Fidelma sniffed in disapproval.

'I have heard that there are such misguided fools among us.'

Spelán blinked.

'Not fools, Sister, not fools,' he corrected softly. 'Many of our blessed saints believed in the efficacy of mortification. They held genuine belief that they must emulate the pain of Christ if they, too, would seek eternal paradise. There are many who will still wear crowns of thorns, who flagellate themselves, drive nails into their hands or pierce their sides so that they might share the suffering of Christ. No, you are too harsh, Sister. They are not fools; visionaries – yes; and, perhaps, misguided in their path.'

'Very well. We will not argue the matter at this stage,

Spelán. What is this to do with what has happened here?'

'Do not mistake my meaning, Sister,' replied Selbach contritely. 'I am not an advocate for the *gortaigid*, those who seek the infliction of such pain. I, too, condemn them as you do. But I accept that their desire to experience pain is a genuine desire to share the pain of the Messiah through which he sought man's redemption. I would not call them fools. However, let me continue. For a while we were a happy community. It did not cross my mind that one among us felt that pain was his path to salvation.'

'There was a *gortaigid* among you?'

The *dominus* nodded.

'I will spare the events that led to it but will simply reveal that it was none other than the venerable Abbot Selbach himself. But Selbach was not of those who simply inflicted pain and punishment upon himself. He persuaded the youthful Brothers we had gathered here to submit to scourgings and whippings in order to satiate his desire to inflict pain and injury so that, he argued, they might approach a sharing of Christ's great suffering. He practised these abominations in secret and swore others to keep that secret on pain of their immortal souls.'

'When was this discovered?' demanded Fidelma, slightly horrified.

Spelán bit his lip a moment.

'For certain? Only this morning. I knew nothing. I swear it. It was early this morning that the body of our youngest neophyte, Sacán, was found. He was fourteen years old. The Brothers found him and it was known that Selbach had taken him to a special place at the far end of the island last night to ritually scourge the boy. So fiercely did he lash the youth that he died of shock and pain.'

The *dominus* genuflected.

Fidelma's mouth tightened.

'Go on. How were you, the *dominus* of this community, unaware of the abbot's action before this morning?'

'He was cunning,' replied Spelán immediately. 'He made the young Brothers take oath each time not to reveal the ritual scourgings to anyone else. He took one young Brother at a time to the far end of the island. A shroud of silence enveloped the community. I dwelt in blissful ignorance.'

'Go on.'

'Selbach had tried to hide his guilt by throwing the poor boy's body over the cliffs last night but the tide washed the body along the rocky barrier that is our shore. It washed ashore early this morning at a point where two of our brethren were fishing for our daily meal.'

He paused and sought another sip of water.

Behind her Lorcán said quietly: 'Indeed, the tide from the headland would wash the body along to the pebble beach.'

'I was asleep when I heard the noise. When I left my cell the Brothers' anger had erupted and they had seized Selbach and lashed him to the quadrangle tree. One of the brothers was flogging him with his own whip, tearing at his flesh . . .'

The *dominus* paused again before continuing.

'And did you attempt to stop them?' inquired Fidelma.

'Of course I tried to stop them,' Spelán replied indignantly. 'I tried to remonstrate, as did another young Brother, Snagaide, who told them they could not take the law into their own hands nor punish Selbach. They must take their complaint to Dún na Séad and place it before the Brehon of The Ó hEidersceoil. But the young Brothers were so enraged that they would not listen. Instead, they seized Snagaide and myself and held us, ignoring our pleas, while they flogged Selbach. Their rage was great. And then, before I knew it, someone had thrust his knife into the back of Selbach. I did not see who it was.

'I cried to them that not only had a crime been done but now great sacrilege. I demanded that they surrender themselves to me and to Brother Snagaide. I promised that I would take them to Dún na Séad where they must answer for their deed but I would speak on their behalf.'

Spelán paused and touched the wound on the side of his head once more with a grimace of pain.

'They argued among themselves then but, God forgive them, they found a determined spokesman in a Brother named Fogach who said that they should not be punished for doing what was right and just in the eyes of God. An eye for an eye, a tooth for a tooth, they argued. It was right for Selbach to have met his death in compensation for the death of young Brother Sacán. He demanded that I should swear an oath not to betray the events on the island, recording the deaths as accidents. If I protested then they would take the currach and seek a place where they could live in peace and freedom, leaving me and Snagaide on the island until visited by Lorcán or some other boatman from the mainland.'

'Then what happened?' urged Fidelma after the *dominus* paused.

'Then? As you might expect, I could not make such an oath. Their anger spilt over while I remonstrated with them. More for the fear of the consequences than anger, I would say. One of their number knocked me on the head. I knew nothing else until I came to with the young Sister and the boatman bending over me.'

Fidelma was quiet for a while.

'Tell me, Spelán, what happened to your companion, Brother Snagaide?'

Spelán frowned, looking around as if he expected to find the Brother in a corner of the cell.

'Snagaide? I do not know, Sister. There was a great deal of shouting and arguing. Then everything went black for me.'

'Was Brother Snagaide young?'

'Most of the brethren, apart from myself and Selbach, were but youths.'

'Did he have fair hair?'

Spelán shook his head to her surprise. Then it was not Snagaide who lay dead on the strand.

'No,' Spelán repeated. 'He had black hair.'

'One thing that still puzzles me, Spelán. This is a small island, with a small community. For two years you have lived here in close confines. Yet you say that you did not know about the sadistic tendencies of Abbot Selbach; that each night he took young members of the community to some remote part of the island and inflicted pain on them, yet you did not know? I find this strange.'

Spelán grimaced dourly.

'Strange though it is, Sister, it is the truth. The rest of the community were young. Selbach dominated them. They thought that pain brought them nearer salvation. Being sworn by the Holy Cross never to speak of the whipping given them by the abbot, they remained in silence. Probably they thought that I approved of the whippings. Ah, those poor boys, they suffered in silence until the death of gentle, little Sacán . . . poor boy, poor boy.'

Tears welled in the *dominus'* eyes.

Sister Sárnat reached forward and handed him the cup of water.

Fidelma rose silently and left the cell.

Lorcán followed after her as she went to the quadrangle and stood for a moment in silent reflection.

'A terrible tale, and no mistake,' he commented, his eyes raised absently to the sky. 'The Brother is better now, however, and we can leave as soon as you like.'

Fidelma ignored him. Her hands were clasped before her and she was gazing at the ground without focusing on it.

'Sister?' prompted Lorcán.

Fidelma raised her head, suddenly becoming aware of him.

'Sorry, you were saying something?'

The boatman shrugged.

'Only that we should be on our way soon. The poor Brother needs to be taken to Chléire as soon as we can do so.'

Fidelma breathed out slowly.

'I think that the poor Brother . . .' she paused and grimaced. 'I think there is still a mystery here which needs to be resolved.'

Lorcán stared at her.

'But the explanation of Brother Spelán . . .?'

Fidelma returned his gaze calmly.

'I will walk awhile in contemplation.'

The boatman spread his hands in despair.

'But, Sister, the coming weather . . .'

'If the storm comes then we will remain here until it passes.' And, as Lorcán opened his mouth to protest, she added: 'I state this as a *dálaigh* of the court and you will observe that authority.'

Lorcán's mouth drooped and, with a shrug of resignation, he turned away.

Fidelma began to follow the path behind the community, among the rocks to the more remote area of the island. She realised that this would have been the path along which, according to Spelán, Abbot Selbach took his victims. She felt a revulsion at what had been revealed by Spelán, although she had expected some such explanation from the evidence of the lacerated backs of the two young Brothers she had seen. She felt loathing at the ascetics who called themselves *gortaigid*, those who sought salvation by bestowing pain on themselves and others. Abbots and bishops condemned them and they were usually driven out into isolated communities.

Here, it seemed, that one evil man had exerted his will on a bunch of youths scarcely out of boyhood who had sought the religious life and knew no better than to submit to his will until one of their number died. Now those youths had fled the island, frightened, demoralised and probably lost to the truth of Christ's message of love and peace.

In spite of general condemnation she knew that in many abbeys and monasteries some abbots and abbesses ordered strict rules of intolerable numbers of genuflections, prostrations and fasts. She knew that Erc, the bishop of Slane, who had been patron of the blessed Brendan of Clonfert, would take his acolytes to cold mountain streams, summer and winter, to immerse themselves in the icy waters four times a day to say their prayers and psalms. There was the ascetic, Mac Tulchan, who bred fleas on his body and, so that his pain might be the greater, he never scratched himself. Didn't Finnian of Clonard purposely set out to catch a virulent disease from a dying child that he might obtain salvation through suffering?

Mortification and suffering. Ultan of Armagh was one of the school preaching moderation to those who were becoming indulgently masochistic, ascetics who were becoming fanatical torturers of the body, wrenching salvation through unnatural wants, strain or physical suffering.

She paused in her striding and sat down on a rock, her hands demurely folded in front of her, as she let her mind dwell on the evidence. It certainly appeared that everything fitted in with Spelán's explanation. Why did she feel that there was something wrong? She opened her *marsupium* and drew out the piece of cloth she had found ensnared on the belt hook of the youthful Sacán. It had obviously been torn away from something and not from the boy's habit. And there was a wooden cup, which had dried out now, which she had found on the floor of the oratory. It had obviously been used for an infusion of herbs.

She suddenly saw a movement out of the corner of her eye, among the rocks. She swung round very fast. For a moment her eyes locked into the dark eyes of a startled youth, the cowl of his habit drawn over his head. Then the youth darted away among the rocks.

'Stop!' Fidelma came to her feet, thrusting the cup and cloth into her *marsupium*. 'Stop, Brother, I mean you no harm.'

But the youth was gone, bounding away through the rocky terrain.

With an exasperated sigh, Fidelma began to follow, when

the sound of her name being called halted her.

Sister Sárnat came panting along the path.

'I have been sent by Brother Spelán and Lorcán,' she said. 'Lorcán entreats you to have a care of the approaching storm, Sister.'

Fidelma was about to say something sarcastic about Lorcán's concern but Sárnat continued.

'Brother Spelán agrees we should leave the island immediately and report the events here to the Abbot of Chléire. The Brother is fully recovered now and he is taking charge of things. He says that he recalls your purpose here was to bring a letter from Ultan to the Abbot Selbach. Since Selbach is dead and he is *dominus* he asks that you give him the letter in case anything requires to be done about it before we leave the island.'

Fidelma forgot about the youth she was about to pursue.

She stared hard at Sister Sárnat.

The young novitiate waited nervously, wondering what Fidelma was staring at.

'Sister . . .' she began nervously.

Fidelma sat down on the nearest rock abruptly.

'I have been a fool,' she muttered, reaching into her *marsupium* and bringing out the letters she was carrying. She thrust back the letter addressed to the Abbot of Chléire and tore open Ultan's letter to Selbach, to the astonished gaze of Sister Sárnat. Her eyes rapidly read the letter and her features broke into a grim smile.

'Go, Sister,' she said, arising and thrusting the letter back into the *marsupium*. 'Return to Brother Spelán. Tell him and Lorcán that I will be along in a moment. I think we will be able to leave here before the storm develops.'

Sárnat stared at her uncertainly.

'Very well, Sister. But why not return with me?'

Fidelma smiled.

'I have to talk to someone first.'

★ ★ ★

195

A short while later Fidelma strode into the cell where Spelán was sitting on the cot, with Lorcán and Maenach lounging nearby. Sister Sárnat was seated on a wooden bench by one wall. As Fidelma entered, Lorcán looked up in relief.

'Are you ready now, Sister? We do not have long.'

'A moment or two, if you please, Lorcán,' she said, smiling gently.

Spelán was rising.

'I think we should leave immediately, Sister. I have much to report to the Abbot of Chléire. Also . . .'

'How did you come to tear your robe, Spelán?'

Fidelma asked the question with an innocent expression. Beneath that expression, her mind was racing for she had made her opening arrow-shot into the darkness. Spelán stared at her and then stared at his clothing. It was clear that he did not know whether his clothing was torn or not. But his eyes lighted upon a jagged tear in his right sleeve. He shrugged.

'I did not notice,' he replied.

Fidelma took the piece of torn cloth from her *marsupium* and laid it on the table.

'Would you say that this cloth fitted the tear, Lorcán?'

The boatman, frowning, picked it up and took it to place against Spelán's sleeve.

'It does, Sister,' he said quietly.

'Do you recall where I found it?'

'I do. It was snagged on the hook of the belt of the young boy, Sacán.'

The colour drained from Spelán's face.

'It must have been caught there when I carried the body from the strand . . .' he began.

'*You* carried the body from the strand?' asked Fidelma with emphasis. 'You told us that some of the young Brothers fishing there saw it and brought it back and all this happened before you were awakened after they had tied Selbach to the tree and killed him.'

Spelán's mouth worked for a moment without words coming.

'I will tell you what happened on this island,' Fidelma said. 'Indeed, you did have a *gortaigid* here. One who dedicated his life to the enjoyment of mortification and suffering but not from any pious ideal of religious attainment . . . merely from personal perversion. Where better to practise his disgusting sadism than a hermitage of youths whom he could dominate and devise tortures for by persuading them that only by that pain could they obtain true spirituality?'

Spelán was staring malignantly at her.

'In several essentials, your story was correct, Spelán. There was a conspiracy of secrecy among the youths. Their tormentor would take them one at a time, the youngest and most vulnerable, to a remote part of the island and inflict his punishment, assuring the boy it was the route to eternal glory. Then one day one of the youths, poor little Sacán, was beaten so severely that he died. In a panic the tormentor tried to dispose of his evil deed by throwing the body over the cliffs. As he did so, the hook on the boy's belt tore a piece of cloth from the man's robe. Then the next morning the body washed ashore.'

'Utter nonsense. It was Selbach who . . .'

'It was Selbach who began to suspect that he had a *gortaigid* in his community.'

Spelán frowned.

'All this is supposition,' he sneered, but there was a fear lurking in his dark eyes.

'Not quite,' Fidelma replied without emotion. 'You are a very clever man, Spelán. When Sacán's body was discovered, the youths who found him gathered on the shore around it. They did not realise that their abbot, Selbach, was really a kindly man who had only recently realised what was going on in his community and certainly did not condone it. As you said yourself, the conspiracy of silence was such that the youthful brothers thought that you were acting with Selbach's approval. They thought that mortification was a silent rule of the community. They decided to flee from the island there and then. Eight of them launched the currach and rowed away, escaping from what had become for them an accursed place . . .'

Lorcán, who had been following Fidelma's explanation with some astonishment, whistled softly.

'Where would they have gone, Sister?'

'It depends. If they had sense they would have gone to report the matter to Chléire or even to Dún na Séad. But, perhaps, they thought their word would be of no weight against the abbot and *dominus* of this house. Perhaps these innocents still think that mortification is an accepted rule of the Faith.'

'May I remind you that I was knocked unconscious by these same innocents?' sneered Spelán.

Maenach nodded emphatically.

'Indeed, Sister, that is so. How do you explain that?'

'I will come to that in a moment. Let me tell you firstly what happened here. The eight young brothers left the island because they believed everyone else supported the rule of mortification. It was then that brother Fogach came across the body and carried it to the oratory and alerted you, Spelán.'

'Why would he do that?'

'Because Brother Fogach was not your enemy, nor was Brother Snagaide. They were your chosen acolytes who had actually helped you carry out your acts of sadism in the past. They were young and gullible enough to believe your instructions were the orders of the Faith and the Word of God. But inflicting punishment on their fellows was one thing, murder was another.'

'You'll have a job to prove this,' sneered Spelán.

'Perhaps,' replied Fidelma. 'At this stage Fogach and Snagaide were willing to help you. You realised that your time was running out. If those brothers reported matters then an official of the church, a *dálaigh*, would be sent to the island. You had to prepare your defence. An evil scheme came into your mind. It was still early. Selbach was still asleep. You persuaded Snagaide and Fogach that Selbach was responsible in the same way that you had persuaded their fellows that Selbach approved of this mortification. You told them that Selbach had flogged Sacán that night – not you – and now he must be ritually scourged in turn. Together you awoke Selbach and took him and tied him to that tree. You knew exactly what you were going to do but first you whipped that venerable old man.

'In his pain, the old man cried out and told your companions the truth. They listened, horrified at how they had been misled. Seeing this, you stabbed the abbot to stop him speaking. But the abbot's life would have been forfeit anyway. It was all part of your plan to hide all the evidence against you, to show that you were simply the dupe of Selbach.

'Snagaide and Fogach ran off. You now had to silence them. You caught up with Fogach and killed him, smashing his skull with a stone. But when you turned in search of Snagaide you suddenly observed a currach approaching. It was Lorcán's currach. But you thought it was coming in answer to the report of the eight brothers.

'You admitted that you were a trained apothecary. You hurried to your cell and mixed a potion of herbs, a powerful sleeping draught which would render you unconscious within a short time. First you picked up a stone and smote your temple hard enough to cause a nasty-looking wound. But Maenach, who knows something of a physician's art, told us that he would not have expected you to be unconscious from it. In fact, after you had delivered that blow, you drank your potion and stretched yourself in the oratory where I found you. You were not unconscious from the blow but merely in a deep sleep from your potion. You had already worked out the story that you would tell us. It would be your word against the poor, pitiful and confused youths.'

Fidelma slowly took out the cup and placed it on the table.

'That was the cup I found lying near you in the oratory. It still smells of the herbs, like mullein and red clover tops, which would make up the powerful sleeping draught. You have jars of such ingredients in your cell.'

'You still can't prove this absurd story,' replied Spelán.

'I think I can. You see, not only did Abbot Selbach begin to suspect that there was a *gortaigid* at work within his community but he wrote to Ultan of Armagh outlining his suspicions.'

She took out the letter from Ultan of Armagh.

Spelán's eyes narrowed. She noticed that tiny beads of sweat were gathering on his brow for the first time since she had begun to call his bluff. She held the letter tantalisingly in front of her.

'You see, Spelán, when you showed yourself anxious to get your hands on this letter, I realised that it was the piece of evidence I was looking for; indeed, that I was overlooking. The letter is remarkably informative, a reply to all Selbach's concerns about you.'

Spelán's face was white. He stared aghast at the letter as she placed it on the table.

'Selbach named me to Ultan?'

Fidelma pointed to the letter.

'You may see for yourself.'

With a cry of rage that stunned everyone into immobility, Spelán suddenly launched himself across the room towards Fidelma with his hands outstretched.

He had gone but a few paces when he was abruptly halted as if by a gigantic hand against his chest. He stood for a moment, his eyes bulging in astonishment, and then he slid to the ground without another word.

It was only then that they saw the hilt of the knife buried in Spelán's heart and the blood staining his robes.

There was a movement at the door. A young, dark-haired youth in the robes of a religieux took a hesitant step in. Lorcán, the first to recover his senses, knelt by the side of Spelán and reached for a pulse. Then he raised his eyes and shook his head.

Fidelma turned to the trembling youth who had thrown the knife. She reached out a hand and laid it on his shaking arm.

'I had to do it,' muttered the youth. 'I had to.'

'I know,' she pacified.

'I do not care. I am ready to be punished.' The youth drew himself up.

'In your suffering of mind, you have already punished yourself enough, Brother Snagaide. These here,' she gestured towards Lorcán, Maenach and Sárnat, 'are witnesses to Spelán's action which admitted his guilt. Your case will be heard before the Brehon in Chléire and I shall be your advocate. Does not the ancient law say every person who places themselves beyond the law is without the protection of the law? You slew a violator of the law and therefore this killing is justified under the Law of the *Fenechus*.'

She drew the youth outside. He was scarcely the age of credulous and unworldly Sister Sárnat. Fidelma sighed deeply. If she could one day present a law to the council of judges of Ireland she would make it a law that no one under the age of twenty-five could be thrust into the life of the religious. Youth needed to grow to adulthood and savour life and understand something of the world before they isolated themselves on islands or in cloisters away from it. Only in such sequestered states of innocence and fear of authority could evil men like Spelán thrive. She placed a comforting arm around the youth's shoulder as he fell to heart-retching sobbing.

'Come, Lorcán,' Fidelma called across her shoulder. 'Let's get down to the currach and reach Inis Chléire before your storm arrives.'

Sister Sárnat emerged from the cell, holding the letter which Fidelma had laid on the table.

'Sister . . .' She seemed to find difficulty in speaking. 'This letter from Ultan to Selbach . . . it does not refer to Spelán. Selbach didn't suspect Spelán at all. He thought that mortification was just a fashion among the youthful Brothers.'

Fidelma's face remained unchanged.

'Selbach could not bring himself to suspect his companion. It was a lucky thing that Spelán didn't realise that, wasn't it?'

The Poisoned Chalice

❧

T he last thing Sister Fidelma of Kildare had expected,
during her pilgrimage to the Eternal City of Rome, was
to see murder committed in front of her eyes in a quiet little
backstreet church.

As any citizen of Rome would have expected, Sister
Fidelma, like every discerning *barbarus* on their first visit,
was duly impressed by the immensity of the city. As neither
a Hellene nor a Roman, the term 'barbarian' was, however, a
pedantry when it applied to the young Irish religieuse. Her
Latin was more polished than most of Rome's citizens and
her literary knowledge was certainly more extensive than
many scholars. She was the product of Ireland's distinguished colleges, which were so renowned throughout
Europe that in Durrow alone there were to be found the sons
and daughters of kings and princelings from no fewer than
eighteen different countries. An education in Ireland was a
distinction that even the scions of the Anglo-Saxon kings
would boast of.

Fidelma had come to Rome to present *the Regula
coenabialis Cill Dara*, the Rule of the House of St Brigid,
in Kildare, to be approved and blessed by the Holy Father
at the Lateran Palace. She had been waiting to see an
official of the Papal household for several days now. To
while away the time, she, like the many thousands of other

pilgrims who poured into the city, spent her time in touring the ancient monuments and tombs of the city.

From the *xenodochia*, the small hostel for foreign pilgrims close by the oratory of the Blessed Prassede, where she was lodging, she would walk down the hill to the Lateran Palace each morning to see whether she was to be received that day. She was becoming irritated as the days passed by without word. But there were so many people, from so many different countries – some she had not known existed – crowding into the palace to beg audience that she stoically controlled her frustration. Each day she would leave the palace in resignation to set off in search of some new point of interest in the city.

That morning she had chosen to visit the small *ecclesia* dedicated to the Blessed Hippolytus, which lay only a short walk from her hostel. Her purpose was for no other reason than the fact that it held the tomb of Hippolytus. She knew that her mentor, Abbot Laisran of Durrow, was an admirer of the work of the early Church Father and she had once struggled through the text of *Philosophoumena*, to debate with Laisran on this refutation of the Gnostic teachings. She knew that Laisran would be impressed if she could boast a visit to the very tomb of Hippolytus.

A mass was being celebrated as she took her place at the back of the tiny *ecclesia*, a small place which could hold no more than two or three dozen people. Even so, there were only half-a-dozen scattered about with bowed heads, hearing the priest intoning the solemn words of the ritual.

Fidelma examined her co-religionists with interest. The sights and sounds of Rome were still new and intriguing to her. She was attracted by a young girl in the forefront of the worshippers. Fidelma could see only her profile emerging from a hood which respectfully hid the rest of her obviously well-shaped head. It was a delicate, finely chiselled, attractive face. Fidelma could appreciate its discreet beauty. Next to her was a young man in the robes of a religieux. Even though Fidelma could not see his face fully, she saw that he was good-looking and seemed to reflect something of the girl's features. Next to him stood a lean, weather-tanned young man, dressed in the clothes of a seaman but in the manner she had often seen adopted by sailors from Gaul. This young man did not look at all content with life. He was scowling; his expression fixed. Behind these three stood a short, stocky man in the rich robes of a senior religieux. Fidelma had seen enough of the abbots and bishops of Rome to guess that he was of such rank. In another corner was a nervous-looking, swarthy man, corpulent and richly attired and looking every inch a prosperous merchant. At the back of the church stood the final member of the congregation, a young man attired in the uniform of the *custodes* of Rome, the guardians of law and order in the city. He was darkly handsome, with a somewhat arrogant manner, as, perhaps, befitted his soldierly calling.

The deacon, assisting in the offering, rang a small bell and the officiating priest raised the chalice of wine and intoned: 'The blood of Christ!' before moving forward to join the deacon, who had now taken up a silver plate on which the consecrated Host lay.

The small congregation moved forward to take their places in line before the priest. It was the handsome young religieux who took the first position, receiving the Host, placing it in his mouth and moving forward to receive the wine from the chalice held in the hands of the priest. As he turned away, his young female companion moved forward, being the next in line, to receive the sacrament.

Even as the religieux turned back to the congregation, his face suddenly distorted, he began to choke, his mouth gaping open, his tongue thrusting obscenely forward. A hand raised to his throat as the colour of his agonised features went from red to blue. The eyes were wide and staring. Sounds came from him that reminded Fidelma of the squealing of a pig about to be slaughtered.

Before the horrified gaze of the rest of the congregation, the young man fell to the floor, his body writhing and threshing for several moments. Then it was suddenly still and quiet.

There was no sound for a moment or two. Everyone stood immobile with shock.

A moment later, the shriek of the young woman rent the air. She threw herself forward onto the body. She was on her knees crying and screaming in a strange language made incomprehensible by her distress.

As no one seemed capable of moving, Sister Fidelma came quickly forward.

'Do not touch the wine nor the bread,' she instructed the priest, who was still holding the chalice in his hands. 'This man has been poisoned.'

She felt, rather than saw, the heads of the people turn to stare at her. She glanced round observing expressions ranging from bewilderment to surprise.

'Who are you to give orders, Sister?' snapped a rough voice. It was the arrogant young *custos* pushing forward.

Fidelma raised her glinting green eyes to meet his dark suspicious ones.

'I hold no authority here, if that is what you mean. I am a stranger in this city. But in my own country I am a *dálaigh*, an advocate of the law courts, and know the effects of virulent poison when I see it.'

'As you say, you hold no authority here,' snapped the *custos*, clearly a young man who felt the honour of his rank and nationality. 'And I . . .'

'The Sister is right, nevertheless, *custos*.'

The voice that interrupted was quiet, modulated but authoritative. It was the short, stocky man who spoke.

The young guard looked disconcerted at this opposition.

'I *do* hold authority here,' continued the short man, turning to Fidelma. 'I am the Abbot Miseno and this *ecclesia* is part of my jurisdiction.'

Without waiting for the guard's response, Abbot Miseno glanced at the officiating priest and deacon. 'Do as the Sister says, Father Cornelius. Put down the wine and bread and ensure no one else touches it.'

Automatically, the priest obeyed, accompanied by the deacon, who placed his tray of bread carefully on the altar.

Abbot Miseno glanced down to the sobbing girl.

'Who was this man, daughter?' he demanded gently, bending down to place a hand on her shoulder.

The girl raised tear-stained eyes to him.

'Is he . . .?'

Miseno bent further to place his fingers against the pulse in the man's neck. The action was really unnecessary. One look at the twisted, frozen features would have been enough to confirm that the young religieux was beyond all human aid. Nevertheless, the action was probably designed as a reassurance for the girl. The abbot shook his head.

'He is dead, daughter,' he confirmed. 'Who was he?'

The girl began sobbing uncontrollably again and could not answer.

'His name was Docco. He was from Pouancé in Gaul.'

It was the young Gaulish seaman, who had been standing with the religieux and the girl, who answered him.

'And you are?' asked Abbot Miseno.

'My name is Enodoc. I was a friend of Docco's and also from Gaul. The girl is Egeria, Docco's sister.'

The Abbot Miseno stood for a moment, his head bowed in thought. Then he glanced up and surveyed Sister Fidelma with some speculation in his eyes.

'Would you come with me a moment, Sister?'

He turned and led the way into a corner of the church, out of earshot of the others. Fidelma followed him in curiosity.

In the corner the abbot turned, keeping his voice low.

'I studied at Bobbio, which was founded fifty years ago by Columban and his Irish clerics. I learnt much about your country there. I have heard about the function of your law system and how a *dálaigh* works. Are you truly such a one?'

'I am a qualified advocate of the law courts of my country,' replied Fidelma simply, without any false pride, wondering what the abbot was driving at.

'And your Latin is fluent,' observed Miseno absently.

Fidelma waited patiently.

'It is clear that this monk, Docco, was poisoned,' went on Miseno after a moment's pause. 'Was this an accident or was there some deliberate plot to kill him? I think it behoves us to find out as soon as possible. If this story went abroad I shudder to think what interpretation would be given to it. Why, it might even stop people coming forward to receive the blessed sacrament. I would be grateful, Sister, if you would use your knowledge to discover the truth of this matter before we have to report this to higher authorities.'

'That will not please the young *custos*,' Fidelma pointed out, with a slight gesture towards the impatient young guard. 'He clearly thinks that he is better suited for this task.'

'He has no authority here. I have. What do you say?'

'I will make inquiries, Abbot, but I cannot guarantee any result,' Fidelma replied.

The abbot looked woeful for a moment and spread his hands in a helpless gesture.

'The culprit must be one of this company. You are trained in such detection. If you could do your best . . .?'

'Very well. But I am also one of this company. How can you be sure that I am not responsible?'

Abbot Miseno looked startled for a moment. Then he smiled broadly.

'You entered the *ecclesia* towards the end of the service and stood at the back. How could you have placed the poison in the bread or wine while it was on the altar before the eyes of us all?'

'True enough. But what of the others? Were they all here throughout the service?'

'Oh yes. I think so.'

'Including yourself?'

The rotund abbot smiled wryly.

'You may also count me among your suspects until you have gained knowledge to the contrary.'

Fidelma inclined her head.

'Firstly, then, I need to check how this poison was administered.'

'I will inform the impatient young *custos* that he must be respectful to you and obey your judgements.'

They returned to the group standing awkwardly around the body of the dead Gaul, whose head was still being cradled in the arms of his sobbing sister.

The abbot cleared his throat.

'I have asked the Sister to conduct an inquiry into the cause of this death,' he began without preamble. 'She is eminently qualified to do so. I trust you will all,' he paused slightly, and let his eyes dwell on the arrogant young *custos*, 'cooperate with her in this matter for it has my blessing and ecclesiastical authority.'

There was a silence. Some glances of bemusement were cast towards her.

Fidelma stepped forward.

'I would like you all to return to the positions you were occupying before this happened.' She smiled gently down at the girl. 'You do not have to, if you wish, but there is nothing that you can do for your brother except truthfully answer the questions that I shall ask you.'

The Gaul, Enodoc, bent forward to raise the young girl to her feet, coaxing her away from the body of her brother, then gently guided her back to her place. There was a reluctant shuffling as the rest of the congregation complied.

Fidelma moved forward to the altar. She bent to the silver plate with its pieces of bread, the Host, and taking a piece sniffed at it suspiciously. She cautiously examined the rest of the bread. There was nothing apparently amiss with it. She turned to the chalice still full of the Eucharist wine and sniffed. She could not quite place the odour. However, it was bitter and even its smell caught at the back of her throat, making her gasp and cough sharply.

'It is as I thought,' she announced, 'the wine has been poisoned. I do not know what poison it is but the fumes are self-evident. It is highly dangerous and you have all seen its instant effect so I should not have to warn you further.'

She turned and sought out the young guard.

'Bring two stools and place them . . .' she turned and sought out an isolated corner of the *ecclesia*, 'place them over there. Then go and stand by the door and prevent anyone entering or leaving until I call for you.'

The young warrior looked outraged and glanced towards the abbot. Abbot Miseno merely gestured with a quick motion of his hand for the young man to comply.

'I will speak with you first, Deacon,' Fidelma said, turning towards the spot where the guard had placed the chairs.

Once seated Fidelma examined the deacon. He was not more than twenty years old. A youth with dark hair and a rather ugly face, the eyes seeming too close together and the brows heavy. His jowl was blue with badly shaved stubble.

'What is your name?'

'I am Tullius.'

'How long have you served here?'

'Six months.'

'As deacon, it would be your job to prepare the wine and bread for the blessing. Is this so?'

'Yes.'

'And did you do so today?'

'Yes.'

'Tell me about the wine.'

The deacon seemed disconcerted.

'In what way?'

'Tell me about the wine in the chalice. Where it came from, how it was poured and whether it was left unguarded at any time.'

'The wine is bought locally. We keep several *amphorae* below the *ecclesia*, in the vaults, where it is stored. This morning I went down into the vaults and filled a jug. Then, when I observed the numbers attending the service, I poured the wine into the chalice for the blessing. This is the usual custom. The same procedure is made for the bread. Once the wine and bread are blessed and the transubstantiation occurs then no piece of the Host nor of the blood of Christ must be discarded. It must all be consumed.'

Among the Irish churches, the taking of the bread and wine was regarded merely as a symbolic gesture in remembrance of the Christ. Rome, however, had started to maintain that the blessing actually changed the substance into the literal flesh and blood of Christ. Fidelma's sceptical smile was not derogatory to the new doctrine but a reflection as to how the poisoned wine could possibly be regarded as the physical blood of the Saviour. And who, she wondered, would now volunteer to consume it?

'So, Tullius, you poured the wine from the jug into the chalice once you had ascertained how many people were attending the service?'

'That is so.'

'Where is this jug?'

'In the sacristy.'

'Take me there and show me.'

The young deacon rose and led the way to a door behind the altar. This was an apartment of the *ecclesia* where the sacred utensils and vestments of the priest were kept.

Fidelma peered around the small room. It was no larger than six feet wide and twelve feet in length. A second doorway, leading to a flight of stone steps descending into the gloom of the vaults, stood almost behind the door which gave ingress into the *ecclesia* itself. At the far end of the sacristy stood a third door, with a small diamond-shaped window in its centre, which, she could see, led to the outside of the building. Clothes were hung on pegs and there were icons and some books on shelves. There was also a bench with some loaves of bread and a wine jug on it. Fidelma bent over the jug and sniffed. There was no bitter odour. Cautiously, she reached down into the jug with her forefinger and dipped it in the wine. Withdrawing it, she sniffed again and then placed it between her lips. There was no bitter taste. Clearly, then, the wine had been poisoned only after it had been poured into the chalice.

'Tell me, Tullius, the chalice, which was used today, is it the same chalice that is used at every service?'

The deacon nodded.

'And the chalice was standing here, in the sacristy, when you brought up the jug of wine from the vaults?'

'Yes. I had purchased the bread on my way to the *ecclesia*, as I usually do. I came in here and placed the loaves ready to cut into small pieces. Then I went down to the vault and poured the jug of wine and brought it up here. I placed it by the chalice. Then Abbot Miseno entered and, as I recall, passed directly through the sacristy to join the congregation. When I judged it was a small attendance, I poured the wine accordingly.'

Fidelma frowned thoughtfully.

'So Abbot Miseno had already passed into the *ecclesia* before you poured the wine into the chalice?'

'He had.'

'And are you saying that at no time did you leave this sacristy after you had brought up the jug of wine and poured it into the chalice?'

'I judged the attendance while standing at the door. While I was doing this Father Cornelius came in. In fact, he did so not long after the abbot.'

'Father Cornelius being the priest who officiated?'

'Yes. He changed his vestments for the service while I poured the wine into the chalice. I then returned to check if anyone else had joined the congregation.'

'Then, at that point, your back was towards the chalice? It

was not in your field of vision the whole time?'

'But there was no one in the sacristy with me except . . .'

'Except Father Cornelius?'

The deacon's mouth had snapped shut and he nodded glumly.

'Let me get this picture clear. Father Cornelius changed his vestments as you were standing at the door examining those entering the *ecclesia*?'

'Yes. I remember warning him that Abbot Miseno had already entered.'

'*Warning* him?' Fidelma was quick to spot the word.

'The abbot is in charge of this *ecclesia* as well as several others in the vicinity. However, he and Father Cornelius were . . . how can I say it? . . . Their views did not coincide. Abbot Miseno has been trying to remove Father Cornelius from this church. That is no secret.'

'Do you know why?'

'It is not for me to say. You may address that question to Abbot Miseno and Father Cornelius.'

'Very well. What then?'

'Father Cornelius was annoyed. In fact, I think he was in an evil temper when he arrived. Anyway, he pushed by me and went straight to Abbot Miseno. I saw them speaking together. I would say that the conversation was not friendly. The appointed hour for the service came and I rang the bell as usual. Father Cornelius then went to the altar to start the service.'

Fidelma leant forward.

'Let me clarify this point: you say that you poured the wine into the chalice while Father Cornelius was changing his vestments; that you then went to stand by the door, turning your back on the chalice?'

'Yes. I think so.'

'Think? You are not sure?'

'Well . . .' the deacon shrugged, 'I would not take oath on it. Perhaps I poured it just after he left the sacristy.'

'Not before he left?'

'I cannot be sure now. This matter has been a shock and I am a little confused as to the order of events.'

'Can you be sure whether there was anything else in the chalice when you poured the wine?'

'The chalice was clean.' The deacon's voice was decisive on this point.

'There was no coating on the chalice, no clear liquid which you might have missed at the bottom?' pressed Fidelma.

'Absolutely not. The chalice was clean and dry.'

'How can you be so sure when you admit to confusion over events?'

'The ritual, which all deacons in this office fulfil, is that before the wine is poured, a small piece of white linen is taken and the inside of the chalice is polished. Only then is the wine poured.'

Fidelma felt frustrated.

The wine had been poisoned. It had been poisoned while it was in the chalice and not before. Yet the only time that the chalice was out of sight for a moment, according to the deacon, was when Father Cornelius had entered the sacristy. That had been the only opportunity to introduce poison into the chalice. But the deacon was not sure whether the priest had left before or after he poured the wine.

'What happened then?' she prompted Tullius, the deacon.

'The service was ready to start. I took the tray of bread and carried it to the altar. Then I returned for the chalice . . .'

Fidelma's eyes sparkled with renewed interest.

'So the chalice stood here on its own while you carried the bread to the altar?'

The deacon was defensive.

'It was here only for a few seconds and I had left the door open between the sacristy and altar.'

'Nevertheless, it stood unobserved for a short while. During that period anyone might have entered the outer door and poisoned the wine, leaving before you noticed them.'

'It is possible, I suppose,' acceded the deacon. 'But they would have had to have been quick to do so.'

'What then? You carried the wine to the altar?'

'Yes. Then the service commenced. The chalice stood in full view of everyone during the service until the moment Father Cornelius blessed it and the Gaulish religieux came forward to receive communion.'

'Very well.'

Fidelma led the way back to where the small congregation were still sitting in silence. She felt their eyes upon her, suspicious and hostile. She dismissed the deacon and motioned for the priest, Father Cornelius, to join her.

'You are Father Cornelius, I believe?'

'I am.' The priest looked tired and was clearly distressed.

'How long have you been priest here?'

'For three years.'

'Do you have any idea how poison was introduced into the Eucharist wine?'

'None. It is an impossible thing.'

'Impossible?'

'Impossible that anyone would dare to perform such a sacrilege with the Eucharist.'

Fidelma sniffed slightly.

'Yet it is obvious that someone did. If people are out to murder, then a matter of sacrilege becomes insignificant compared with the breaking of one of God's commandments,' she observed dryly. 'When Tullius, the deacon, brought the wine from the sacristy, was it placed on the altar?'

'It was.'

'It stood there in full sight of everyone and no one went near it until you blessed it and raised the chalice, turning to administer the sacrament to the first communicant?'

'No one went near it,' affirmed the priest.

'Did you know who would be the first communicant?'

Father Cornelius frowned.

'I am not a prophet. People come to receive the sacrament as and when they will. There is no order in their coming.'

'What was the cause of your differences with Abbot Miseno?'

Father Cornelius blinked.

'What do you mean?' There was a sudden tone of anxiety in his voice.

'I think my Latin is clear enough,' Fidelma replied phlegmatically.

Father Cornelius hesitated a moment and then gave a shrug.

'Abbot Miseno would prefer to appoint someone else to my office.'

'Why?'

'I disagree with the teachings of Augustine of Hippo, that everything is preordained, which is now a doctrine of our church. I believe that men and women can take the initial and fundamental steps towards their salvation, using their own efforts. If men and women are not responsible for their own good or evil deeds, then there is nothing to restrain them from an indulgence in sin. To argue, as Augustine has, that no matter what we do in life, God has already preordained everything so that it is already decided if our reward is heaven or hell, is to imperil the entire moral law. For my heresy, Abbot Miseno wishes to have me removed.'

Fidelma felt the harsh passion in the man's voice.

'So? You would describe yourself as a follower of Pelagius?'

Father Cornelius drew himself up.

'Pelagius taught a moral truth. I believe men and women have the choice to become good or evil. Nothing is preordained. How we live our lives determines whether we are rewarded by heaven or hell.'

'But Pope Innocent declared Pelagius to be a heretic,' Fidelma pointed out.

'And Pope Zosimus declared him innocent.'

'Later to renounce that decision,' smiled Fidelma thinly. 'Yet it matters not to me. Pelagius has a special place in the philosophy of the church in my country for he was of our blood and faith. Sufficient to say, Abbot Miseno holds to the teachings of Augustine of Hippo?'

'He does. And he would have me removed from here because I do not.'

'Yet Abbot Miseno has the authority to appoint whomsoever he likes as priest of this *ecclesia*?'

'He has.'

'Then surely he has the authority to dismiss you without argument?'

'Not without good cause. He must justify his actions to the bishop.'

'Ah yes. In Rome bishops have more authority than abbots. This is not so in Ireland. Yet, on the matter of Pelagius, surely heresy, even a just heresy, is cause enough?'

'But I do not openly preach the teachings of Pelagius nor those of Augustine. They are a subject for my conscience. I perform my duties to my congregation without complaint from them.'

'So you have shown the abbot no good cause to dismiss you?'

'None.'

'But Abbot Miseno has suggested that you resign from this church?'

'He has.'

'And you have refused.'

'I have.'

'Did you know the Gaul who died?'

Again Cornelius blinked at the sudden change of subject of her questioning.

'I have seen him several times before.'

'Several times?'

'Himself and his sister. I believe that they are pilgrims

217

staying in a nearby *xenodochia*. They have attended the mass here each day.'

'And the other Gaul, who seems so friendly with the girl?'

'I have seen him only once, yesterday. I think he has only recently arrived in Rome.'

'I see.'

'Sister, this is a great mystery to me. Why should anyone attempt to poison the wine and cause the death of all the communicants in the church today?'

Fidelma gazed thoughtfully at him.

'Do you think that the wine was meant to be taken by all the communicants?'

'What else? Everyone would come to take the bread and wine. It is the custom.'

'But not everyone did. The poison was so quick in its action that undoubtedly only the first person who took it would die and his death would have served as a warning to the others not to drink. That is precisely what happened.'

'Then if the wine were meant only for the Gaul, how could the person who poisoned the wine know that he would be the first to come forward to take it?'

'A good point. During the time that the Gaul attended the services here, did he take communion?'

'Yes.'

'Was he always in the same place in the church?'

'Yes, I believe so.'

'And at what point did he usually come forward to take the wine and bread?'

Cornelius' eyes widened slightly as he reflected on the question.

'He was always the first,' he admitted. 'His sister was second. For they were both in the same position before the altar.'

'I see. Tell me, did you enter the church via the sacristy?'

'Yes.'

'Was the deacon, Tullius, already there?'

'Yes. Standing by the door trying to estimate the numbers attending the service.'

'Had he poured the wine into the chalice?'

'I do not know,' confessed Father Cornelius. 'Tullius told me that Miseno had arrived and I went to see him. I think Tullius had the jug in hand as I left the sacristy.'

Fidelma rubbed her chin thoughtfully.

'That is all, Father. Send Abbot Miseno across to me.'

The abbot came forward smiling and seated himself.

'What news? Are you near a resolution?'

Fidelma did not return his smile.

'I understand that you wished to remove Father Cornelius?'

Abbot Miseno pulled a face. A curious, protective gesture.

'I have that authority,' he said defensively. 'What has that to do with this matter?'

'Has Father Cornelius failed in his duties?' Fidelma ignored his question.

'I am not satisfied with them.'

'I see. Then the reason you wish him removed has nothing to do with Father Cornelius' personal beliefs?'

Abbot Miseno's eyes narrowed.

'You are clearly a clever investigator, Fidelma of Kildare. How do you come to know so much?'

'You said that you knew the manner in which a *dálaigh*, an advocate of the laws of my country, acted. It is, as you know, my job to ask questions and from the answers to make deductions. I say again, has the removal of Cornelius anything to do with the fact of his beliefs?'

'In truth, I am liberal about these matters,' replied Abbot Miseno. 'However, Cornelius will tell you otherwise.'

'Why, then, do you wish him removed?'

'Cornelius has been here three years. I do not believe that he has fulfilled his functions properly. There are stories that he keeps a mistress. That he flouts more than one doctrine of our church. His deacon, a worthy soul, keeps this flock together in spite of Father Cornelius. And now Christ Himself has demonstrated clearly that Cornelius is unworthy of the priesthood.'

'How so?' Fidelma was intrigued at the Abbot Miseno's logic.

'The matter of the poisoned Eucharist wine.'

'Do you accuse Father Cornelius of being the poisoner?' Fidelma was astonished at the apparent directness of the accusation.

'No. But if he had been a true priest, then the transubstantiation would have taken place and the wine would not have been poisoned. It would have become the blood of Christ even though it contained poison, for the blessing would have purified it.'

Fidelma was nonplussed at this reasoning.

'Then it would, indeed, have been a miracle.'

Abbot Miseno looked annoyed.

'Is not the fact of transubstantiation a miracle, Sister, one that is performed every day in all churches of Christendom?'

'I am no theologian. I was taught that the matter was a symbolism and not a reality.'

'Then you have been taught badly. The bread and wine, when blessed by a true and pure priest, truly turns into the blood and flesh of Our Saviour.'

'A matter of opinion,' observed Fidelma distantly. She indicated the corpulent and richly attired man who sat apart from everyone else. 'Tell that man to come to me.'

Abbot Miseno hesitated.

'Is that all?'

'All for the moment.'

With a sniff of annoyance at being so summarily dismissed, the abbot rose and made his way to the corpulent man and spoke to him. The man rose and came hesitantly forward.

'This matter is nothing to do with me,' he began defensively.

'No?' Fidelma looked at the man's pouting features. 'And you are . . .?'

'My name is Talos. I am a merchant and have been a member of this congregation for many years.'

'Then you are just the person to answer my questions,' affirmed Fidelma.

'Why so?'

'Have you known Father Cornelius for some time?'

'Yes. I was attending this congregation before he became priest here.'

'Is he a good priest?'

The Greek merchant looked puzzled.

'I thought this questioning was to be about the poisoning of the wine?'

'Indulge me,' Fidelma smiled. 'Is he a good priest?'

'Yes.'

'Are you aware of any complaints about him? Any conduct that would not become his office?'

Talos looked awkwardly at his feet. Fidelma's eyes glinted.

'I am personally not aware of anything.'

'But you have heard some story?' she pressed.

'Tullius has told me that there have been complaints, but not from me. I have found Father Cornelius to be a conscientious priest.'

'Yet Tullius said that there were complaints? Was Tullius one of the complainants?'

'Not that I am aware. Yet I suppose that it would be his job to pass on the complaints to the abbot. He must also be conscientious in his job. Indeed, he would have cause to be.'

'I do not understand.'

Talos grimaced.

'Tullius has been studying for the priesthood and will be ordained on the day after tomorrow. He is a local boy. His family were not of the best but he had ambition enough to overcome that. Sadly, the gods of love have played him an evil trick.'

'What do you mean by that?'

Talos looked surprised and then he smiled complacently.

'We are people of the world,' he said condescendingly.

'You mean that he prefers the company of his own sex?'

'Exactly so.' She saw the Greek's eyes glance disapprovingly across the *ecclesia* and, without turning her head, followed the direction of the look to the young *custos*.

Fidelma sniffed. There were no laws against homosexuality under the auspices of the Brehons.

'So when he is ordained,' she went on, 'he will move on to his own church?'

'That I would not know. I would presume so. This church cannot support two priests. As you see, it boasts only a small congregation, most of whom are well known to each other.'

'Yet the Gauls are strangers here.'

'That is true. But the dead religieux and his sister were staying in a hostel across the street and had been attending here during the week. The other, he had been here once. There was only one other complete stranger here today – you.'

'You have been most helpful, Talos. As you return to your place, would you ask Enodoc, the Gaul, to come here?'

Talos rose and left hastily, performing his task perfunctorily on the way back to his position.

The Gaul had been comforting the girl. Fidelma watched as the young man leant forward and squeezed the arm of the girl, whose head hung on her breast, as if she were asleep. She had ceased her sobbing.

'I know all about the advocates of the Brehon laws,' remarked the young man pleasantly, as he seated himself. 'We, in Gaul, share a common ancestry with you of Ireland as well as a common law.'

'Tell me about yourself,' Fidelma invited distantly, ignoring the friendly overture.

'My name is . . .'

'Yes, that I know. I also know from whence you come. Tell me what is your reason for visiting Rome.'

The young man still smiled pleasantly.

'I am the captain of a merchant ship sailing out of the city of the Veneti in Armorica. It is as a trader that I am in Rome.'

'And you knew the monk named Docco?'

'We came from the same village.'

'Ah. And you are betrothed to the girl, Egeria?'

The young man started with a frown.

'What makes you ask this?'

'The way you behave to her is that of a concerned lover not a stranger nor that of a mere friend.'

'You have a perceptive eye, Sister.'

'Is it so?'

'I want to marry her.'

'Then who prevents you?'

Again Enodoc frowned.

'Why do you presume that anyone prevents me?'

'Because of the way you defensively construct your sentence.'

'Ah, I see. It is true that I have wanted to marry Egeria. It is true that Docco, who is the head of his family, did not want her to marry me. We grew up in the same village but there is enmity between us.'

'And yet here you are in Rome standing together with Docco and his sister before the same altar,' observed Fidelma.

'I did not know Docco and Egeria were in Rome. I met them by chance a few days ago and so I made up my mind to argue my case further with Docco before I rejoined my ship to sail back to Gaul.'

'And was that what you were doing here?'

Enodoc shrugged.

'In a way. I was staying nearby.'

'Forgive me, but the port of Ostia, the nearest port of Rome, is a long way from here. Are you telling me that you, the captain of your ship, came to Ostia and then, hearing by chance that Docco and Egeria were in Rome, made this long journey here to find them?'

'No. I had business to transact in Rome and left my ship at Ostia. I needed to negotiate with a merchant for a cargo. Yet it is true that I found Egeria and Docco simply by chance.'

'I am told that you have been to this *ecclesia* before.'

'Yes; but only once. That was yesterday when I first encountered Egeria and Docco in the street and followed them to this place.'

'It was a strange coincidence.'

'Coincidences happen more often than we give them credit. I attended the service with them yesterday.'

'And was your plaint successful?'

Enodoc hesitated.

'No, Docco was as firmly against my marriage to Egeria as ever he had been.'

'Yet you joined them again today?'

'I was leaving for Ostia today. I wanted one more chance to plead my case with Docco. I love Egeria.'

'And does she love you?'

Enodoc thrust out his chin.

'You will have to ask her that yourself.'

'I intend to do so. Where did you meet them this morning? Did you come to the *ecclesia* together, or separately?'

'I had some business first and then went to their lodgings. They had already left for the church and so I followed.'

'At what time did you get here?'

'A moment or so before the service started.'

'And you came straight in and joined them?'

'Yes.'

'Very well. Ask Egeria to come and sit with me.'

Clearly despondent, Enodoc rose to his feet and went back to the girl. He spoke to her but seemed to get no response. Fidelma noticed that he put his hand under her arm, drew her to her feet and guided her to where Fidelma was sitting. She came unprotestingly but was apparently still in a stupefied state.

'Thank you,' Fidelma said, and reached forward to take the girl's hand. 'This is a great shock for you, I know. But I need to ask some questions. Be seated now.' She turned and gazed up at Enodoc. 'You may leave us.'

Reluctantly the Gaulish seaman departed.

The girl had slumped on the stool before Fidelma, head bowed.

'Your name is Egeria, I believe?'

The girl simply nodded.

'I am Fidelma. I need to ask some questions,' she repeated again. 'We need to discover who is responsible for this terrible deed.'

The girl raised her tear-stained eyes to Fidelma. A moment or two passed before she seemed to focus clearly.

'It cannot bring back Docco. But I will answer, if I can.'

'You were very fond of your brother, I take it?'

'He was all I had. We were orphans together.'

'He was protective of you?'

'I am . . . *was* younger than he and he raised me when our parents were killed during a Frankish raid. He became the head of my family.'

'What made you come to Rome?'

'It was a pilgrimage that we had long talked about.'

'Did you expect Enodoc to be here?'

The girl shook her head.

'Do you love Enodoc?'

Egeria looked at her without answering for a moment or two and then shook her head slowly.

'Enodoc came from our village. He used to be our friend when we were children. I liked him as a friend but no more

225

than that. Then he went to sea. He is captain of a merchant ship. I hardly see him. But whenever we meet, he seems to think he has a claim on me.'

'Indeed; he thinks that he is in love with you.'

'Yes. He has said so on several occasions.'

'But you are not in love with him?'

'No.'

'Have you told him so? Have you told him clearly?'

'Several times. He is a stubborn man and convinced himself that it was Docco who stood against him. That Docco had the ability to make up my mind for me.'

'I see. Are you telling me that he thought that it was only Docco that was an obstacle to marriage with you?'

The girl nodded and then her eyes widened a fraction.

'Are you saying . . .?'

'I am merely asking questions, Egeria. When did you meet Enodoc today?'

'When he arrived for the service.'

'You and your brother were already in the *ecclesia*, I take it?'

She nodded.

'You had taken up your position at the front?'

'Yes.'

'Did your brother normally take that position?'

Egeria sniffed a little and wiped a tear from her eye.

'Docco always liked to be the first to take the ritual of the Eucharist and so he liked to place himself near the priest. It was a habit of his, even at home.'

'I see. At what stage did Enodoc join you?'

'A few moments before the service began. I thought that he had finally accepted the situation but then he appeared, breathless and flustered as if he were in a hurry. I thought that the priest, Father Cornelius, was going to admonish him because he had halted the opening of the service while Enodoc took his place.'

Fidelma frowned.

'Why so? I came very late into the service yet Father Cornelius did not halt the service for me.'

'It was because Enodoc entered at the back of the altar and crossed in front of the priest to take his position with us.'

Fidelma could not speak with surprise for a moment.

'Are you saying that Enodoc entered the *ecclesia* through the sacristy?'

Egeria shrugged.

'I do not know. He entered through that door.' She turned and pointed to the door of the sacristy.

Fidelma was silent for a while.

'Return to your place, Egeria. I will not be long now. Please ask Enodoc to come back to me.'

Enodoc was as pleasant as before.

'You have been selective with your truths, Enodoc,' Fidelma opened.

The young man frowned.

'How so?'

'Docco was not the only person to stand in your way to marriage with Egeria.'

'Who else did so?' demanded the Gaul.

'Egeria herself.'

'She told you that?' The young man flushed.

'Yes.'

'She does not really mean it. She may say so but it was merely Docco speaking. Things will be different now.'

'You think so?'

'She is distraught. When her mind clears, she will know the truth.' He was confident.

'Perhaps. You did not mention that you entered this *ecclesia* through the sacristy.'

'You did not ask me. Is it important?'

'Why did you choose that unorthodox way of entering?'

'No mystery to that. I told you that I had to see a merchant this morning. I finished my business and came hurrying to the church. I found myself on the far side of the building and heard the bell toll for the opening of the service. It would have taken me some time to walk around the building, for there is a wall which is a barrier along the road. To come from the back of the church to the main doors takes a while, and I saw the door to the sacristy so I entered it.'

'Yet you had only been in this *ecclesia* once before. You must have a good memory.'

'It does not take much memory to recall something from the previous day, which was when I was here.'

'Who was in the sacristy when you entered?'

'No one.'

'And what did you do?'

'I came straight through into the *ecclesia*.'

'Did you see the chalice there?'

Enodoc shook his head. Then his eyes widened as he saw the meaning to her questions. For a moment, he was silent, his mouth set in a tight line. His tanned features reddened but he overcame his obvious indignation.

'I am sure that the chalice was already on the altar because as I entered the priest was starting the service.'

Fidelma met his gaze and held it for a moment.

'You may return to your place.'

Fidelma sat thinking for some moments and then she rose and walked towards the doors where the young *custos* stood. The young man watched her with narrow-eyed suspicion.

'What is your name?' she asked as she came to face him.

'Terentius.'

'Do you usually attend the services in this *ecclesia*?'

'My house is but a short walk away and my position as a member of the *custodes* is to ensure that law and order prevail in this area.'

'How long have you performed that duty?'

'Two years now.'

'So you have known Father Cornelius since you have been here?'

'Of course.'

'What is your opinion of Father Cornelius?'

The guard shrugged.

'As a priest, he has his faults. Why do you ask?'

'And your opinion of Tullius? Do you know him?'

She saw the young man flush.

'I know him well. He was born here in this district. He is conscientious in his duties. He is about to be ordained.'

She detected a slight tone of pride.

'I am told Tullius is from a poor family. To be honest, I am given to believe that his is a family known to the *custodes*.'

'Tullius has long sought to dissociate himself from them. Abbot Miseno knows that.'

'Had the service started, when you arrived here?'

'It had just begun. I was the last to arrive . . . apart from yourself.'

'The Gaulish seaman . . . had he already entered the church?' Fidelma asked.

The guard frowned.

'No. As a matter of fact, he came in just after I did but through the sacristy.'

'You came in through the main doors, then?'

'Of course.'

'How soon after everyone else did you enter the church?'

'Not very long. As I was approaching along the street, I saw Abbot Miseno outside the building. I saw him arguing with Father Cornelius. They were standing near the sacristy door as I passed. The abbot turned in, then, after he had stood a moment or two, Father Cornelius followed.'

'Do you know what they were arguing about?'

The young soldier shook his head.

'Then you came into the *ecclesia*? What of the Gaul?'

'A moment or so later. Father Cornelius was about to start the service, when he came in. We were halfway through the service when you yourself entered.'

'That will be all for the moment.'

Fidelma turned in deep thought and made her way to Abbot Miseno.

The abbot watched her approach with impatience.

'We cannot afford to take long on this matter, Sister Fidelma. I had heard that you advocates of the Brehon Court were quick at getting to the truth of the matter. If you cannot demonstrate who killed this foreign religieux, then it will reflect badly on that reputation.'

Fidelma smiled thinly.

'Perhaps it was in hope of that event that you so quickly suggested my involvement in this matter?'

Abbot Miseno flushed in annoyance.

'Do you suggest . . . ?'

Fidelma made a dismissive gesture with her hand.

'Let us not waste time in rhetoric. Why were you arguing with Father Cornelius outside the sacristy?'

Miseno's jaw clamped tightly.

'I had demanded his resignation from this office.'

'He refused to resign?'

'Yes.'

'And you came into the church through the sacristy? Did Father Cornelius follow you?'

'Yes. He had changed his vestments and suddenly came out of the sacristy, straight to me and tried to renew the argument. Luckily, Tullius rang the bell for the service to start. I had just told him that I would do everything in my power to see him relieved of his position.'

'Everything?'

Miseno's eyes narrowed.

'What do you imply?'

'How far would you go to have him removed?'

'I will not deign to answer that.'

'Silence often speaks as loudly as words. Why do you dislike Father Cornelius so much?'

'A priest who betrays the guiding principles of . . .'

'Cornelius says that you disapprove of him because he holds to the teachings of Pelagius. Many of us do. But you claim that it is not that but more personal matters that make him fit not to be priest here.'

'Why are you concentrating on Father Cornelius?' demanded Miseno. 'Your task was to find out who poisoned the Gaulish religieux. Surely you should be looking at the motives for his killing?'

'Answer my question, Abbot Miseno. There must have been a point when you approved Cornelius in this office.'

Miseno shrugged.

'Yes. Three years ago I thought he was appropriate to the task and a conscientious priest. I do not mind admitting that. It has been during the last six months that I have had disturbing reports.'

Fidelma tugged thoughtfully at her lower lip.

'And where do these reports emanate from?'

Abbot Miseno frowned.

'I cannot tell you that. That would be a breach of confidence.'

'Did they come from a single source?'

Miseno's expression was enough to confirm the thought. Fidelma smiled without humour.

'I suspect the reports came from the deacon, Tullius.'

Abbot Miseno stirred uncomfortably. But he said nothing.

'Very well. I take the fact that you do not deny that as an affirmative.'

'All very well. So it was Tullius. As deacon it was his duty to inform me if anything was amiss.'

'And your task to certify that Tullius was giving you accurate information,' observed Fidelma. 'Did you do so?'

Abbot Miseno raised an eyebrow.

'Verify the reports?'

'I presume that you did not simply take Tullius at his word?'

'Why would I doubt him? Tullius is in the process of

taking holy orders, under my supervision. I can trust the word of Tullius.'

'The word of someone currently seeking ordination, you mean? Such a person would not lie?'

'That's right, absolutely not. Of course they would not lie.'

'But a priest, already ordained, would lie? Therefore, you could not take Cornelius' word? Surely there is a contradictory philosophy in this?'

'Of course I don't mean that!' snapped Abbot Miseno.

'But that is what appears to be happening. You took Tullius' word over that of Cornelius.'

'The accusation was that Cornelius had dishonoured the priesthood by taking a mistress.'

'Talos suggests that Tullius takes male lovers. You indicate that you know of this. The conclusion there is that not only did you take the word of a deacon against a priest, but you preferred to condemn a man on the grounds that he had a female lover or mistress while supporting a young man who is said to have a male lover. Why is one to be condemned and the other to be accepted in your eyes?'

Abbot Miseno set his jaw firmly.

'I am not Tullius' lover, if that is what you are implying. Tullius is under my patronage. He is my protégé.'

'Are you retracting your claim that Tullius had a male lover?'

'You have spoken to the young *custos*.' It was a statement rather than a question.

'Do you admit you are prejudiced in your judgement?'

'Are you saying that Tullius lied to me? If so, what proof do you have?'

'As much proof as you have to say that he told the truth.'

'Why should he lie to me?'

'You are about to ordain him. I suspect that you now intend him to replace Cornelius here?'

Abbot Miseno's face showed that her guess was right.

'But what has this to do with the death of the Gaul?'

'Everything,' Fidelma assured him. 'I think I am now ready to explain what happened.'

She turned and called everyone to come forward to the place before the altar.

'I can tell you why Docco, a visitor to this country and this city, died and by whose hand.' Her voice was cold and precise.

They appeared to surge forward, edging near to her with expectant expressions.

'Sister Fidelma!' It was Egeria who spoke. 'We know there was only one person who wanted my brother dead. Everyone else here was a stranger to him.'

Enodoc's face was white.

'This is not true. I would never harm anyone . . .'

'I don't believe you!' cried Egeria. 'Only you had reason to kill him.'

'What if Docco was killed simply because he was the first to take the sacrament?' interrupted Fidelma.

There was a tense silence.

'Go on,' urged Abbot Miseno in an icy tone.

'Docco was not singled out as a victim. Any of us might have been the victim. The intention was to discredit Father Cornelius.'

There was an angry glint in Abbot Miseno's eyes and they narrowed on Fidelma.

'You will have to answer for these accusations . . .'

'I am prepared to do so. It was something that the abbot said that gave me an idea of the true motive of this terrible deed. He said that if Father Cornelius had been a true priest, then once the wine was blessed and the transubstantiation occurred, the poison would have been rendered harmless when the wine became the Blood of Christ. The motive of this crime was to demonstrate that Father Cornelius was unworthy to hold office.'

Father Cornelius stood gazing at her in awe.

Fidelma went on.

'For some time the deacon, Tullius, had been feeding stories to Abbot Miseno about the misconduct of Cornelius, stories which Cornelius categorically denies. But Abbot Miseno was convinced. Tullius was his protégé and could do no wrong in the abbot's eyes. Furthermore, Miseno was about to ordain Tullius and, as a priest, he would need his own *ecclesia*. What better than to give him this church . . . once Cornelius had been removed. But Cornelius was not going without a fight. Any accusations of misconduct would have to be argued before the local bishop.'

'Who are you accusing?' demanded Cornelius, intervening. 'Miseno or Tullius?'

'Neither.'

Her answer was met with blank looks.

'Then whom?'

'Terentius of the *custodes*!'

The young man took a step backwards and drew his short ceremonial sword.

'This has gone far enough, barbarian!' he cried in anger. 'I am a Roman. No one will believe you.'

But Tullius was moving forward.

'What have you done, Terentius?' he cried in a high-pitched voice. 'I loved you more than life, and you have ruined everything.'

He ran as if to embrace Terentius and then seemed to freeze in mid-stride. It was clearly not meant to happen but the young deacon had inadvertently run forward onto the sword which the *custos* had been holding defensively in front of him. Tullius gave a gurgling cry, blood gushed from his mouth and he fell forward.

Enodoc reached forward and snatched the sword from the guard's hand. There was no struggle. The *custos* stood frozen in shock staring down at the body of his friend.

'But I did it for you, Tullius!' he wailed, suddenly sinking to his knees and reaching for the hand of the corpse. 'I did it for you.'

A short time later Fidelma sat with Father Cornelius and Abbot Miseno.

'I was not sure whether Tullius and Terentius had planned this together, or even whether you might be part of the plan yourself, Abbot Miseno,' she said.

Miseno looked pained.

'I might be a fool, one of ill judgement, but I am not a murderer, Sister.'

'How did you realise that Terentius was the murderer?' demanded Father Cornelius. 'I cannot understand this.'

'Firstly, the motive. It was easy to eliminate the fact that Docco was an intended victim. There were too many improbables, too many coincidences had to happen to ensure that the Gaul was the first and only victim. So I had to look for another motive. That motive was not so obscure and, as I said, it was Abbot Miseno's interpretation of the fact of transubstantiation which gave me a clue. The motive was to discredit you, Father Cornelius. Who would benefit from that? Obviously Tullius the deacon.'

'So why did you think Tullius was innocent?'

'Because if he had been involved he would have given himself a better alibi, for, it appeared at first, only he had the opportunity to poison the wine. Then I learnt that Tullius had a male lover. It became clear that it was Terentius, the *custos*.'

'Yes, but what made you so sure he was the murderer?'

'He was the only other person with opportunity. And, most importantly, he lied. He said that he had entered the church by the main doors just before the Gaulish seaman. He also told me that he had been coming along the street and saw you both quarrelling on the path to the sacristy.'

'Well that was no lie, we were arguing,' Miseno confirmed.

'Surely, you were. But the sacristy, where that argument took place, as Enodoc told me, is entered by a path on the other side of this church. You have to walk a long way round to enter the main doors. Enodoc didn't have time to do so, so blundered through the sacristy into the church.'

'I do not follow.'

'If Terentius had seen you both arguing then he was on the path outside the sacristy and therefore he was on the far side of the building. What was he doing there? Why did he not come through the sacristy, like Enodoc, knowing the service was about to start? He had been there enough times with Tullius. No, he came in through the main doors.

'He had seen your quarrel and gone to the sacristy door. Watching through the window, he waited until he saw Tullius take the bread into the *ecclesia*; then he slipped in and poisoned the wine and left, hurrying round the church to come in by the main doors and thus giving himself an alibi.'

'And he did this terrible deed purely in order to help Tullius become priest here?' asked Miseno, amazed.

'Yes. He had reasoned out that it did not matter who was killed by the poison, the end result was that you would believe that Cornelius was not fit to be a priest because the transubstantiation had not happened. That would ensure Tullius became priest here. That plan nearly succeeded. Love makes people do insane things, Miseno. Doesn't Publilius Syrus say: *amare et sapere vix deo conceditur*? Even a god finds it hard to love and be wise at the same time.'

Miseno nodded. '*Amantes sunt amentes*,' he agreed. 'Lovers are not sane.'

Fidelma shook her head sorrowfully.

'It was a sad and unnecessary death. More importantly, Abbot Miseno, it is, to my mind, a warning of the dangers of believing that what was meant as symbolism is, in fact, a reality.'

'There we will have to differ on our theology, Fidelma,' sighed Miseno. 'But our Faith is broad enough to encompass differences. If it is not – then it will surely perish.'

'*Sol lucet omnibus*,' Fidelma replied softly, with just a touch of cynicism. 'The sun shines for everyone.'

Tarnished Halo

❧

Father Allán looked up with a frown from his interrupted devotions as Sister Fidelma opened the door of his *cubiculum* unannounced.

'I am told that you have urgent need of a lawyer,' she said without preamble.

As he scrambled from his knees, making a hasty genuflection to the crucifix that hung on the wall and before which he had been praying, she noticed that his face was graven in lines of anxiety. Once on his feet he turned and surveyed the young religieuse who stood poised within the door frame. From the surprise on his face, she was clearly not what he had been expecting. She was tall, with rebellious strands of red hair escaping from her *cabhal* or head-dress; her figure, lithe and vital, clearly indicated a joy in living, scarcely concealed by her habit.

'Are you the *dálaigh* whom I was told to expect?' Father Allán's voice held an incredulous tone.

'I am Fidelma of Kildare, an advocate of the courts,' affirmed Fidelma. 'I am qualified to the rank of *Anruth*.'

The Father Superior blinked. The qualification of *Anruth* was only one degree below the highest qualification obtainable either at the ecclesiastic or secular universities of the five kingdoms of Ireland. He swallowed as he eventually remembered his etiquette and thrust out a hand to invite the religieuse in.

'Welcome, Sister. Welcome to our community of piety and peace . . .'

Fidelma interrupted the ritual greeting with a slight cutting motion of her hand.

'Not so peaceful, I am told,' she observed drily. 'I was informed by the Abbot of Lios Mór Mochuda that murder has been committed within these walls and that you have need of the services of a *dálaigh*. I came as soon as I could.'

Father Allán's lips compressed into a thin line.

'Not exactly within these walls,' he countered pedantically. 'Come, walk with me in our gardens and I will endeavour to explain matters.'

He led the way from the tiny grey monastic building which was perched on a rocky outcrop thrusting itself above a forest, and beside which a winding river meandered. The small religious community had a breathtaking view across the green vegetation towards distinct blue-hazed mountain peaks.

There was a small enclosed garden at the back of a dry-stone-built oratory. A young Brother was hard at work hoeing in a far corner. Father Allán led the way to a granite wall, well out of earshot of the young man, and seated himself. It was midday and the sun was warming and pleasant on the skin. Fidelma followed his example, perching herself on the wall.

'Now . . .?' she prompted.

'There has, indeed, been murder committed here, Fidelma of Kildare,' confirmed Father Allán, his tone heavy with sorrow.

'Who was killed, when and now?'

Father Allán waited a moment, as if to gather his thoughts before he spoke.

'Brother Moenach was killed. Perhaps you have heard of him?'

'We are many miles from Kildare,' observed Fidelma. 'Why would I have heard of this Brother Moenach?'

'He was a saintly youth,' sighed Father Allán. 'Yes, a veritable saint. He was a lad of eighteen summers but so steeped in wisdom, in poetry and in song; so serene and calm of nature was he that he was surely blessed by the Living God. His charity and sweet disposition were renowned as much as his musical accomplishments. Abbots and chieftains, even the King of Cashel, sought his musical talent to create solace for their spirits.'

Fidelma raised a cynical eye at Father Allán's enthusiasm for the virtues of Moenach.

'So an eighteen-year-old member of your house, Brother Moenach, was killed?' she summarised.

The Father Superior of the settlement nodded.

'When?'

'It happened a week ago.'

Fidelma exhaled deeply. That meant that there was little evidence for her to see. And doubtless Brother Moenach had been decently buried many days ago. But she had promised the Abbot of Lios Mór Mochuda that she would investigate this affair, for the tiny community fell within his ecclesiastical jurisdiction.

'How?'

'It was a village woman named Muirenn who killed him. We have her locked up to be taken before the chieftain for summary justice . . .'

'After she has been given a proper hearing before the local Brehon,' interrupted Fidelma. 'But I ask "how" not "who".'

Father Allán frowned.

'I do not follow.'

Fidelma restrained her irritation.

'Tell me the facts about this incident as you know them.'

'One evening, Brother Aedo came running to find me. It was shortly before vespers, as I recall. He had been

241

returning through the forest from the village with some vegetables for the settlement when he saw a movement through the trees to one side of the path. Curiosity prompted him to investigate. To his horror, in a clearing, he came upon the body of young Moenach. Kneeling beside him was an old woman of the village, Muirenn. She was holding a rock in her hand. There was blood on the stone and on the head of young Moenach. Brother Aedo fled and came straightaway to tell me of this terrible thing . . .'

'Fled? Yet you tell me that Muirenn is an old woman? What put such fear into a man of God?'

The Father Superior wondered whether Fidelma was being sarcastic but could not make up his mind.

'Muirenn turned on his approach with such a ghastly look on her face that Aedo was afraid for his life,' Father Allán explained. 'If Muirenn could kill Moenach then she could equally kill Aedo.'

'Her guilt is supposition at the moment. Then what? What after Aedo reported the matter to you?'

'Some of us went to the spot. Moenach was still lying there. His skull had been smashed in from behind. A bloodstained rock was lying where Muirenn had apparently discarded it. We hunted for her and found her hiding in her *bothán* in the village . . .'

'Hiding? Why would she return to her own cabin and her own village? Surely she would have known that she had been seen and recognised? It would be the last place to hide. And how was she hiding? Was she concealed somewhere in the cabin?'

Father Allán shook his head with a soft breath of vexation.

'I do not pretend to understand the workings of her mind. We caught her in her *bothán*, seated before her own hearth. We have been holding her for your interrogation, pending trial before the Brehon.'

'Hardly "hiding", from what you tell me,' observed

Fidelma somewhat scornfully. 'And did she admit culpability for the crime and volunteer a reason why she killed Moenach?'

The Father Superior sniffed deprecatingly.

'She claimed to have no knowledge at all of the murder although we have an eye-witness.'

'An eye-witness?' Fidelma's voice was sharp. 'Who is your eye-witness?'

Father Allán looked pained as if dealing with a dim-witted pupil. 'Why, Brother Aedo of course.'

'But you told me that he was only an eye-witness to this woman kneeling by the side of Moenach and holding a bloody rock in her hand. That is not an eye-witness to the actual murder.'

Father Allán opened his mouth to protest and then, seeing the angry glint in Fidelma's eyes . . . were they green or light blue? . . . he fell silent. When annoyed, her eyes seem to dance with a curious ice-coloured fire.

'I don't pretend to be learned in law,' he said stubbornly. 'I have no time for such nuances.'

'The law text of the *Berrad Airechta* states clearly that a person can only give evidence about what he or she has seen or heard and what does not take place before a witness's eyes is irrelevant. Nor can hearsay evidence be accepted.'

'But it was obvious . . .' began Father Allán.

'I am here to deal with law, not supposition,' snapped Fidelma. 'And as a *dálaigh*, I would counsel you to be more careful with the words you choose. Tell me more about this . . . this saintly youth.'

Father Allán heard the slight sarcastic emphasis in her voice. He hesitated a moment, wondering if he should chide her mocking tone but finally decided to ignore it.

'He was the son of a chieftain of the Uí Fidgente. He displayed a rare gift as a musician, playing the *cruit* like an angel would play a harp. His poetry was sweet and pure. He was given to us for his fosterage when he was seven years of age and, after reaching the age of choice last year, he decided to stay on with us as a member of our community.'

'So he had a reputation as a musician?'

'He would be invited to attend the feastings of chieftains and abbots for miles about here,' Father Allán repeated.

'But what sort of person was he?'

'A pleasing person. Kind, wise, considerate of his brethren and of all who met him. He would always go out of his way to please his superiors and attend their needs. He was especially fond of animals and . . .'

'Was he beyond all human frailties, then?'

Father Allán took her question seriously and shook his head. With a sniff, Fidelma stood up. The set smile on her face was somewhat false. Father Allán was too full of angelic visions of his acolyte to be of further use to her.

'I would now speak with the woman, Muirenn,' she said. 'After that, I wish to see Brother Aedo.'

The Father Superior slid reluctantly from his seat on the wall and indicated that she should follow him to a corner of the settlement buildings.

Muirenn sat in a corner of the small *cubiculum*, perched on the edge of the cot which she had been provided for a bed. She looked up defiantly as Fidelma entered. She was a small, reed-like woman, with angry dark eyes, a thrusting jaw and a tumble of greying black hair. She was not really old but it could not be rightfully claimed that she was of middle age.

'I am Fidelma, a *dálaigh* of the courts,' announced Fidelma as she entered. She had asked Father Allán to leave her alone with the prisoner.

The woman, Muirenn, snorted.

'You have come to punish me for something I did not do,' she growled. There was anger in her voice, not fear.

'I am come here to discover the truth,' Fidelma corrected her mildly.

'You whining religieux have already decided what is the

244

truth. You should return from whence you came if you mean simply to confirm Allán's prejudices.'

Fidelma sat down instead.

'Tell me your story,' she invited. 'You are from the village below this settlement?'

'God curse the day that the religieux started to build here,' muttered the woman.

'I am told that you are a widow? That you have no children but help the village apothecary. Is this the truth?'

'It is so.'

'Then tell me your story.'

'I was in the forest, gathering herbs and other plants for medications. I heard a cry nearby. I pushed forward to see what I could see. In a small clearing I saw a young religieux lying face down on the ground. On the far side of the clearing the bushes rustled, marking the passage of someone leaving the clearing. I thought I might help the young boy. I knelt down and I saw that it was too late. His skull had been smashed in beyond repair. I automatically picked the rock up that lay near his head; it was covered in blood.

'It was then that I heard a gasp behind me. I turned and saw another young religieux standing at the edge of the clearing staring at me. I scrambled to my feet and fled in terror back to my *bothán*.'

Fidelma raised an eyebrow.

'Why would you run in terror when you beheld a young Brother standing there? Surely the natural thing would have been to seek his help?'

Muirenn scowled in annoyance.

'I ran in terror because I thought he was the murderer come back.'

'Why would you think that?' demanded Fidelma. 'He was clearly a member of this community.'

'Exactly so. When I first entered the clearing and saw the bushes closing over the retreating figure, I caught a glance of his back. He was wearing the brown robe of a religieux. Moenach was killed by a member of his own community. I did not kill him.'

Outside the cell Father Allán glanced expectantly at Fidelma.

'Do you still wish to see Brother Aedo or have you concluded your investigation?'

Was there eagerness in his voice? He seemed so anxious that she simply endorse his claim that Muirenn was guilty. Fidelma pursed her lips and gazed at him for a moment before replying.

'I have just begun my investigation,' she replied softly. 'Tell me, how many Brothers reside in this community?'

'What has that to do . . .?' Father Allán bit his tongue as he saw the furrows on her brow deepen and caught the angry flash of fire in her eyes. 'There are ten Brothers altogether.'

'Did Brother Moenach have any special companions here?'

'We are all companions of each other,' sniffed the Father Superior. 'Companions in the service of Christ.'

'Was he liked equally by everyone in the community?' she tried again.

'Of course,' snapped Father Allán. 'And why wouldn't he be?'

Fidelma suppressed a sigh.

'Has his *cubiculum* been cleared?' she asked, deciding to try another tack.

'I believe so. Brother Ninnedo would know. He is tending the garden there.' He pointed to where the fair-haired young monk was trimming a bush across the grassy slopes. 'Come, I will . . .'

Fidelma held up a hand.

'I can see him. You need not trouble yourself, Father Allán. I will speak to him. I will find you when I am ready. Alert Brother Aedo to my intention to see him after I have spoken to Brother Ninnedo.'

She turned and made her way towards the young man, who was bent industriously to his work.

'Brother Ninnedo?'

The young man glanced up. He looked uncomfortable. His eyes darted towards the disappearing figure of Father Allán behind her.

'I am a *dál*—' Fidelma began to introduce herself.

The young man interrupted before Fidelma could explain.

'You are a *dálaigh*. I know. The community has been expecting you for some days since.'

'Good. And do you know why I am here?'

The young man simply nodded.

'I understand that you shared a *cubiculum* with Brother Moenach. I suppose you knew him well?'

Fidelma was surprised when she saw a positive expression of repugnance cross the young man's face.

'I knew him well enough.'

'But you did not like him?' she asked quickly.

'I did not say so,' replied Ninnedo defensively.

'You did not have to. Why didn't you like him? According to Father Allán, this Brother Moenach was little short of a saint.'

Ninnedo laughed bitterly.

'I did not like him because he was an evil person and not fit to serve the Living God. He could fool Father Allán. He could fool many people who were so complacent in office that they did not recognise a fawning sycophant who purposely flattered their vanity. But I and Brother Fogartach had to share a *cubiculum* with him and knew his evil ways.'

Fidelma stood with her head slightly to one side, slightly surprised at the young man's articulate vehemence.

'How long did you know him?'

'We were fostered together, Sister. A long time.'

'And did you hate him all that time?'

'Mostly.'

'So, tell me, in what way did he manifest evil? You accuse

247

him of being a fawning sycophant. Well, we are all, in some ways, flattering to those in power over us. That hardly constitutes evil.'

Ninnedo pressed his upper teeth against his lower lip, frowning a little, before he spoke.

'Father Allán would have Moenach as a saint. It would do me little good to speak plainly.'

'You are not speaking to Father Allán but a *dálaigh* of the courts. Speak only the truth and by truth you shall be rewarded.'

Ninnedo shifted uneasily at her sharp tone.

'Very well, Sister. Moenach was a liar, a thief and a lecher.'

Fidelma raised her eyebrows.

'If so, how could he disguise such vices from Father Allán?'

'He had the look of a cherub and could speak sweetly when the need arose. Often people cannot see beyond appearances. And he had an ability to make sweet music. He could fool people. But now and then that mask of innocence would slip. He was evil.'

'Can you cite proof, for hearsay evidence is inadmissible under the law.'

'Proof? He would steal anything he coveted. He stole from me and he stole from Brother Nath. Why, there used to be a Brother Follamon in our community until a few months ago. Moenach coveted a bejewelled cup belonging to Father Allán. He could not control his desires and he stole it. Father Allán launched a search for it. Moenach realised that he could not get away with the theft so he planted it in the cot of Brother Follamon so that it would be found and blame placed on him.'

'What happened?'

'Father Allán simply had Follamon expelled from the community.'

'Why wasn't Moenach reported to the Father? If you knew and Brother Nath knew, why didn't Father Allán accept your evidence?'

Ninnedo laughed again. There was no humour in his voice.

'You do not realise just how entrenched is the good Father's belief in Moenach. Nath told him, for Nath knew what had happened. Father Allán simply accused Nath of jealousy and threatened his expulsion as well.'

'But Moenach's position could not be maintained simply by Father Allán's prejudice alone? There must be others who agreed with Father Allán's views?'

Ninnedo sniffed bitterly.

'Oh yes. Moenach fooled some of the Brothers. That fool Aedo, for example.'

'Aedo who discovered the body with the old woman Muirenn kneeling by it?'

'The same. He was so shocked and prostrate by grief that, when he arrived back here with the news of what he had seen, he took to his bed for several days.'

'So? Aedo did not accompany Father Allán and the Brothers in search of Muirenn?'

'He did not.'

'And apart from some of these Brothers, Moenach fooled other people as well?'

'He had the same influence with many local chieftains and even abbots.'

'But you and Nath recognised him as evil?'

'We knew his ways, Sister. In fact, he seemed to delight in our knowing how he was fooling people like the Father Superior. He would challenge us to report him, knowing full well that we would not be believed.'

'Did you not support Nath against Father Allán?'

'Little use that was,' sniffed Ninnedo.

There came the sound of a distant bell.

'I must go,' Ninnedo said and moved off rapidly.

Fidelma stood for a moment watching him stride away and then she turned in search of Father Allán.

'You did not tell me that Moenach was not well liked by everyone.'

The Father Superior stared angrily.

'Who did not like him?' he demanded. 'Ninnedo, I suppose?'

'I also speak of Brother Nath.'

'Nath!' Father Allán's mouth drooped. 'So Ninnedo told you of that matter?'

Fidelma did not reply.

'Sister Fidelma, you know as well as I, that in spite of our vows and dedication to the service of the Living God, we do not suddenly become more than human, nor do we become incorrupt.'

'What are you saying?'

'That I am aware of the accusations of Nath and Ninnedo. I have known them for many years, ever since they came here to be fostered with Moenach. They all grew up together but as men sometimes take a dislike to each other, so too with boys. I knew of their jealousies and dislike of Moenach.'

'Yes? And to what reason did you attribute it?'

'Who knows? When a boy is as talented and pure as Moenach, he will have many enemies.'

'And are you so sure that their accusations were unfounded?'

'I knew Moenach since he was seven years old. He was beyond reproach.'

'Although you do admit that none of us is incorruptible?' Fidelma could not help the sarcastic thrust.

Father Allán did not rise to the bait.

'Moenach was someone special. It was a great pain for me to see Nath's jealousy.'

'I want to talk to Brother Nath.'

Father Allán gestured awkwardly.

'But he . . . he has absconded. Did Ninnedo not mention this to you?'

Fidelma gazed blankly at him for a moment.

'Nath has disappeared?'

'Yes. No one has seen him for the last week.'

Fidelma caught her breath to suppress a surge of anger.

'Are you telling me that Brother Nath disappeared a week ago? And it was a week ago that Brother Moenach was murdered. Why was I not informed of this before?'

Father Allán's face whitened.

'But Muirenn slew Moenach. Why would you be interested in a headstrong young man who has slunk away from the community?'

'Why was I not informed about this?' repeated Fidelma. 'Has any investigation been made into what has happened to Nath?'

Father Allán shrugged helplessly.

'He broke his vows and absconded. That is all.'

'Tell Brother Ninnedo to join me at once.'

Father Allán blinked, hesitated and moved off.

Ninnedo arrived with surly face. Father Allán stood behind him, watching anxiously.

'I want the full truth, Ninnedo,' Fidelma told him. 'And I want it now.'

'I have spoken the truth.'

'Yet you did not tell me that your friend Nath has been missing since the day of the killing of Moenach.'

Ninnedo blanched but contrived a stubborn expression.

'Are you accusing him of killing Moenach and running off?' he muttered. 'Everyone says Muirenn slew Moenach.'

'It is my role to find out the truth. Do you know where Nath is?'

Ninnedo stared at her. It was the young Brother who dropped his eyes first. He shook his head.

'Speak to Ainder, the daughter of Illand,' he muttered.

'Who is Ainder?' Fidelma asked.

Father Allán moved uneasily from one foot to the other.

'Ainder is a young girl of the village who washes the clothes of the community. She lives with her father, Illand, who oversees our gardens.'

Fidelma turned her gaze back to Brother Ninnedo.

'Why should I speak with this Ainder?'

'It is not my place to anticipate what she will say to you,' the young man replied spiritedly, attempting to copy Fidelma's style.

Fidelma stared at Ninnedo's stubborn features and sighed.

'Where will I find this Ainder?'

'The *bothán* of Illand is at the bottom of the hill,' interrupted the Father Superior. 'Seek her there, Sister Fidelma.'

She decided to ask Brother Aedo to accompany her in order to show her the spot where Moenach was killed and to confirm his story of the finding of the body. He was a simple ingenuous youth and had nothing else to add. He confirmed that he had been so distressed on his return to the community that he could do no more than report the matter to the Father Superior before becoming incapacitated by a surfeit of emotion. Father Allán and three other Brothers had left immediately to find Moenach and search for the woman Muirenn. Fidelma, looking round the small clearing, did not expect to find anything to assist her at the site. Nevertheless, it helped to fix the location of the crime in her mind. Without Brother Aedo's help, it would have been impossible to pinpoint the exact spot for there were many such little clearings amidst the great forest. She bade Aedo return to the hilltop community and continued on down the hill.

There was a small cabin at the bottom of the hill as Father Allán had said. A line of freshly laundered clerical robes were hanging to dry on a rope line strung between two trees. An elderly but sturdily built man was picking apples from one of the trees. He turned and watched suspiciously as Fidelma approached.

'Is this the home of Ainder, daughter of Illand?'

'I am Illand,' replied the man. 'My daughter is inside.'

'I am Fidelma of Kildare. I wish to speak with your daughter.'

The man hesitated before gesturing towards the cabin.

'You are welcome, Fidelma. But my daughter is not well . . .'

'But well enough to see the Sister,' interrupted a soft soprano voice.

A young girl, fair-haired and slim, and no more than fourteen years of age, stood framed in the doorway of the cabin.

'Please, father,' the girl said with hurried insistence before he could argue. 'I am at the age of choice.'

Fidelma glanced carefully at her, wondering why the girl had to point out her right to make her own decision.

Illand shrugged expressively.

'I have things to attend to,' he muttered in a surly tone and, picking up his basket of apples, moved off.

The girl turned to Fidelma with a pale face but determined chin.

'You must be the *dálaigh* whom Father Allán was waiting for,' she said. 'Why do you seek me out?'

'I am told you are laundress for the community,' returned Fidelma. 'Do you live here with your mother and father?'

A scowl flitted across the girl's face.

'My mother is many years in the place of truth,' she replied, using the Irish euphemism meaning that her mother was dead.

'I am sorry.'

'No need for sorrow,' said the girl.

Without another word, Ainder turned and went into the *bothán*, beckoning Fidelma to follow. She sat in the chair which Ainder indicated. The young girl sat opposite her and examined her carefully.

'I am glad that you are a woman and a young one.'

Fidelma raised her eyebrows in surprise.

'Why so?'

'I think you are here to ask me about Nath.'

'What do you know of Brother Nath?'

253

'He wishes to marry me.'

Fidelma blinked and sighed.

'I see.' Members of religious communities could and did get married under the Law of the *Fenechus*. 'So Nath is in love with you?'

'He is.'

There was a slight emphasis in her voice which contained a hidden 'but'.

'But your father disapproves?' hazarded Fidelma.

'Oh no!' The words were ejaculated hurriedly. 'He does not know.'

'You know that Nath has disappeared?'

Ainder nodded, eyes on the ground.

'You knew that Brother Moenach was murdered and that Brother Nath disappeared on the same day? Things look bad for him.'

Ainder seemed bewildered.

'But didn't the old woman, Muirenn, kill Moenach?' she demanded.

'That is what I am here to find out. What do you know of Nath's disappearance?'

The girl hesitated and then sighed deeply.

'Nath was frightened when Moenach was killed. You see, no one believes how evil Moenach really was. He had caused Brother Follamon to be expelled by his deception.'

'How did you know of this?'

'I grew up here, under the shadow of Father Allán's community. My father tends their garden and, after my mother died, I am laundress for the community. I knew most of the brothers. Follamon, Nath, Ninnedo and Moenach were all fostered together and when they reached the age of choice last year they all decided to stay on in the community of Father Allán. They all knew each other well enough. Follamon, Nath and Ninnedo became my friends.'

'But not Moenach?'

The girl shuddered.

'No!' Her voice was emphatic. Too emphatic.

'Why did you dislike Moenach?'

The girl raised her eyes to Fidelma. Two bright red spots coloured her cheeks. Then she lowered her gaze and spoke with studied care.

'I will not keep the truth from you, Sister. The day before Moenach was killed, he attacked me.'

Fidelma started.

'He attacked you?'

'He raped me.'

Fidelma noticed that she used the word *forcor* which indicated a forcible rape, a physical attack, distinguished in law from *sleth*, which covered all other forms of sexual intercourse with a woman without her consent.

'Explain to me the circumstances, Ainder. And let me warn you that this is a serious allegation.'

Ainder's face hardened.

'It is serious for me, for who now will pay my *coibche*?'

A husband gave a *coibche* or 'bride-price' which was shared between a bride and her guardian in law, usually her father. The 'bride-price' was related to the virginity of the bride and if the bride was not a virgin then humiliation and financial loss resulted.

'Very well. Tell me your story,' invited Fidelma.

'I was taking a basket of laundry up to the community. Moenach came upon me. He hated me because he knew Nath loved me. He insulted me and then knocked me to the ground and raped me. Afterwards . . . he said if I spoke of the matter no one would believe me for it was well known in the community that he was trusted of abbots and kings.'

'Was it an actually physical assault?' Fidelma pressed. 'You realise the differences between *forcor* and *sleth*?'

'Moenach was strong. I could not prevail against him. It was a physical attack.'

'And you told Nath about this?'

The girl paused a moment, examining Fidelma's face from under lowered eyelids, and then nodded quickly.

'I see. And Nath was angry, of course?'

'I have never seen him so angry.'

'When was this? How long before Moenach was killed?'

'He did not kill Moenach.'

Fidelma smiled thinly.

'I did not make such an accusation. But what makes you so emphatic?'

'He would not. It is not in Nath's nature.'

'It is in the nature of all men given the right motive. Answer my question then, how long before Moenach was killed did you tell Nath of this attack?'

'It was on the same afternoon that Moenach died. Scarcely an hour before.'

'When did you learn of Moenach's death? ' Fidelma asked.

'Why . . .' the girl frowned, 'it was when Father Allán and some others of the community came searching for the old woman Muirenn. But Father Allán said that Muirenn had been seen with the murder weapon in her hand.'

'Did you see Nath afterwards?'

Ainder appeared reluctant to speak and so Fidelma pressed the question again.

'That very evening,' the girl replied unwillingly. 'He came to me and was frightened. He had heard the news but was afraid for himself.'

'He must have known Muirenn was suspected. What made him run away?'

'Because he thought that he would be suspected. His dislike of Moenach was well known. And Nath believed that should the news of Moenach's attack on me come out, whether it was believed or not, he would be singled out as a suspect in the murder.'

Fidelma looked at the girl sadly.

'Certainly, Nath is now more of a suspect than the old

woman, Muirenn. Which makes me ask, why have you told me this story so readily, Ainder, when it makes things look so bad for Nath?'

The girl looked aggrieved at the question.

'I tell it because it is the truth and are we not taught that the truth stands against all things? Nath cannot continue to hide forever. I cannot marry with an outlaw forever hiding in the fastnesses and shadows of this land. I have urged Nath to surrender himself many times and rely on truth as his shield.'

Fidelma sat back and regarded the girl thoughtfully.

'You realise just how bad the situation is for Nath if he does not return to be heard before me?'

'I do. I believe that he should do so and that the truth will free him.'

'If that is so, will you tell me where Nath is hiding?'

The girl dropped her eyes to the ground. She did not speak for a long while. Then she sighed, as if making up her mind.

'Can I bring Nath to you?'

'It is all the same to me,' Fidelma replied indifferently. 'Just so long as he presents himself before me.'

'Then I will bring him to Muirenn's *bothán* at dusk.'

Fidelma did not really expect Brother Nath to turn up that evening. Somehow she did not really trust the credulous attitude of Ainder. She had been waiting in Muirenn's cabin for half an hour before she heard Ainder's voice call softly.

Fidelma was seated in a chair beside the grey remnants of the dead turf fire.

Ainder's shadowy figure stood for a while framed in the doorway.

Fidelma rose and lit a candle.

It was then she saw the pale young man in the robes of a religieux standing nervously behind the young woman.

'And so you are Nath?' she asked.

Ainder drew the young man into the cabin by her hand and quickly closed the door.

'I have told him not to fear you, Sister Fidelma, but only to speak the truth.'

Fidelma studied the young man. He was fresh-faced, tousle-haired and had a look of bemusement as if he were caught in a stream of events over which he had no control. Something maternal stirred in Fidelma for the youth had the vacant expression of a little boy lost and alone in a frightening forest. She shook herself to rid her mind of the emotion.

She gestured for him to sit down.

'Tell me your story, Nath,' she invited, also seating herself.

'Little to tell,' the boy said quietly. 'I love Ainder and wish to marry her. Moenach was always an enemy to me, to me and to my other brethren. He was a bully always, as a child and as a youth. He delighted in actions that harmed us but like most bullies he knew how to ingratiate himself to his betters. Father Allán would not hear a word against him. Moenach engineered the expulsion of Follamon . . .'

'I know about this. I have talked with Brother Ninnedo.'

Nath gave her an intense look.

'Then you know what Moenach was really like?'

'I know what I have been told. So when Ainder came to you and told you what had happened, you were in a great rage?'

Nath lowered his head and sighed.

'I rage still. Sister, I do not regret Moenach's death. We are taught to forgive our enemies, them that do us ill. I cannot find it in my heart to do so. I rejoice in his death. I approve his ultimate punishment. My heart is exuberant. My mind tells me, however, that this is not the law nor the path of the Living God.'

'Did you kill him?'

'No!' The word was ejaculated like a rasping breath.

'Then why did you run away? Muirenn had been taken prisoner and the rest of the community thought the guilt lay at her door. Why bring suspicion down on your head?'

Nath looked bewildered.

'There were many who did not believe in Muirenn's guilt and believed that Father Allán was using her as an easy scapegoat to protect Moenach's reputation.'

'If they knew Muirenn to be innocent, they must have known someone to be guilty. By running, you provided a suspect.'

Nath shook his head. 'Knowing that it is impossible for someone to kill does not mean that one must have know-ledge of who committed the deed.'

'That is true,' conceded Fidelma. 'You, for instance, knew Muirenn not to be guilty of the deed. You claim that you, too, are innocent. Why should you be believed any more than Muirenn?'

'Father Allán said . . . I thought it for the best until I could make myself heard before a Brehon.'

'What did Father Allán say?' demanded Fidelma sharply.

Nath hesitated.

'When Ainder told me her story, I went straightaway to tell Father Allán. As before, he did not believe me. He fell into a terrible rage and it was some time before he calmed himself. He would not believe anything against his favourite. He told me to go away and never speak of it again. Later, when I heard Moenach was dead, I feared Father Allán would blame me.'

'So Father Allán knew that Ainder accused Moenach of rape?' mused Fidelma. 'And you, Nath, you blindly ran into hiding even though you must have realised that, in the meantime, your running away would compound any suspi-cions of your own guilt?'

'But there was no suspicion,' interposed Ainder, 'for everyone thought that Muirenn had committed the deed.'

Fidelma nodded thoughtfully.

'That is what puzzles me. On Brother Aedo's word, Father Allán had Muirenn imprisoned until my coming. You say that many did not believe her guilty but the entire community seemed apparently satisfied to have the old woman locked up and the assumption of her guilt left until my arrival. I still find it hard to understand why, knowing this, you, Nath, did not return to your community and await my arrival like the rest? Why draw attention to yourself by running away . . . unless you had something to hide?'

Nath looked blank while Ainder was agitated and defiant.

'The truth, Nath!' snapped Fidelma when neither of them spoke. 'I no longer want to indulge in your games.'

The young man raised his shoulders in a shrug of helplessness.

'We thought it for the best . . .'

Fidelma glanced at Ainder. Her lips were compressed and she was staring at the ground. Abruptly, a thought dawned in Fidelma's mind.

'Ainder told you to go into hiding, didn't she?' She asked the question sharply, without warning.

Nath started nervously and raised his head to look at Ainder.

'Look at me, Nath!' Fidelma said sharply. 'Tell me the truth and you will have nothing to fear.'

The young religieux hung his head.

'Yes. Ainder advised it was for the best.'

'Why?'

'It was Ainder who came to me with the news that Moenach had been slain. When I told her that I had already told Father Allán about Moenach's attack on her, she felt that no one would ever believe her any more than they believed me when I told people that Moenach was the culprit who stole Father Allán's cup. But she feared that suspicion might fall on me for the killing because of what I had told Father Allán. He knew I hated Moenach. I agreed that I should hide until the whole affair was over or until a learned Brehon arrived who might view my case with sympathy.'

'That was stupid. If Muirenn had been found guilty, that would have weighed heavily on your conscience.'

'I would not have let that happen. I would have returned,' protested Nath.

'Returned? And what excuse would you have offered for your absence? You would have willingly returned to exchange places with Muirenn? That I find hard to believe.'

'Believe it or not, it is the truth.' The young cenobite looked defiant.

Fidelma turned reprovingly to Ainder.

'That was foolish advice which you gave to Nath.'

The young girl raised her chin pugnaciously.

'I thought it best at the time,' she answered.

Fidelma gazed thoughtfully at the girl.

'I believe you did.'

She rose and turned towards the door.

'I am returning to see Father Allán now. You should return to the community, Nath. You have told me the truth.'

Father Allán rose awkwardly as Sister Fidelma entered his *cubiculum.*

'Will you tell me why you killed Moenach, or shall I tell you?' she demanded with an abruptness that left him staring open-mouthed at her. Her voice was cold, impersonal.

Father Allán blinked and his jaw slackened at the unexpectedness of the question. Before he could protest innocence, Fidelma added with emphasis: 'I know you did it. It would save time if we dispensed with any false protestations. I first suspected when I heard that after Brother Aedo had arrived here with the news, he was so distraught that he could not lead you to the spot. Yet you unerringly led the way to where Moenach's body was, in spite of the fact that there are many similar glades and dells in the forest; even if Aedo had given you the best directions in the world, you might have hesitated before you found the body.'

A bewildering variety of expressions chased one across the face of the Father Superior. Then, as he realised that

Fidelma was coldly determined, he sat down abruptly and spread his hands helplessly.

'I loved Moenach!'

'Hate is often simply the other side of love,' observed Fidelma.

The Father Superior hung his head.

'I raised Moenach from a boy. I was his foster father before the law. He had everything a young man could want, good looks, talent and a way of bending everyone to his will, of deceiving everyone into believing his goodness and piety . . .'

'Not quite everyone,' Fidelma pointed out.

'I know. I know,' sighed Father Allán, his shoulders hunched. 'I should have listened to his fellow cenobites a long time ago. I should have listened. But I was prejudiced and stopped up my ears when they told me the truth.'

'What changed you?'

'I tried to deceive myself for a long time about Moenach. Then Nath came to me with the terrible news of what Moenach had done to Ainder. I could not allow the evil that I had nurtured to continue. If he were capable of this as a boy, what evil lay in store in the future?'

'What happened?'

'I dismissed Nath, pretending that I did not believe him. I knew that Moenach had gone down to the village and so I hurried immediately down the path and waited for him. The rest was simple. He had no suspicions. I drew his attention to something on the ground and while he was bending to examine it, I picked up a rock and hit him, again and again until . . .'

'Then Muirenn happened to come on the scene . . .?'

'I heard someone coming along the forest path. I hurried away as quickly as I could.'

'And poor Muirenn saw the form of a religieux hastening away from the scene. You left the old woman there to be blamed for Moenach's death.'

'I did not wish that. My soul has been in purgatory ever since.'

'Yet you did not speak up when Brother Aedo claimed that she was the murderess? You went along with it and added to the evil of your deed by arresting her and calling for a Brehon to try her.'

'I am a human being,' cried Father Allán. 'I am not beyond sin if self-preservation is a sin.'

Fidelma pursed her lips as she gazed at him. 'Your attempt to shift the blame to the innocent and stand by while the innocent suffered is a sin.'

'But my deed was not evil. I have cleansed the world of an evil that once I nurtured in the mistaken belief of its goodness.' Father Allán had recovered his composure. His features were scornful, almost boastful now. 'I believed that Muirenn might prove her innocence. But if Muirenn was innocent then suspicion should not fall on me. Nath had foolishly been persuaded to disappear. He might have been blamed. Everyone knew how he hated Moenach.'

Fidelma felt troubled. There was something about this puzzle that did not fit exactly together. A piece of the puzzle was still missing. She accepted that Father Allán had struck the blows that killed Moenach. However, why would Father Allán, who had not previously accepted Brother Nath's word about Moenach, nor, indeed, the word of any of those who had tried to warn the Father Superior about Moenach, suddenly accept Nath's story of Ainder's rape to the extent that he went straightaway and killed Moenach? Something did not fit.

Suddenly Fidelma's mouth split into an urchin grin of satisfaction.

An hour later she presented herself at the cabin of Illand.

Ainder greeted her at the doorway.

'I will not keep you long, Ainder,' Fidelma said. 'I want to clarify one point. You told me that Nath loved you?'

Ainder nodded with a frown of curiosity.

'But you did not return his love,' Fidelma continued calmly. 'You never returned it. You only used him.'

Ainder flashed an angry glance at Fidelma. She saw the grim signs of knowledge in the eyes of the religieuse.

'Father Allán is under arrest for the murder of Moenach. Muirenn is released and no suspicion falls on Nath whose only crime was that he was easily led.'

For a while Ainder said nothing. Then she seemed to explode in emotion.

'Nath was weak, untalented. Allán was a chieftain's son with position and a reputation. I, we . . .'

She suddenly realised the implication of what she had confessed to. Her shoulders hunched and then she said in a small-girl voice: 'What will happen to me now?'

Fidelma did not feel pity for this child-woman. Ainder did not love Father Allán any more than she had loved Nath. She had been using Father Allán simply as a means of changing her station in life. It had been Father Allán who had become infatuated with the girl. So besotted with her that when he heard that Moenach had raped the girl, and had it confirmed from her lips, he had waylaid the young man and killed him. The rage that Nath had witnessed had not been for his accusation against Moenach but for Moenach's crime against Ainder. It was a rage born of jealousy.

That much might have been understandable as a justification for killing Moenach. But Father Allán and Ainder together had conspired to lay the blame on two innocent people. Muirenn might well have proved her innocence and so they had plotted to use the guileless fascination of Nath for Ainder and manipulate him into guilty behaviour. Ainder had cynically deceived and exploited the enamoured youth.

'You will be tried for complicity in the murder of Moenach,' replied Sister Fidelma.

'But I am only a . . .'

'A young girl?' finished Fidelma drily. 'No. As you have previously remarked, you are at the age of choice and considered responsible in law. You will be tried.'

Fidelma gazed a moment at the hatred on the girl's face. She was thinking of the infatuated Brother Nath and the love-sick Father Allán. *Grá is gráin* – love or hate, even the words came from the same root. What was it that the great poet Dallán Forgaill once wrote? Love and hatred were hatched from the same egg.

The Horse that Died for Shame

ॐ

'Horse racing,' observed the Abbot Laisran of Durrow, 'is a cure for all the ills of humankind. It is a surrogate for people's aggression and for their greed. We would find the world a harsher place without its institution.'

The abbot was a short, rotund, red-faced man with an almost exuberant sense of humour. In fact, the abbot's features were permanently fixed in a state of jollity for he was born with that rare gift of fun and a sense that the world was there to provide enjoyment to those who inhabited it.

Sister Fidelma of Kildare, walking at his side, answered his philosophical pronouncement with an urchin-like grin which seemed to belie her calling as a member of the religieuses of the community of Kildare.

'I doubt that Archbishop Ultan would agree with you, Laisran,' she responded, raising a hand to her forehead in a vain attempt to push back the wisps of red hair which escaped beneath her head-dress.

The abbot's lips quirked in amusement as he gazed at his one-time protégée, for it had been Laisran who had urged Fidelma to study law under the renowned Brehon, Morann of Tara, and, when she had reached the qualification of *Anruth*, one degree below the highest rank of learning, becoming an advocate of the courts of law, he had persuaded her to join the community of Brigid.

'But the Bishop Bressal would agree with me,' he countered. 'He has two horses which he races regularly and he is not averse to placing wagers on them.'

Sister Fidelma knew that Bressal, who was bishop to Fáelán of the Uí Dúnlainge, king of Laighin, was a keen supporter of the sport but, then, there were few to be found in the five kingdoms of Éireann who were not. Even the ancient word for a festival in Éireann, *aenach*, meant 'the contention of horses', when people came together to discuss weighty matters, to race their horses, to place wagers, to feast, to make merry and generally indulge in celebrations. Only recently had Ultan of Armagh, the archbishop and primate, begun to denounce the great fairs as contrary to the Faith for, so he claimed, the fairs were merely an excuse for the people to indulge in idolatry and pagan dissoluteness. Mostly, his denouncements were ignored, even by his own clergy, for the ancient customs were so instilled in the people's lives that it would take more than one man's prejudice to alter or dilute them.

In fact, Ultan's pronouncements were being ignored that very day by Abbot Laisran and Sister Fidelma as they strolled through the crowds gathering for the Aenach Lifé, the great annual fair held on the plain which, since the days of the High King Conaire Mór, had been called the Curragh Lifé, or 'the race course of the Lifé', after the name of the broad river flowing close by, twisting under the shadow of Dún Aillin. Indeed, was it not recorded that the saintly Brigid, who had founded Fidelma's own community at nearby Kildare, had raced her own horses on this very plain? The Curragh was now the most celebrated race course in all the five kingdoms and the Aenach Lifé attracted people from all the corners of Éireann. Each year, the King of Laighin himself would come to officially open the proceedings as well as to race his own champion horses there.

Fidelma, smiling, waved away a youth trying to sell them hot griddle cakes, and glanced at her elderly companion.

'Have you seen Bishop Bressal this morning?'

'I heard that he was here earlier,' Laisran replied, 'but I have not seen him. He is racing his favourite horse, Ochain, today. However, I have seen the bishop's jockey, Murchad, laying heavy wagers on himself to win with Ochain. At least Murchad shares the bishop's faith in himself and his horse.'

Fidelma pursed her lips reflectively.

'Ochain. I have heard of that beast. But why name a horse "moaner"?'

'I understand that Ochain utters a moaning sound as it senses that it is about to win. Horses are intelligent creatures.'

'More intelligent than most men, oftimes,' agreed Fidelma.

'Between ourselves, certainly more intelligent than the good bishop,' chuckled Laisran. 'He is openly boasting that he will win the race today against Fáelán's own horse, which does not please the king. They say the king is in a sour mood at his bishop's bragging.'

'So Fáelán is also racing today?'

'His best horse,' confirmed the abbot. 'And, in truth, there is little doubt of the outcome, for the king's champion Illan is in the saddle and with Aonbharr beneath his thighs, no team in Laighin will even come near . . . not even Murchad and Ochain. And, indeed, the fact that Illan is riding the king's horse is doubtless a matter of displeasure for Bishop Bressal.'

'Why so?' Fidelma was interested in Laisran's gossip.

'Because Illan used to train and race Bressal's horses before the king of Laighin offered him more money to train and ride Aonbharr.'

'Aonbharr, eh?' Fidelma had heard of the king's horse. So fleet was it that the king had named it after the fabulous horse of the ancient god of the oceans, Manánnan Mac Lir, a wondrous steed which could fly over land and sea without missing a pace. 'I have seen this horse race at the Curragh last year and no one could best it. This horse of Bressal's

269

better be good or the bishop's boasting will rebound on him.'

Abbot Laisran sniffed cynically.

'You have been away travelling this year, Fidelma. Perhaps you have not heard that there is something of a feud now between the king and his bishop. Four times during the last year Bressal has presented horses at races to run against the king's champion horse and his jockey. Four times now he has been beaten. Bressal is mortified. He has become a man with an obsession. He thinks that he is being made a fool of, especially by his former trainer and jockey. Now he has one aim, to best the king's horse and Illan in particular. The trouble is that his very efforts are making him a laughing stock.'

Abbot Laisran raised an arm and let his hand describe a half circle in the air towards the throng around them.

'I reckon a goodly proportion of these people have come here to see Bressal humiliated yet again when Aonbharr romps past the winning post.'

Fidelma shook her head sadly.

'Did I not say that horses had more sense than men, Laisran? Why must a simple pleasure be turned into warfare?'

Laisran suddenly halted and turned his head.

Pushing towards them, and clearly hurrying to make contact with them, was a young man in the livery of the Baoisgne, the king of Laighin's élite warrior guard. There was anxiety on his youthful features. He halted before them awkwardly.

'Forgive me, Abbot Laisran,' he began and then turned directly to Fidelma. 'Are you Sister Fidelma of Kildare?'

Fidelma inclined her head in acknowledgement.

'Then would you come at once, Sister?'

'What is the matter?'

'It is the wish of the king, Fáelán himself.' The young man glanced quickly round before lowering his voice so that he would not be overheard by the surrounding crowds.

'Illan, the king's champion jockey, has been found . . . dead. The king's horse, Aonbharr, is dying. The king believes that there has been foul play and has caused Bishop Bressal to be arrested.'

Fáelán of the Uí Dúnlainge, King of Laighin, sat scowling in his tent. Fidelma and Laisran had been escorted to the veritable township of tents which had been set up for the king and chieftains and their ladies alongside the course. Often entire families would camp at the Curragh during the nine days of the meeting. Behind the tents of the nobles were the tents of the trainers, riders and owners of lesser status as well as the tents which served as stables for their horses.

Fáelán of the Uí Dúnlainge was a man approaching his fortieth year. His dark features, black hair and bushy eyebrows made his features saturnine. When he scowled, his face took on the appearance of a malignant spirit which caused many a person to quail in his presence and stand uneasy.

Abbot Laisran, however, who had accompanied Fidelma, stood imperturbably smiling at the king, hands folded in his robes. He was acquainted with Fáelán and knew his grim features disguised a fair and honourable man. At Fáelán's side sat his queen, the beautiful Muadnat of the burnished hair; tall and sensual, the tales of her amours were legend. She was richly dressed with a jewelled belt and dagger sheath at her waist, such as all noble ladies carried. But, Fidelma noticed curiously, the sheath was empty of its small ceremonial dagger. The queen looked dejected, as if she had been given to a recent fit of weeping.

Behind the king and queen stood the *tánaiste*, heir-presumptive, a nephew of Fáelán's name Énna; and beside him was his wife, Dagháin. They were both in the mid-twenties. Énna was a handsome, though morose man, while his wife was almost nondescript at first glance, fashionably dressed yet without the same care as her queen for Fidelma noticed that her dress was mud-stained and dishevelled.

Even the bejewelled belt and sheath looked scuffed and its ceremonial dagger fitted badly. She seemed ill at ease and impatient.

Fidelma stood before the king, waiting with her hands quietly folded before her.

'I have need of a Brehon, Sister,' began Fáelán. 'Énna, here,' he motioned with his head towards his *tánaiste*, 'Énna told me that you were on the course with the Abbot Laisran.'

Fidelma still waited expectantly.

'Have you heard the news?' Énna interrupted his king who controlled a look of annoyance at the breach of protocol. As Fidelma turned her gaze, Fáelán continued before she could reply to the question.

'My champion jockey has been murdered and an attempt has been made to kill my best horse. The horse doctor tells me that the beast is already dying and will be dead before noon.'

'This much your guard told me,' Fidelma said. 'Also, I am informed that Bishop Bressal has been arrested.'

'On my orders,' confirmed the king. 'There is no one else who benefits from this outrage but Bressal. You see . . .'

Fidelma stayed his explanation with a small impatient gesture of her hand.

'I have heard of your disputes over the matter of horse racing. Why do you send for me? You have your own Brehon?'

Fáelán blinked at her unceremonious address.

'He is not in attendance today,' explained the king. 'And it is only permitted that a Brehon should decide whether there are grounds to hold the bishop so that he may be taken before the law courts. In the case of a bishop, who better qualified to this task than a *dálaigh* who is also a member of the religious?'

'Then let me hear the facts,' Fidelma assented. 'Who discovered the body of your jockey?'

'I did.'

It was Dagháin who spoke. She was, now that Fidelma had time to assess her closely, a rather plain-looking girl, blonde of hair, and with features which seemed without animation. The eyes were grey and cold but they did not shy away from her level gaze.

'Let me hear your story.'

Dagháin glanced towards the king as if seeking permission and, after he had nodded approvingly, she turned to Fidelma.

'It was an hour ago. I had just arrived for the races. I went into Illan's tent. I found Illan's body on the floor. He was dead. So I hurried to find my husband, who was with the king, and told them what I had seen.'

Dagháin's voice was matter of fact, without guile.

Fidelma examined her closely.

'Let us go through this more carefully,' she smiled. 'You arrived from where?'

It was Énna who answered.

'My wife and I had been staying at Dún Ailinn. I came on here early this morning to meet with Fáelán.'

Fidelma nodded.

'And what made you go directly to Illan's tent instead of coming to find your husband?'

Did Dagháin blush and hesitate a little?

'Why, I went first to see the horse, Aonbharr. He was raised in my husband's stables before he was sold to the king. I saw that he looked unwell and went to tell Illan.'

'And found him dead?'

'Yes. I was shocked. I did not know what to do and so I ran here.'

'Did you fall in your haste?' asked Fidelma.

'Yes, I did,' admitted the girl with a puzzled expression.

'And that would explain the disarray of your dress?' Fidelma's question was more rhetorical, but the woman nodded in hasty relief.

'I see. What was the cause of Illan's death, were you able to see? And how was he lying?'

Dagháin reflected.

'On his back. There was blood on his clothing but I did not see anything else. I was too intent to inform my husband.'

A sob caused Fidelma to glance up quickly to where the king's wife, Muadnat, was sitting, dabbing at her eyes with a piece of lace.

'You will forgive my wife,' interposed Fáelán quickly. 'She has a horror of violence and Illan was one of our household. Perhaps she can withdraw? She has no knowledge of these events and so cannot help your deliberations.'

Fidelma glanced at the woman and nodded. Muadnat forced a small grimace of relief and gratitude, rose and left with her female attendant.

Fidelma then turned to Énna.

'Do you agree with this record thus far?'

'It is as my wife says,' he confirmed. 'She came into our tent, where I was talking with Fáelán, in a state of distress telling us exactly what she has now told you.'

'And what did you do?'

Énna shrugged.

'I called some guards and went to the tent of Illan. He lay dead on the floor as Dagháin has described.'

'He was lying on his back?'

'That is so.'

'Very well. Continue. What then? Did you look for the cause of death?'

'Not closely. But it appeared that he had been stabbed in the lower part of the chest. I left a guard there and went with a second guard to the stable tent and saw Aonbharr. As Dagháin had said, the horse was obviously distressed. Its legs were splayed apart and its head depressed between its shoulders. There was froth around its muzzle. I know enough of horses to know that it was poisoned in some way. I called Cellach, the horse doctor, and told him to do what he could for the beast. Then I came back to report to Fáelán.'

Fidelma now turned to the king.

'And do you, Fáelán of the Uí Dúnlainge, agree that this is an accurate account thus far?'

'Thus far, it is as Dagháin and Énna have related,' confirmed the king.

'What then? At what point did you come to believe that the culprit responsible for these events was your own bishop, Bressal?'

Fáelán gave a loud bark of cynical laughter.

'At the very point I heard the news. This year my bishop has become obsessed with beating my horse, Aonbharr. He has made vain boasts, has wagered heavily and, indeed, is deeply in debt. He has put forward a horse to race Illan in the main race of today, a horse named Ochain. It is a good horse but it would not have stood a chance against Aonbharr. It became obvious that Bressal could not afford to lose against me. If Illan and Aonbharr did not run, then Ochain would win. It is as simple as that. And Bressal hated Illan, who was once his jockey.'

Fidelma smiled softly.

'It is a well-conceived suspicion but there is not enough evidence here to arrest nor charge a man, Fáelán. If it is only this suspicion which has caused your action, then my advice is to free Bressal immediately lest he cite the law against you.'

'There is more,' Énna said quietly, and motioned to the warrior of the Baoisgne who stood at the flap of the tent. The man went out and called to someone. A moment later, a large man with a bushy beard and rough clothes entered and bowed to the king and his *tánaiste*.

'Tell the Brehon your name and station,' Énna ordered.

The big man turned to Fidelma.

'I am Angaire, hostler to Bishop Bressal.'

Fidelma raised an eyebrow but controlled all other expression on her features.

'You are not a member of Bressal's community in Christ,' she observed.

'No, Sister. The bishop employed me because of my expertise with horses. I train his horse Ochain. But I am no religieux.'

Angaire was a confident man, smiling and sure of himself.

'Tell Sister Fidelma what you have told us,' prompted Énna.

'Well, Bressal has often boasted how Ochain would beat Aonbharr at this race and he has laid heavy wagers upon the outcome.'

'Get to the main point,' pressed Fáelán irritably.

'Well, this morning, I was preparing Ochain . . .'

'You were to ride him in this race?' interrupted Fidelma. 'I thought . . .'

The big man shook his head.

'Bressal's jockey is Murchad. I am only Ochain's trainer.'

Fidelma motioned him to continue.

'Well, I told Bressal that it was my opinion, having seen Aonbharr in a trial run yesterday, that Ochain would have difficulty in catching the beast on the straight. Bressal went berserk. I have never seen a man so angry. He would not listen to me and so I withdrew. Half-an-hour later I was passing the tent of Illan . . .'

'How did you know it was Illan's tent?' demanded Fidelma.

'Easy enough. Each jockey has a small banner outside showing the emblem of the owner of the horse he rides. The insignia of owners are important at such gatherings as this.'

Fáelán interrupted: 'This is true.'

'As I passed the tent I heard voices raised in anger. I recognised Bressal's voice at once. The other I presumed to be that of Illan.'

'What did you do?'

Angaire shrugged.

'No business of mine. I went on to Murchad's tent to advise him how best to handle the race, though I knew he had little chance against Illan.'

'Then?'

'As I was leaving Murchad's tent I saw . . .'

'How much later was this?' interjected Fidelma again.

Angaire blinked at the interruption.

'Ten minutes probably. I can't recall. Murchad and I did not speak for very long.'

'So what did you see?'

'I saw Bressal hurrying by. There was a red welt on his cheek. His face was suffused with anger. He did not see me. Furthermore, he was carrying something concealed under his cloak.'

'What sort of something?'

'It could have been a long, thin knife.'

Fidelma drew her brows together.

'What makes you say that? Describe what you saw exactly.'

'He held something long and thin in one hand, hidden under his cloak, it was no more than nine inches long but I have no idea of the width.'

'So you cannot take oath that it was a knife?' snapped Fidelma. 'I am not here to listen to surmise and guesses but only facts. What then?'

Angaire looked aggrieved for a moment and then shrugged.

'I went about my business until I heard a guard telling someone that Illan had been found dead in his tent. I felt it my duty to tell the guard what I knew.'

'That guard came to me,' Énna agreed. 'I later verified Angaire's story with him.'

'And I had Bressal arrested,' confirmed Fáelán as if it ended the matter.

'What has Bressal replied to these charges?' Fidelma asked.

'He has refused to speak until a Brehon is sent for,' the king replied. 'When Énna told me that you were on the course, I sent for you. Now you know as much as we. I think

I have the right to hold the bishop for trial. Will you see Bressal now?'

Fidelma surprised them by shaking her head.

'I will see the body of Illan. Has a physician been in attendance?'

'None, since Illan is dead.'

'Then one needs to be sent for. I want Illan's body examined. While that is being done, I shall see the horse, Aonbharr, and this horse doctor . . . what name did you say?'

'Cellach,' the king said. 'He attends all my horses.'

'Very well. Your guard may escort me to the place where the animal is stabled.' She turned to Abbot Laisran, who had remained quiet during the entire proceedings. 'Will you accompany me, Laisran? I have need of your advice.'

Outside as they walked in the direction which the warrior of the Baoisgne conducted them, Fidelma turned to Laisran.

'I wanted to speak to you. I noticed that Queen Muadnat seemed to be very upset by the death of Illan.'

'Your perception is keen, Fidelma,' agreed Laisran. 'For example, I did not even notice the disarray of Dagháin's clothes until you mentioned it. But Muadnat has obviously been weeping. The death of Illan has upset her.'

Fidelma smiled thinly.

'That much I know. You know more of the gossip of the court, however. Why would she be so upset?'

'Muadnat is a handsome woman with, by all accounts, a voracious appetite in sexual matters. Perhaps I should say no more for Fáelán is a tolerant monarch.'

'You are still speaking in riddles, Laisran,' sighed Fidelma.

'I am sorry. I thought you might have heard of Illan's reputation as a ladies' man. Illan was only one of many lovers who has graced the queen's entourage.'

When Fidelma and Laisran reached the stable tent in which Aonbharr was, the horse was lying on its side, its great breath coming in deep grunting pants. It was clearly nearing the end. A few men were gathered around it and one of these was Cellach, the horse doctor.

He was a thin man with a brown weather-beaten face and he regarded the sister with large, sad grey eyes. He was obviously upset by the suffering of the animal.

'Aonbharr is dying,' he replied to Fidelma's question.

'Can you confirm that the horse has been poisoned?'

Cellach grimaced angrily.

'It has. A mixture of wolfsbane, ground ivy leaves and mandrake root. That is my diagnosis, Sister.'

Fidelma stared at Cellach in surprise.

The man sniffed as he saw her scepticism.

'No magic in that, Sister.'

He reached toward the horse's muzzle and gently prised it open. There were flecks of blood and spittle around the discoloured gums. Amidst this mucus Fidelma could see speckles of the remains of feed.

'You can see the remnants of these poisons. Yes, someone fed the horse on a potent mixture.'

'When would such feed have been administered?' she asked.

'Not long ago,' replied Cellach. 'Within the last hour or so. Such a mixture on this beast would have an almost instantaneous effect.'

Fidelma laid a gentle hand on the big animal's muzzle and stroked it softly.

The great soft brown eyes flickered open, stared at her and then the beast let out a grunting breath.

'Are there no other signs of violence inflicted on it?' she asked.

Cellach shook his head.

'None, Sister.'

'Could Aonbharr have eaten some poisonous plants by accident?' asked Laisran.

Cellach shrugged.

'While tethered in its stable here? Hardly likely, Abbot. Even in the wilderness, horses are intelligent and sensitive creatures. They usually have a sense of things that will harm them. Apart from the fact that one would not find mandrake root nor wolfsbane around these parts. And how could it crush ivy leaves? No, this was a deliberate act.'

'Is there no hope for the animal?' asked Fidelma sadly.

Cellach grimaced and shook his head.

'It will be dead by noon,' he replied.

'I will see Illan's body now,' Fidelma said quietly, turning towards the tent of the king's jockey.

'Are you Sister Fidelma?'

As Fidelma entered the tent of Illan she found a religieuse straightening up from the body of the man who lay on his back on the floor. The woman was big boned with large hands and an irritable expression on her broad features. On Fidelma's acknowledgement she went on: 'I am Sister Eblenn, the apothecary from the community of the Blessed Darerca.'

'Have you examined the body of Illan?'

Sister Eblenn made a swift obeisance to Laisran as he entered the tent before answering Fidelma.

'Yes. A fatal stabbing. One wound in the heart.'

Fidelma exchanged a glance with the abbot.

'Is there sign of the knife?'

'The wound was not made by a knife, Sister.' The apothecary was confident.

Fidelma controlled her irritation at the pause.

'Then by what?' she demanded, when there had been a sufficient silence and the religieuse had made no attempt to amplify her statement.

Sister Eblenn pointed to the table. A broken arrow lay on it. It was the front half of the arrow, about nine inches, of the shaft and head. It was splintered where the shaft had been snapped in two.

Fidelma reached forward and took up the section of arrow. She could see that it was covered with blood and it was clear that Sister Eblenn had taken it from the wound.

'Are you telling us that Illan was stabbed in the heart with this arrow?' intervened Abbot Laisran. 'Stabbed, you say, not shot with the arrow?'

Sister Eblenn pursed her lips and regarded him dourly.

'Have I not said so?' she asked petulantly.

Fidelma's voice was brittle.

'No; so far you have not explained matters at all. Tell us what you have discovered and be specific.'

Eblenn blinked. She was obviously unused to people questioning her. She was given to assuming knowledge on the part of others and did not explain herself clearly. She flushed angrily at the rebuke.

'The dead man,' she began slowly, speaking in wooden but distinct tones, like a child explaining the obvious, 'was stabbed in the heart. The instrument was this arrow. Whoever killed him thrust the arrow under the rib cage, avoiding the sternum and thrusting with some force upwards so that it entered the heart. Death was instantaneous. There was little bleeding.'

'Why do you discount the arrow being shot into the body?' insisted Abbot Laisran.

'The angle of incision is of such a degree that it would be impossible unless the archer was standing five feet away and shooting upwards at a forty-five degree angle at least five feet below the target. There is also the fact that the arrow snapped in two. I believe the impact of the blow, the arrow gripped hard in the hand of the attacker, was the cause of its breaking.'

'I presume that you cut out the arrowhead?'

Eblenn pursed her thin lips and shook her head.

'The head is part of the shaft, simply a carved wooden point. I did not cut the arrow out at all but merely pulled it out. As it went in, so it came out. It was easy enough.'

Fidelma sighed deeply.

'So that when you came to examine the body, the arrow was in two pieces? One in the body, the other . . . where was that exactly?'

Sister Eblenn looked suddenly startled and peered around as if seeking the answer.

'I do not know. I presume it is somewhere about.'

Fidelma bit her lip. Extracting information from Sister Eblenn was like fishing for trout. One had to cast about blindly.

For a moment or two she stood looking down at the arrow. She became aware that Sister Eblenn was speaking.

'What?'

'I said, I must return to my apothecary's tent. I have already had one theft this morning and do not want to chance another.'

Fidelma swung round with sudden interest.

'What was taken from your tent?'

'Some herbs, that is all. But herbs cost money.'

'And these herbs – were they mandrake root, wolfsbane and crushed ivy?'

'Ah, you have spoken to the lady Dagháin.'

Fidelma's eyes rounded slightly.

'What has the lady Dagháin to do with this matter?'

'Nothing. She was passing my tent just after I discovered the theft. I asked her to inform her husband as the *tánaiste* has charge of the royal guards.'

'When exactly was this?'

'Just after the breakfast hour. Early this morning. Queen Muadnat had come by requesting a balm for a headache. It was soon after that I noticed the herbs were gone. Then, as I was going to breakfast, I saw the lady Dagháin and told her.'

After Sister Eblenn had left, still showing some bewilderment, Laisran grimaced.

'So now we know where the killer obtained the poison from.'

Fidelma nodded absently. While Laisran watched silently, she lowered herself to her knees and began to examine the body. Then she motioned Laisran to join her.

'Look at the wound, Laisran,' she said. 'It seems our Sister Eblenn is not as perceptive as she should be.'

Laisran peered closely to where Fidelma indicated.

'No pointed arrowhead made that wound,' he agreed after a moment. 'It is more of a gash, such as a broad-bladed knife would have made.'

'Exactly so,' agreed Fidelma.

For a while she searched all around the body in ever increasing circles to cover the whole floor of the tent. There was nothing on the floor except for a leather *cena*, a medium-sized bag, which she placed on a table top. She could not find what she was expecting to discover and climbed back to her feet. She took up the splintered arrow again and stared at it as if perplexed. Then she thrust it into the *marsupium* or purse which she always carried.

She gazed down to study Illan's features for a final time. Laisran was right; he had been a handsome young man. But his face was a little too handsome to attract her. She could imagine the self-satisfaction of his expression while he was in life.

Abbot Laisran coughed, as if to remind her of his presence.

'Do you have any ideas?' he asked.

She smiled at her old mentor.

'None that makes sense at this moment.'

'While you have been examining the corpse, I have examined this *cena* which you found in a corner of the tent. I think that you'd better look in it.'

Frowning, Fidelma did so. There was a mixture of herbs inside. She picked out a handful and sniffed suspiciously. Then she turned to Laisran with wide eyes.

'Are they what I suspect them to be?' she asked.

'Yes,' confirmed Laisran. 'Mandrake root, wolfsbane and ivy leaves. Moreover, there is a small insignia on the *cena* and it is not the same one as I noticed on Sister Eblenn's apothecary's bag.'

Fidelma pursed her lips as though to whistle but did not do so.

'This is a mystery that goes deep, Laisran,' she reflected slowly. 'We must discover the owner of the insignia.'

Énna suddenly entered the tent.

'Ah, there you are, Sister. Have you seen enough here?'

'I have seen all that I can see,' Fidelma replied.

She gestured down at Illan's body. 'A sad end for one who was so young and talented in his profession.'

Énna sniffed deprecatingly.

'Many a husband would not agree with you, Sister.'

'Ah? You mean the queen?' Laisran smiled.

Énna blinked rapidly and looked embarrassed. Many knew of the gossip of Muadnat's affairs but none in the court circle would openly discuss them.

'Doubtless,' he turned to Fidelma, 'you will want to see Bishop Bressal now? He is upset that you have not gone directly to see him.'

Fidelma suppressed a sigh.

'Before we do so, Énna, perhaps you can help. I believe, as *tánaiste*, that you have a knowledge of insignia, don't you?'

Énna made an affirmative gesture.

'What insignia is this?' Fidelma showed him the *cena* Laisran had discovered.

Énna didn't hesitate.

'That is the insignia of Bishop Bressal's household.'

Fidelma's lips thinned while Laisran could not hold back an audible gasp.

'I would not wish to keep the good bishop waiting longer than is necessary,' Fidelma said, with soft irony in her voice. 'We will see him now.'

'Well, Bressal, tell me your story,' invited Fidelma as she seated herself before the agitated portly figure of the king of Laighin's bishop. Bressal was a large, heavily built man, with pale, baby-like features and a balding head. One of the first things she noticed was that Bressal had a red welt on his left cheek.

Bressal frowned at the young religieuse before glancing across to acknowledge Abbot Laisran who had followed her into the tent and taken a stand with folded arms by the tent flap. The only other occupant of the tent was a tall warrior of Bressal's personal household, for the bishop's rank and position entitled him to a bodyguard.

'You have seated yourself in my presence without permission, Sister,' Bressal thundered ominously.

Fidelma regarded him calmly.

'I may be seated in the presence of any provincial king without permission,' she informed him icily. 'I am a *dálaigh*, an advocate of the courts, qualified to the level of *Anruth*. Therefore, I can sit even in the presence of the High King, though with his permission. I am . . .'

Bressal waved a hand in annoyance. He was well informed on the rules of the rank and privileges of the Brehons.

'Very well *Anruth*. Why were you not here sooner? The sooner I am heard, the sooner I can be released from this outrageous imprisonment.'

Fidelma eyed the bishop with distaste. Bressal was certainly a haughty man. She could well believe the stories that she had heard about him and this vanity of racing against the King of Laighin's horse.

'If you wish speed and urgency in this matter, it would be better to answer my questions without interpolating any of your own. Now, to this matter . . .'

'Is it not clear?' demanded the bishop with outrage in his voice. 'Fáelán is trying to blame me for something that I have not done. That much is simple. He has probably done this evil deed himself to discredit me, knowing my horse would have beaten his.'

Fidelma sat back with raised eyebrows.

'Counter accusations come better when you can demonstrate your own innocence. Tell me of your movements this morning.'

Bressal bit his lip and was about to argue, then he shrugged and flung himself onto a chair.

'I came to the race track with my personal guard, Sílán,' he gestured to the silent warrior. 'We came straightaway to see Ochain, my horse.'

'Who had brought Ochain here?'

'Why, Angaire, my trainer, and Murchad, my rider.'

'At what time was this? Tell me in relationship to the finding of Illan's body.'

'I do not know when it was discovered but I was here about an hour before that oaf Fáelán had me arrested.'

'And did you see anyone else apart from Angaire and Murchad in that time?'

Bressal sniffed in annoyance.

'There were many people at the track. Many who might well have seen me but who they were I cannot remember.'

'I mean, did you engage with anyone else in conversation; anyone in particular . . . Illan himself, for example?'

Bressal stared back at her and then shook his head. She could see that he was lying by the light of anxiety in his dark eyes.

'So you did not speak to Illan this morning?' pressed Fidelma.

'I have said as much.'

'Think carefully, Bressal. Did you not go to his tent and speak with him?'

Bressal stared at her and a look of guilty resignation spread over his features.

'A man of God should not lie, Bressal,' admonished Laisran from the entrance. 'Least of all, a bishop.'

'I did not kill Illan,' the man said stubbornly.

'How did you obtain that recent scar on your left cheek?' Fidelma demanded abruptly.

Bressal raised his hand automatically.

'I . . .' He stopped suddenly, apparently unable to think of an adequate reply. His shoulders slumped and he seemed to grow smaller in his chair, looking like a defeated man.

'Truth is the best refuge in adversity,' Fidelma advised coldly.

'It is true that I went to Illan's tent and argued with him. It is true that he struck me.' Bressal's voice was sullen.

'And did you strike him back?'

'Is it not written in the Gospel of Luke: "Unto him that smiteth thee on the one cheek offer also the other"?' parried Bressal.

'That which is written is not always obeyed. Am I to take it that you, who are obviously a man who is not poor in spirit, did not retaliate when Illan struck you?'

'I left Illan alive,' muttered Bressal.

'But you did strike him?'

'Of course I did,' snapped Bressal. 'The dog dared to strike me, a prince and bishop of Laighin!'

Fidelma sighed deeply.

'And why did he strike you?'

'I . . . roused his anger.'

'Your argument was to do with the fact that he had once been your rider and had left your service to ride for Fáelán?'

Bressal was surprised.

'You seem to know many things, Sister Fidelma.'

'So how did you leave Illan?'

'I hit him on the jaw and he fell unconscious. Our conversation had thus ended and so I left. I did not kill him.'

'How did the argument arise?'

Bressal hung his head shamefully but having embarked on the path of truth he decided to maintain it to the end.

'I went to his tent to offer him money to stand down from the race and return his allegiance to me.'

'Did anyone else know of your intention to bribe Illan?'

'Yes; Angaire did.'

'Your trainer?' Fidelma thought hard for a moment.

'I told Angaire that I was not happy with the way he was training my horse, Ochain. I told him that if I could persuade Illan to return, then he could look elsewhere for a job. In all my races this year, Angaire has failed to provide me with a winner.'

Fidelma turned to the silent warrior within the tent.

'How much of this story can you confirm, Sílán?'

For a moment the warrior stared at her in surprise. He glanced to Bressal, as if seeking his permission to speak.

'Tell them what happened this morning,' snapped Bressal.

Sílán stood stiffly before Fidelma, his eyes focused in the middle distance and his voice wooden in its recital.

'I came to the Curragh at . . .'

'Have you been personal guard to the bishop for a long time?' interrupted Fidelma. She disliked rehearsed speeches and when she sensed one she liked to interrupt and put the reciter out of stride.

'I have,' replied the surprised guard. 'For one year, Sister.'

'Go on.'

'I came to the Curragh not long after dawn to help set up the bishop's tent.'

'Did you see Illan at this time?'

'Surely. There were many people here already. The bishop, also Angaire, Murchad, Illan, even Fáelán and his queen and the *tánaiste* . . .'

Fidelma was not looking at his face. Her eyes had fastened thoughtfully on the quiver at the guard's side. One arrow seemed shorter than the others. Its feathered flight seemed to be sinking into the quiver among the other arrows.

'Turn out your quiver!' she suddenly ordered.

'What?'

Sílán was gazing at her, clearly amazed at her behaviour. Even Bressal was staring as if she had gone mad.

'Turn out the arrows in your quiver and place them on the table here before me,' instructed Fidelma.

Frowning, the warrior did so with no further hesitation.

Fidelma seized upon a shaft of an arrow. It was snapped off and only some six inches with its tail feathered flight remained. There was no need for Fidelma to look for the other half among the rest of the arrows.

They watched in silent fascination as Fidelma took from her *marsupium* the section of the arrow which had been found by Sister Eblenn in the body of Illan. She carefully brought the two pieces together before their fixed gaze. They fitted almost perfectly.

'You seem to be in a great deal of trouble, Sílán,' Fidelma said slowly. 'The head of your arrow was buried in the wound that killed Illan.'

'I did not do it!' gasped the warrior in horror.

'Is this one of your arrows?' Fidelma asked, holding out the two halves.

'What do you mean?' interrupted Bressal.

Laisran came forward with interest.

'The design on the flights are the same.'

Sílán was nodding.

'Yes, it is obviously one of my arrows. Anyone will tell you that it bears the emblem of the bishop's household.'

Fidelma turned to Laisran.

'Place the *cena* that we found in Illan's tent on the table, Laisran.'

The abbot did as she bid him.

Fidelma pointed to the insignia.

'And this emblem, being the same as on the arrow flight, is also the emblem of Bishop Bressal?'

Bressal shrugged.

'What of it? All the members of my household carry my insignia. Such bags as these are saddle bags, freely available among those who serve my stables.'

'Would it surprise you that this contains the mixture of poisonous herbs used to poison Aonbharr?'

Sílán and Bressal were silent.

'It could be argued that Sílán killed Illan and poisoned Aonbharr on the orders of his master, Bishop Bressal,' suggested Fidelma as if musing with an idea.

'I did not!'

'And I gave him no such order,' cried Bressal, his face turning white in horror.

'If you confessed that you were acting on the orders of Bressal,' Fidelma went on, speaking softly to Sílán, 'little blame would attach to you.'

Sílán shook his head stubbornly.

'I had no such orders and did not do this thing.'

Fidelma turned to Bressal.

'The evidence was circumstantial in the first place, Bishop. Yet, circumstantial as it is, it is against you. The evidence of this arrow and the *cena*, containing the poisons, now seems hard to refute.'

Bressal was clearly perturbed. He turned to Sílán.

'Did you slay Illan of your own volition?' he demanded.

The warrior shook his head violently and turned pleading eyes upon Fidelma. She could see the innocence in his face. The guard was clearly shocked at the evidence against him and his bishop.

'I am at a loss to explain this,' he said inadequately.

'Tell me, Sílán, have you carried your quiver of arrows all morning?'

Sílán paused to give thought to the question.

'Not all morning. I left my quiver and bow in the bishop's tent most of the morning while I had errands to run.'

'What kind of errands?'

'To find Murchad, for example. I found him talking with Angaire near Illan's tent at the time we saw the lady Dagháin come out, white-faced, and go running to her tent. I remember that Angaire passed some unseemly and lewd remark. I left Angaire and returned here with Murchad.'

'So the quiver of arrows was in this tent while you went to find the bishop's jockey at the bishop's request?' Fidelma summed up. 'The bishop was alone in the tent, then?'

Once more a look of indignation caused Bressal's face to flush.

'If you are saying that I took an arrow and went to kill Illan . . .' he began.

'Yet you were alone in this tent at that time?'

'Some of the time,' admitted Bressal. 'Sílán left his weapons most of the morning and we were constantly in and out of the tent. Also, there were visitors coming and going. Why, even Fáelán and his wife, Muadnat, were here for a moment.'

Fidelma was surprised. 'Why would he come here? You had become bitter rivals.'

'Fáelán merely wanted to boast about Aonbharr.'

'Was that before or after you had your argument with Illan?'

'Before.'

'And Muadnat was with him?'

'Yes. Then Énna came by.'

'What for?'

'To beg me to withdraw Ochain from the race, saying my argument with Fáelán was an embarrassment to the kingdom. This was pointless. Angaire and Murchad were here as well . . .'

'Was Énna's wife, the lady Dagháin, one of your visitors?' queried Fidelma.

The bishop shook his head.

'However, if you are looking for an opportunity to take an arrow and kill Illan, why, several people had that opportunity.'

'And what about the *cena* full of poison herbs?'

'All I can say is that it bears my insignia but I have no knowledge of it.'

Fidelma smiled thinly and turned to Laisran. 'Walk with me a moment.'

Bressal stared at her in outrage as she made to leave his tent.

'What do you propose to do?' he demanded.

Fidelma glanced across her shoulder towards him.

'I propose to finish my investigation, Bressal,' she said shortly, before stepping through the flap, followed by the bewildered Laisran.

Outside, Fáelán had posted several of his élite guards to keep the bishop a prisoner.

'You do not like the good bishop,' Laisran reflected once they were outside.

Fidelma gave her urchin-like grin.

'The bishop is not a likeable man.'

'And the evidence weighs heavily against him,' went on Laisran, as he fell into step with the religieuse. 'Surely that evidence is now conclusive?'

Fidelma shook her head.

'If Bressal or Sílán had used the arrow to kill Illan then neither would have kept hold of the incriminating half of the arrow so that it could be found so easily.'

'But, it makes sense. Either one of them could have stabbed Illan with the arrow. Then, realising that the design on the flight would betray them, they broke off the arrow and took the incriminating part away with them . . .'

Fidelma smiled gently. 'Leaving the *cena* with the poison and its insignia conspicuously in Illan's tent? No, my good mentor, if they were that clever then they would have simply destroyed the arrow. There are enough braziers in which to have burnt it. Why place it invitingly back in the quiver where it would easily be discovered? And they would have rid themselves of the *cena*. Also, my friend, in the excitement you have forgotten the very fact that neither Bressal nor Sílán appears to be aware of, and which demonstrates their innocence.'

Laisran looked bewildered.

'What fact?'

'The fact that the arrow was placed in the wound after Illan was dead in order to mislead us. The fact that Illan was killed by a dagger thrust and not by stabbing with the arrow.'

Laisran clapped a hand to his head. He had forgotten that very point in the agitation of Fidelma's cross-examination of Bressal and Sílán.

'Are you suggesting that there is some plot to make Bressal appear guilty?'

'I am,' confirmed Fidelma.

Laisran looked at her thunderstruck.

'Then who . . .?' His eyes widened. 'Surely you are not suggesting that the king . . .? Are you saying that Fáelán might have feared that his horse would not win against Bressal's horse and so he contrived this intricate plot . . .?'

Fidelma pursed her lips.

'Your hypothesis is good but there is more work to be done before it can be used in argument.'

Énna was suddenly blocking their path.

'Have you seen Bressal, Sister?' he greeted, and when she nodded he smiled grimly. 'Has he now confessed his guilt?'

Fidelma regarded him for a moment.

'So you believe him to be guilty?'

Énna stood back in surprise.

'*Believe?* Surely there is no doubt?'

'Under our laws, one must be proven guilty of the offence unless one confesses that guilt. Bressal does not accept any guilt. My investigation must show proof against him.'

'Then that is not difficult.'

'You think not?' Énna looked uncomfortable at her mocking tone. 'I would have everyone concerned now gather in Fáelán's tent: Bressal, Sílán, Angaire, Murchad, Fáelán and Muadnat, yourself and Dagháin. There I will reveal the result of my investigation.'

As Énna hurried away, Fidelma turned to Laisran.

'Wait for me at Fáelán's tent, I will not be long.' At Laisran's look of interrogation, she added: 'I have to look for something to complete my speculation.'

★ ★ ★

At Fidelma's request they had all crowded into the tent of Fáelán of the Uí Dúnlainge, King of Laighin.

'This has been a most perplexing mystery,' she began when the king signalled her to speak. 'What seemed simple at first began to become mysterious and obscure. That was until now.'

Fidelma smiled broadly at them.

'And now?' It was Fáelán who prompted her.

'Now all the pieces of the puzzle fit together. Firstly, the evidence against Bressal is overwhelming.'

There was a gasp of outrage from Bressal.

'It is not true. I am not guilty,' he protested indignantly.

Fidelma raised her hand for silence.

'I did not say that you were. Only that the evidence against you was overwhelming. However, if you had been guilty, or, indeed, if Sílán had carried out the deed for you, then you would have known that Illan had not been stabbed with an arrow but with a dagger. Only the real killer knew this and the person who placed the arrow in the wound. The arrow was a false scent planted in an attempt to lay a path to Bressal. It was obvious, therefore, that someone wanted me to find that evidence and draw the inevitable but wrong conclusion.'

Bressal gave a deep sigh and relaxed for the first time. Sílán, behind him, looked less defensive.

'I first approached this matter from the viewpoint of the motive, which seemed obvious,' went on Fidelma. 'What immediately sprang to all minds was the idea that both Illan and the horse, Aonbharr, had been killed to prevent them taking part in the race today. Who would benefit by this? Well, Bressal, of course, for his horse, Ochain, and Murchad, his jockey, were the only serious contenders in the race other than Illan and Aonbharr. So if Bressal was not guilty, who could it have been? Who would benefit? Was it Murchad, who had laid a large wager on his winning? Laisran had already witnessed Murchad earlier this morning placing heavy wagers on himself to win.'

'No law against that!

Murchad had flushed angrily but Fidelma ignored him and went on: 'Obviously it was not Murchad for he did not have a motive. He would only have collected his winnings if he had won the race which essentially meant taking part in it. If he had murdered Illan, poisoned Aonbharr and left the trail of false clues to Bressal, then it would be obvious that Bressal would be arrested and his horse and Murchad would be disqualified from racing. That being so, Murchad would have forfeited his wager.'

Murchad nodded slowly in agreement and relief. Fidelma went blithely on.

'If not Murchad, what of Angaire, the trainer? He was not doing well for Bressal and had been told this very morning that Bressal was going to get rid of him. Bressal had made no secret of the fact that he had gone to see Illan in an attempt to persuade him to return to his stable and ride for him instead of Fáelán. Angaire had a better motive than Murchad.'

Angaire shifted uneasily where he stood. But Fidelma continued.

'You see, sticking to the line of argument about the horse race as the motive, there was only one other person with a motive who might benefit from putting the blame on Bressal.'

She turned towards Fáelán, the king. He stared at her in astonishment which swiftly grew into anger.

'Wait,' she cut his protests short. 'Such a plot was too convoluted. Besides everyone was of the opinion that Aonbharr could out-distance Ochain. There was no challenge there to be worried about. So there was no motive.'

She paused and looked around at their perplexed faces.

'It eventually became clear that the killing of Illan was not caused by rivalries on the race track. There was another motive for that crime. But was it the same motive as that for poisoning Aonbharr?'

They were all silent now, waiting for her to continue.

'The motive for Illan's death was as ageless as time. Unrequited love. Illan was young, handsome and his reputation among women was such that he had many lovers. He picked them up as one might pick up flowers, kept them until the affair withered and then threw them away. Am I not right?'

Fáelán was pale and he glanced surreptitiously at Muadnat.

'That is no crime, Fidelma. In our society, many still take second wives, husbands or lovers.'

'True enough. But one of the flowers which Illan had picked was not ready to be discarded. She went to his tent this morning and argued with him. And when he spurned her, when he said he would have no more to do with her, she, in a fit of rage, stabbed him to death. All it needed was one swift dagger blow under the rib cage.'

'If this is so,' said Énna, quietly, 'why would she go to such lengths to put the blame on Bressal? Why poison Aonbharr? The laws of our society allow leniency to those who perpetrate such crimes of passion.'

Fidelma inclined her head.

'A case could be made that any non-fatal injury inflicted by the woman in such circumstances does not incur liability. Our laws recognise the stirring of uncontrollable passion in such circumstances. In the matter of death she would be fined her victim's honour price only. No other punishment would be necessary.'

'Then why, if this were so, did the woman conceal her crime, for the concealment brings forth greater punishment?' repeated Énna.

'Because there were two separate villainies at work here and one fed off the initial deed of the other,' replied Fidelma.

'I don't understand. Who killed Illan?' Fáelán again glanced uneasily at his wife. 'You say it was a woman. By attempting to conceal the crime such a woman, no matter her rank, if found guilty would be placed into a boat with one paddle and a vessel of gruel and the mercy of God. Sister Fidelma,' his voice suddenly broke with passion, 'is it Muadnat of whom you speak?'

Fáelán's wife sat as if turned to stone.

Fidelma did not reply immediately but drew out of her *marsupium* a belt with a bejewelled ceremonial sheath. There was a small dagger in it. She took out the dagger and handed it to Muadnat.

'Does the dagger belong to you, my lady?'

'It is mine,' Muadnat replied grimly.

Fáelán gasped in horror, as if his worst fears were confirmed.

'Then . . .?' he began. Fidelma was shaking her head.

'No, Dagháin killed Illan.'

There was a gasp of astonishment from the company and all eyes turned on the flushed face of Énna's wife. Dagháin sat stunned for a moment by the revelation. Then, as if in a dream, she slowly rose to her feet and looked about her, as if searching someone out. 'Liar! Betrayer!' she hissed venomously. Fidelma glanced quickly in the direction of the woman's gaze and felt satisfied.

Dagháin now turned towards her and cursed her in a way which left no one in doubt as to her guilt. Énna had simply collapsed into a chair, immobile with shock.

After Dagháin had been removed to a place of confinement, Fidelma had to raise her hands to quell the questions that were thrown at her.

'Dagháin was seen coming to the Curragh early this morning. The apothecary, Sister Eblenn, saw her soon after she had been robbed which was just after breakfast. Dagháin therefore lied when she said that she had come later in the morning to the course. That lie alerted my suspicions. A suspicion which was increased when I realised that the arrow was not the murder weapon but the wound had been made by a dagger. When I first came before Fáelán, Muadnat had been wearing a ceremonial dagger sheath yet there was no dagger in it.'

'This I don't understand,' Fáelán said. 'Surely this would lay suspicion on Muadnat?'

'Indeed, I was suspicious for a while, that I admit. But it was obvious to my eye that the dagger in Dagháin's sheath was too small to fit comfortably. That I had to work out. Then I realised that she, at some stage, had put Muadnat's dagger in her sheath, is that not so?'

Muadnat spoke softly.

'She wanted an apple to calm her nerves and asked me for the loan of my dagger, saying she had mislaid her own. It was only a moment ago that I realised Dagháin had not returned it.'

'Dagháin,' Fidelma went on, 'in her description of the finding of Illan, said that she had run straight to tell Énna. Yet she was seen running from his tent directly to her own. I searched her tent a moment ago. Thankfully, she had discarded her ceremonial belt and sheath. I was confirmed in my suspicion that the dagger did not belong to her but was that of Muadnat.'

'Then where was Dagháin's own dagger?' demanded Laisran, intrigued.

'I found it where I suspected it would be, the blade still covered with Illan's blood. It was in Angaire's saddle bag.'

Angaire, with a cry of rage, made to jump to the tent door, but one of the Baoisgne, the king's guards, stayed him with a drawn sword to his chest. Fidelma continued without taking any notice of the drama.

'While Angaire did not kill Illan, he did poison Aonbharr, and then tried to place the guilt for both deeds on Bressal by planting the arrow and *cena* as evidence. Angaire's actions obscured the real murderer of Illan. You see Angaire knew that he was about to be discarded by Bressal. I have already given you his motive. Bressal had been quite open in his intention to replace Angaire. Indeed, even though Illan had refused Bressal's offer to return to his stable, Angaire's days as trainer were still numbered.

'Angaire had, I believe, already devised a plan to hurt Bressal. I believe his original intention was to poison Ochain. For that end, he stole some poisonous plants from the tent of Sister Eblenn early this morning. Then the mysteries of Fate itself took over. Angaire overheard Bressal arguing with Illan. But the plot did not occur to him then.

'It was only when he was with Murchad and Sílán a little while later that he saw Dagháin fleeing from Illan's tent. Her dress was dishevelled and the ceremonial dagger missing. She fled to her own tent. He made a lewd remark, an automatic remark. His companions, Sílán and Murchad, were leaving. Perhaps even before then the thought struck him that his unthinking remark might be true and what if . . . his mind was thinking about the missing dagger.

'He went to Illan's tent. There was Dagháin's knife buried in Illan's chest. His suspicion was right. He took out the knife with the idea growing in his mind. Here was his chance to get even with Bressal and to secure a future lucrative role for himself in the service of Dagháin. He hurried to her tent, showed her the knife, which he kept as a hold over her. He told her to wait a while before she should find her husband and tell him the story which she has subsequently told us. The reason for her to be in Illan's tent was that she had noticed that Aonbharr was ill. This was Angaire's addition, providing a perfect excuse and an essential part of his intrigue.

'Then he hurried to Bressal's tent, furtively took an arrow from Sílán's quiver, broke it in two, and left one half in the quiver. The other he took, together with his *cena* full of poisonous herbs, and hurried to his task. He fed Aonbharr the poison. Then he went into Illan's tent and thrust the forward section of the broken arrow into the wound. He left the *cena* in plain sight. The false trail was laid.

'Thus two separate villainies were at work, coming together over the one great crime. And who is the greater villain – Dagháin, a pitiful, rejected woman, or Angaire, petty and vengeful, whose spite might have led to an even greater crime? I tell you this, Fáelán, when the time comes for Dagháin to be tried before the courts, I would like to be retained as her advocate.'

'But what made you connect Dagháin with Illan?' demanded Fáelán.

'Énna himself indicated that his wife had had an affair with Illan by a chance remark. You knew of the affair, didn't you, Énna?'

Énna glanced up from his chair, red-eyed with emotional exhaustion. He nodded slowly.

'I knew. I did not know that she was so besotted with Illan that she would resort to such means to keep him when he finally rejected her,' he whispered. 'Fáelán, I will stand down as your *tánaiste*. I am not worthy now.'

The King of Laighin grimaced.

'We will talk of this, Énna,' he said, with considerable discomfiture, studiously ignoring his wife, Muadnat. 'I am not without sympathy for your situation. There are doubtless several victims in this terrible drama. Yet I still do not understand why Dagháin would do this thing. She was the wife of a *tánaiste*, heir presumptive to the throne of the Laighin, while Illan was merely a jockey. How could she behave thus simply because Illan rejected her for a new lover?'

The question was aimed at Fidelma.

'There is nothing simple about the complexity of human emotions, Fáelán,' replied Fidelma. 'But if we are to seek the real victim then it is the poor beast Aonbharr. Truly, Aonbharr was a horse that died in an attempt to conceal the shame of others.'

A trumpet sounded outside.

Fáelán bit his lip and sighed.

'That is the signal for me to open the afternoon's race . . . my heart is not in it.'

He rose and automatically held out his arm to Muadnat, his wife. She hesitated before taking it, not looking at her husband. There would be much to mend in that relationship, thought Fidelma. Then Fáelán turned and called to his bishop:

'Bressal, will you come with us? Stand alongside me while I open the proceedings so that the people will clearly see that we are together and are not enemies? As neither of our horses can now enter this race, let us show unity to our people for this day at least.'

Bressal hesitated before nodding his reluctant agreement.

'I'll send your fee to Kildare, Fidelma,' Fáelán called over his shoulder. 'I thank God we have Brehons as wise as you.'

After they had left the tent, Énna slowly rose. He stared at Fidelma and Laisran with sad eyes for a moment.

'I knew she was having an affair. I would have stood by her, even resigned my office for her as I will now. I would not have divorced nor rejected her had she come to me with the truth. I will continue to stand by her.'

Fidelma and Laisran silently watched him leave the tent.

'Sad,' remarked Fidelma. 'It is, indeed, a sad world.'

They left the tent and began walking through the shouting, carefree masses, milling towards the race course. Fidelma smiled thinly at Laisran.

'As you were saying, Laisran, horse racing is a cure for all the ills of humankind. It is a surrogate for people's aggression and for their greed.'

Laisran grimaced wryly but was wisely silent before the cynical gaze of his protégée.

At the Tent of Holofernes

∽

S ister Fidelma halted her mare where the track curved
round the shoulder of the hill and gazed down at the
broad valley below. The placid light-blue strip of a river
wound its way through the valley, among the green culti-
vated clan lands of the Uí Dróna. She saw the grey granite
walls of the *ráth*, which was her goal, and her dust-stained
features formed into a tired smile of anticipation. She had
been four days on the road from the monastery of Durrow.
She was tired and uncomfortable with the dust of travel. Yet
it was not simply the prospect of the comforts of a bath,
fresh clothes, and a rest from being on horseback that caused
her to smile. It was the thought of seeing Liadin again.

Fidelma had been an only daughter with elder brothers,
and Liadin, her childhood friend, had been as a sister to her.
The bonding had been strong. They had reached the 'age of
choice' together when they had, under law, become women.
At that time Fidelma had become *anamchara*, the 'soul
friend', to Liadin: her spiritual guide according to the
practice of the faith in Ireland.

Now, in her pocket, there reposed an urgent message from
Liadin which had been delivered to Fidelma at Durrow a
week ago. It read: 'Come at once! I am greatly troubled.
Liadin.' Now as she reached her journey's end, Fidelma felt
both anticipation at the reunion and apprehension.

Fidelma had not seen her friend for several years. Their paths had eventually separated, for Fidelma had gone to Tara to continue her studies while Liadin had taken the path of marriage.

Fidelma remembered Liadin's trepidation at marriage, for it had been Liadin's father, a petty chieftain of Cashel, who had agreed to an arranged marriage as a matter of political expedience. Liadin's wish had been to become a teacher. She had a good knowledge of Greek and Latin and other studies. The marriage was to a foreign chieftain. He was a Gaul named Scoriath of the Fir Morc who had been driven into exile from his own lands. Scoriath had been granted sanctuary in the clan lands of the Uí Dróna in Laigin. It was the chieftain of the Uí Dróna who had interceded with Liadin's father and persuaded him of the political and financial advantage in marrying his daughter to the Gaulish warrior. He had made Scoriath captain of his bodyguard.

At the time, Fidelma's heart had been heavy for her unfortunate soul-friend, forced into such a marriage. Their paths continued on separate courses as Fidelma pursued her studies, eventually being admitted as a *dálaigh*, an advocate, of the law courts of Ireland.

After Liadin's marriage, Fidelma had met her friend only once and she was replete with happiness for she had, in spite of expectations, fallen in love with her husband. Fidelma had been astonished at her friend's transformation. Liadin and Scoriath's joining, so far as Fidelma could assess from her friend's enthusiasm, was that of a vine to a tree. Fidelma rejoiced in her friend's happiness and in the subsequent birth of her son. Then their paths separated again.

The child must be three years old now, Fidelma reflected, guiding her mount towards the fortress of the Uí Dróna. What could ail Liadin to make her send such a message?

Fidelma had observed that the man had been watching her approach for an hour, ever since she had rounded the

shoulder of the hill and ridden carefully down into the valley
towards the dark, brooding walls of the fortress. He lounged
by the gate of the *ráth* with folded arms and made no
attempt to change his position as she approached and halted
her mount.

'What do you seek here?' he demanded gruffly.

Fidelma gazed down at him with irritation.

'Is this the *ráth* of the Uí Dróna?' she demanded.

The man motioned assertively with his head.

'Then I demand entrance.'

'On what business?'

'On my own business.' Her voice was soft but dangerous.

'I am Conn, *tanist* of the Uí Dróna. My business is to
know your business here,' was the implacable response. A
tanist was the heir-elect of a chieftain.

Fidelma was unperturbed. 'I am come to see Liadin. I am
Fidelma of Kildare.'

Fidelma was aware of a momentary change of expression
on the man's face. She had a curious feeling that it was a
look of relief but it was gone before she was sure. The *tanist*
shifted his weight upright.

'I regret, Sister, that Liadin is being heard before the
Brehon Rathend even as we speak.'

Sister Fidelma's features re-formed into an expression of
surprise.

'Being *heard*? Do you mean that she pleads a case in law
before the Brehon?'

The *tanist* hesitated. 'In a way. She pleads her innocence.'

'Innocence? Of what is she accused?'

'Liadin is accused of the murder of her husband, Scoriath
of the Fir Morc, and of her own son.'

The Brehon Rathend was tall and thin, with pale, bloodless-
looking skin. The learned judge had hooded dark eyes with
shadowy pouches under them which seemed to suggest that
he was a man unused to sleep. The lines of his face

certainly denoted that he was a man who had little sense of humour. His entire expression was one of controlled irritation. The whole measured up to an expression of ill-health and ill-humour.

'By what authority do you interrupt this trial, Sister?' he demanded querulously as he came into the chamber where Fidelma had been conducted. Fidelma told him of her qualification as a *dálaigh*.

'Is Liadin of the Uí Dróna represented by an advocate?' she demanded.

'No,' he replied. 'She refuses to plead.'

'Then I am here to plead her case for her. I would request a postponement of the hearing for twenty-four hours that I may consult with Liadin . . .'

Rathend grimaced diffidently.

'This will be difficult. Besides, how do you know she will accept your advocacy?'

Fidelma glared hard at the Brehon. Rathend tried to return her gaze but eventually dropped his eyes uncomfortably.

'Even if she accepts your advocacy, everyone has already gathered to hear the opening arguments,' he explained lamely.

'The purpose of the hearing is for justice to be done not for the convenience of an audience. The opening of the hearing can be delayed under law.'

A slight colour tinged the sallow cheeks of the thin Brehon. He was about to reply when the door of the room burst open abruptly and a young woman entered. Fidelma quickly appraised her and had to admit that she was attractive in spite of a prominent aquiline nose, sallow skin, and dark hair which made her rather foreign in appearance. Her dark eyes flashed vivaciously. That she was a woman of rank was obvious.

'What does this delay mean, Rathend?' The dark eyes fell on Fidelma and registered suspicion. 'Who is this?'

'Sister Fidelma is an advocate come to plead Liadin's case,' Rathend said obsequiously.

A flush of annoyance tinged the woman's cheeks.

'Then you are late in coming here, Sister.'

Fidelma let her gaze move almost languidly over the shorter woman's haughty features.

'And you are . . .?' she asked softly, reminding Rathend of his breach of etiquette and causing the woman's flush of annoyance to intensify.

'This is Irnan, chieftainess of the Uí Dróna,' Rathend supplied quickly. 'You stand in her *ráth*.'

Fidelma let a smile deepen the corners of her mouth and she inclined her head in acknowledgement of the woman's rank rather than in deference.

'Whether I am late or early, Irnan of the Uí Dróna, the point is that I am here and justice must be served.' A *dálaigh* of Fidelma's rank of *Anruth* could speak on equal terms with a provincial king and could even sit in the presence of the High King himself, though only at the latter's invitation. Fidelma turned back to Rathend. 'I shall need to consult with Liadin to arrange her defence. I need twenty-four hours' delay before the opening arguments.'

'Defence?' Was there a bitter humour in Irnan's interruption. 'What defence can there be for this woman?'

Fidelma barely glanced at her.

'I shall be able to inform the court of my defence once I have had access to Liadin.'

'The case is clear,' Irnan snapped. 'Liadin killed her husband and her son.'

'For what reason?' demanded Fidelma.

'It was an arranged marriage. Perhaps Liadin hated Scoriath?' the chieftainess sniffed. 'Who knows?'

'A weak reason when she could have sought the redress of law. And why kill the child? What mother would kill her own child? Why, indeed, kill after three and a half years of marriage if, as you say, it was in pique at an arranged marriage?'

Irnan's eyes flashed with uncontrolled anger. Her tone told Fidelma that here was a woman used to being firmly in control of a situation and obeyed without question. Opposition was something that Irnan was clearly unused to.

'I am not on trial here, Sister. I cannot answer your questions.'

'Someone will have to answer them,' replied Fidelma calmly. She turned to the Brehon again. 'To that end, will you grant the postponement?'

Rathend seemed to glance at Irnan before responding. Fidelma saw, from the corner of her eye, the chieftainess shrug. Rathend sighed and inclined his head in affirmative.

'Very well, Sister. You have twenty-four hours before the court sits to hear the charges. Be warned that the charge is that of *fingal*, kin-slaying, and is so grave in this instance that we are not talking of compensation in terms of an *eric* fine. If Liadin is judged guilty, so heinous is this crime that she will be cast adrift on the high seas in an open boat without oars, sail, food, or water. And if she survives, if she is cast ashore by the will of God, on whosoever's shore she lands, that person has the right of life and death over her. That is the judgement prescribed by law.'

Sister Fidelma knew well the penalty for extreme cases of murder.

'Only if she's found guilty,' she added softly.

Irnan let out a sharp bray of laughter.

'There is little doubt of that.'

She turned and swept from the room, leaving Rathend gazing in unhappy confusion after her.

The two women broke apart from their embrace. Fidelma's eyes were troubled as she gazed at the face of her friend. Liadin was shorter than Fidelma, with a shock of chestnut hair, pale skin, and dark brown eyes that seemed almost black from a distance. Her face was strained, the flesh under the eyes was dark with worry, the skin almost bloodless and etched with lines.

'Fidelma! Praise the saints that you have come at last. I

had given you up. I did not kill Scoriath nor my son Cunobel.'

'No need to convince me,' Fidelma replied quickly. 'I have succeeded in getting a postponement of your trial for twenty-four hours. You must now tell me everything so that I will know best how to defend you.'

Liadin let out a small sob.

'My mind has not worked since I heard the terrible news of Scoriath's death. I have been numbed with shock and could not believe that I was being accused. Somehow I thought I would awake from all this . . . that . . .'

Fidelma squeezed her friend's hand as her voice trailed off.

'I will do your thinking for you. Simply tell me the facts as you know them.'

Liadin wiped her tears and forced a smile.

'I feel such hope now. But I know so little.'

'When we last met, you told me you were very happy with Scoriath. Had anything changed since then?'

Liadin shook her head vehemently. 'We were blessed with contentment and a fine child.'

'Was Scoriath still commander of the bodyguard of the chieftainess of the Uí Dróna?'

'Yes. Even when Irnan succeeded her father, Drón, as chieftainess of the clan a month ago, Scoriath continued as her commander. But he was considering giving up war and simply working his own land.'

Fidelma pursed her lips. She could not help but recall the hostility which Irnan had displayed towards Liadin.

'Was there any conflict of personality? What of the *tanist*? Was there enmity with the heir-elect?'

'Conn? No, there was no animosity between Scoriath and Conn.'

'Very well. So let us turn to the facts of the death of Scoriath and your son.' Time enough to commiserate with her friend later.

'It happened a week ago. I was not here at the time.'

'Explain. If you were not here, on what grounds are you accused of carrying out the deed? Start at the beginning.'

Liadin made a little gesture of helplessness.

'On the day it happened I had left Scoriath and the child here and had ridden to visit a sick relative, my aunt Flidais. The illness was minor and when I reached her dwelling I found her past any danger and almost entirely well. It had been nothing but a slight chill. So I returned here, reaching the fortress in the late evening about an hour after sunset. As I made my way to our chambers Conn came out of our apartments and seized me.'

'Seized you? Why?'

'It is all so hazy now. He was shouting that Scoriath was slain along with my son. I could not believe it. He seemed to be accusing me.'

'For what reason?'

'He had found a bloodstained knife and clothing, my clothes hidden in my private chamber. Scoriath and my son had been found in our chambers – stabbed to death.'

'You immediately denied responsibility?'

Liadin nodded fiercely. 'How could anyone think a mother could slaughter her own child?'

Fidelma pursed her lips and shrugged.

'Alas, it has been known, Liadin. We have to look at things as logically as we can. Did they have any other grounds to accuse you?'

Liadin hesitated a moment.

'There came another witness against me. A house servant, Branar, came forward and said she had witnessed Scoriath and me in argument that very day.'

'Witnessed? And had she?'

'Of course not. I had not seen Branar that day.'

'So she lied? How could she claim to have seen this argument then?'

'She said that she had *heard* it,' corrected Liadin after a moment's thought. 'She said that she was passing our bedchamber door and she heard our voices raised in angry exchanges. She then thought it prudent to depart. I denied it but no one would believe me.'

'Who brought you the news of your aunt's illness?'

'A monk from the monastery of the Blessed Moling, which is not far from here. A Brother named Suathar.'

'And who saw you leave the *ráth* to visit your aunt?'

'Many people. It was midday when I left.'

'So it was well known that you had left the *ráth*.'

'I suppose so.'

'And who saw you arrive back that night?'

'Conn, of course, when he seized me.'

Fidelma frowned slightly.

'He saw you arrive through the gate, you mean? And then seized you later?'

Liadin shook her head in bewilderment.

'No. I meant that he saw me at the time he seized me at the door of my chambers.'

'So no one saw you actually arrive back? So far as people were concerned, you could have come back much earlier that evening. You travelled on horse. How about the stable boys?'

Liadin looked worried.

'Ah. I see what you mean. No one was about in the stable at the time. I unsaddled my own horse. I am afraid that no one saw me arrive back.'

'But your aunt will witness the time that you left her?'

'My aunt has come here already to testify but Rathend says this matters little. No one disputes that I went to see my aunt, nor that I returned that evening. They say, however, that I could have arrived back earlier, that I went straight to Scoriath, slew him, and then my child and was going to sneak back out into the night to feign a later arrival, hoping that the bodies would have been found before my return.'

Fidelma chewed her lower lip in thought.

'It seems indeed, that Branar is then central to the argument of your guilt, for she presents us with a motive; the motive being that your relationship with Scoriath was not what you claimed it to be. If the quarrel was not between Scoriath and yourself then either Branar is mistaken or lying. Was Scoriath seen by anyone after this alleged quarrel?'

'Of course,' Liadin said at once. 'Cunobel was with Branar all afternoon while Scoriath was attending Irnan at the assembly of the clan and while I was away from the *ráth*. The assembly rose at sunset. But what of the knife, and bloodied clothes in my chamber?'

'Anyone can plant such evidence. And there is an obvious contradiction there. You would hardly leave such evidence in your chamber and be sneaking back out into the night to gain an alibi, would you?'

Liadin paused to reflect on the logic and then she nodded with a faint smile.

'I hadn't thought of that.'

Fidelma gave her an encouraging grin.

'You see? Already we find a lack of logic in the arguments against you. The case against you seems so circumstantial. Has anyone put forward an argument as to why you should want to slay your own husband and your child? Have they ascribed a motive, a reason why you argued with Scoriath and why you would have killed him and your son?'

'Rathend believes I did it in some uncontrolled fit of jealousy.'

Fidelma looked hard at her friend.

'And did you have reason for jealousy?' she asked softly.

Liadin raised her chin defiantly, a hot colour on her cheeks.

'With Scoriath? Never!'

'So did he have enemies? As commander of the bodyguard, and as a foreigner in this land, he was surely bound to have created animosities. But was there anyone in particular that you know of?'

Liadin was frowning reflectively.

'None that I can name. But Scoriath became morose a few weeks ago and would not tell me what ailed him. All that Scoriath said was something I found very strange. We were talking about his giving up command of Irnan's bodyguard. As I said, he had decided to give up the profession of warfare and farm his own land. But he was brooding and depressed. As we were talking, he suddenly said, 'I will become a farmer unless the Jewess has plans to destroy our peace.'

Fidelma's eyes widened.

'The *Jewess*? Who did he mean?'

Liadin shrugged.

'I have no idea. I know of no Jewess in the kingdom.'

'You asked him to explain, of course?'

'I did, but he laughed it away and said it was nothing but a bad joke.'

'Can you repeat exactly what he said, and the manner in which he said it?'

Liadin did so. It did not make matters clearer.

Sister Fidelma rose to her feet, her brows drawn together. Then, she focused on her friend's worried features and smiled to reassure her.

'There is a mystery here, Liadin. Something curious that itches my mind, like a bug bite. I cannot yet scratch. I must investigate further. Do not worry. All will be well.'

Conn, the *tanist* of the Uí Dróna, stood awkwardly in front of Sister Fidelma, occasionally shifting his weight from one leg to another, trying to maintain an expressionless countenance. He was a fair-haired and handsome man.

Seated to one side was the Brehon Rathend, who, as the law ordained, had to attend any questioning of witnesses, excepting the questioning of the accused person, before the trial. His job was to observe and not to question nor even participate unless the *dálaigh* did not abide by the rules set forth for pretrial interrogations.

313

'Tell me about the events which led to your arresting Liadin.'

The young warrior cleared his throat and spoke woodenly, as if having learnt a lesson by rote.

'I found the weapon that killed Scoriath in the bedchamber of . . .'

'From the beginning,' Fidelma interrupted with annoyance. 'When did you last see Scoriath? See him alive, that is?'

Conn considered for a moment.

'On the evening of the day on which he was killed. It was the day of the clan assembly, the feast day of the blessed Mochta, the disciple of Patrick. That afternoon Scoriath, myself, and some other warriors were in attendance to our chieftainess, Irnan, at the assembly hall. An hour before sunset, the assembly dispersed so that each could return home before the hour of darkness.'

'Was that the last time you saw Scoriath alive?'

'It was, Sister. Everyone returned to their homes. Later Irnan's messenger came to me and said that he was looking for Scoriath, for Scoriath had been summoned by the chieftainess. The messenger said that he had gone to his chambers but could find no one.' The fair-haired young man paused and frowned, massaging his forehead with his fingers as if the act would conjure memory. 'I knew this to be strange for Scoriath had a child, and if he were not in his house then his wife and child or servant would be there.'

He paused as if seeking approval from Fidelma. She simply motioned him to continue.

'I went to the house with the messenger. No one answered in response to our knocking. I opened the door and went in. I cannot describe it. I felt something was wrong. A small oil lamp, whose light I could see through a crack in the door, burned in the bedchamber. I went to the door and pushed it open.' He genuflected hastily. 'There I found Scoriath face downward on the floor. Blood still gushed from a terrible wound in his neck.'

'*Still* gushed?' Fidelma interrupted quickly.

Conn nodded.

'Obviously he had not long been dead. I turned the body slightly and saw that his throat had been cut. Then, by the door of a small side chamber, was the body of Scoriath's child, Cunobel. He, too, was dead from several wounds in the chest. Blood stained the entire room.'

The *tanist* paused to swallow nervously.

'I saw that the side chamber door, a chamber where the child slept, and which Scoriath's wife used for her personal toilet, stood ajar. I noticed a trail of blood leading into the chamber. I followed this trail of droplets and it led me to a chest. Inside the chest was a knife, still sticky with blood, and a bloodstained outer garment which belonged to Liadin.'

He was silent for so long that Fidelma felt she had to prompt him. 'And then?'

'I sent the messenger back to Irnan to tell her what had been discovered. There was no doubt in my mind that Liadin was answerable for this foul deed.'

'Why?'

The fair-haired man blinked.

'Why?' he repeated as if surprised at the question being asked. 'Because, Sister, I found the knife and the garment. They were hidden in a chest in Liadin's room. The garment belonged to Liadin. I had often seen her wearing it.'

' "Hidden" is hardly an exact description, Conn,' Fidelma observed. 'A trail of blood led you to the chest.'

He shrugged. 'The bloodstains probably went unnoticed in Liadin's panic to hide the objects of her guilt.'

'Perhaps. But that is supposition. If you had done this deed, would you have gone into your personal chamber to hide the weapon and bloodstained garment? Even without the bloody trail, someone would surely be bound to examine that room later?'

Conn looked confused.

'Perhaps you are right, Sister. But surely no one else

could have done the deed, and that for a very good reason.'

Fidelma raised an eyebrow quizzically.

'What is that reason?'

'Scoriath was a warrior. A man of strength as well as full of a warrior's guile. Yet he turned his back on his murderer, allowed them to reach around his neck and slit his throat. The incision was made in the left side of the neck and the blade drawn along the throat to the right side. No one could have been placed in such a position to perform the deed unless Scoriath trusted them very well. Only a woman with whom Scoriath was intimate could be so trusted.'

For a few minutes Fidelma sat considering.

'Could the wound not have been made by a left-handed person, facing Scoriath?' mused Fidelma.

Conn blinked again. It was obviously a habit which signalled reflection on a question.

'But Liadin is right-handed.'

'Just so,' Fidelma remarked softly.

'And,' Conn continued, ignoring her point, 'if the murderer stood in front of Scoriath, he surely would have defended himself from the attack with ease.'

Fidelma mentally conceded the point.

'Continue, Conn. You say that you sent the messenger back to Irnan. What then?'

'I was surveying the scene when I heard a noise outside the building. I moved to the door, wrenched it open, and found Liadin attempting to sneak back into the building, presumably in an attempt to retrieve the knife and garment from her chamber.'

'That is surmise on your part,' Fidelma admonished.

Conn shrugged indifferently.

'Very well, I found Liadin outside the door and I arrested her. Irnan came soon afterwards with Rathend, the Brehon. Liadin was taken away. That is all I know.'

'Did you know Scoriath well?'

'Not well, save that he was captain of the guard.'

'Were you jealous of him?'

Conn appeared bewildered by the abrupt question.

'Jealous?'

'Scoriath was a foreigner,' Fidelma explained. 'A Gaul. Yet he had achieved high office among the Uí Dróna. Did it not annoy you to see a foreigner so well treated?'

'He was a good man, an excellent champion. It is not my place to question the decisions reached by the councils of the king nor those of my chief. He was a good warrior. As for high office . . . I am the heir-elect to the chieftainship, so why should I be jealous of him?'

'And what was your relationship with Liadin?'

Did a faint colour suffuse his cheeks?

'I have no relationship,' he said gruffly. 'She was Scoriath's wife.'

'A good wife, to your knowledge?'

'I suppose so.'

'A good mother?'

'I have no knowledge of such things. I am unmarried.'

'If she had murdered Scoriath as you suggest, do you not question the fact that she also murdered her own child . . . a three-year-old boy?'

Conn was stubborn.

'I can only state what I know.'

'Did Scoriath ever say anything about a Jewess to you?'

Conn was again apparently bewildered by this abrupt change of tack.

'Never. I have never heard of a woman of that religion in these parts, though it is said that many Jewish traders frequent the port of Síl Maíluidir on our southern coast. Irnan spent some of her youth there and may have an answer for you about such things.'

The servant, Branar, was a raw-boned, fresh-faced girl with wide guileless-looking blue eyes, and a permanent expression of confusion. She was no more than a year or two beyond the age of choice. Sister Fidelma smiled encouragingly at her and bade her be seated. Rathend sat in place, looking a trifle irritated. Branar had been escorted to the chamber by her mother but Fidelma had refused to allow the old woman to remain with her daughter during the interrogation, showing her to a side chamber. Rathend thought that Fidelma might have showed some compassion for the young girl and allowed the mother to remain. Branar was nervous and awed by the proceedings.

'How long have you been a servant to Liadin and Scoriath?' Fidelma opened.

'Why, not even a year, Sister.' The girl bobbed her head nervously as she sat. Her confused, somewhat frightened gaze travelled from Fidelma to the stony-faced Brehon and then back to Fidelma.

'A year? Did you enjoy working for them?'

'Oh yes. They were kind to me.'

'And you liked your work?' inquired Fidelma.

'Oh yes.'

'And you had no problems with either Liadin or Scoriath? Were there no arguments between them and you?'

'No, I was quite happy.'

'Was Liadin a caring wife and mother?'

'Oh yes.'

Fidelma decided to attempt another tack.

'Do you know anything about a Jewess? Did Scoriath know such a woman?'

For the first time Rathend raised an eyebrow in surprise and glanced at Fidelma. But he kept silent.

'A Jewess? No.'

'What happened on the day Scoriath was killed?'

The girl looked troubled for a moment and then her face lightened.

'You mean about the argument I heard? I went that morning to clean the house of Liadin and Scoriath as I usually did. They were in the bedchamber with the door closed, but their voices were raised in a most terrifying argument.'

'What were they saying?'

'I could not make out what was being said. The door was closed.'

'Yet you could clearly identify their voices and knew that they were engaged in a violent quarrel, is that it?'

'It is. I could hear only the tones of their voices raised in anger.'

Fidelma gazed at the ingenuous face of the house servant.

'You only heard Liadin's voice through a closed door but can identify it clearly?'

The girl's nod was emphatic.

'Very well. Do you think that you know my voice by now?'

The girl hesitated suspiciously but then nodded.

'And you would know your own mother's voice?'

The girl laughed nervously at the apparent stupidity of the question.

Sister Fidelma rose abruptly.

'I am going into the other room. I will close the door and will speak at the top of my voice. I want you to see if you can hear what I say.'

Rathend sighed. He clearly felt that Fidelma was pursuing too theatrical an approach.

Fidelma went into the next room and closed the door behind her. Branar's mother rose uncertainly as she entered.

'Is your questioning over, Sister?' she asked in a puzzled tone.

Fidelma smiled softly and shook her head.

'I want you to say anything that comes into your head, but say it as loud as you can. It is an experiment.'

The woman stared at Sister Fidelma as if she were mad but, at a nod from Fidelma, began talking a mixture of sense and gibberish as loud as she could until Fidelma signalled her to silence. Fidelma then opened the door and called to Branar. The girl rose uncertainly.

'Well,' smiled Fidelma, 'what did you hear?'

'Oh, I heard you speaking loudly, Sister, but I could not understand all you said.'

Fidelma smiled broadly now.

'But you did hear *my* voice?'

'Oh yes.'

'Clearly my voice?'

'Oh yes.'

Fidelma turned and pushed the door open. Branar's mother shuffled nervously forward, as perplexed as her daughter.

'The voice you heard was your own mother's voice, Branar. Are you still sure you wish to swear that it was Liadin who was arguing with Scoriath behind the closed door?'

The chambers where Liadin and Scoriath had dwelt were a set of rooms in the fortress not far from the stable buildings beyond the central gate. Three chambers constituted the dwelling; a living room, a bedchamber leading off it, and, with access from the bedchamber, a smaller chamber in which Liadin's young son had his bed and in which Liadin apparently stored her clothes.

The rooms now seemed cold and bleak, although they were filled with items which once spelt homeliness and comfort. Perhaps it was the lack of a fire in the hearth and the gloom of the day that enhanced the chill.

Rathend led the way, crossing the floor of the room in which meals were cooked and eaten; where an iron cauldron hung on a spit over the dead grey ashes.

'Scoriath was slain in this room,' Rathend explained, showing the way into the large bedchamber.

The granite blocks of the walls were covered with tapestries. There were no windows, and the room was dark. Rathend bent and lit a tallow candle. There was a large, ornately carved bed. The bedclothes, a jumbled mess of linen and blankets, were stained with what was obviously dried blood.

'Scoriath was lying there. The child, Cunobel, was found just by the door of the smaller chamber,' Rathend explained.

Fidelma noted the dark stains crossing the floor to the small arched door which led off the chamber. She saw, by the doorway, that there was a slightly larger pool of dried blood. But the stains also led beyond the chamber door.

She walked into the smaller chamber with Rathend, who held aloft the tallow candle, following her. The trail of dried blood led to a large wooden trunk as Conn had said it had. She noticed some footprints in the dried blood. They were large and must have been made by Conn during his investigation, obscuring the original footprints of the killer.

'That was the trunk in which Liadin's bloodstained garment was found together with the knife,' the Brehon said. 'Next to the trunk was a small cot in which the boy, Cunobel, must have slept. There are no bloodstains there so we can conclude that the child was slain where he was found.'

Fidelma did not reply but returned to the main bedchamber and examined it again.

'What are you looking for, Sister?' ventured Rathend.

'I do not know . . . yet.' Fidelma stopped suddenly, noticing a book satchel hanging from a peg. She reached into it and drew out a moderate-sized volume. She gazed with interest at the patterned binding, frowning slightly as she noted a few dark stains which spoilt the careful artistry of the leatherwork.

Reverently she placed it on a nearby table and motioned for Rathend to hold the candle higher.

'Why,' she said softly, opening the first page, 'it is a copy of the *Hexapla* of Origenes. What would Scoriath or Liadin be doing with this?'

The Brehon sighed impatiently.

'There is no law against the ownership of books.'

'But it is unusual,' insisted Fidelma as she turned the

pages. It was a collection of Hebrew religious texts which Origenes, head of the Christian school of Alexandria, had copied three centuries before. He had rendered the text in parallel columns, in Hebrew, Greek and then in Latin.

Fidelma frowned suddenly. Someone had marked a passage in a textual section entitled '*Apokrupto*'. Fidelma dredged her knowledge of Greek. It meant 'hidden texts'. She read the passage with a frown. The story told of how the Assyrian king, Nebuchadnezzar, sent his army against the Israelites. The army was commanded by an invincible general named Holofernes. As the Assyrian army lay encamped around the Israelite city of Bethulia a young Jewish maiden named Judith went to the Assyrian camp and was brought before Holofernes. She seduced him and then, afterwards, as he lay in a drunken slumber, she cut off his head and returned to her own people, who took heart by this sign, rushed upon the invading army, and routed them.

Fidelma smiled to herself. It was a story worthy of the ancient Irish bards, for it was once believed that the soul reposed in the head and the greatest sign of respect was to sever the head of one's enemy. Fidelma's eyes suddenly widened. Judith. Her eye travelled from the Hebrew text to the Greek and then to the Latin. She caught her breath as she realised the meaning of the name Judith – it meant Jewess.

Why had the passage been marked? What had Scoriath meant when he told Liadin that he would give up his warrior's role and become a farmer unless the 'Jewess' prevented him? Scoriath was a foreigner and, in a way, commander of an army as Holofernes had been. Also, Scoriath's head had nearly been severed. Was there some bizarre meaning to this?

Slowly she replaced the book under the puzzled gaze of the Brehon.

'Have you seen all you wish?'

'I wish,' Fidelma replied, raising her head, 'to see the genealogist of the Uí Dróna.'

★ ★ ★

'You now say that you wish to question the chieftainess of the Uí Dróna? What has she to do with this matter?'

It was an hour later and Rathend and Fidelma were seated in the great hall of the fortress.

'That is for me to discover,' replied Fidelma. 'I have the right to call Irnan for examination. Do you deny it?'

'Very well.' Rathend was clearly reluctant. 'But I hope you know what you are doing, Fidelma of Kildare.'

Irnan came in after a short, uneasy period of waiting. Rathend leapt to his feet as the chieftainess entered.

'Why am I summoned, Rathend?' Irnan's voice was irritable and she chose to ignore Fidelma. But it was Fidelma who replied to her.

'How long was Scoriath your lover, Irnan?'

A pin falling to the ground would have been heard for several seconds after Fidelma had spoken.

The face of the swarthy woman blanched, the lips thinned. An expression of shock etched her features.

Rathend was staring at Fidelma as if he could not believe what he had heard.

Suddenly, as if her bones and muscles would no longer support her, Irnan seemed to fold up on a nearby chair, her gaze, combining consternation and fear, not leaving Fidelma's imperturbable features. As she did not reply, Fidelma continued.

'Before your birth, I am told that your father, Drón, travelled to the port of Síl Maíluidir. His aim was to encourage some merchants of the clan to open trade there. While at the port he met a Phoenician merchant who had a beautiful daughter. Drón married her and they had a child. The child was yourself. Your mother was named Judith – the Jewess. She survived your birth by only a few months. When she died your father then brought you back here, where you were raised.'

'That story is no secret,' replied Irnan sharply. 'Molua, the genealogist, doubtless told it to you.'

'When did Scoriath tell you that he no longer loved you and wanted to resign his command and be a simple farmer?'

Irnan had apparently recovered her composure and chuckled drily.

'You do not know everything, *dálaigh* of the court. Scoriath did love me and told me as much on the day his wife slew him for jealousy.'

Fidelma found herself having to control her surprise at the sudden candour of Irnan's response.

'Scoriath loved me, but he was a man of honour.' Irnan's words were like acid. 'He did not want to harm Liadin nor his young son and so he told me that he would not divorce his wife. He would stay with them.'

'That provided you with a motive for killing him,' Fidelma pointed out.

'I loved Scoriath, I would never have harmed him.'

'So you would have us believe that you accepted the situation?'

'Scoriath and I were lovers from the first day that he arrived among us. My father, who was then chieftain, found out. While he admired Scoriath as a warrior, my father wanted me to marry an Irish prince of wealth. I think he was more determined that I should do so because of the fact that I was my mother's daughter and he wanted to compensate for my foreign blood. He then forced Scoriath into an arranged marriage with Liadin. Scoriath did not love her.'

Irnan paused and stared reflectively at the fire for a moment before drawing her dark eyes back to the graven features of Fidelma.

'When my father died, I became the Uí Dróna. I was then free to do as I willed. I urged Scoriath to divorce Liadin, making fair settlement on her and the child. He, however, was a man of honour and refused. He did not want to hurt Liadin. So we remained lovers.

'Then came the news of how Scoriath and his son were

slain. It was so obvious who did it and why. Liadin must have found out and killed him in jealous passion.'

Sister Fidelma gazed thoughtfully at Irnan.

'Perhaps it is too obvious a conclusion? We must take your word alone as to Scoriath's attitudes. You could just as easily have slain Scoriath because he rejected your love.'

Irnan's jaw came up pugnaciously.

'I do not lie. This is all I have to say.' Irnan stood up. 'Have you done with your questions?'

'All for the time being.'

The chieftainess turned and, without another glance at the unhappy Rathend or at Fidelma, strode from the room.

Fidelma sighed. There was something itching at the back of her memory.

Rathend was about to break the silence when the door of the hall opened and a nervous youth in the brown homespun robes of a religieux entered.

'Is the Brehon Rathend here?' he began nervously and then, catching sight of Fidelma, he bobbed his head nervously, '*Bene vobis*, Sister.'

'I am Rathend,' the Brehon said. 'What do you wish?'

'I am Suathar of the monastery of the Blessed Moling. I came to seek the return of the book we loaned to Scoriath. I was told that before I can reclaim the book, I must have your permission.'

Fidelma looked up swiftly.

'Scoriath borrowed the copy of Origenes's *Hexapla* from your monastery's library?'

'Yes; a week ago, Sister,' agreed the young man.

'Did Scoriath request the loan of this book in person?'

Suathar shook his head, puzzled by the question.

'No. He sent a message and asked that the book be delivered the next time someone came to the *ráth* of the Uí Dróna. I had to come here six days ago because the aunt of the lady Liadin was ill and requested me to bring her to nurse her. I gave the book to Liadin.'

Rathend had handed the book satchel to the monk.

'You'd best check to see whether all is in order,' Fidelma invited as the young man began his thanks.

The monk hesitated, pulled out the leather-bound book, turning it over in his hands. Then he opened it.

'Has someone made a mark on the story of Holofernes?' prompted Fidelma.

'The mark was not there when I left it,' agreed the young monk. 'Also,' he hesitated. 'The dark, brownish stains on the leather binding were not there before. They look like the imprint of the palm of a hand.'

Fidelma exhaled sharply, rebuking herself for her blindness. She took the book and, after a moment's examination, placed her hand palm down over the dark stain to assess the measurement of the imprint.

'I have been a fool!' she said softly, as if to herself. Then she drew herself up again. 'Suathar, is the work of Origenes one that is popular?'

'Not popular. As you must know, Sister, it is only of passing interest to we of the Faith because the Hebrew texts, which the great Origenes put together, are of a questionable nature, being the stories which we now call "The Apocrypha", from the Greek word.'

Fidelma raised a hand impatiently to silence him.

'Just so. Nowhere else is the story of Judith and Holofernes to be found?'

'None that I know of, Sister.'

'Has the lady Liadin ever visited your library at the monastery?'

Suathar pursed his lips in thought.

'Yes. Several weeks ago.'

Fidelma turned with a grave face to the Brehon.

'I have finished my inquiries, Rathend. I need only to see Liadin once more. The case may be heard tomorrow.'

'Then you will be entering a "not guilty" plea for the lady Liadin?' asked Rathend.

Fidelma shook her head at the startled Brehon.

'No. I shall be making a plea of "guilty". Liadin has been clever, but not clever enough.'

Before Sister Fidelma entered Liadin's small cell, she turned to Conn, the commander of the guard, whom she had asked to accompany her, and told him to remain outside the door in case he was needed.

As Liadin rose with bright expectation on her face, Fidelma positioned herself just inside the door with folded arms.

'I will defend you, Liadin,' she began coldly without preamble, 'but only to seek some mitigation for your guilt. It has been hard for me to believe that you would attempt to use me in this evil plot.'

When the horror of realisation at what Fidelma had said began to spread across her features, Liadin opened her mouth to protest.

'I know it all,' Fidelma interrupted. 'You appealed to my intellectual vanity with a number of false clues which you thought would lead me to suspect Irnan. Above all, you relied on my human weakness, that of my long friendship with you, to convince me that you could never have done this deed.'

Liadin's face was suddenly drained of emotion and she sat back on the cot abruptly.

'You learnt that Scoriath had never loved you,' went on Fidelma relentlessly. 'You learnt that he was having an affair with Irnan. The crime was well planned. If you could not have him, neither would Irnan. You hatched a cunning double plot. You decided to kill him and send for me, leaving me a false trail so that I would defend you by following that trail to Irnan.'

'How could I do that?' The girl was defiant.

'You had discovered the story of Irnan's parentage and it put you in mind of the story of Holofernes. You were always a good Greek scholar and decided to use that as the intellectual bait which you knew would appeal to my imagination.

You checked the story in the *Hexapla* by Origenes on a visit to the library of the monastery of Moling. When the time was right, you sent to ask Suathar, in Scoriath's name, to bring the book which would provide me with the next clue after you had dropped into your conversation with me that Scoriath was afraid of someone called the "Jewess".'

Fidelma paused and gazed sadly at her friend.

'You took the book and hung it in the chamber. One unexpected thing occurred. You were overheard by Branar having a row with Scoriath. But that turned out to be no problem because, having convinced myself so firmly of your innocence, I cleverly used a trick to dismiss Branar's information to my own satisfaction. Cleverness when used with prejudice is a formidable thing.

'You went off to your aunt. Later you returned unnoticed to the *ráth* and entered your chambers. There was Scoriath. He had no cause to suspect you, and you struck him from behind. Perhaps it was then that you remembered . . . in the row that morning you had neglected to plant the main piece of evidence needed for me to follow the trail. You had neglected to mark the passage about Judith and Holofernes. You did so then, for there was blood which stained the leather binding and went unnoticed.

'Then,' Fidelma went on remorselessly, 'then you went to hide in the stables and wait until Conn discovered the bodies. You appeared, pretending to have just returned from your aunt. You knew that you would be accused, but you had already sent for me and laid your false trail. The thing that was irritating my mind was the fact that you must have sent for me before the murder to allow me to reach here on time.'

'It is not true,' Liadin's voice was broken now. 'Even if I did kill Scoriath for jealousy, there is a flaw in your arguments and one I think you know in your heart.'

Fidelma raised her head and returned her friend's gaze. Did she detect a triumph in that gaze?

'And what is that?' she asked softly.

'You know that I would not be capable of killing my own son. While you have that doubt you will do all you can to argue my case and clear me of this crime.'

'You are right,' Fidelma admitted. 'I know that you could not have killed your son.'

Fidelma heard a movement outside the cell but did not take her eyes from Liadin's triumphant gaze.

'Come in, Conn,' she called quietly and without turning her head. 'Tell me why you had to kill Liadin's little son.'

The fair-haired young *tanist* entered the cell with his sword drawn.

'For the same reasons that I must now kill you,' he replied coldly. 'The plot was more or less as you have described it. There was a slight difference. I was the leading spirit. Liadin and I were lovers.'

Liadin had begun crying softly, realising the truth was finally out.

'I wanted my freedom from Scoriath to go with Conn. I knew Scoriath would not divorce me, for he was a man of principles. So there was no alternative. I had to make you believe that he was having an affair with Irnan . . .'

Fidelma raised an eyebrow in cynicism.

'Are you telling me that you did not know that Scoriath and Irnan were really lovers?'

Liadin's look of startled surprise told Fidelma that she did not.

'Then you did not know that Scoriath would have divorced you had you simply asked him? Or that he remained with you only because of what he considered was his duty to you and his son?'

Liadin stood frozen in horror. Then she stammered 'But Conn . . . Conn said . . . Oh God! If only I had known . . . then all this could have been avoided. Conn and I could have been together without guilt.'

'That would not be so, would it, Conn, *tanist* of the Uí Dróna?'

The young man's expression was sullenly defiant.

'You see,' Fidelma went on, speaking to Liadin, 'Conn was using you, Liadin. He persuaded you to work out the plan to implicate Irnan because if I followed your false trail and could demonstrate that Irnan was implicated, or at least was a suspect in Scoriath's death, then she would have had to relinquish the chieftaincy of the Uí Dróna. A chieftain must be without blemish or suspicion. Who would benefit from that but the *tanist* – the elected heir?'

Liadin had turned to Conn in disbelief.

'Deny it!' she cried. 'Say it is not so!'

Conn shrugged arrogantly.

'Why gamble just for love when one can take power as well? We laid out the plot as you have deduced it, Fidelma of Kildare. Except for one thing. I also slew Scoriath. And when the child stumbled into the room and saw me, I had to kill him as I must now kill you . . .'

Conn raised his sword.

Fidelma flinched, closing her eyes. She heard Liadin scream! The blow was not delivered. She opened her eyes to find that Liadin was clinging to Conn's sword arm while Rathend and two warriors crowded the cell to disarm and drag the struggling young man away.

Liadin collapsed into a sobbing heap on the cot.

Rathend was standing gazing at Fidelma with a look of admiration in his eyes.

'So you were right, Fidelma of Kildare. How could you have been so sure?'

'I was not sure. Only my instinct was sure. I was certain that Liadin could not have killed her son but that weighed against my certainty that it was Liadin who set the elaborate series of false clues for me to follow, knowing how they would appeal to my vanity for solving mysteries. I was faced with two conflicting certainties. That meant Liadin had an accomplice, and in that accomplice one could look for motive. I began to suspect Conn when he willingly provided me with the next link about Irnan and the Jewess connection.

'Poor Liadin, even when she knew that Conn had slain her child, she continued to go through with this plot for love of him. A strong thing, this blindness of love.'

She glanced compassionately at her friend.

'Only when I realised the width of the palm print on the book satchel was that of a male hand did things make sense. Conn, in setting the murder scene, had to make sure that Liadin had left the clue in its proper place and, in doing so, he left his own clue there. The plan needed my participation to follow the false clues. I was late in arriving here and found that Conn was looking for my coming. At the time I wondered why he was relieved when I arrived.'

Rathend sighed softly.

'So Conn persuaded his lover to participate in the crime, making her believe it was all for love while all the time he merely sought power?'

'Liadin is guilty, but not so guilty as Conn, for he played on her emotions as a fiddler plays upon his instrument. Ah, Liadin, Liadin!' Fidelma shook her head. 'No matter how well one thinks one knows someone, there is always some dark recess of the mind that even the closest of friends may never reach.'

'She saved your life, though. That will stand in mitigation when she is judged.'

'If only Scoriath had been honest with her,' Fidelma sighed. 'If Scoriath had confessed his affair with Irnan and told Liadin that he wanted a divorce, she would not have been led into this fearful plot.'

'It seems that Scoriath brought his own fate upon himself,' ventured Rathend.

'He was probably a coward to emotion,' agreed Fidelma as they turned from the cell, leaving the sobbing Liadin alone. 'Men often are. *Deus vult!*'

'God wills all things,' echoed Rathend hollowly.

A Scream from the Sepulchre

೪೪

I t was the evening of All Saints' Day and Tressach, a warrior of the guard of the royal palace of Tara, home of Sechnasach, High King of Ireland, was unhappy. That evening he had drawn the most unpopular duty, which was to act as sentinel in that area of the palace complex where generations of High Kings were buried. Rows of carved granite memorials marked the mounds where many of the great monarchs were interred, often with their chariots, armour, and such grave goods as were needed to help them on their journey to the Otherworld.

Tressach felt uncomfortable that this duty fell to his lot on this night of all nights. The evening of All Saints or All Hallows as some now named it, was an ancient observance which many still called the Samhain Festival even though the five kingdoms had long accepted the new Faith of Christendom. Samhain, according to ancient tradition, was the one night of the year when the mystic realms of the Otherworld became visible to the living and when the souls of the dead could enter the living world to wreak vengeance on anyone who had wronged them in life. So strong was this belief among the people that even when the new faith entered the land it could not be suppressed. The Christians therefore incorporated the ancient festival by creating two separate celebrations. All Saints' Day was set aside as a day

333

when the saints, known and unknown, were glorified, and the following day, All Souls, was given to the commemoration of the souls of the faithful dead.

Tressach shivered slightly in the cold evening air as he approached the walled-off compound of graves, far away from the main palace buildings which made up the High King's capital. Autumn was departing with rapidity and the first signs of winter, the white fingers of a creeping evening frost, were permeating across the sacred hills of Royal Meath.

Tressach paused as he contemplated the path that he had to take between the darkened mounds with their granite stone portals. They called this 'the avenue of the great kings', for here were entombed some of the most famous of ancient rulers. There was the imposing tomb of Ollamh Fodhla, the fortieth king, who gathered the laws of Ireland and established a *féis*, or convention, which sat at Tara every three years at the feast of Samhain. This was when judges, lawyers, and administrators gathered to discuss the laws and revise them. Indeed, Tressach knew that hosts of judges and lawyers had already descended on Tara, for the convention fell this very year. They would start their deliberations in the morning.

Here, also, was the imposing tomb of Macha Mong Ruadh, Macha of the Foxy Hair, the seventy-sixth monarch and the only woman to have ruled all Ireland. Beyond were the tombs of Conaire the Great, of Tuathal the Legitimate, of Art the Solitary, of Conn of the Hundred Battles, and of Fergus of the Black Teeth. Tressach could reel off the names of those who inhabited the graves like a litany. How the mighty were laid low.

Yet, why a warrior needed to waste his time patrolling this resting place of the dead was a mystery to Tressach. What need was there to guard this desolate place and why this night of all the dark autumnal nights? Tressach would have preferred to be somewhere else . . . anywhere else.

At least he had a lantern, but its light gave him little comfort. He began to walk with a quick pace as he passed down the darkened aisle between the tombs. The quicker he completed his task so that – in good conscience – he could report to his commander that he had walked through the compound, the better. The thought that, at the end of his vigil, there would be a mug of *cuirm*, a strong mead, acted as an added incentive.

He turned a corner and conscience made him pause near a row of tombs for an inspection. He held his lantern before him. He owed it to his commander and his pride as a warrior to make a cursory check at each vantage point. His eyes fell on a newly dug grave and he found himself suppressing a shiver. He knew that Garbh, the keeper of the cemetery, whose duties included the maintenance of the graves and the digging of new tombs, had been working here over the last two days. Although the grave was unfinished and empty, Tressach felt a morbid fascination as he stared at the yawning black hole with its piled dark earth around it. His imagination began to run riot and fearful childhood fantasies clutched at his mind. Any moment something fearful could raise itself out of that black pit. He genuflected and turned abruptly away.

Here, at the end of the row of more modern tombs, stood a mound set slightly apart. This type of grave was ancient and called a *dumma*. It was surrounded by a circle of granite pillar stones notched in Ogham, the ancient Irish writing which was falling into disuse since the new faith had brought Latin script into the land. Had it not been so dark, Tressach knew that one would have seen that this tomb was more richly endowed than the others. Under its grey stone portals were heavy oak doors, panelled in copper and bronze and reinforced with iron. The panels were studded with patterning of gold and silver.

It was one of the oldest of the graves at Tara. In fact, according to the chroniclers, it was some fifteen hundred years old. It was the tomb of the twenty-sixth High King, Tigernmas, known as 'Lord of Death', for he was one of the most warlike of the ancient kings and had won thrice-nine battles in a single year. During his reign, so the old storytellers claimed, the first gold and silver mines were discovered and worked in Ireland. Tigernmas had become a rich and powerful king. It was he who had ordained that the people should wear clothes of varied colours to denote their clans and social status.

Of all the tombs that Tressach would have to pass this fearsome evening, he was most apprehensive of the tomb of Tigernmas. The old annalists had it that Tigernmas had forsaken the ancient gods and turned to worship an idol dedicated to blood and vengeance. Sacrifices were made at the feast of Samhain on the plain of Magh Slecht. Because of this, a terrible disaster had overtaken Tigernmas. He and all his followers died of a strange illness and his body was then returned to Tara to be interred in this last resting place of kings.

Tressach knew the story well and wished, for at least this night, that he could expunge it from his imagination. He clasped his sword hilt more firmly with one hand as he held the lantern high with the other. It gave him comfort. He was about to hurry on past the tomb of Tigernmas when a scream poleaxed him. His limbs lost all form of movement. It was a muffled cry, a strangled cry of pain.

Then an agonised voice distinctly cried: 'Help me! God help me!'

Tressach broke into a cold sweat, unable to move, unable to make a sound from his suddenly constricted and dry throat.

There was no question in his mind that the cry had come from the long-sealed tomb of Tigernmas.

The Abbot Colmán, spiritual adviser to the Great Assembly of the chieftains of the five kingdoms of Ireland, a thickset, ruddy-faced man in his mid-fifties, rose to greet the young religieuse who had just entered his chamber. She was tall, with grey-green eyes and strands of red hair escaping from under her head-dress.

'Sister Fidelma! It is always good to see you here at Tara. Alas, you do not often bless us with a visit.'

He came forward with both hands outstretched.

'*Dominus tecum*,' replied the religieuse solemnly, observing protocol. But the smiling abbot shook his head, gripped her hands warmly, and guided her to a chair beside the fire. They were old friends but it had been some time since their last meeting.

'I was wondering whether we should see you here this year for the convention. All the other judges and lawyers have already arrived.'

Sister Fidelma, of the house of Brigid of Kildare, grimaced wryly.

'It would have been remiss of me to fail to attend, for there are many contentious matters that I want to debate with the Chief Brehon.'

Abbot Colmán smiled happily and offered Fidelma a drink of mulled imported Gaulish wine. When she indicated her acceptance he took down a pottery amphora, emptying some of the red wine into a jug, then, taking a red-hot poker from the fire, he dipped it into the sizzling liquid. He poured a measure into a silver goblet.

The evening was chill and Fidelma appreciated the warm liquid.

'Is it really three years since you were last at Tara?' inquired the abbot, shaking his head in mock disbelief as he seated himself in the chair opposite her.

'It does seem a lifetime ago,' agreed Fidelma.

'The king still speaks with wonder of how you solved the mystery of his stolen sword.'

'How is Sechnasach, the king? Is he well? And his family, do they prosper?'

'They are all well, *Deo gratias,*' the abbot said piously. 'But I hear that much has happened to you since.'

He was interrupted by a sharp rap on the door.

The abbot made an apologetic glance towards Fidelma and bade the caller enter.

It needed no expertise to see that the warrior who stood there was in some state of shock. In spite of his sheepskin cloak, his body shook as if with intense cold and his face was white. The lips quivered almost uncontrollably. His dark eyes flickered from the abbot to the young religieuse and back again.

'Well, man,' Colmán said sharply. 'Out with it. What is it you seek?'

'Lord Abbot,' the man hesitated. His voice was a mumble.

Colmán heaved an impatient sigh.

'Speak up, man!'

'I am Tressach of the palace guard. My captain, Irél, has sent me to fetch you. There has been an incident . . .'

Tressach's voice trailed nervously away.

'An incident?' queried Colmán. 'What incident?'

'There has been an incident in the cemetery of the High Kings. Irél requests that you should attend immediately.'

'Why? What incident?' Colmán obviously did not enjoy the prospect of having to leave the warmth of his hearth and wine. However, the abbot was both an officer of the royal court and an ecclesiastical adviser, and any incident affecting spiritual matters at Tara, in which the upkeep of the cemetery was included, came under his jurisdiction.

Sister Fidelma had been examining the nervous warrior under lowered brows as she sipped her wine. The man was clearly in a state of extreme unease. The abbot's abrupt manner was not helping him. She placed her goblet on the table and smiled reassuringly up at him.

'Tell us what has happened and then we may see how best we can help.'

The warrior spread his arms helplessly as he turned to her.

'I was on guard. By the tombs, that is. This very evening, I was on guard. Abruptly there came a scream from the tomb of Tigernmas . . .'

'*From* the tomb?' queried Fidelma sharply.

'From inside the tomb, Sister.' The warrior lent emphasis to the statement by genuflecting. 'I heard a voice crying distinctly for God to help it. I was in mortal fear. I can fight with men but not with the wandering tormented souls of the dead.'

Colmán was tut-tutting. His face showed scepticism.

'Is this some mischievous prank? I am well aware what night this is.'

But Fidelma could see that humour was not in the fearful face of the warrior.

'Go on,' invited Fidelma. 'What did you do?'

'Do, Sister? I hastened away as fast as I could from that accursed place. I ran to report to my captain, Irél. At first, like the abbot, he did not believe me. He and another warrior took me back to the tomb. Oh, by my soul, Sister! The voice came again. It was fainter than before but still crying for help. Irél heard it and so did the other warrior who accompanied us.'

It was plain Colmán still did not believe him.

'What is it Irél wants me to do?' he demanded cynically. 'Go there and pray for the souls of the dead?'

'No. Irél is one not given to a belief in wandering spirits. My captain wants permission to open the tomb. He believes that someone is inside and hurt.'

The abbot looked aghast.

'But that tomb has not been opened in fifteen hundred years,' he protested. 'How could anyone be inside?'

'That's what Garbh told him,' agreed the warrior.

'Garbh?' queried Fidelma.

'The keeper of the cemetery. My captain, Irél, sent for him and requested that he open the doors of the tomb.'

'And did Garbh do so?' asked the abbot, irritably.

'No. He refused unless Irél obtained higher authority. That is why Irél sent me to you, to seek your permission.'

'Quite right. This is a matter of seriousness,' Colmán muttered. 'The decision to open tombs is not one a soldier – even the captain of the palace guard – can make. I'd better come along and see this Irél, your captain.' Colmán rose to his feet and glanced at Fidelma. 'If you will forgive me, Sister . . .'

But Fidelma was rising also.

'I think I will come with you,' she said quietly. 'For if a voice comes from a sealed tomb, then someone must have been able to enter it . . . or else, God forbid, it is indeed a spirit calling to us.'

They found Irél, the sombre-faced captain of the palace guard, standing outside the tomb with another warrior. There was a third man there, a stocky man with rippling muscles who was clad in a workman's leather jerkin and trousers. He had pugnacious features and was arguing with the captain. The man turned as they approached and, with relief on his face, greeted Abbot Colmán by name.

'I am glad that you have come, my lord Abbot. This captain is demanding that I break open this tomb. Such an act is sacrilege and I have refused unless ordered to do so by a churchman of authority.'

Irél stepped forward and saluted the abbot.

'Has Tressach explained the matter to you?' His voice was curt.

The abbot glanced disdainfully at him.

'Can we hear this voice?' Colmán's tone was sarcastic and he cocked an ear as if to listen.

'We have not heard it since I sent for Garbh,' replied Irél, keeping his irritation in check. 'I have been trying to get Garbh to open the tomb, for every moment is urgent. Someone may be dying in there.'

The man called Garbh laughed drily.

'Look at the doors. Not opened in fifteen hundred years. Whoever died in there, died over a millennium ago.'

'Garbh, as keeper of the cemetery, is within his rights to refuse your request,' Abbot Colmán explained. 'I am not sure that even I can give such permission.'

It was then that Sister Fidelma stepped forward.

'In that case, I shall give the order. I think we should open the tomb immediately.'

Colmán swung round and frowned at Fidelma.

'Do you take this matter seriously?'

'That an experienced captain of the guard and a warrior take it so should be enough reason to accept that they heard something. Let us see if this is so.'

Irél looked at the young religieuse in surprise while Garbh's features were forming into a sneer of derision.

Colmán however sighed and motioned to Garbh to start opening the doors of the tomb.

'Sister Fidelma is a *dálaigh*, an advocate of the law courts, and holds the degree of *Anruth*,' he explained to them in order to justify his action. 'She has the authority.'

Garbh's eyes flickered imperceptibly. It was the only indication that he made in recognition of the fact that the young religieuse held a degree which was only one below the highest legal qualification in the land. Irél's shoulders seemed to relax as if in relief that a decision had finally been made.

It took some time for Garbh to smash open the ancient locks of the door and swing them open.

As they pressed forward there were some gasps of astonishment.

Just inside the door was the body of a man.

They could see that this was no ancient body. It was the body of a man who was but recently dead. From his back there protruded a length of wood with which he had clearly been shot or stabbed. It was like the shaft of an arrow but without feathered flights. He lay face-down behind the doors, hands stretched out as if attempting to open the doors from the inside. They could see that his fingernails were torn and bleeding where he had scraped at the door in his terror. And his face! The eyes were wide with fear, as if he had been confronted by some evil power of darkness.

Tressach shivered violently. 'God look down on us!'

Garbh was rubbing his chin in bewilderment.

'The tomb was securely sealed,' he whispered. 'You all saw the seals on the door. It has been sealed for fifteen hundred years.'

'Yet this man was inside trying to break out.' Fidelma pointed out the obvious. 'He was apparently dying even as Irél was ordering the tomb to be opened. It was his dying cries, that Tressach and Irél heard.'

Irél glanced towards Sister Fidelma.

'This is hardly a sight for a Sister of the Faith,' he protested as he saw her moving forward.

'I am a *dálaigh*,' she reminded him. 'I shall take charge of this investigation.'

Irél glanced questioningly to Abbot Colmán, who nodded slightly and the captain stood aside to allow Fidelma to enter the tomb. She ordered the lanterns to be held up to illuminate the area.

Fidelma moved forward curiously. She had heard all the stories of Tigernmas, the infamous High King, who had ordered his druids to be put to death and turned to the worship of a gigantic idol. Generations of children had been frightened into obedience with tales of how the evil king's soul would ascend from the Otherworld and take them off unless they obeyed their parents. And now she stood at the door of his tomb, unopened since his body had been placed in it countless generations ago. It was not an inviting place. The air was stale, dank, and smelling of rotting earth and vegetation. A noxious, unclean atmosphere permeated the place.

The first thing she noticed, was that the body was of a man of middle years, somewhat plump, with well-kempt white hair. She examined the torn and bleeding hands and looked at the softness of the fingers and the palms. He was clearly someone not used to manual work. She examined his clothing. Apart from the dust and dirt of the tomb and the stains of blood from his wound, they were the clothes of someone of rank. Yet he wore no jewellery, no symbols of office, and when she examined the leather purse attached to the belt around his waist, she found only a few coins in it.

Only when she had conducted this scrutiny did she turn to examine his face. She tried to ignore the terrible mask of dread on it. Then she frowned and called for a lantern to be held more closely, studying the features with some dim memory tugging at her mind. The features seemed familiar to her.

'Abbot Colmán, please look at this man,' she called. 'I have a feeling that I should know him.'

Colmán moved forward somewhat unwillingly and bent down beside her.

'Christ's wounds!' exclaimed the abbot, forgetting his calling. 'It is Fiacc, the Chief Brehon of Ardgal.'

Fidelma nodded grimly. She knew that she had seen the man's features before. The chief judge of the clan of Ardgal was one of the learned judges of the country.

'He must have been here to attend the convention,' breathed Colmán.

Fidelma rose and dusted her clothing. 'The more important thing to discover is what he was doing here at all,' she pointed out. 'How did a respected judge come to be in a tomb which has never been opened in generations and get himself stabbed to death?'

'Witchcraft!' supplied Tressach in a breathless tone.

Irél glanced at his subordinate with a look of derision.

'Don't the teachings of Patrick's first council tell us there is no such thing as witchcraft?' he rebuked, before turning to Fidelma. 'There must be an explanation for this, Sister.'

Fidelma smiled appreciatively at the man's pedestrian approach.

'There is an explanation for everything,' she agreed, as she let her eyes wander into the interior of the tomb. 'Sometimes it is not easily seen, however.' Then she turned back to Colmán. 'Would you consult with the steward of the convention and see if Fiacc was in attendance and whether he was due to speak?'

Colmán hesitated only a moment before hurrying away on his task.

Fidelma bent again to the corpse. There was no disputing the cause of death. The shaft of wood, like an arrow, was stuck in the back of the corpse under the shoulder blade.

'The worst place to try to stab a man,' sniffed Irél. 'To stab him in the back,' he added when Fidelma glanced up questioningly at him. 'You can never be sure of inflicting a mortal wound. There are too many bones in the way of a vital organ, any of which might deflect the blow. It is better to stab from the front, in and up under the rib cage.'

He spoke with the relish of a warrior.

'So you would say that whoever delivered the blow was an amateur when it came to killing?' asked Fidelma drily.

Irél considered the point.

'Not necessarily. The implement has been inserted slightly to the side and with an abrupt thrust towards the heart. The killer knew what he was about. He was aiming to pierce the heart immediately. Nevertheless, the victim lived on for a while. If he had not we would never have heard his cries and discovered the body.'

'You are very observant, Irél. But why do you ascribe the killing to a man?'

Irél shrugged indifferently.

'It is logical. Look at the depth at which the wood is buried in the flesh. It would take strength to thrust it in so far.'

Fidelma could not fault the logic. But she was examining

the shaft of wood with more interest. It was a piece of aspen, some eighteen inches or more in length, and it was inscribed with Ogham characters. She ran her finger over the cut letters, feeling the faint stickiness of the sap. The words meant 'The gods protect us'. It was now obvious what it was. The aspen wand was called a *fé* – an instrument by which corpses and graves were measured. It was generally regarded as an unlucky object and no one would willingly touch a *fé* unless they had need to.

Even Fidelma felt that she had to summon a special courage before she reached over and yanked the piece of wood from the corpse of Fiacc. She immediately saw that it was no ordinary *fé*. Where the shaft had been driven in, it had been whittled into a sharp point and, when she'd wiped the blood on the clothes of the corpse, her eyes narrowed as she observed that this point had been hardened by fire.

Tressach, standing nearby, was gazing aghast at Fidelma's handling of the wooden *fé*.

'Sister,' he reproached, 'it is highly unlucky to handle that. And to handle the very *fé* that measured this tomb for Tigernmas . . .'

Fidelma did not reply. She rose to examine the rest of the tomb.

It was an oval-shaped chamber cut into a mound of earth with its floors flagged with stones while granite blocks lined the walls and were placed so that they formed a natural archlike structure across the entire roof. The length of the tomb was about fifteen feet, and its width a little more than twelve. Fidelma was thankful that the open doors of the tomb had allowed fresher, chill evening air to dispel the fetid atmosphere.

There was no need to ask where the remains of Tigernmas were. At the far end of the tomb, in a central position, stood an upright, rusting iron frame. In it, almost crumbled to pieces, were the remains of a skeleton. There were some fragments of clothing on it; a metal belt buckle and a rusty

sword had fallen nearby. It had been the custom for the
ancients to bury their chieftains and great rulers standing
upright and facing their enemies, sword clasped in their dead
hand. This iron cage had obviously been designed to keep
the corpse upright in the burial chamber. By this method, it
was said the aura of the dead was supposed to protect the
living. The skull of the skeleton had fallen to one side in the
cage so that its eyeless sockets appeared to be staring with
malignant force in the direction of the dead Fiacc. The
skeletal grin seemed to be one of satisfaction. Fidelma felt
irritated at the way her imagination interpreted these images.

To one side of the tomb were the rotting remains of a
chariot. This would be the king's most cherished vehicle, left
there to help transport him to the Otherworld. Jars and
containers of what had once been his favourite foods and
drink stood nearby, large bronze and copper containers made
by skilled craftsmen.

Fidelma moved forward and her foot caught at something.
She bent down and picked up a small but weighty bar of
metal. Having examined it closely by Irél's lantern, she
realised that it was silver. She set it down carefully, and as
she did so she saw a few brooches scattered about. They
were of semiprecious jewels set in gold mountings. Again, it
was the custom to bury a portion of wealth with a great
chieftain, for he would also need some means to help him in
his journey to the Otherworld. Frowning thoughtfully,
Fidelma continued to examine the rest of the tomb.

By the beam of the lantern, Fidelma noticed that a small
trail of blood led from a point before the iron cage of the
skeleton to where the corpse of Fiacc lay before the doors.
She could also see scratch marks on the granite floor.

Irél, standing beside her, articulated her thoughts.

'He was obviously stabbed while standing by the cage and
then contrived to drag himself to the doors.'

Fidelma did not bother to glance at him.

'Obviously,' she replied shortly.

346

At the entrance of the tomb, Garbh, the keeper of the cemetery, was standing with Tressach and the other warrior, watching her progress with fascination.

'Speaking of things obvious, does it not surprise you that there is so little dust and dirt on the floor of this tomb?' she asked Irél. 'It is almost as if it had been recently swept.'

Irél stared at her, wondering whether she was making a joke. But she had passed on, examining the floor and looking carefully at one of the stone slabs that made up its surface. She pointed to the scratch marks across the floor.

'Bring your lantern closer,' she instructed. 'What do you make of those?'

The captain shrugged. 'It is probably where the floor stones were scored by ropes while they were being dropped into place.'

'Exactly so,' agreed Fidelma quietly. 'And have you noticed anything else that is curious about this sepulchre?'

Irél glanced quickly around but shook his head.

'Tigernmas, although he subsequently developed an evil reputation, is accredited as the king who first encouraged gold and silver to be smelted and works of great art to be produced in this land.'

'I have heard the stories,' replied Irél.

'And it was the custom of our people to place grave goods in the tombs, together with symbols of their wealth and power.'

'That much is well known,' acknowledged Irél, slightly irritated at Fidelma for not addressing the more urgent problem.

'Apart from a few golden brooches and a silver bar, which I see lying on the floor there as if they were hurriedly discarded, where are the riches that one would have expected to find in this tomb? It is singularly devoid of any such items.'

Irél tried to see some connection that Fidelma's remark might have with the murder of Fiacc but failed. He was not interested in the customs of ancients.

'Is that significant?' he asked.

'Perhaps.'

Fidelma walked back to the corpse and looked down at it once more. There was a movement outside and Abbot Colmán came hurrying back.

'Fiacc was certainly due to attend the convention tomorrow,' he confirmed. 'The steward says that Fiacc and his wife, Étromma, arrived in Tara a few days ago. However, and this is interesting, there was a problem, for, the steward says, Fiacc was to be heard before the Chief Brehon to answer charges which, if proved, would have debarred him from practice as a judge.'

'A special hearing?' Fidelma had heard nothing about such a contentious matter. She cast a final look around the tomb before returning her gaze to Colmán.

'Does the steward have details of the charges against Fiacc?'

'Only that it was something to do with malpractice. Only the Chief Brehon has the details.'

'Has Étromma been informed of her husband's death?'

'I took it upon myself to send word to her.'

'Then I think I should go and speak with her.'

'Is that necessary? She will be distraught. Perhaps tomorrow would be a more suitable time?'

'It is necessary to see her now in order to clear up this mystery.'

Abbot Colmán spread his hands in acquiescence.

'Very well. What about . . .?' He did not finish but gestured towards the tomb.

It was Garbh who finished the question. 'Shouldn't the body of this man be removed so that I can seal the tomb?'

'Not for the moment,' replied Fidelma. 'Irél, have a guard mounted outside the tomb. Everything is to be left as it is until I order otherwise. Hopefully, I shall have resolved the mystery before midnight. Then the tomb can be resealed.'

She left the tomb and began to walk slowly and thoughtfully back through the graves of the High Kings. She paused for a moment waiting for Abbot Colmán to catch up with her. He had stopped to issue final instructions to Irél. Her eyes flickered towards the yawning pit of a freshly dug grave and suppressed a shiver. Colmán came panting along a moment later and together they walked leisurely towards the lights of the main palace complex.

Étromma was surprisingly young to be the wife of a middle-aged judge. She was scarcely more than eighteen years old. She sat stiffly but in complete control of herself. There was little sign of anguish or of grieving on her features. The cold, calculating blue eyes stared with hostility at Fidelma. The lips were thinned and pressed together. A small nerve twitching at the corner of her mouth was the only sign of expression on her features.

'I was divorcing Fiacc. He was about to be disbarred and he had no money,' she replied coldly to a question Fidelma had asked her.

Fidelma was seated before her, while Abbot Colmán stood nervously by the fire.

'I do not see how the two things fit together, Étromma,' she commented.

'I do not want to spend my life in poverty. It was an agreement between us. Fiacc was an old man. I married him only for security. He knew that.'

'What about love?' queried Fidelma mildly. 'Had you no feelings for him?'

For the first time Étromma smiled, a humourless parting of her lips. 'Love? What is that? Does love provide financial security?'

Fidelma sighed softly.

'Why was Fiacc facing disbarment from practice as a judge?' Fidelma chose a new tack.

'During this last year he had made many wrong judgements. He was, as you know, judge of the Ardgal. After so many wrong judgements, he was no longer trusted by the people. He had made himself destitute from the continual payment of compensation.'

Fidelma knew that a judge had to deposit a pledge of five *séd*, or ounces of silver, for each case he tried as a surety against error. If, on appeal by the defendant to higher judges, a panel of no fewer than three more experienced judges, a judge was found to have made an error, then this pledge was confiscated and the judge ordered to pay further compensation of one *cumal*, the equivalent of the value of three silver *séd*.

'How many wrong judgements had your husband made this last year, then? How could he have become poverty-stricken?'

'There were eleven wrong judgements during this last year.'

Fidelma's eyebrows raised in surprise. Eighty-eight silver *séd*, which could buy nearly thirty milch cows, was a staggering sum to have to pay out in compensation in a single year. No wonder there was talk of disbarring Fiacc.

'He was to be heard before the Chief Brehon to answer the fact that he had gone into debt to pay fines and to answer for his competence as a judge,' Étromma added.

'Are you saying that he had borrowed money to pay?'

'That is why I was divorcing him.'

Fidelma realised that a judge who turned to moneylenders to support him would certainly be disbarred if he could not present a valid argument to endorse his actions. Clearly, Fiacc had been in considerable trouble.

'So your husband was worried about his situation?'

Étromma chuckled drily.

'Worried? No, he was not. At least not recently.'

'Not worried?' pressed Fidelma sharply.

'He tried to stop me divorcing him by claiming that it was only a temporary matter and that he was not really destitute. He said that he was expecting money shortly and, after that, if the people did not want him as judge, he would be rich enough to live without working.'

'Did he explain where the money was coming from? How would he pay off his debts and find the money to live for the rest of his life in any degree of comfort?'

'He did not explain. Nor did I care. I think he was just a liar or a fool. It was his problem. He knew that if he lied to me and he was disbarred and shown to be penniless then I would leave. It was as simple as that. I was not going to recall my application for divorce.'

Fidelma tried to conceal her dislike of the cold, commercial attitude of the young woman.

'You were not at all interested where your husband would suddenly obtain money, if he actually did so?'

'I knew he would not. He was a liar.'

'At what point did he become confident that he would manage to obtain money to pay his debts?'

The woman Étromma reflected for a moment.

'I suppose that he started to brag that he was going to overcome this problem a day or so ago. Yes, it was yesterday morning.'

'You mean that he was worried until yesterday morning?'

'Precisely so.'

'When did you both arrive here at Tara?'

'Four days ago.'

'And during that time, Fiacc was concerned? Then yesterday morning his attitude changed?'

'Yes, I suppose so.'

'Did he meet with anyone here?'

Étromma shrugged. 'He was known to many people here. I was not interested in his friends.'

'I mean, was there anyone in particular with whom he spent some time at Tara? Was there anyone who could be described as a close friend or confidant?'

'Not so far as I know. He was a solitary man. I do not think he met with anyone here. He kept to himself. The only thing that I know he did was go for walks on his own in the graveyard of the High Kings.' Étromma paused to sniff. 'I thought he was getting maudlin. But, as I said, yesterday he came back grinning like a cat who had found a dish of cream. He assured me that things would be all right. I knew he was a liar, so I was not going to alter my plans to leave him.'

Fidelma stood up abruptly.

'I will not express my condolences, Étromma,' she said with emphasis. 'Doubtless you do not expect them. You are obviously more concerned with the financial arrangements. Fiacc was still your husband when he met his death. Your husband was murdered. I think I now know who the murderer is and, if proven, the compensation due for the slaying of your husband, as a Brehon of lower rank, is three *séd* of silver. It is not a fortune but it will keep you momentarily from poverty, and doubtless you will soon find someone else to support you.'

Abbot Colmán followed her unhappily along the corridors of the palace towards his chamber. 'You were harsh, Sister. After all, she has just been widowed and is only eighteen years old.'

Fidelma was indifferent.

'I meant to be harsh. She felt nothing for Fiacc. He was merely a source of income for her. She proclaims her motto without shame – *lucri bonus est odor ex requalibet.*'

Colmán grimaced. 'Sweet is the smell of money obtained from any source. Isn't that from Juvenal's *Satires*?'

Fidelma smiled briefly.

'Send for Irél, Tressach, and Garbh to come to your chamber. I think I can now solve this problem.'

It was not long before the three men crowded curiously into the abbot's chamber.

Fidelma was seated in a chair before the fire while Colmán stood with his back to it, a little to one side. His hands were clasped behind his back.

'Well now.' Fidelma raised her head and regarded them each in turn before addressing the warrior, Tressach. 'How long have you been a guard at Tara, Tressach?'

'Three years, Sister.'

'And how long have you patrolled the compound containing the tombs of the High Kings?'

'One year.'

'And you, Irél? You are captain of the guards of Tara. How long have you been here?'

'I entered the service of the High Kings some ten years ago. Conall Cáel was still High King then. I have been captain here for the last year.'

She looked from one to another and shook her head sadly.

'And how long has Sechnasach been High King?' she continued.

Irél frowned, not understanding the logic of this question. He regarded Fidelma as if she were joking. But her expression was completely serious.

'How long? You must know that, Sister. Everyone does. It was three years ago when the joint High Kings, Diarmuid and Blathmac, died of the Yellow Plague within a week of one another. That was when Sechnasach became High King.'

'Three years ago?' pressed Fidelma.

'You must remember, Fidelma,' interrupted Colmán, wondering how she could have forgotten. 'You were in Tara on that occasion yourself.' But she ignored him and continued to direct her questions to Irél.

'And is the High King in good health?'

'To my knowledge, thanks be to God,' Irél replied, becoming slightly defensive.

'And his family?' continued Fidelma remorselessly. 'Are they in good health?'

'Indeed, the High King is blessed.'

'I told you as much myself when you arrived earlier,' frowned Colmán, wondering if Fidelma was losing her memory.

'So what is the purpose of the new grave being dug behind the tomb of Tigernmas?'

The question was asked so softly that it took a moment or two for its implication to sink in. Fidelma's fiery green eyes were fixed on the keeper of the cemetery.

Garbh's mouth dropped open and he began to stutter. Then he hung his head in silence.

'Hold him,' instructed Fidelma calmly. 'He is to be held for premeditated murder and grave robbery.'

With astonished expressions, Irél and Tressach moved close to the side of the keeper of the cemetery.

Fidelma now rose languidly to her feet and gazed sorrowfully at Garbh. 'There has been no death of a High King or any member of his family during the last three years. Sechnasach is still young and healthy. Why then dig a new grave in the cemetery of the High Kings? Will you explain, Garbh, or shall I?'

Garbh remained silent.

'You started digging the grave in order to construct a small passage into the tomb of Tigernmas, didn't you, Garbh?'

'For what purpose would one want to enter an ancient tomb?' demanded Colmán, chagrined that he had not spotted such an obvious matter as the new grave.

'To rob the tomb, of course,' replied Fidelma. 'Where were all the gold, silver, and jewels that would have been buried with Tigernmas? Only a single silver bar and some gold jewellery lay discarded on the floor of the burial chamber. Tigernmas was a king of many legends. But it was well known that he ruled a rich court. Following the custom of our ancestors, rich grave goods would have been placed there to serve him in the Otherworld.'

Irél was looking shamefaced. Fidelma had pointed out this very fact to him and it had not registered.

'But there is much to be explained,' he pointed out. 'How did the judge, Fiacc, come to be there? Had he spotted Garbh's intention and tried to catch him?'

Fidelma shook her head. 'It was Fiacc's idea to rob the tomb in the first place. Fiacc had married a mercenary young woman. He had also made several mistakes in judgement and had become destitute through the payment of compensation. He was desperately in debt. He needed money badly. He needed money prior to his hearing before the Chief Brehon tomorrow. Money to cover his debts and money to keep his capricious young wife. It was Fiacc's idea to rob the tomb of Tigernmas, which, according to the chroniclers, contained great riches. But how was he to do it on his own?'

'Do you have the explanation?' Colmán asked.

'When he arrived at Tara, Fiacc spent a day or so in the cemetery examining the tomb. He realised there was only one way to get access without attracting attention. He enlisted the aid of Garbh, the keeper of the graves. Once Garbh saw the simplicity of the plan greed took over. Money is always a great incentive.

'Garbh was always in the cemetery, repairing tombs. It was Garbh's job to dig the graves when a High King or his family died. No one was bothered when Garbh started to dig a grave near the sepulchre of Tigernmas. No one even thought to ask why he was digging a grave. Everyone saw Garbh at what was presumed to be his usual lawful task.

'Garbh and Fiacc broke into the tomb of Tigernmas this evening. When you come to examine the new grave which Garbh has dug and which he meant to fill in tomorrow, you will find traces of a short tunnel into the tomb. It will come up under the floor, under one of the granite slabs. One of those slabs, Irél, with the scratch marks on it which you so rightly observed had been made by ropes used to reset it into its proper place in the floor. The plan was that Garbh and Fiacc would extract the riches and reseal the passage so that no one would know that the tomb had even been entered. A few items were overlooked in the haste to extract everything. A bar of silver and some jewellery were left behind. But that was all!'

'How did Fiacc die?' demanded Irél, trying to follow the story.

'Was it the curse of Tigernmas that struck him down?' Tressach asked fearfully.

'Fiacc died,' replied Fidelma coldly, 'because Garbh decided that he did not want to share the easy money that had come his way. Having been shown the almost effortless way to gain riches, Garbh wanted those riches for himself. He waited until he and Fiacc had removed all the loot from the tomb and were cleaning up. Fiacc, you see, being a judge, was very meticulous about his planning. In case some accident caused the tomb to be opened, he had decided that the dust on the floor, which would show evidence of their activity and might provide a clue to their identity, should be swept away.'

Irél groaned. Again Fidelma had pointed this out to him and it had not registered as important.

'Go on,' he urged. 'You have told us why Fiacc died. Now tell us how exactly he died?'

'It was after the spoils had been removed and the cleaning finished that Garbh, using a *fé*, the measuring stick for graves, stabbed Fiacc in the back and thought he had killed him. He then left the tomb, resealed the entrance, and went back to the grave he was digging, perhaps filling in the tunnel after him. We shall see that later. I would imagine that he has stored his spoils in or near his cabin.'

Garbh shifted uneasily at this and Fidelma smiled in satisfaction.

'Yes, Irél, I think you will find the treasure of Tigernmas hidden at Garbh's cabin.'

'But Fiacc was not killed immediately,' Tressach interrupted. 'Garbh left him wounded in the tomb when he resealed it.'

'Garbh did not realise this. He thought he had killed Fiacc. The wound made Fiacc pass out. He was badly hurt. He was dying. But he came to consciousness and realised that he was sealed in the darkened tomb. He realised, in terror, that he himself was entombed. He gave a scream of dread, which you, Tressach, in passing the tomb, heard. He began to drag himself to the wooden doors, crying in desperation. Not knowing that Tressach had heard his scream, he began to scrabble at the doors until, in that fearful moment of horror, death overtook him.'

'I did not mean to kill him. It was an argument,' Garbh said slowly, speaking now for the first time and admitting guilt. 'It was Fiacc who wanted the greater part of the wealth for himself. He said that he would only give me a small portion of the spoils. When I demanded a fair and equal share, he attacked me. He picked up the old grave measure and attacked me and I defended myself. In the struggle, he was stabbed. I was not responsible for the murder. You cannot punish me for that.'

Fidelma shook her head.

'Oh no, Garbh. You plotted to kill Fiacc from the very beginning. As soon as Fiacc had explained the plan to you, you decided that you wanted all the spoils from the tomb. You kept Fiacc alive long enough for him to be of help in gaining entrance to the tomb and taking out the treasure. You planned to kill him and leave him in the tomb, hoping that no one would ever open the tomb again. Your mistake was twofold: firstly, not ensuring that he was dead when you left him, and secondly, vanity.'

'You cannot prove I set out to kill Fiacc!' cried Garbh. 'If I had meant to kill him I would have taken a weapon into the tomb. Fiacc was killed by an old grave measurement left lying in the tomb. Even Irél will bear witness to that.'

Irél reluctantly nodded in agreement.

'That seems so, Sister. It was a *fé* that killed Fiacc. You know that. And there was Ogham carved on it. I know the ancient script. It read, "May the gods protect us". The reference to the *gods* and not *God* shows that it belonged to the pagan tomb. It must have been lying in the burial chamber.'

'Not so. The grave measure was made by Garbh,' insisted Fidelma. She pointed to the table in the abbot's room on which she had already laid the *fé* taken from the tomb.

'That was not the *fé* that measured the tomb of Tigernmas. Look at it closely. The wood is new. The Ogham notches are clean-cut. Examine the cuts. There are traces of sap still drying. Whoever cut this, cut it within the last twenty-four hours.'

Colmán had picked up the stick, taking care to genuflect to keep himself from harm at the handling of such an unlucky instrument, and examined it carefully.

'The piece of aspen is still in sap,' he confirmed wonderingly.

'Garbh had burnt a point on it to ensure that it was hard and able to be used as a dagger. He carved some Ogham on it as an afterthought. That was his vanity. He had taken notice of Fiacc's exhortation to detail and thought of a great joke to play on him. If the tomb was ever excavated, they would find Fiacc with an ancient pagan *fé* stuck into his heart. Garbh was too clever for his own good. It was easy to see that the *fé* was new-cut. And it proves that Garbh premeditated the murder. He prepared his murder weapon before he entered the tomb. It was not a spur-of-the-moment argument.'

Garbh said nothing. The blood had drained from his features.

'You may take him away now,' Fidelma instructed Irél. 'And you may make the arrangements to reseal the tomb . . . but after the treasures of Tigernmas are replaced in it.' She grinned impishly. 'It would not do, this night of all nights, to provoke the spirit of Tigernmas by keeping back any of his gold or silver, would it?'

Abbot Colmán was pouring more mulled wine and handed the goblet to Fidelma. 'A sorry story, indeed,' he sighed. 'An avaricious official and a corrupt judge. How can such wickedness be explained?'

'You forget Étromma in that summation,' replied Fidelma. 'She was the catalyst who made Fiacc's need of money so desperate and who started this chain of events. It was her lack of love, her selfishness, and above all, her greed that caused this human tragedy. It is said in the book of Timothy: *radix omnium malorum est cupiditas.*'

'The love of money is the root of all evil,' translated Abbot Colmán and then bent his head in agreement.

Invitation to a Poisoning

❧

The meal had been eaten in an atmosphere of forced politeness. There was a strained, chilly mood among the diners. There were seven guests at the table of Nechtan, chieftain of Múscraige. Sister Fidelma had noticed the unlucky number immediately she had been ushered into the feasting hall for she had been the last to arrive and take her seat, having been delayed by the lure of a hot bath before the meal. She had inwardly groaned as she registered that seven guests plus Nechtan himself made the unfavourable number of eight seated at the circular table. Almost at once she had silently chided herself for clinging to old superstitions. Nevertheless she conceded that an oppressive atmosphere permeated the hall.

Everyone at the table that evening had cause to hate Nechtan.

Sister Fidelma was not one to use words lightly for, as an advocate of the law courts of the five kingdoms as well as a religieuse, she used language carefully, sparingly and with as much precision in meaning as she could. But she could think of no other description for the emotion which Nechtan aroused other than an intense dislike.

Like the others seated around the table, Fidelma had good cause to feel great animosity towards the chieftain of the Múscraige.

Why, then, had she accepted the invitation to this bizarre feast with Nechtan? Why had her fellow guests also agreed to attend this gathering?

Fidelma could only account for her own acceptance. In truth, she would have refused the invitation had Nechtan's plea for her attendance not found her passing, albeit unwillingly, through his territory on a mission to Sliabh Luachra, whose chieftain had sent for her to come and judge a case of theft. As one qualified in the laws of the Brehons to the level of *Anruth*, only one degree below the highest grade obtainable, Fidelma was well able to act as judge when the occasion necessitated it.

As it turned out, Daolgar of Sliabh Luachra, who also had cause to dislike Nechtan, had similarly received an invitation to the meal and so they had decided to accompany one another to the fortress of Nechtan.

Yet perhaps there was another reason behind Fidelma's half-hearted acceptance of the invitation, a more pertinent reason; it was that Nechtan's invitation had been couched in very persuasive language. He begged her forgiveness for the harm that he had done her in the past. Nechtan claimed that he sought absolution for his misdeeds and, hearing that she was passing through his territory, he had chosen this opportune moment to invite her, as well as several of those whom he had injured, to make reparation to them by asking them to feast with him so that, before all, he could make public the contrite apology. The handsomeness of the language was such that Fidelma had felt unable to refuse. Indeed, to refuse an enemy who makes such an apology would have been against the very teachings of the Christ. Had not the Apostle Luke reported that the Christ had instructed: 'Love your enemies, do good to them which hate you, bless them that curse you, and pray for them which despitefully use you, and unto him that smiteth thee on the one cheek offer also the other . . .'?

Where would Fidelma stand with the Faith if she refused

to obey its cardinal rule; that of forgiveness of those who had wronged her?

Now, as she sat at Nechtan's feasting table, she observed that her dislike of Nechtan was shared by all her fellow guests. At least she had made a Christian effort to accommodate Nechtan's desire to be forgiven but, from the looks and glances of those around her, from the stilted and awkward conversation, and from the chilly atmosphere and tension, the idea of forgiveness was not the burning desire in the hearts of those who sat there. A different desire seemed to consume their thoughts.

The meal was drawing to a close when Nechtan rose to his feet. He was a middle-aged man. At first glance one might have been forgiven for thinking of him as a jolly and kindly man. He was short and plump, his skin shone with a child-like pinkness, though his fleshy face sagged a little around the jowls. His hair was long, and silver in colour, but combed meticulously back from his face. His lips were thin and ruddy. Generally, the features were pleasant enough but hid the cruel strength of character which had marked his leadership of the Múscraige. It was when one stared directly into his ice-blue eyes that one realised the cold ruthlessness of the man. They were pale, dead eyes. The eyes of a man without feeling.

Nechtan motioned to the solitary attendant, who had been serving wine to the company, to refill his goblet from the pitcher which stood on a side table. The young man filled his vessel and then said quietly: 'The wine is nearly gone. Shall I have the pitcher refilled?' But Nechtan shook his head and dismissed him with a curt gesture so that he was alone with his guests.

Fidelma inwardly groaned again. The meal had been embarrassing enough without the added awkwardness of a speech from Nechtan.

'My friends,' Nechtan began. His voice was soft, almost cajoling, as he gazed without warmth around him. 'I hope I

363

may now call you thus, for it has long been in my heart to seek you all out and make reparation to each of you for the wrong which you have suffered at my hands.'

He paused, looking expectantly around, but was met only with silence. Indeed, Fidelma seemed to be the only one to raise her head to meet his dead eyes. The others stared awkwardly at the remains of the meal on their plates before them.

'I am in your hands tonight,' went on Nechtan, as if oblivious to the tension around the table. 'I have wronged you all . . .'

He turned to the silent, elderly, nervous-looking man who was seated immediately to his left. The man had a habit of restively chewing his nails, a habit which Fidelma thought disgusting. It was a fact that, among the professional classes of society, well-formed hands and slender tapering fingers were considered a mark of beauty. Fingernails were usually carefully cut and rounded and most women put crimson stain on them. It was also considered shameful for a professional man to have unkempt nails.

Fidelma knew that the elderly man was Nechtan's own physician which made his untidy and neglected hands twice as outrageous and offensive in her eyes.

Nechtan smiled at the man. It was a smile, Fidelma thought, which was merely the rearrangement of facial muscles and had nothing to do with feeling.

'I have wronged you, Gerróc, my physician. I have regularly cheated you of your fees and taken advantage of your services.'

The elderly man stirred uncomfortably in his seat but then shrugged indifferently.

'You are my chieftain,' he replied stiffly.

Nechtan grimaced, as if amused by the response, and turned to the fleshy but still handsome middle-aged woman who sat next to Gerróc. She was the only other female at the table.

'And you, Ess, you were my first wife. I divorced you and drove you from my house by false claims of infidelity when all I sought was the arms of another younger and more attractive woman who took my fancy. By seeking to convict you of adultery I unlawfully stole your dowry and inheritance. In this, I wronged you before our people.'

Ess sat stony-faced; only a casual blink of her eyes denoted that she had even heard Nechtan's remark.

'And seated next to you,' Nechtan went on, still turning sunwise around the circle of the table, 'is my son, *our* son, Dathó. Through injustice to your mother, Dathó, I have also wronged you, my son. I have denied you your rightful place in this territory of the Múscraige.'

Dathó was a slim young man of twenty; his face was graven but his eyes – he had his mother's eyes and not the grey, cold eyes of his father – flashed with hatred at Nechtan. He opened his mouth as though to speak harsh words but Fidelma saw that his mother, Ess, laid a restraining hand on his arm and so he simply sniffed, thrust out his jaw pugnaciously but made no reply. It was clear that Nechtan would receive no forgiveness from his son nor his former wife.

Yet Nechtan appeared unperturbed at the reactions. He seemed to take some form of satisfaction in them.

Another of the guests, who was seated opposite Ess – Fidelma knew him as a young artist named Cuill – nervously rose from his seat and walked round the table, behind Nechtan, to where the pitcher of wine stood and filled his goblet, apparently emptying the jug, before returning to his seat.

Nechtan did not seem to notice him. Fidelma only half-registered the action. She continued to meet Nechtan's cold eyes steadily with her stormy green ones, and raised a hand to thrust back the wisps of red hair which crept from under her head-dress.

'And you, Fidelma of Cashel, sister of our king

Colgú . . .' Nechtan spread his hands in a gesture which seemed designed to extend his remorse. 'You were a young novice when you came to this territory as one of the retinue of the great Brehon Morann, chief of the judges of the five kingdoms. I was enamoured by your youth and beauty; what man would not be? I sought you out in your chamber at night, abusing all laws of hospitality, and tried to seduce you . . .'

Fidelma raised her jaw; a tinge of red showed on her cheeks as she recalled the incident vividly.

'Seduce?' Her voice was icy. The term which Nechtan had used was a legal one – *sleth* – which denoted an attempted intercourse by stealth. 'Your unsuccessful attempt was more one of *forcor*.'

Nechtan blinked rapidly and for a moment his face dissolved into a mask of irritation before resuming its pale, placid expression. *Forcor* was a forcible rape, a crime of a violent nature, and had Fidelma not, even at that early age, been accomplished in the art of the *troid-sciathagid*, the ancient form of unarmed combat, then rape might well have resulted from Nechtan's unwelcome attention. As it was, Nechtan was forced to lie indisposed for three days after his nocturnal visit and bearing the bruises of Fidelma's defensive measures.

Nechtan bowed his head, as if contritely.

'It was a wrong, good Sister,' he acknowledged, 'and I can only admit my actions and plead for your forgiveness.'

Fidelma, in spite of her internal struggle, reflecting on the teachings of the Faith, could not bring herself to indicate any forgiveness on her part. She remained silent, staring at Nechtan in ill-concealed disgust. A firm suspicion was now entering her mind that Nechtan, this evening, was performing some drama for his own end. Yet for what purpose?

Nechtan's mouth quirked in a fleeting gesture of amusement, as if he knew her angry silence would be all the response that he would receive from her.

He paused a moment before turning to the fiery, red-haired man seated on her left. Daolgar, as Fidelma knew, was a man of fierce temper, given to action rather than reflection. He was quick to take offence but equally quick to forgive. Fidelma knew him as a warm-hearted, generous man.

'Daolgar, chieftain of Sliabh Luachra and my good neighbour,' Nechtan greeted him, but there seemed irony in his tone. 'I have wronged you by encouraging the young men of my clan to constantly raid your territory, to harass your people in order to increase our lands and to steal your cattle herds.'

Daolgar gave a long, inward sniff through his nostrils. It was an angry sound. His muscular body was poised as if he were about to spring forward.

'That you admit this thing, a matter known to my people, is a step in the right direction towards reconciliation, Nechtan. I will not let personal enmity stand in the way of a truce between us. All I ask is that such a truce be supervised by an impartial Brehon. Needless to say, on behalf of my people, compensation for the lost cattle, the deaths in combat, must also be agreed . . .'

'Just so,' Nechtan interrupted curtly.

Nechtan now ignored Daolgar, turning to the young man who, having filled his goblet, had resumed his place.

'And now to you, Cuill, I have also made grievous injury, for our entire clan knows that I have seduced your wife and taken her to live in my house to the shame of your family before our people.'

The young, handsome man was sitting stiffly on the other side of Daolgar. He tried to keep his composure but his face was red with a mixture of mortification and a liberal amount of wine. Cuill was already known to Fidelma by reputation as a promising decorative artist whose talents had been sought by many a chieftain, bishop and abbot in order to create monuments of lasting beauty for them.

'She allowed herself to be seduced,' Cuill replied sullenly. 'Only in seeking to keep me ignorant of the affair was harm done to me. That matter was remedied when she left me and went to dwell in your house, forsaking her children. Infatuation is a terrible thing.'

'You do not say "love"?' queried Nechtan sharply. 'Then you do not concede that she loves me?'

'She was inspired with a foolish passion which deprived her of sound judgement. No. I do not call it love. I call it infatuation.'

'Yet you love her still.' Nechtan smiled thinly, as if purposely mocking Cuill. 'Even though she dwells in my house. Ah well, have no fear. After tonight I shall suggest that she returns to your house. I think my . . . infatuation . . . with her is ended.'

Nechtan seemed to take amusement from the young man's controlled anger. Cuill's knuckles showed white where he gripped the sides of his chair. But Nechtan seemed to tire of his ill-concealed enjoyment and now he turned to the last of the guests – the slim, dark-haired warrior at his right side.

'So to you, Marbán.'

Marbán was *tánaiste*, heir elect to Nechtan's chieftaincy. The warrior stirred uncomfortably.

'You have done me no wrong,' he interrupted with a tight, sullen voice.

Nechtan's plump face assumed a woebegone look.

'Yet I have. You are my *tánaiste*, my heir apparent. When I am gone, you will be chieftain in my stead.'

'A long time before that,' Marbán said, evasively. 'And no wrong done.'

'Yet I have wronged you,' insisted Nechtan. 'Ten years ago, when we came together before the clan assembly so that the assembly could choose which of us was to be chief and which was to be *tánaiste*, it was you who the assembly favoured. You were the clear choice to be chieftain. I discovered this before the assembly met and so I paid bribes to many in order that I might be elected chieftain. So I came to office while you, by default, became the second choice. For ten years I have kept you at my side when you should have ruled in my place.'

Fidelma saw Marbán's face whiten but there was no registration of surprise on his features. Clearly the *tánaiste* already knew of Nechtan's wrongdoing. She saw the anger and hatred pass across his features even though he sought to control the emotions.

Fidelma felt that she had no option but to speak up and she broke the silence by clearing her throat. When all eyes were turned on her she said in a quiet, authoritative tone:

'Nechtan of the Múscraige, you have asked us here to forgive you certain wrongs which you have done to each of us. Some are a matter for simple Christian forgiveness. However, as a *dálaigh*, an advocate of the courts of this land, I have to point out to you that not all your misdeeds, which you have admitted freely at this table, can be dealt with that simply. You have confessed that you should not legally be chieftain of the Múscraige. You have confessed that, even if you were legally chieftain, you have indulged in activities which did not promote the commonwealth of your people, such as encouraging illegal cattle raids into the territory of Daolgar of Sliabh Luachra. This in itself is a serious crime for which you may have to appear before the assembly and my brother, Colgú, King of Cashel, and you could be dismissed from your office . . .'

Nechtan held up his plump hand and stayed her.

'You had ever the legal mind, Fidelma. And it is right that you should point out this aspect of the law to me. I accept your knowledge. But before the ramifications of this feast of forgiveness are felt, my main aim was to recognise before you all what I have done. Come what may, I concede this. And now I will raise my goblet to each and every one of you, acknowledging what I have done to you all. After that, your law may take its course and I will rest content in that knowledge.'

He reached forward, picked up his goblet and raised it in salutation to them.

'I drink to you all. I do so contritely and then you may have joy of your law.'

No one spoke. Sister Fidelma raised a cynical eyebrow at Nechtan's dramatic gesture. It was as if they were watching a bad play.

The chieftain swallowed loudly. Almost immediately the goblet fell from his hand and his pale eyes were suddenly wide and staring, his mouth was open and he was making a terrible gasping sound, one hand going up to his throat. Then, as if a violent seizure racked his body, he fell backwards, sending his chair flying as he crashed to the floor.

For a moment there was a deadly stillness in the feasting hall.

It was Gerróc, the chieftain's physician, who seemed to recover his wits first. He was on his knees by Nechtan in a moment. Yet it didn't need a physician's training to know that Nechtan was dead. The contorted features, staring dead eyes, and twisted limbs showed that death had claimed him.

Daolgar, next to Fidelma, grunted in satisfaction.

'God is just, after all,' he remarked evenly. 'If ever a man needed to be helped into the Otherworld, it was this man.' He glanced quickly at Fidelma and half-shrugged as he saw her look of reproach. 'You'll pardon me if I speak my mind, Sister? I am not truly a believer in the concept of forgiveness of sins. It depends much on the sins and the perpetrator of them.'

Fidelma's attention had been distracted by Daolgar but, as she was turning back towards Gerróc, she noticed that young Dathó was whispering anxiously to his mother Ess, who was shaking her head. Her hand seemed to be closed around a small shape hidden in her pocket.

Gerróc had risen to his feet and was glaring suspiciously at Daolgar.

'What do you mean "*helped* into the Otherworld",
Daolgar?' he demanded, his tone tight with some suppressed emotion.

Daolgar gestured dispassionately.

'A figure of speech, physician. God has punished Nechtan in his own way with some seizure. A heart-attack, or so it appears. That was help enough. And as for whether Nechtan deserved to be so stricken – why, who around this table would doubt it? He has wronged us all.'

Gerróc shook his head slowly.

'It was no seizure brought on by the whim of God,' he said quietly. Then he added: 'No one should touch any more of the wine.'

They were all regarding the physician with confusion, trying to comprehend his meaning.

Gerróc responded to their unarticulated question.

'Nechtan's cup was poisoned,' he said. 'He has been murdered.'

After a moment's silence, Fidelma rose slowly from her place and went to where Nechtan lay. There was a blue tinge to his lips, which were drawn back, revealing discoloured gums and teeth. The twisted features of his once cherubic face were enough for her to realise that his brief death agony had been induced in a violent form. She reached towards the fallen goblet. A little wine still lay in its bowl. She dipped her finger in it and sniffed at it suspiciously. There was a bitter-sweet fragrance which she could not identify.

She gazed up at the physician.

'Poison, you say?' She did not really need such confirmation.

He nodded quickly.

She drew herself up and gazed round at the disconcerted faces of her fellow guests. Bewildered though they were, not one did she see there whose face reflected grief or anguish for the death of the chieftain of the Múscraige.

Everyone had risen uncertainly to their feet now, not knowing what to do.

It was Fidelma who spoke first in her quiet, firm tone.

'As an advocate of the court, I will take charge here. A crime has been committed. Each one in this room has a motive to kill Nechtan.'

'Including yourself,' pointed out young Dathó immediately. 'I object to being questioned by one who might well be the culprit. How do we know that you did not poison his cup?'

Fidelma raised her eyebrows in surprise at the young man's accusation. Then she considered it slowly for a moment before nodding in acceptance of the logic.

'You are quite right, Dathó. I also had a motive. And until we can discover how the poison came to be in this cup, I cannot prove that I did not have the means. Neither, for that matter, can anyone else in this room. For over an hour we have been at this table, each having a clear sight of one another, each drinking the same wine. We should be able to reason how Nechtan was poisoned.'

Marbán was nodding rapidly in agreement.

'I agree. We should heed Sister Fidelma. I am now chieftain of the Múscraige. So I say we should let Fidelma sort this matter out.'

'You are chieftain unless it can be proved that you killed Nechtan,' interrupted Daolgar of Sliabh Luachra with scorn. 'After all, you were seated next to him. You had motive and opportunity.'

Marbán retorted angrily: 'I am now chieftain until the assembly says otherwise. And I say that Sister Fidelma also has authority until the assembly says otherwise. I suggest that we resume our places at the table and allow Fidelma to discover by what means Nechtan was poisoned.'

'I disagree,' snapped Dathó. 'If she is the guilty one then she may well attempt to lay the blame on one of us.'

'Why blame anyone? Nechtan deserved to die!' It was Ess, the former wife of the dead chieftain, who spoke sharply. 'Nechtan deserved to die,' she repeated emphatically. 'He deserved to die a thousand times over. No one in this room would more gladly see him dispatched to the Otherworld than I. And I would joyfully accept responsibility for the deed if I had done it. Little blame to whoever did this deed. They have rid the world of a vermin, a parasite who has caused much suffering and anguish. We, in this room, should be their witnesses that no crime was committed here, only natural justice. Let the one who did this deed admit to it and we will all support their cause.'

They all stared cautiously at one another. Certainly none appeared to disagree with Ess's emotional plea but none appeared willing to confess to the deed.

Fidelma pursed her lips as she considered the matter under law.

'In such a case, we would all need to testify to the wrongs enacted by Nechtan. Then the guilty one would go free simply on the payment of Nechtan's honour price to his family. That would be the sum of fourteen *cumal* . . .'

Ess's son, Dathó, interrupted with a bitter laugh.

'Perhaps some among us do not have a herd of forty-two milch cows to pay in compensation. What then? If compensation is not paid, the law exacts other punishment from the guilty.'

Marbán now smiled expansively.

'I would provide that much compensation merely to be rid of Nechtan,' he confessed without embarrassment. With Nechtan's death, Fidelma noticed, the usually taciturn warrior was suddenly more decisive in manner.

'Then,' Cuill, the young artist who had so far been silent, leant forward eagerly, 'then whoever did this deed, let them speak and admit it, and let us all contribute to exonerating them. I agree with Ess – Nechtan was an evil man who deserved to die.'

There was a silence while they examined each other's faces, waiting for someone to admit their guilt.

'Well?' demanded Daolgar, impatiently, after a while. 'Come forward whoever did this and let us resolve the matter and be away from this place.'

No one spoke.

It was Fidelma who broke the silence with a low sigh.

'Since no one will admit this deed . . .'

She did not finish for Marbán interrupted again.

'Better it was admitted.' His voice was almost cajoling. 'Whoever it was, my offer to stand behind them holds. Indeed, I will pay the entire compensation fee.'

Sister Fidelma saw Ess compressing her lips; her hand slid to the bulge on her thigh, her slender fingers wrapping themselves around the curiously shaped lump which reposed in her pocket. She had began to open her mouth to speak when her son, Dathó, thrust forward.

'Very well;' he said harshly. 'I will admit to the deed. I killed Nechtan, my father. I had more cause to hate him than any of you.'

There was a loud gasp of astonishment. It was from Ess. She was staring in surprise at her son. Fidelma saw that the others around the table had relaxed at his confession and seemed relieved.

Fidelma's eyes narrowed as she gazed directly into the face of the young man.

'Tell me how you gave him the poison?' she invited in a conversational voice.

The young man frowned in bewilderment.

'What matters? I admit the deed.'

'Admission must be supported by evidence,' Fidelma countered softly. 'Let us know how you did this.'

Dathó shrugged indifferently.

'I put poison into his cup of wine.'

'What type of poison?'

Dathó blinked rapidly. He hesitated a moment.

'Speak up!' prompted Fidelma irritably.

'Why . . . hemlock, of course.'

Sister Fidelma shifted her gaze to Ess. The woman's eyes had not left her son since his confession. She had been staring at him with a strained, whitened face.

'And is that a vial of hemlock which you have in your thigh pocket, Ess?' Fidelma snapped.

Ess gave a gasp and her hand went immediately to her pocket. She hesitated and then shrugged as if in surrender.

'What use in denying it?' she asked. 'How did you know I had the vial of hemlock?'

Dathó almost shouted: 'No. I asked her to hide it after I had done the deed. It has nothing to do—'

Fidelma raised a hand and motioned him to silence.

'Let me see it,' she pressed.

Ess took a small glass vial from her pocket and placed it on the table. Fidelma reached forward and picked it up. She took out the stopper and sniffed gently at the receptacle.

'Indeed, it is hemlock,' she confirmed. 'But the bottle is full.'

'My mother did not do this!' cried Dathó angrily. 'I did! I admit as much! The guilt is mine!'

Fidelma shook her head sadly at him.

'Sit down, Dathó. You are seeking to take the blame on yourself because your mother had a vial of hemlock on her person and you suspect that she killed your father. Is this not so?'

Dathó's face drained of colour and his shoulders dropped as he slumped back into his seat.

'Your fidelity is laudable,' went on Fidelma compassionately. 'However, I do not think that your mother, Ess, is the murderess. Especially since the vial is still full.'

Ess was staring blankly at Fidelma. Fidelma responded with a gentle smile.

'I believe that you came here tonight with the intention of trying to poison your former husband as a matter of vengeance. Dathó saw that you had the vial which you were attempting to hide after the deed was done. I saw the two of you arguing over it. However, you had no opportunity to place the hemlock in Nechtan's goblet. Importantly, it was not hemlock that killed him.'

She turned, almost sharply. 'Isn't that so, Gerróc?'

The elderly physician started and glanced quickly at her before answering.

'Hemlock, however strong the dose, does not act instantaneously,' he agreed pedantically. 'This poison was more virulent than hemlock.' He pointed to the goblet. 'You have already noticed the little crystalline deposits, Sister? It is realgar, what is known as the "powder of the caves", used by those creating works of art as a colourant but, taken internally, it is a quick-acting poison.'

Fidelma nodded slowly as if he were simply confirming what she knew already and then she turned her gaze back to those around the table. However, their eyes were focused towards the young artist, Cuill.

Cuill's face was suddenly white and pinched.

'I hated him but I would never take a life,' he stammered. 'I uphold the old ways, the sanctity of life, however evil it is.'

'Yet this poison is used as a tool by artists like yourself,' Marbán pointed out. 'Who among us would know this other than Gerróc and yourself? Why deny it if you did kill him? Have we not said that we would support one another in this? I have already promised to pay the compensation on behalf of the person who did the deed.'

'What opportunity had I to put it in Nechtan's goblet?' demanded Cuill. 'You had as much opportunity as I had.'

Fidelma raised a hand to quell the sudden hubbub of accusation and counter-accusation.

'Cuill has put his finger on the all-important question,' she said calmly but firmly enough to silence them. They had all risen again and so she instructed: 'Be seated.'

Slowly, almost unwillingly, they obeyed.

Fidelma stood at the spot in which Nechtan had sat.

'Let us consider the facts,' she began. 'The poison was in the wine goblet. Therefore, it is natural enough to assume that it was in the wine. The wine is contained in that pitcher there.'

She pointed to where the attendant had left the wine pitcher on a side table.

'Marbán, call in the attendant, for it was he who filled Nechtan's goblet.'

Marbán did so.

The attendant was a young man named Ciar, a dark-haired and nervous young man. He seemed to have great trouble in speaking when he saw what had happened in the room and he kept clearing his throat nervously.

'You served the wine this evening, didn't you, Ciar?' demanded Fidelma.

The young man nodded briefly. 'You all saw me do so,' he confirmed, pointing out the obvious.

'Where did the wine come from? Was it a special wine?'

'No. It was bought a week ago from a Gaulish merchant.'

'And did Nechtan drink the same wine as was served to his guests?'

'Yes. Everyone drank the same wine.'

'From the same pitcher?'

'Yes. Everyone had wine from the same pitcher during the evening,' Ciar confirmed. 'Nechtan was the last to ask for more wine from the pitcher and I noticed that it was nearly empty after I filled his goblet. I asked him if I should refill it but he sent me away.'

Marbán pursed his lips, reflectively.

'This is true, Fidelma. We were all a witness to that.'

'But Nechtan was not the last to drink wine from that pitcher,' replied Fidelma. 'It was Cuill.'

Daolgar exclaimed and turned to Cuill.

'Fidelma is right. After Ciar filled Nechtan's goblet and

left, and while Nechtan was talking to Dathó, Cuill rose from his seat and walked around Nechtan to fill his goblet from the pitcher of wine. We were all concentrating on what Nechtan had to say; no one would have noticed if Cuill had slipped the poison into Nechtan's goblet. Cuill not only had the motive, but the means and the opportunity.'

Cuill flushed. 'It is a lie!' he responded.

But Marbán was nodding eagerly in agreement.

'We have heard that this poison is of the same material as used by artists for colouring their works. Isn't Cuill an artist? And he hated Nechtan for running off with his wife. Isn't that motive enough?'

'There is one flaw to the argument,' Sister Fidelma said quickly.

'Which is?' demanded Dathó.

'I was watching Nechtan as he made his curious speech asking forgiveness. But I observed Cuill pass behind Nechtan and he did not interfere with Nechtan's goblet. He merely helped himself to what remained of the wine from the pitcher, which he then drank, thus confirming, incidentally, that the poison was placed in Nechtan's goblet and not the wine.'

Marbán was looking at her without conviction.

'Give me the pitcher and a new goblet,' instructed Fidelma, irritably.

When it was done she poured the dregs which remained in the bottom of the pitcher into the goblet and considered them a moment before dipping her finger in them and gently touching her finger with her tongue.

She smiled complacently at the company.

'As I have said, the poison is not in the wine,' she reiterated. 'The poison was placed in the goblet itself.'

'Then how was it placed there?' demanded Gerróc in exasperation.

In the silence that followed, Fidelma turned to the attendant. 'I do not think that we need trouble you further, Ciar, but wait outside. We will have need of you later. Do not mention anything of this matter to anyone yet. Is that understood?'

Ciar cleared his throat noisily.

'Yes, Sister.' He hesitated. 'But what of the Brehon Olcán? He has just arrived. Should I not inform him?'

Fidelma frowned.

'Who is this judge?'

Marbán touched her sleeve.

'Olcán is a friend of Nechtan's, a chief judge of the Múscraige. Perhaps we should invite him in? After all, it is his right to judge this matter.'

Fidelma's eyes narrowed.

'Was he invited here this night?' she demanded.

It was Ciar who answered her question.

'Only after the meal began. Nechtan requested me to have a messenger sent to Olcán. The message was to ask the judge to come here.'

Fidelma thought rapidly and then said: 'Have him wait then but he is not to be told what has happened here until I say so.'

After Ciar had left she turned back to the expectant faces of her erstwhile meal guests.

'So we have learnt that the poison was not in the wine but in the goblet. This narrows the field of our suspects.'

Daolgar of Sliabh Luachra frowned slightly.

'What do you mean?'

'Simply that if the poison was placed in the goblet then it had to be placed there after the time that Nechtan drained one goblet of wine and when he called Ciar to refill his goblet. The poison had to be placed there after the goblet was refilled.'

Daolgar of Sliabh Luachra leant back in his chair and suddenly laughed hollowly.

'Then I have the solution. There are only two others in this room who had the opportunity to place the poison in

Nechtan's goblet,' he said smugly.

'And those are?' Fidelma prompted.

'Why, either Marbán or Gerróc. They were seated on either side of Nechtan. Easy for them to slip the poison into the goblet which stood before them while we were concentrating on what he had to say.'

Marbán had flushed angrily but it was the elderly physician, Gerróc, who suffered the strongest reaction.

'I can prove that it was not I!' he almost sobbed, his voice breaking pathetically in indignation.

Fidelma turned to regard him in curiosity.

'You can?'

'Yes, yes. You have said that we all had a reason to hate Nechtan and that implies that we would all therefore wish him dead. That gives every one of us a motive for his murder.'

'That is so,' agreed Fidelma.

'Well, I alone of all of you knew that it was a waste of time to kill Nechtan.'

There was a pause before Fidelma asked patiently: 'Why would it be a waste of time, Gerróc?'

'Why kill a man who was already dying?'

'*Already* dying?' prompted Fidelma after the exclamations of surprise had died away.

'I was physician to Nechtan. It was true that I hated him. He cheated me of my fees but, nevertheless, as physician here, I lived well. I did not complain. I am advancing in years now. I was not going to imperil my security by accusing my chieftain of wrongdoing. However, a month ago, Nechtan started to have terrible headaches, and once or twice the pain was so unbearable that I had to strap him to his bed. I examined him and found a growth at the back of the skull. It was a malignant tumour for within a week I could chart its expansion. If you do not believe me, you may examine him for yourselves. The tumour is easy to discern behind his left ear.'

Fidelma bent over the chief and examined the swelling behind the ear with repugnance.

'The swelling is there,' she confirmed.

'So, what are you saying, Gerróc?' Marbán demanded, seeking to bring the old physician to a logical conclusion.

'I am saying that a few days ago I had to tell Nechtan that it was unlikely he would see another new moon. He was going to die anyway. The growth of the tumour was continuing and causing him increased agony. I knew he was going to die soon. Why need I kill him? God had already chosen the time and method.'

Daolgar of Sliabh Luachra turned to Marbán with grim satisfaction on his face.

'Then it leaves only you, *tánaiste* of the Múscraige. You clearly did not know that your chieftain was dying and so you had both the motive and the opportunity.'

Marbán had sprung to his feet, his hand at his waist where his sword would have hung had they not been in the feasting hall. It was a law that no weapons were ever carried into a feasting hall.

'You will apologise for that, chieftain of Sliabh Luachra!'

Cuill, however, was nodding rapidly in agreement with Daolgar's logic.

'You were very quick to offer your newfound wealth as chieftain to pay the compensation should anyone else confess. Had they done so, it would have solved a problem, wouldn't it? You would emerge from this without a blemish. You would be confirmed as chieftain of the Múscraige. However, if you were guilty of causing Nechtan's death then you would immediately be deposed from holding any office. That is why you were so eager to put the blame on to me.'

Marbán stood glowering at the assembly. It was clear that he now stood condemned in the eyes of them all. An angry muttering had arisen as they confronted him.

Sister Fidelma raised both her hands to implore silence.

'Let us not quarrel when there is no need. Marbán did not kill Nechtan.'

There was a brief moment of surprised silence.

'Then who did?' demanded Dathó angrily. 'You seem to be playing cat and mouse with us, Sister. If you know so much, tell us who killed Nechtan.'

'Everyone at this table will concede that Nechtan was an evil, self-willed man who was at war with life. As much as we all had reason to hate him, he hated everyone around him with equal vehemence.'

'But who killed him?' repeated Daolgar.

Sister Fidelma grimaced sorrowfully.

'Why, he killed himself.'

The shock and disbelief registered on everyone's faces.

'I had begun to suspect,' went on Fidelma, 'but I could find no logical reason to support my suspicion until Gerróc gave it to me just now.'

'Explain, Sister,' demanded Marbán wearily, 'for I cannot follow the same logic.'

'As I have said, as much as we hated Nechtan, Nechtan hated us. When he learnt that he was to die anyway, he decided that he would have one more great revenge on those people he disliked the most. He preferred to go quickly to the Otherworld than to die the lingering death which Gerróc doubtless had described to him. If it takes a brave man to set the boundaries to his own life, then Nechtan was brave enough. He chose a quick-acting poison, realgar, delighting in the fact it was a substance that Cuill, the husband of his current mistress, often used.

'He devised a plan to invite us all here for a last meal, playing on our curiosity or our egos by saying that he wanted to make public reparation and apology for those wrongs that he had done to us. He planned the whole thing. He then recited his wrongdoing against us, not to seek forgiveness, but to ensure that we all knew that each had cause to hate him and seek his destruction. He wanted to plant seeds of suspicion in all our minds. He made his recitation of wrongdoing sound more like a boast than an apology. A boast and a warning.'

Ess was in agreement.

'I thought his last words were strange at the time,' she said, 'but now they make sense.'

'They do so now,' Fidelma endorsed.

'What were the words again?' queried Daolgar.

'Nechtan said: "And now I will raise my goblet to each and every one of you, acknowledging what I have done to you all. After that, your law may take its course and I will rest content in that knowledge . . . I drink to you all . . . and then you may have joy of your law.'

It was Fidelma who was able to repeat the exact words.

'It certainly does not sound like an apology,' admitted Marbán. 'What did he mean?'

It was Ess who answered.

'I see it all now. Do you not understand how evil this man was? He wanted one or all of us to be blamed for his death. That was his final act of spite and hatred against us.'

'But how?' asked Gerróc, confused. 'I confess, I am at a loss to understand.'

'Knowing that he was dying, that he had only a few days or weeks at most, he set his own limits to his lifespan,' Fidelma explained patiently. 'He was an evil, spiteful man, as Ess acknowledges. He invited us to this meal, knowing that, at its close, he would take poison. As the meal started, he asked Ciar, the attendant, to send for his own judge, Brehon Olcán, hoping that Olcán would find us in a state of confusion, each suspecting the other, and come to a wrong decision that one or all of us were concerned in his murder. Nechtan killed himself in the hope that we would be found culpable of his death. While he was talking to us he secreted the poison in his own goblet.'

Fidelma looked around the grim faces at the table. Her smile was strained.

'I think we can now speak with the Brehon Olcán and sort this matter out.'

She turned towards the door, paused and looked back at those in the room.

'I have encountered much wrongdoing in this world, some of it born of evil, some born of desperation. But I have to say that I have never truly encountered such malignancy as dwelt in the spirit of Nechtan, sometime chieftain of the Múscraige.'

It was the following morning as Fidelma was riding in the direction of Cashel that she encountered the old physician, Gerróc, at a crossroads below the fortress of Nechtan.

'Whither away, Gerróc?' she greeted with a smile.

'I am going to the monastery of Imleach,' replied the old man gravely. 'I shall make confession and seek sanctuary for the rest of my days.'

Fidelma pursed her lips thoughtfully.

'I would not confess too much,' she said enigmatically.

The old physician gazed at her with a frown.

'You know?' he asked sharply.

'I know a boil which can be lanced from a tumour,' she replied.

The old man sighed softly.

'At first I only meant to put fear into Nechtan. To make him suffer a torment of the mind for a few weeks before I lanced his boil or it burst of its own accord. Boils against the back of the ear can be painful. He believed me when I pretended it was a tumour and he had not long to live. I did not know the extent of his evil mind nor that he would kill himself to spite us all.'

Fidelma nodded slowly.

'His blood is still on his own hands,' she said, seeing the old man's troubled face.

'But the law is the law. I should make confession.'

'Sometimes justice takes precedence over the law,'

Fidelma replied cheerfully. 'Nechtan suffered justice. Forget the law, Gerróc, and may God give you peace in your declining years.'

She raised a hand, almost in blessing, turned her horse and continued on her way towards Cashel.

Those that Trespass

❧

'The matter is clear to me. I cannot understand why the abbot should be bothered to send you here.'

Father Febal was irritable and clearly displeased at the presence of the advocate in his small church, especially an advocate in the person of the attractive, red-haired religieuse who sat before him in the stuffy vestry. In contrast to her relaxed, almost gentle attitude, he exuded an attitude of restlessness and suspicion. He was a short, swarthy man with pale, almost cadaverous features, the stubble of his beard, though shaven, was blue on his chin and cheeks and his hair was dark like the colour of a raven's wing. His eyes were deep set but dark and penetrating. When he expressed his irritability his whole body showed his aggravation.

'Perhaps it is because the matter is as unclear to the abbot as it appears clear to you,' Sister Fidelma replied in an innocent tone. She was unperturbed by the aggressive attitude of the priest.

Father Febal frowned; his narrowed eyes scanned her features rapidly, seeking out some hidden message. However, Fidelma's face remained a mask of unaffected candour. He compressed his lips sourly.

'Then you can return to the abbot and report to him that he has no need for concern.'

Fidelma smiled gently. There was a hint of a shrug in the position of her shoulders.

'The abbot takes his position as father of his flock very seriously. He would want to know more details of this tragedy before he could be assured that he need not concern himself. As the matter is so clear to you, perhaps you will explain it to me?'

Father Febal gazed at the religieuse, hearing for the first time the note of cold determination in her soft tones.

He was aware that Sister Fidelma was not merely a religieuse but a qualified advocate of the Brehon Law courts of the five kingdoms. Furthermore, he knew that she was the young sister of King Colgú of Cashel himself, otherwise he might have been more brusque in his responses to the young woman. He hesitated a moment or two and then shrugged indifferently.

'The facts are simple. My assistant, Father Ibor, a young and indolent man, went missing the day before yesterday. I had known for some time that there had been something troubling him, something distracting him from his priestly duties. I tried to talk to him about it but he refused to be guided by me. I came to the church that morning and found that the golden crucifix from our altar and the silver chalice, with which we dispense the communion wine, were both missing. Once I found that Father Ibor had also vanished from our small community here, it needed no great legal mind to connect the two events. He had obviously stolen the sacred objects and fled.'

Sister Fidelma inclined her head slowly.

'Having come to this conclusion, what did you do then?'

'I immediately organised a search. Our little church here is attended by Brother Finnlug and Brother Adag. I called upon them to help me. Before entering the order, Finnlug was master huntsman to the Lord of Maine, an excellent tracker and huntsman. We picked up the trail of Ibor and followed it to the woods nearby. We were only a short distance into the woods when we came across his body. He was hanging from the branch of a tree with the cord of his habit as a noose.'

Sister Fidelma was thoughtful.

'And how did you interpret this sight?' she asked quietly.

Father Febal was puzzled.

'How should I interpret this sight?' he demanded.

Fidelma's expression did not change.

'You tell me that you believe that Father Ibor stole the crucifix and chalice from the church and ran off.'

'That is so.'

'Then you say that you came across him hanging on a tree.'

'True again.'

'Having stolen these valuable items and run off, why would he hang himself? There seems some illogic in this action.'

Father Febal did not even attempt to suppress a sneer.

'It would be as obvious to you as it was to me.'

'I would like to hear what you thought.' Fidelma did not rise to his derisive tone.

Father Febal smiled thinly.

'Why, Father Ibor was overcome with remorse. Knowing that we would track him down, realising how heinous his crime against the Church was, he gave up to despair and pronounced his own punishment. He therefore hanged himself. In fact, so great was his fear that we would find him still alive, he even stabbed himself as he was suffocating in the noose, the knife entering his heart.'

'He must have bled a lot from such a wound. Was there much blood on the ground?'

'Not as I recall.' There was distaste in the priest's voice as if he felt the religieuse was unduly occupied with gory details. 'Anyway, the knife lay on the ground below the body where it had fallen from his hand.'

Fidelma did not say anything for a long while. She remained gazing thoughtfully at the priest. Father Febal glared back defiantly but it was he who dropped his eyes first.

'Was Father Ibor such a weak young man?' Fidelma mused softly.

'Of course. What else but weakness would have caused him to act in this manner?' demanded the priest.

'So? And you recovered both the crucifix and chalice from his person, then?'

A frown crossed Father Febal's features as he hesitated a moment. He made a curiously negative gesture with one hand.

Fidelma's eyes widened and she bent forward.

'You mean that you did not recover the missing items?' she pressed sharply.

'No,' admitted the priest.

'Then this matter is not at all clear,' she observed grimly. 'Surely, you cannot expect the abbot to rest easy in his mind when these items have not been recovered? How can you be so sure that it was Father Ibor who stole them?'

Fidelma waited for an explanation but none was forth-coming.

'Perhaps you had better tell me how you deem this matter is clear then?' Her voice was acerbic. 'If I am to explain this clarity to the abbot, I must also be clear in my own mind. If Father Ibor felt that his apprehension was inevitable and he felt constrained to inflict the punishment of death on himself when he realised the nearness of your approach, what did he do with the items he had apparently stolen?'

'There is one logical answer,' muttered Father Febal without conviction.

'Which is?'

'Having hanged himself, some wandering thief happened by and took the items with him before we arrived.'

'And there is evidence of that occurrence?'

The priest shook his head reluctantly.

'So that is just your supposition?' Now there was just a hint of derision in Fidelma's voice.

'What other explanation is there?' demanded Father Febal in annoyance.

Fidelma cast a scornful glance at him.

'Would you have me report this to the abbot and inform him that he need not worry? That a valuable crucifix and a chalice have been stolen from one of his churches and a priest has been found hanged but there is no need to worry?'

Father Febal's features grew tight.

'I am satisfied that Father Ibor stole the items and took his own life in a fit of remorse. I am satisfied that someone then stole the items after Ibor committed suicide.'

'But I am not,' replied Fidelma bitingly. 'Send Brother Finnlug to me.'

Father Febal had risen automatically in response to the commanding tone in her voice. Now he hesitated at the vestry door.

'I am not used . . .' he began harshly.

'I am not used to being kept waiting,' Fidelma's tone was icy as she cut in, turning her head away from him in dismissal. Father Febal blinked and then banged the door shut behind him in anger.

Brother Finnlug was a wiry-looking individual; his sinewy body, tanned by sun and wind, proclaimed him to be more a man used to being out in all sorts of weather than sheltering in the cloisters of some abbey. Fidelma greeted him as he entered the vestry.

'I am Fidelma of . . .'

Brother Finnlug interrupted her with a quick, friendly grin.

'I know well who you are, lady,' he replied. 'I saw you and your brother, Colgú the King, many times hunting in the company of my Lord of Maine.'

'Then you know that I am also an advocate of the courts and that you are duty bound to tell me the truth?'

'I know that much. You are here to inquire about the tragic

death of Father Ibor.' Brother Finnlug was straightforward and friendly in contrast to his superior.

'Why do you call it a tragic death?'

'Is not all death tragic?'

'Did you know Father Ibor well?'

The former huntsman shook his head.

'I knew little of him. He was a young man, newly ordained and very unsure of himself. He was only here about a month.'

'I see. Was he the newest member of the community? For example, how long has Father Febal been here?'

'Father Febal has been priest here for seven years. I came here a year ago and Brother Adag has been here a little more than that.'

'I presume that the members of your little community were on good terms with one another?'

Brother Finnlug frowned slightly and did not reply.

'I mean, I presume that there was no animosity between the four of you?' explained Fidelma.

Finnlug's features wrinkled in an expression which Fidelma was not able to interpret.

'To be truthful, Father Febal liked to emphasise his seniority over us. I believe he entered the Church from some noble family and does not forget it.'

'Was that attitude resented?'

'Not by me. I was in service to the Lord of Maine. I am used to being given orders and to obeying them. I know my place.'

Was there a slight note of bitterness there? Fidelma wondered.

'If I recall rightly, the Lord of Maine was a generous man and those in his service were well looked after. It must have been a wrench for you to leave such an employer to enter religious life?'

Brother Finnlug grimaced.

'Spiritual rewards are often richer than temporal ones. But, as I say, I have been used to service. The same may be said for Brother Adag, who was once a servant to another lord. But he is somewhat of a simpleton.' The monk touched his forehead. 'They say such people are blessed of God.'

'Did Father Ibor get on well with Father Febal?'

'Ah, that I can't say. He was a quiet young man. Kept himself to himself. I do not think he liked Father Febal. I have seen resentment in his eyes.'

'Why would he be resentful? Father Febal was the senior of your community. Father Ibor should have recognised his authority without question.'

The monk shrugged.

'All I can say is that he was hostile to Father Febal's authority.'

'Why do you think that he stole the items from the church?' Fidelma asked the question sharply.

Brother Finnlug's expression did not alter.

He simply spread his arms.

'Who can say what motivates a person to such actions? Who can know the deep secrets of men's hearts?'

'That is what I am here to discover.' Fidelma replied dryly. 'Surely, you must have an idea? Even to hazard a guess?'

'What does Father Febal say?'

'Does it matter what he says?'

'I would have thought that he was closer to Father Ibor than either Brother Adag or myself.'

'Closer? Yet you said there was hostility between them.'

'I did not mean close in the manner of friends. But they were priests together. Of similar social backgrounds, unlike Adag and me. As Brothers of this community, our task was more like that of servants in this church rather than the equals of Fathers Febal and Ibor.'

'I see.' Fidelma frowned thoughtfully. 'I am sure the abbot will be distressed to learn that this is the way your community is governed. We are all servants of God and all one under His Supreme Power.'

'That is not exactly the Faith which Father Febal

espouses.' Now there was clearly bitterness in his voice.

'So you do not know why Ibor might have stolen the items?'

'They were items of great value. They would never be poor on the proceeds of that wealth.'

'*They?*'

'I mean, whoever stole the items.'

'You have a doubt that Father Ibor stole them, then?'

'You are sharp, Sister. Alas, I do not have the precise way with words that you do.'

'Why do you think Father Ibor hanged himself having fled with these valuable items?'

'To avoid capture?'

'Your reply is in the form of a question. You mean that you are not sure of this fact either?'

Brother Finnlug shrugged.

'It is difficult for me to say. I cannot understand why a priest should take his life in any event. Surely no priest would commit such a sin?'

'Would you say that you cannot be sure that Father Ibor took his life?'

Brother Finnlug was startled.

'Did I say that?'

'You implied it. Tell me, in your own words, what happened during the last two days. Had there been any tension between Ibor and Febal or anyone else?'

Finnlug set his jaw firmly and stared at her for a moment.

'I did hear Father Ibor arguing the night before he disappeared.'

Fidelma leant forward, encouragingly.

'Arguing? With Father Febal?'

Brother Finnlug shook his head.

'I cannot be sure. I passed his cell and heard his voice raised. The other voice was quiet and muffled. It was as if Father Ibor had lost his temper but the person he was arguing with was in control.'

'You have no idea who this other person was?'

'None.'

'And you heard nothing of the substance of the argument?'

'I caught only a few words here and there.'

'And what were these words?'

'Nothing that makes sense. Ibor said: "It is the only way". Then he paused and after the other person said something, he replied, "No, no, no. If it has to end, I shall not be the one to end it". That was all I heard.'

Fidelma was quiet as she considered the matter.

'Did you interpret anything from these words, especially in the light of what subsequently happened?'

Brother Finnlug shook his head.

The door of the vestry suddenly opened and Father Febal stood on the threshold, his features wearing a peculiar look of satisfaction. He was clearly a man who had heard some news which pleased him.

'We have found the thief who took the crucifix and chalice from Father Ibor,' he announced.

Brother Finnlug rose swiftly to his feet. His eyes flickered from Father Febal to Sister Fidelma. Fidelma saw something within his expression but could not quite interpret it. Was it fear?

'Bring the thief forth,' she instructed calmly, remaining seated.

Father Febal shook his head.

'That would be impossible.'

'Impossible?' asked Fidelma with a dangerous note to her voice.

'The thief is dead.'

'You'd best explain,' Fidelma invited. 'In detail. Does this thief have a name?'

Father Febal nodded.

'Téite was her name.'

There was a deep intake of breath from Brother Finnlug.

'I take it that you knew her, Brother Finnlug?' Fidelma turned her head inquiringly.

'We all did,' replied Father Febal shortly.

'Who was she?'

'A young girl who lived not far from our community in the forest. She was a seamstress. She sewed garments and laundered clothes for us.'

'Where was she found and how was she identified as the thief?'

'Her cabin is within a short distance of where we found Father Ibor,' explained the priest. 'I understand from Brother Adag that she had picked up some garments from the community and when she did not return with them this morning, as she had arranged, Brother Adag went to her cabin and found her . . .'

Fidelma raised a hand to silence him.

'Let Brother Adag come forth and tell me his story in his own words. It is proper that I hear this matter at first hand. You and Brother Finnlug may wait outside.'

Father Febal looked uncomfortable.

'I think that you had better be warned, Sister.'

'Warned?' Fidelma's head came up quickly to stare at the priest.

'Brother Adag is slightly simple in nature. In many ways his mind has not matured into adulthood. His role in our community is to do simple manual tasks. He . . . how shall I explain it? . . . has a child's mind.'

'It might be refreshing to speak with one who has remained a child and not developed the contrived attitudes of an adult,' Fidelma smiled thinly. 'Bring him hither.'

Brother Adag was a handsome youth but clearly one who was used to taking orders rather than thinking for himself. His eyes were rounded and seemed to hold an expression of permanent innocence; of inoffensive naïveté. His hands were calloused and showed that he was also a man used to manual work.

'You found the body of the woman, Téite, in her cabin, so I am told?'

The young man drew his brows together as if giving earnest consideration to the question before answering.

'Yes, Sister. When she did not arrive here at midday, with some garments which she had collected yesterday and promised to deliver, Father Febal sent me to fetch them. I went to her cabin and she was lying stretched on the floor. There was blood on her clothing. She had been stabbed several times.'

'Ah? So Father Febal sent you to her cabin?'

The youth nodded slowly.

'How old was this woman, Téite? Did you know her?'

'Everyone knew her, Sister, and she was eighteen years and three months of age.'

'You are very exact.' Fidelma smiled at his meticulous diction, as if he considered each word almost before he uttered it.

'Téite told me her age and, as you ask me for it, I told you.' It was a simple statement of fact.

'Was she pretty?'

The youth blushed a little. He dropped his eyes.

'Very pretty, Sister.'

'You liked her?' pressed Fidelma.

The young man seemed agitated. 'No. No, I didn't.' He protested. His face was crimson.

'Why ever not?'

'It is the Father's rule.'

'Father Febal's rule?'

Brother Adag hung his head and did not reply.

'Rule or not, you still liked her. You may tell me.'

'She was kind to me. She did not make fun like the others.'

'So, what persuaded you that she had stolen the crucifix and chalice from Father Ibor?'

The young brother turned an ingenuous look upon her.

'Why, the chalice was lying by the side of her body in the cabin.'

Fidelma hid her surprise.

'The chalice only?' She swallowed hard. 'Why would someone enter her cottage, kill her and leave such a valuable item by the body?'

Brother Adag clearly did not understand the point she was making. He said nothing.

'What did you do after you found the body?' she continued after a pause.

'Why, I came to tell Father Febal.'

'And left the chalice there?'

Brother Adag sniffed disparagingly.

'I am not stupid. No, I brought it with me. Father Febal has been searching for it these last two days. I brought it back to Father Febal for safekeeping. I even searched for the crucifix but could not find it there.'

'That is all, Adag. Send Father Febal in to me,' Fidelma instructed the youth.

The priest entered a moment later and sat down before Fidelma without waiting to be asked.

'A sad tale,' he muttered. 'But at least the matter should be cleared up to your satisfaction now. You may return to give your report to the abbot.'

'How well did you know this woman, Téite?' asked Fidelma, without commenting.

Father Febal raised his eyebrows a moment and then sighed.

'I have known her since she was a small girl. I went to administer the last rites when her mother died. Téite had barely reached the age of choice then. However, she had a talent with a needle and therefore was able to make a good living. She has lived within the forest these last four years to my knowledge and often repaired or made garments for our community.'

'Did Father Ibor know her?'

Febal hesitated and then gave an odd dismissive gesture with his hand.

'He was a young man. Young men are often attracted to young women.'

Fidelma glanced at the priest curiously.

'So Father Ibor was attracted to the girl?' she asked with emphasis.

'He was in her company more than I found to be usual. I had occasion to reprimand him.'

'Reprimand him? That sounds serious.'

'I felt that he was neglecting his duties to be with the girl.'

'Are you telling me that there was a relationship between Father Ibor and this girl?'

'I am not one to judge such a matter. I know only that they were frequently in one another's company during the past few weeks, almost since the time he arrived at our little community. I felt that he was ignoring his obligation to his community. That is all.'

'Did he resent your admonition?'

'I really have no idea whether he resented my telling him or not. That was not my concern. My concern was to bring him to an awareness of what was expected of him in this community.'

'You did not have an argument about it?'

'An argument? I am . . . I *was* his superior and when I told him of my concern that should have been an end to the matter.'

'Clearly it was not an end to it,' observed Fidelma.

Father Febal gave her an angry look.

'I do not know what you mean.'

'The events that have unfolded since you told Father Ibor that he was spending too much time with Téite have demonstrated that it was not an end to the matter,' Fidelma pointed out coldly. 'Or do you have some other interpretation of these events?'

Father Febal hesitated.

'You are right. You are implying that the two of them were in the plot to steal the artefacts from the church and, having done so, Father Ibor was overcome with remorse and killed himself . . .' The priest's eyes suddenly widened. 'Having killed the girl first,' he added.

Fidelma stroked the side of her nose with a forefinger reflectively.

'It is an explanation,' she conceded. 'But it is not one that I particularly favour.'

'Why not?' demanded the priest.

'The hypothesis would be that the young priest was so enamoured of the girl that they decided to run away, stealing the valuable objects as a means of securing themselves from want and poverty. We would also have to conclude that, having reached as far as the girl's cabin, the young priest is overcome with remorse. He quarrels with the girl and stabs her to death. Then, leaving the precious chalice by her body, yet curiously hiding the crucifix, he wanders into the forest and, after travelling some distance, decides he is so distressed that he hangs himself. Furthermore, while hanging, while suffocating to death, he is able to take out a knife and stab himself through the heart.'

'What is wrong with that surmise?'

Fidelma smiled thinly.

'Let us have Brother Adag back here again. You may stay, Father Febal.'

The ingenuous young monk stood looking from Fidelma to Father Febal with an unstudied innocence.

'I am told that it was you who saw Téite when she came to the community yesterday?'

The boy was thoughtful.

'Yes. It is my task to gather the clothes that need washing or mending and prepare a bundle for Téite.'

'And this you did yesterday morning?'

'Yes.'

'Téite collected them? These were garments for sewing?'

'And two habits for washing. Father Febal and Brother Finnlug had given me . . . They had been torn and one bloodied in the search for Father Ibor.'

'Let me be sure of this,' interrupted Fidelma. 'Téite collected them yesterday morning?'

Brother Adag looked across at Father Febal, dropped his eyes and shifted his weight from one foot to another.

'Yes, yesterday morning.'

'You are sure that she collected them *after* the search had been made for Father Ibor then?'

'Yes. Father Ibor was found the day before.'

'Think carefully,' snapped Father Febal, irritated. 'Think again.'

The young monk flushed and shrugged helplessly.

Father Febal sniffed in annoyance.

'There you are, Sister, you see that little credit may be placed on this simpleton's memory. The clothes must have been taken before we found Father Ibor.'

The young monk whirled around. For a moment Fidelma thought that he was going to attack Father Febal for both hands came up, balled into clenched fists. But he kept them tight against his chest in a defensive attitude. His face was red and there was anger in his eye.

'Simple I may be but at least I cared for Téite.' There was a sob in his voice.

Father Febal took an involuntary step backwards.

'Who did not care for Téite?' Fidelma prompted gently. 'Father Ibor?'

'Of course he did not care. But she cared for him. She loved him. Not like . . .'

The youth was suddenly silent.

'I would take no notice of this boy's foolishness, Sister,' Father Febal interposed blandly. 'We all know what happened.'

'Do we? Since we are talking of people being attracted to this young girl, was Brother Finnlug attracted to her?'

'Finnlug?' Brother Adag grimaced dismissively. 'He has no time for women.'

Father Febal looked pained. 'Brother Finnlug has several faults. Women were certainly not one of them.'

'Faults?' pressed Fidelma with interest. 'What faults does he have then?'

'Alas, if only he had the gift of spirituality we would be

compensated. He was of use to us only in his ability to hunt and gather food for our table. He is not suited to this religious life. Now, I think we have spoken enough. Let us call a halt to this unhappy affair before things are said that may be regretted.'

'We will end it only when we discover the truth of the matter,' replied Fidelma firmly. 'Truth is never to be regretted.' She turned to the youth. 'I know you liked the girl, Téite. Yet now she is dead and has been murdered. Father Febal's rule does not apply now. You owe it to your feelings for her to tell us the truth.'

The boy stuck out his chin.

'I am telling the truth.'

'Of course, you are. You say that Father Ibor did not like Téite?'

'He did not love her as I did.'

'And how did Téite feel about Ibor?'

'She was blinded by Father Ibor's cleverness. She thought that she loved him. I overheard them. He told her to stop . . . stop pestering, that was his word . . . stop pestering him. She thought that she loved him just as Father Febal thought that he loved her.'

The priest rose angrily.

'What are you saying, boy?' he thundered. 'You are crazy!'

'You cannot deny that you told her that you loved her,' Brother Adag replied, not intimidated by the priest's anger. 'I overheard you arguing with her on the day before Father Ibor died.'

Father Febal's eyes narrowed. 'Ah, now you are not so stupid that you forget times and places and events. The boy cannot be trusted, Sister. I would discount his evidence.'

'I loved Téite and can be trusted!' cried Brother Adag.

'I did not love her . . .' Father Febal insisted. 'I do not love anyone.'

'A priest should love all his flock,' smiled Fidelma in gentle rebuke.

'I refer to the licentious love of women. I merely looked after Téite when her mother died. Without me she would not have survived.'

'But you felt, perhaps, that she owed you something?'

Father Febal scowled at her.

'We are not here to speak of Téite but the crime of Father Ibor.'

'Crime? No, I think that we are here to speak of a crime committed against him rather than by him.'

Father Febal paled.

'What do you mean?'

'Téite was murdered. But she was not murdered by Father Ibor. Nor was she responsible for stealing the crucifix or chalice, the latter of which was found so conveniently by her body.'

'How have you worked this out?'

'Send for Brother Finnlug. Then we may all discuss the resolution of this matter.'

They sat in the small vestry facing her: Father Febal, Brother Finnlug and Brother Adag. Their faces all wore expressions of curiosity.

'I grant that people behave curiously,' began Fidelma. 'Even at the best of times their behaviour can be strange. But I doubt that they would behave in the manner that is presented to me.'

She smiled, looking at each of them in turn.

'What is your solution to this matter?' sneered the priest.

'Certainly it would not be one where the murder victim appears alive and well after the murderer has hanged himself.'

Father Febal blinked. 'Adag must be mistaken.'

'No. Father Ibor and the artefacts vanished the day before yesterday? You immediately raised the alarm. Brother Finnlug tracked Ibor through the forest and you found him hanging from a tree. Isn't that right?'

'Quite right.'

'Had he killed Téite, as is now being suggested, before he hanged himself, she could not have come to the community yesterday noon to pick up the garments that needed sewing.'

'Why do you discount the fact that Adag might be confused about the day?'

'Because he gave Téite two habits that had been torn and bloodied in the search for Father Ibor, those worn by you and Finnlug when you found him hanging on the tree. Doubtless they will be found in her cabin to prove the point.' Fidelma paused. 'Am I to presume that no one thought to tell the girl that Ibor had just been discovered having hanged himself? She did think she was in love with him.'

'I did not see the girl,' Father Febal replied quickly. 'Brother Adag did.'

'And Brother Adag admits that he loved Téite,' added Brother Finnlug cynically.

The young man raised his head defiantly. 'I do not deny it. But she didn't return my love; she loved Father Ibor who rejected her.'

'And that made you angry?' asked Fidelma.

'Yes. Very angry!' replied Brother Adag vehemently.

Brother Finnlug turned to gaze at his companion in suspicion.

'Angry enough to kill them both?' he whispered.

'No,' Fidelma replied before Brother Adag could put in his denial. 'Ibor and Téite were not killed in anger, but in cold blood. Weren't they, Brother Finnlug?'

Brother Finnlug turned sharply to her, his eyes suddenly dead.

'Why would I know that, Sister Fidelma?'

'Because you killed them both,' she said quietly.

'That's nonsense! Why would I do that?' exploded the monk, after a moment's shocked silence.

'Because when you stole the crucifix and chalice from the church, you were discovered by Father Ibor. You had to kill him. You stabbed him in the heart and then took the body to

404

the forest where you concocted a suicide by hanging. Then you realised the knife wound could not be hidden and so you left the knife lying by his body. As if anyone, hanging by a cord from a tree, would be able to take out a knife and stab themselves in the heart. How, incidentally, was the poor man able to reach the branch to hang himself? No one has reported to me any means whereby he could have climbed up. Think of the effort involved. The body was placed there by someone else.'

She gazed at Father Febal who was deep in thought. He shook his head, denying he could offer an explanation.

Fidelma returned her gaze to Brother Finnlug.

'You concocted an elaborate plan to deceive everyone as to what had truly happened.'

There was a tension in the vestry now.

'You are insane,' muttered Brother Finnlug.

Fidelma smiled gently.

'You were huntsman to the Lord of Maine. We have already discussed what a generous man he was to those in his service. None went in want, not even when the harvest was bad. When I asked you what reason you had to leave such a gainful employer, you said it was because of your spiritual convictions. Do you maintain that? That you rejected the temporal life for the spiritual?'

Father Febal was gazing at Brother Finnlug in bemusement. The monk was silent.

'You also revealed to me, unwittingly, perhaps, your resentment at the structure of this community. If it was a spiritual life you wanted, this was surely not it, was it?'

Father Febal intervened softly.

'The truth was that Finnlug was dismissed by the Lord of Maine for stealing and we took him in here.'

'What does that prove?' demanded Finnlug.

'I am not trying to prove anything. I will tell you what you did. You had initially hoped to get away with the robbery. The motive was simple, as you told me; the sale of those precious artefacts would make you rich for life. That would appease your resentment that others had power and riches but you did not. As I have said, Ibor discovered you and you stabbed him and took his body to the forest. When you returned, you realised that you had his blood on your clothing.

'The theft was now discovered and Father Febal sought your help. The blood was not noticed. Maybe you put on a cloak to disguise it. You, naturally, led him to Father Ibor's body. Everything was going as you planned. Father Ibor had been blamed for the theft. Now Father Febal was led to believe that Ibor must have killed himself in a fit of remorse. Even the fact that Ibor had been stabbed was explained. The fact there was little blood on the ground did not cause any questions. You, meanwhile, could pretend that the blood-stains on your cloak were received in the search for Ibor. Perhaps you, Finnlug, came up with the idea that the missing crucifix and chalice had been taken by some robber.

'The following day, Téite, unaware, came to collect the sewing and washing. Adag had gathered it as usual, including your habit, the bloodstained one. You had not meant the girl to have it. You hurried to her cottage to make sure she did not suspect. Perhaps you had made your plan even before you went there? You killed her and placed the chalice by her side. After all, the crucifix was such as would still give you wealth and property. It was known that Téite and Ibor had some relationship. Everyone would think the worst. All you had to do was return and bide your time until you could leave the community without arousing suspicion.'

Brother Finnlug's face was white.

'You can't prove it,' he whispered without conviction.

'Do I need to? Shall we go and search for the crucifix? Will you tell us where it is . . . or shall I tell you?' She stood up decisively as if to leave the room.

Brother Finnlug groaned, raising his hands to his head.

'All right, all right. It is true. You know it is still hidden in my cell. It was my chance to escape . . . to have some wealth, a good life.'

Father Febal walked slowly with Fidelma to the gate of the complex of buildings which formed the community.

'How did you know where Brother Finnlug had hidden the crucifix?' he asked.

Sister Fidelma glanced at the grave-looking priest and suddenly allowed a swift mischievous grin to flit across her features.

'I didn't,' she confessed.

Father Febal frowned.

'How did you know then . . .? Know it was Finnlug and what he had done?' he demanded.

'It was only an instinct. Certainly it was a deduction based on the facts, such as they were. But had Brother Finnlug demanded that I prove my accusation, I do not think I would have been able to under the strictures of the proceedings of a court of law. Sometimes, in this business of obtaining proof, more depends on what the guilty person thinks you know and believes that you can prove than what you are actually able to prove. Had Brother Finnlug not confessed, I might not have been able to clear up this business at all.'

Father Febal was still staring at her aghast as she raised her hand in farewell and began to stride along the road in the direction of Cashel.

Holy Blood

❦

'**S** ister Fidelma! How came you here?'

The Abbess Ballgel, standing at the gate of the Abbey of Nivelles, stared at the dusty figure of the young religieuse with open-mouthed surprise.

'I am returning home to Kildare, Ballgel,' replied the tall, slimly built figure, a broad smile of greeting on her travel-stained features. 'I have been in Rome awhile and where else should I come when passing through the land of the Franks on my way to the coast?'

To the surprise of two elderly religieuses standing nearby, the Abbess Ballgel and Sister Fidelma threw their arms around one another and hugged each other with unconcealed joy.

'It is a long time,' observed the abbess.

'Indeed, a long time. I have not seen you since you departed Kildare and left the shores of Éireann to come to this place. Now I am told that you are the abbess.'

'The community elected me to that honour.'

Sister Fidelma became aware that the two sisters who accompanied the abbess were fretting impatiently. She was surprised at their grim faces and anxiety. Abbess Ballgel caught her swift examination of her companions. The group had been leaving the abbey when Fidelma had come upon them.

'I am afraid that you have chosen a bad moment to arrive, Fidelma. We are on our way to the Forest of Seneffe, a little way down the road there. You didn't come by that route, did you?'

Fidelma shook her head.

'No. I came over the hills from Namur where I arrived by boat along the river.'

'Ah!' The abbess looked serious and then she forced a smile. 'Go in and accept our hospitality, Fidelma. I hope to be back before nightfall and then we will talk and catch up on each's other's news.'

Fidelma drew her brows together, sensing a preoccupation in the abbess's voice and manner.

'What is the matter?' she demanded. 'There is something vexing you.'

Ballgel grimaced.

'You had ever a keen eye, Fidelma. A report has just arrived that one of our sisters has been found murdered in the Forest of Seneffe, and another member of our community is missing. We are hurrying there now to discover the truth of this report. So go and rest yourself from your travels and I will join you later.'

Fidelma shook her head quickly.

'Mother Abbess,' she said softly, 'it has been a long time and perhaps you have forgotten. I spent eight years studying law under the Brehon Morann. I have an aptitude for solving conundrums and investigating mysteries. Let me come with you and I will lend you what talent I have to resolve this matter.'

Fidelma and Ballgel had been novices together in the Abbey of Kildare.

'I remember your talent well, Fidelma. In fact, I have often heard your name spoken for we receive many travellers from Éireann here. By all means come with us.'

In fact, Ballgel looked slightly relieved.

'And you may explain the details of this matter as we go,'

Fidelma said, putting down her travelling bag within the gate of the abbey before joining the others.

They set off, walking side by side, with the two other religieuses bringing up the rear.

'Who has been reported murdered?' Fidelma began.

'I do not know. I know that early this morning Sister Cessair and Sister Della set off to the Abbey of Fosse. It is the seventeenth day of March and so they were taking the phial of the Holy Blood of Blessed Gertrude to the Brothers of Fosse for the annual blessing and . . .'

Fidelma laid a hand on her friend's arm.

'You are raising more questions than I can keep pace with, Ballgel. Remember that I am a stranger here.'

The abbess was apologetic. 'Let me start at the beginning then. Twenty-five years ago the ruler of this land, Peppin the Elder of Landen, died. His widow, Itta, decided to devote herself to a religious life and came here, to Nivelles, with her daughter, Gertrude. They built our abbey. When Itta died, the Blessed Gertrude became abbess.

'About that time two Brothers from Éireann, Foillan and Ultan, came wandering and preaching the word of God. They decided to stay and Gertrude granted them lands a few miles from here in Fosse, the other side of the forest of Seneffe. Foillan and Ultan gathered many Irish religious there and some were attracted to our abbey as well. It is said that the Blessed Foillan prophesied that Abbess Gertrude, because she so loved and encouraged the Irish missionaries, would die on the same day that the Blessed Patrick died. And it happened as he said it would seven years ago today.'

Abbess Ballgel grew silent for a while until Fidelma encouraged her to continue.

'So Foillan proved to be a prophet?'

'He did not live to see his prophecy fulfilled for he died four years before his beloved Gertrude. He and his three companions were travelling from his Abbey of Fosse through the very same forest that we are entering – the forest of Seneffe – when they were set upon by robbers and murdered. Their bodies were so well hidden in the forest that it took three months before anyone stumbled across them. Foillan's brother Ultan then became the abbot.

'When the Blessed Gertrude died it was agreed between the two abbeys that, as she was the benefactor of both, each anniversary of her death, a phial of her holy blood, taken from her at death to be held behind the high altar at our abbey, would be taken to the Abbey of Fosse and blessed by the abbot in service with his community and then returned here. This was the task which Sister Cessair and Sister Della set out to fulfil this morning.'

'How did you hear that a sister had been murdered in the forest?'

'When midday came, the time of the service at Fosse, and no members of our community had arrived with the holy blood, Brother Sinsear from the Fosse abbey set out to see what delayed them. He found the dead body of one of the sisters by the roadside. He came straightaway to tell us and then immediately returned to alert the community at Fosse.'

'But you do not know which of the poor sisters was killed?'

The abbess shook her head.

'Brother Sinsear was too agitated to say, but merely told our gatekeeper the news before returning.'

By now they had entered the tall, dark brooding forest of Seneffe. The track was fairly straight, though at times it twisted around rocky outcrops, avoiding streams to find a ford in a more accessible place. The afternoon sun was obliterated by the heavy foliage and the day grew cold around them. Fidelma realised that the highway proved an ideal ambush spot for any robbers and it did not surprise her to hear that lives had been lost along this roadway.

Although Irish religious went out into the world unarmed to preach the Faith, most of them were taught the art of *troid-sciathagid* or battle through defence – a method of defending oneself without the use of weapons. Not many religious, thus prepared, fell to bands of marauding thieves and robbers. Clearly from their names, the two sisters had been Irish and must have known some rudiments of the art for it was the custom to have such knowledge before being allowed to take the holy word from the shores of Éireann into the lands of the strangers.

Now they walked silently and swiftly along the forest track, eyes anxiously scanning for any dangers around them.

'Is it not a dangerous path for young sisters to travel?' observed Fidelma after a while.

'No more so than other places,' her friend replied. 'Do not let the death of Foillan colour your thinking. Since his death a decade ago, the robbers were driven from these parts and there have been no further incidents.'

'Until now,' Fidelma added grimly.

'Until now,' sighed Ballgel.

A moment or two later, they rounded a clump of trees which the path had skirted. Not far away they saw a group of religious. There were four or five and they had a cart with them, harnessed to an ass. They clustered under a gnarled oak whose branches formed a canopy over the pathway, so low that one might almost reach up and grab the lower branches. It made this particular section of the forest path even more gloomy and full of shadows.

A tall, florid man, wearing a large gold cross, and clearly one of authority, saw Abbess Ballgel and came hurrying forward.

'Greetings, Mother Abbess. This is a bad business, a profane business.' He spoke in Latin but Fidelma could hear his Frankish accent.

'Abbot Heribert of Fosse,' Ballgel whispered to Fidelma just out of earshot.

'Where is the body?' Ballgel came straight to the point, also speaking in Latin.

Abbot Heribert looked uncomfortable.

413

'I would prepare yourself . . .' he began.

'I have seen death before,' replied Abbess Ballgel quietly.

He turned and indicated the far side of the oak tree.

Ballgel moved forward in the direction of his hand, followed by Fidelma.

The woman was tied to the oak tree facing away from the path, almost in mockery of a crucifixion. There was blood everywhere. Fidelma screwed her features up in distaste. The woman, who was dressed in the habit of a religieuse, had been systematically mutilated about the face.

'Cut her down!' cried the sharp tone of the Abbess Ballgel. 'At once! Do not leave the poor girl hanging there!'

Two of the monks went forward grimly.

'Who is it?' Fidelma asked. 'Do you recognise her?'

'Oh yes. We have only one sister with hair as golden as that. It is young Sister Cessair. God be merciful to her soul.' She genuflected.

Fidelma pursed her lips thoughtfully. She watched as two male religious cut down the body.

'Wait!' Fidelma called and, turning to the abbess, she said quickly, 'I would examine the body carefully and with some privacy.'

Ballgel raised her eyes in surprise.

'I do not understand.'

'This is a bizarre matter. It might be that she has been . . . brutalised.'

Ballgel passed a hand across her brow as if bewildered but she understood what Fidelma meant.

She called to the monks to set the body down on the ground before the cart and then asked Abbot Heribert to withdraw his men to a respectful distance while Fidelma made her investigation.

Fidelma knelt by the body, noticing that the shade of the oak tree stopped the sun's rays from drying the ground. It was muddy and the mud had been churned by the cart and the footprints of those trampling round. Her attention was momentarily distracted by indentations of two feet at one point which were far deeper than the others, to the extent that water had formed in the hollows. Nevertheless, she ignored the mud and bent over the body. She turned and motioned the Abbess Ballgel to come closer.

'If you will observe and witness my examination, Ballgel,' she called over her shoulder. 'You will observe that the sister's face has been severely mutilated with a knife. The skin has been deliberately marked with a sharp blade, disfiguring it, as if the purpose were to destroy the features of this young girl.'

Ballgel forced herself to look on and nodded, suppressing a soft groan of anguish.

Fidelma bent further to her work before pausing, satisfied as to her physical examination. Then she turned her attention to the small leather *marsupium* which hung at the dead sister's waist. It was not secured with the leather thong that usually fastened such a purse and it was empty.

Fidelma rose to her feet. Next she went to the tree from which the body had been taken and began to look about. With a gasp of triumph she bent down a picked up a torn scrap of paper. There was no writing but a few curious short lines drawn on it. Fidelma frowned and placed it in her own *marsupium*.

Her keen eye then caught a round stone on the ground. It was bloody and pieces of hair and skin were stuck to it.

'What is it?' demanded Abbess Ballgel coming forward.

'That is the instrument with which Cessair was killed,' Fidelma explained. 'Her death was caused by her skull being smashed in and not through the blade of the knife that destroyed her features. At least this was no attack by robbers.'

'How can you be so certain?'

'We have observed that the girl was not sexually molested in any way. Yet this was an attack of hate towards the sister.'

Ballgel stared at her friend in amazement.

'How can you say it was an attack of hate?'

'Let us discount the idea of robbers. The purpose of a thief is to steal. It is true that some thieves have even been known to sexually assault Sisters of the faith. There was no attempt at theft here. The Sister's crucifix of silver still hangs around her neck. It was not a sexual assault. What is left of the motivation which would cause someone to smash her skull, tie her to a tree and mutilate her features? There is surely only hatred left?'

'The Holy Blood of the Blessed Gertrude is not in her *marsupium*,' Ballgel pointed out. 'I have been looking all around for the phial. That is valuable; but above all, where is Sister Della?'

Fidelma grimaced.

'The holy blood may be valuable to you, yes. Not to a thief. There would be no purpose in stealing that if one wanted money.'

'Do thieves and robbers need a purpose?'

'All people need a purpose, even those whom we deem mad follow a logic, which may not be our logic but one of their own creation with its own rules. Once one deciphers the code of that logic then it is as easy to follow as any.'

'And what of Sister Della?'

Fidelma nodded. 'There is the real mystery. Find her and we may find the missing phial. Has a search been made for her?' She asked the question of the abbot.

Abbot Heribert looked sourly at Fidelma.

'Not yet. And who are you?'

'Sister Fidelma is a qualified advocate of our legal courts,' explained Abbess Ballgel hurriedly, seeing the look of derision on the abbot's face.

'Do women have such a status in your country?' he demanded in astonishment.

'Is that so strange?' Fidelma replied irritably. 'Anyway, we waste time. We must find Sister Della for she may be in danger. If Sister Cessair was not robbed, and was not attacked for sexual motives, the alternative is that she was killed from some personal motive which, judging from the savagery of the attack, shows a depth of malice that makes me shudder. Who could have been so angered by her that they would attempt to destroy her beauty? It is as if she were attacked by a jealous lover, for it is known that hate and love are two sides of the same coin.'

Fidelma suddenly saw Abbot Heribert's eyes widened a fraction. She saw him glance swiftly at Ballgel and then drop his gaze.

'Why does the mention of a lover have some special meaning for you?' she demanded.

It was Abbess Ballgel who answered for him.

'Sister Cessair did have a . . . a liaison,' she said quietly.

'It was disgusting!' grunted Abbot Heribert.

'A curious choice of word.' Fidelma's eyes narrowed. 'Disgusting in what way?'

'Abbot Heribert is a firm believer in the concept of celibacy,' explained Ballgel.

'Celibacy is by no means universally approved of by the Church,' Fidelma pointed out. 'There are many double houses where religious of both sexes live and raise their children to the service of God. What is disgusting about that?'

'Paul of Tarsus spoke firmly in favour of celibacy and many other Church Fathers have done so. There are those of us who argue that only through celibacy do we have the power to spread the Faith.'

'I am not here to discuss theology, Heribert. Are you telling me that Cessair was in love with a religieux from your Abbey of Fosse?'

'God forgive him,' Heribert lowered his head piously.

'Only him?' Was there sarcasm in Fidelma's voice. 'Surely forgiveness is universal? Who was this monk?'

'Brother Cano,' replied Ballgel. 'He was a young monk who arrived from Éireann only a few weeks ago. It seems that he and Sister Cessair met and were immediately attracted by one another.'

'And this relationship was disapproved of?'

'It did not matter to me,' Ballgel said hastily. 'Our culture does not forbid such relationships as you have pointed out. Even Kildare, where we studied, was a mixed house.'

'But it mattered to Abbot Heribert,' Fidelma swung round on the tall Frankish prelate.

'Of course it mattered. My Abbey of Fosse is for men of the Faith only. I follow the strict rule of celibacy and expect all members of my community to do the same. I warned Brother Cano several times to cease this disgusting alliance. Abbess Ballgel knew my views. It does not surprise me that this woman of loose morals has paid a bitter price.'

Fidelma raised her eyebrows in surprise.

'That is also an interesting statement. Are you given to much passion over this matter, Father Abbot?'

Heribert frowned suspiciously at her.

'What do you mean?'

'I merely make an observation. Does it worry you that I comment on the passionate tones by which you denounce this poor Sister?'

'I believe in the teachings of Paul of Tarsus.'

'Yet it is not the rule of the Church. Nor, indeed, does the Holy Father denounce those who reject celibacy. It is not even a rule of our Faith.'

'Not yet. But the ranks of those of us who believe in the segregation of men and woman and the rule of celibacy are increasing. One day the Holy Father will have to pay us heed. Already he has suggested that celibacy is the best way forward . . .'

'Until that happens, it is not a rule. Very well, I understand your position now. But we have a murder to be solved. Where is this Brother Cano?'

Abbot Heribert shrugged.

'I understand from brother Sinsear that Brother Cano left

the abbey this morning and was last seen heading along this road. Perhaps he meant to meet Sister Cessair?'

Abbess Ballgel groaned softly.

'If Cano was coming to meet Sister Cessair . . . if he could do this to her . . . we must find Sister Della.'

Fidelma gave her a reassuring smile.

'No one has said that Cano did this as yet,' she observed quietly. 'However, it seems that, as well as the missing Sister, we also have a missing Brother to account for. Perhaps we will find one with the other. Where is this Brother Sinsear?'

A religieux who was standing nearby coughed nervously and took a hesitant step towards her. He was a pale-faced young man, hardly more than an adolescent. His features were taut and he appeared in the grip of strong emotions.

'I am Sinsear.'

Fidelma regarded his flushed, anxious face.

'You appear agitated, Brother.'

'I work with Brother Cano in the gardens of our abbey, Sister. I am his friend. I knew that he had a . . .' he glanced nervously at his abbot, '. . . a passion for Sister Cessair.'

'A passion? You do not have to bandy words, Brother. Was he in love with her?'

'I only knew that they met at regular times in the forest here because of Father Abbot's disapproval of their relationship.'

Abbot Heribert's brows drew together in anger but Fidelma held up a hand to silence him.

'Go on, Brother Sinsear. What are you saying?'

'They had a special meeting spot in a glade not a far distance from here. A woodsman's hut. It occurs to me, in the circumstances, that the hut might be examined.'

'You should have spoken up sooner, Brother,' snapped Abbot Heribert. 'Cano may have fled by now. I see no point in seeking him in that hut.'

'You are presuming that he is guilty of this deed, Heribert,' Fidelma rebuked him. 'Yet I think we should investigate this hut. Do you know the way to it, Brother Sinsear?'

'I think so. There is a small path leading off this track about fifty metres in that direction.' He pointed towards Fosse, and on the far side of the track to the oak tree where Cessair had been found.

'How far into the forest?'

'No more than three hundred metres.'

'Then lead the way. Father Abbot, you may send the rest of the Brothers of your community to escort the Sisters and the body of Cessair back to the Abbey of Nivelles.'

Heribert made to object and then did her bidding.

Brother Sinsear turned pale eyes on Fidelma.

'Could Cano really have done such a terrible deed? Oh God, to maltreat such grace and beauty! Why did she not give her love to one who would appreciate such exquisite . . .'

Abbot Heribert interrupted him.

'Let us get a move on, Brother Sinsear. I expect it will be a waste of time. If Cano killed her then he will not be hiding in a forest hut but will have left the area by now.'

'You are also forgetting the missing Sister Della,' Fidelma pointed out. 'And it is wrong to assume Cano's guilt.'

'Yes, yes,' Heribert snapped. 'Have it your own way.'

With the young Brother Sinsear leading the way, clutching at a newly cut hawthorn stick, they trod a well-worn path through the great forest.

Eventually they came on a little glade, a pleasant spot through which a small stream meandered. By it stood a woodsman's crude hut. The door was shut and there was no sign of life.

Fidelma raised her hand and brought them to a halt on the edge of the glade. As they neared the door of the hut, Fidelma's keen eyes surveyed it quickly. The first thing she noticed was bloodstains on the door jamb and there were several palm prints on the door as if someone had, with bloodied hands, pushed it open. Blood was also on a piece of wood near the door.

They heard a sobbing sound from within.

'Brother Cano!' Sinsear suddenly called. 'The abbot and I are here.'

There was a silence. The sobbing suddenly halted.

'Sinsear?' came a hesitant male voice. 'Thank God! I need help.'

There was another sound now. A feminine cry which sounded as if it were stifled almost immediately.

Fidelma glanced at her companions.

'Stay back. I shall go in first.' She turned and raised her voice. 'Brother Cano? I am Fidelma of Cashel. I have come to help you. I am coming in.'

There was no response.

Slowly Fidelma leant forward, placing her hand near the bloodied imprint and pushed against the door. It swung open easily.

At the far end of the woodsman's hut she saw a young man clad in religious robes, kneeling on the floor. His hair was dishevelled, his eyes red and cheeks stained as if from weeping. He held a piece of bloodstained cloth in his hands. Before him lay the prone figure of a girl. Her eyes were opened and she appeared conscious but her clothes were covered in blood.

Fidelma heard a sound behind her and swung round. She saw Abbot Heribert and the others trying to squeeze behind her and swiftly waved them back.

'Stay there!' she snapped. There was such a power in her voice that they paused. 'I will speak with Cano and Sister Della first.'

Fidelma turned and took a step into the hut.

'I am Sister Fidelma,' she repeated. 'May I attend to Sister Della?'

'Of course,' the young man seemed bewildered.

Fidelma knelt by his side. He had been trying to cleanse her wounds.

'Lie still,' she said, as she examined the wound of the young religieuse. It was to the back of the head. Sister Della had been clubbed in the same fashion as Sister Cessair. Unlike the blow delivered to Cessair's skull, it had not broken the bone. There was, however, a nasty swelling.

'Am I dying, Sister?' The girl's voice was faint.

'No. In a moment we will get you back to the abbey so that you may be properly attended. What can you tell me about the attack on Sister Cessair and yourself?'

'Little enough.'

'A little in these circumstances may mean a lot,' encouraged Fidelma.

'Alas, the little is nothing. Sister Cessair and I were bringing the phial of the Holy Blood of Blessed Gertrude to the Abbey of Fosse. We were walking through the woods. I remember . . .' she paused and groaned. 'I did not hear anyone behind us for we were talking together and . . .' She held up a hand to her head and groaned. 'There came a sharp blow and then I can remember nothing until I came to, lying on the path with a blinding pain in my head. I thought I was alone. I could see no one. I began to look around and then, then I saw Cessair . . .'

She gave a heartrending sob.

'What then?' prompted Fidelma gently.

'I could do nothing for her, except try to get help. I came here and . . .'

'You came here?' Fidelma interrupted quickly. 'Why come to this woodsman's hut? Why not go on to the Abbey of Fosse or back to Nivelles?'

'I knew Cano would be here.' The girl groaned again.

'She knew that I had arranged to meet Cessair here on the journey from Nivelles to Fosse,' interrupted Cano defiantly. 'I am not ashamed of it.'

Fidelma ignored him and smiled down at the girl.

'Rest awhile. It will not be long before we have you safe and your wound attended.'

Only then did she turn to Cano.

'So you were waiting here for Cessair?'

'Cessair and I loved one another. We often met here because Abbot Heribert was vehement against us.'

'Tell me about it.'

'There is not much to tell. I arrived at Fosse about a month ago to join the community. Although there are several Irish religious here and in Nivelles, it is a strange land. They are more inclined to celibacy than we are in Éireann. They do not have the number of mixed houses that we do. Abbot Heribert was fanatical for the rule of celibacy; even though there is no such proscription in the church, he makes it a rule in his abbey. I think I would have left long ago had I not met Cessair.'

'When did you and Cessair meet?'

'The week after I came here. It was Brother Sinsear who introduced me when we were taking produce from Fosse to Nivelles.'

'Brother Sinsear introduced you?'

'Yes. As a gardener, Sinsear often took produce between the two abbeys. He knew many of the religieuses at Nivelles.'

'Did Cessair have any enemies that you knew of?'

'Only Abbot Heribert, when he discovered our relationship.' Cano's voice was bitter. From the doorway, Fidelma heard Heribert's expression of anger.

'Why didn't you leave and move on to a mixed house?'

'We planned to but Abbess Ballgel counselled Cessair against it.'

Fidelma frowned.

'Why would she be against such a plan?'

Cano shrugged.

'She was . . . protective to Cessair. She felt Cessair was too young.'

'More protective than to her other charges?'

'I do not know. All I know is that we were desperate and planning to leave here.'

Fidelma waited a while. Then she said abruptly: 'Did you kill Cessair?'

The young monk raised a tear-stained face to her and there was a haunted look in his eyes.

'How can you ask such a question?'

'Because I am a *dálaigh*, an advocate of the law,' replied Fidelma. 'It is my duty to ask.'

'I did not.'

'Tell me what happened this morning, then.'

'I knew that Cessair and Della were bringing the phial to Fosse for the annual blessing. So we arranged to meet here.'

'Surely that would mean a delay in the bringing of the phial to Fosse? The service was at midday.'

'Cessair was going to persuade Della to take the phial on to Fosse while she joined me here. We only meant to meet briefly to make some arrangements and then Cessair would hasten after Della, pretending she had broken her sandal on the road.'

'What arrangements were you going to make?'

'Arrangements to leave this place. Perhaps to go back to Ireland.'

'I see. So you arrived here . . .?'

'And here I waited. I thought Cessair was late and was about to go down to the main track to see if there was a sign of her when Della came stumbling into the hut. She was almost hysterical and told me what had happened then she passed out. I could not leave her alone and have been trying to return her to consciousness ever since. It is only a moment ago that she regained her senses.'

Fidelma turned to Della.

'Do you agree with this account?'

The girl had raised herself on an elbow: she still looked pale and shaken.

'So far as I am able. I do not remember much at all.'

'Very well. Then I think we should get you to the abbey where you may have the wound tended.' She glanced at Cano who was twisting his hands nervously. Then she remembered something.

'Do you have the phial of blood, Sister Della? The Holy Blood of the Blessed Gertrude?'

Della frowned and shook her head.

'Cessair carried it in her *marsupium*.'

'I see,' replied Fidelma thoughtfully, before turning to the others and waving them forward.

'We will carry Sister Della to Fosse,' she told them. 'There are a few more questions that I wish to ask but we should ensure that Sister Della gets proper treatment for her wound.'

The church and community of Fosse was not as spectacular as some of the abbeys which Fidelma had encountered in her travels. She reminded herself that it was barely twenty years old. It was not more than a collection of timber houses around a large, rectangular wooden church.

Sister Della was immediately taken to the infirmary while the abbot led the abbess and Fidelma to the refectory for refreshments. Brother Sinsear and Brother Cano were told to go to their cells and await the abbot's call.

Abbess Ballgel was the first to break the uneasy silence that had fallen between them. She had seen Fidelma's work before while they had been together at the Abbey of Kildare.

'Well, Fidelma, do you see a solution to this horror? And where is the Holy Blood of Gertrude?'

'Let us summarise what we know. We can eliminate certain things. Firstly, the concept that this action was committed by robbers. I have already given one main reason, that is the mutilation of Cessair. That was done from hate. Secondly, we have the testimony from Della who says that she was walking along talking with Cessair and did not hear or see anything until she was struck from behind.'

'You mean, if there had been robbers waiting in ambush then she would have seen something of them?'

'Just so. The very idea of even a single person creeping unobserved behind someone walking in a forest is, I find, rather a difficult one to accept.'

Abbess Ballgel frowned quickly.

'You claim that Sister Della is lying?'

'Not necessarily. But think of it in this way; think of a forest path strewn with dead leaves, twigs and the like. An animal might move quietly over such a carpet but can a human? Could a man or woman creep up so quickly behind someone walking along then strike them before they knew it?'

'Then we must question the girl further,' snapped Heribert, 'and force her to confess.'

Fidelma looked at him in disapproval.

'Confess to what?'

'Why, the killing of the other girl,' replied Heribert.

Fidelma gave a deep sigh.

'There is another more plausible explanation why Sister Della did not hear her assailant creep up behind her.'

The abbot frowned in anger.

'What game are you playing? First you say one thing and then you say another. I do not follow.'

The Abbess Ballgel intervened as she saw Fidelma's facial muscles go taut and her eyes change colour.

'Fidelma is a qualified advocate used to these puzzles. I suggest we allow her to follow her path of reasoning.'

The abbot sat back, his face set in a sneer.

'Proceed, then.'

'Before I come back to that point, let us proceed along another route. The savagery with which Sister Cessair was attacked, the fact that her features were mutilated, the fact that Sister Della was left unmarked except for the blow that laid her unconscious, means that Cessair was, indeed, singled out particularly in this attack. She was, as I said before, attacked out of some great malice towards her.'

'It is logical, Fidelma,' agreed the abbess.

'Then we must consider who had such a hatred of Cessair.'

She paused and allowed them to consider her proposal in silence.

'Well, we can eliminate almost everyone,' the abbess smiled briefly.

'How so?'

'Brother Cano was her lover. Sister Della was her closest friend in the abbey. Cessair made no enemies . . . except . . .'

She suddenly hesitated.

'Except?' encouraged Fidelma gently.

The abbess had dropped her eyes.

It was Abbot Heribert who flushed with anger.

'Except me, you mean?' He rose to his feet. 'What are you implying? Because I uphold the teaching of celibacy? Because I forbid any liaison with women among the members of my community? Because I urged the abbess to forbid Sister Cessair to see Brother Cano as I had forbidden him to meet with her? Are these things to be thrown at me in accusation that I murdered her?'

'Did you?'

Fidelma asked the question so quietly that for a long time it seemed that the abbot had not heard her.

'How dare you!'

'I dare because I must,' replied Fidelma calmly. 'Keep your bluster to yourself, Abbot. We are here discover the truth not to engage in games of vanity.'

Heribert went red in the face. He was inarticulate with rage.

The Abbess Ballgel leant forward.

'Abbot Heribert, we are simply intelligent people trying to resolve a problem. Our pride and self-regard should not impinge on that process for we are seeking the truth and the truth alone.'

Abbot Heribert blinked.

'I resent being accused . . .'

'I did not accuse you, Heribert,' Fidelma replied. 'Your unthinking pride did so. But, since you have raised this matter yourself, I put it to you that you certainly had no liking for Cessair.'

He stared at her and then shrugged.

'I have made that evident. No. I disliked her for she was a distraction to Brother Cano. Indeed, she was a distraction to all the young men in my community. I have even seen young men like Brother Sinsear moonstruck in her presence.'

'My mentor, the Brehon Morann of Tara, used to say: it is easier to become a monk in one's old age,' sighed Fidelma.

Abbess Ballgel hid a smile.

'Anyway,' Fidelma continued, 'as abbot you were expecting Sisters Cessair and Della to arrive at Fosse at noon or so I am led to believe?'

'Not precisely. I was expecting two sisters of Abbess Ballgel's community to arrive but I did not know who they would be. Had I known one was going to be Sister Cessair . . .'

'What would you have done?'

'I should have stopped her coming to mislead Brother Cano further into temptation's way.'

'Cano was misled?' queried Fidelma. 'I thought he was in love with Cessair?'

The abbot stirred uncomfortably.

'Women are the temptresses by which the saintly fall from grace.'

He did not meet Fidelma's flashing anger. But, Fidelma, realising it was impossible to overcome the misogynist prejudice, decided to ignore the remark.

'Ballgel, why did you choose Cessair and Della to bring the phial of blood for the service this morning?'

'Why?'

'Someone knew that Cessair was going to be walking along that forest track.'

The eyes of the abbess widened.

'Why, it was Sister Della who came to me last night and asked if she be allowed to take the phial for the blessing. She also asked me if she could choose a companion to accompany her.'

'You did not know that she would choose Cessair?'

'As a matter of fact,' smiled the abbess, 'I presumed that she would. They have been inseparable companions.'

'You knew that she would choose Cessair to accompany her through the forest of Seneffe even though the abbot disapproved of Cessair? Isn't that strange?'

'Not at all. I am like you, Fidelma. I refuse to be dictated to as to who I can send here or there.'

Abbot Heribert's mouth set in a grim line. He was clearly displeased but did not say anything.

'So Sister Della was the only other person who knew Cessair would go with her, apart from yourself, Ballgel?'

Abbess Ballgel looked carefully at her friend.

'You will remember, Fidelma,' she said softly, 'that you arrived at Nivelles only a short time after Brother Sinsear had brought us the dreadful news.'

Fidelma smiled sympathetically.

'I do remember. And you need hardly remind me that you would have had no time to have done the deed. Besides, it would be very difficult for an abbess to absent herself from her abbey for the time needed to do carry out this murder. I also presume that you would have had no motive either?'

Before Ballgel could respond, Abbot Heribert interrupted.

'It would similarly be difficult for an abbot to absent himself from his abbey,' he said shortly.

'I had not forgotten, Heribert,' Fidelma said solemnly. 'Tell us, as a matter of record, where you were about noon?'

Abbot Heribert shrugged.

'I will play the game to the end,' he said heavily. 'Today, being the anniversary of the death of the Blessed Gertrude, we have a midday Angelus followed by a service of remembrance, not only for Gertrude but in memory of the Blessed Foillan whom she allowed to build our abbey. The phial of the holy blood is brought to the abbey just before the midday Angelus bell is sounded.

'At ten minutes before midday I was standing with several brothers awaiting the appearance of the two sisters, who usually carry the phial from Nivelles. I did not know who they would be. When midday came and the bell was tolled, I thought that the only thing to do was proceed with the service, although without the phial.'

'Did you not send anyone to look for the Sisters?'

'I was informed that Brother Sinsear had already left to escort the Sisters through the forest. So I did not need to.'

'I see. Go on.'

'Well, we performed the service and when it was over there was still no sign of the Sisters nor of Brother Sinsear.'

'Brother Sinsear had come straight to Nivelles to alert us,' pointed out Ballgel.

'It was some time before Brother Sinsear returned,' agreed Heribert, 'and told us the appalling news and we immediately set out to the forest. We had barely reached there when you arrived.'

'I see. Will you send for Brother Sinsear?'

It was moments before they were joined by the young monk. The youth made an effort to overcome the nervous twisting of his hands by placing them behind his back.

'It is a terrible business,' he began, breaking the silence.

'I know that you are upset,' Fidelma smiled gently. 'After all, it is your close friend who stands in some danger. The finger of suspicion points in his direction.'

'Brother Cano might be possessed of a temper but he would never . . . never . . .'

'He was quick tempered?' Fidelma interrupted.

Brother Sinsear hung his head.

'I should not have said that. I meant . . .'

'It is true,' observed Abbot Heribert. 'I have rebuked him a couple of times for his turbulent moods.'

'Well, all I want from you, Brother Sinsear, are the details about today. I understand that you left the abbey go to in search of the two Sisters bringing the phial of holy blood? At what time was this?'

'Some time before midday, I think. Yes, it was half an

hour before the midday Angelus bell sounded because that was when the phial was due to be at the abbey.'

'Were you instructed to do so?'

Brother Sinsear shook his head.

'No. But knowing Cessair . . . well, I knew she would be in no hurry.'

There was a brief silence.

'You *knew* that one of the two sisters would be Cessair?' pressed Fidelma. 'How did you know?'

'Why, Brother Cano told me. We had few secrets. He left to go to the woodsman's hut where he and Cessair usually met. I knew that this would delay them bringing the phial to the abbey. That was why I set off in good time to meet them and encourage them to hurry. Alas, I was too late.'

'You found Cessair dead?'

'I did. She was tied to the tree even as you saw her.'

'And Sister Della?'

'There was no sign of her. So I hurried straight to Nivelles to alert Abbess Ballgel.'

'Why did you do that?' Fidelma asked.

'Why?'

'There were other options. Why not rush back to Fosse and alert the Abbot Heribert?'

Sinsear grimaced.

'It is well known that Nivelles is closer to that point in the forest than is Fosse. I thought it more expedient to bring the news to Nivelles and then return to alert Fosse.'

'Have you been friends with Cano from the time he arrived in Fosse?'

'He was assigned to help me in the gardens and we became friends.'

'Yet you knew Cessair before Cano arrived?'

'I have met Cessair and Della as well as many others of the sisters of Nivelles. There is much intercourse between the abbeys. You see, I am employed in the gardens and my job is to take fruit and vegetables to Nivelles once a week.'

'Brother Sinsear is perfectly correct,' interrupted Heribert. 'Members of our community often go to Nivelles to help them with the heavy building work and the upkeep of their fields and crops. In fact, Brother Sinsear took produce to Nivelles only yesterday afternoon. Ah, and didn't Brother Cano accompany you?'

Brother Sinsear flushed and nodded reluctantly.

Fidelma pursed her lips thoughtfully.

'There is a further question that I must now ask Sister Della. Please wait for me here.'

In the infirmary, Sister Della, although pale-faced and weak, was looking much improved.

'Sister Della,' Fidelma began without preamble. 'There is only one question I need ask you. Why did you especially ask to be allowed to take the phial of holy blood to Fosse today?'

'Sister Cessair asked me to.'

'Cessair, eh? Then it was not your idea?'

'No. Neither was it her idea, to be truthful. She knew that there would be some argument with the abbot who disliked her and was reluctant to go. However, Brother Cano had especially asked her to come . . .'

'How had he asked? Had he not seen her yesterday?'

'No. He sent a message, for there is always someone coming or going between our two abbeys. He sent a note to Cessair asking her to come early to the hut so that he could spent a few moments with her to discuss their future.'

'Did you approve of her meetings with Cano?'

'I was Cessair's friend. I know that there is no stopping the stupidities that love brings with it. And I thought it was only one question that you wished to ask?'

'So it was. Is this the note?' She pulled out the piece of torn paper from her *marsupium*.

Sister Della glanced at it and shrugged.

'I do not read Ogham,' she said. 'But I think it is part of the note. Cano and Cessair used the ancient form of Irish writing to write cryptic notes to one another.'

Fidelma turned back to the refectory.

'I think I have the solution to this mystery,' she announced as Abbess Ballgel and Abbot Heribert gazed up as she re-entered the refectory.

'Who then is guilty?' demanded Heribert.

'Ask Brother Cano to come here. You will remain, Brother Sinsear.'

'Brother Cano,' Fidelma began when the young man arrived, 'the future looks bleak for you.'

Cano grimaced in resignation.

'The future is empty for me,' he corrected. 'Without Cessair my life is indeed an abyss filled with pain.'

'Why did you ask Cessair to meet you today?'

'I have told you already. So that we could plan to go away together and find a mixed house where we could live and work and, God willing, raise our children in His service.'

'Whose idea was that?'

'Mine.'

'I thought that someone else might have suggested it to you as a solution to your problems,' Fidelma said quietly.

Cano frowned.

'It matters not who suggested it. That was the purpose of our rendezvous.'

'It does matter. Wasn't it Brother Sinsear who suggested that you should plan to leave here?'

'Perhaps. Sinsear has been a good friend. He saw that there was no future for us here.'

'You went with Brother Sinsear to Nivelles last evening to take garden produce. Why didn't you speak with Cessair then?'

'We arrived during the evening service and as there was no excuse to delay at Nivelles, I wrote Cessair a note in Ogham suggesting the meeting. I knew that Cessair could read the ancient Irish writing so I put the instructions in that note and left it with the gatekeeper.'

'Yes. It all fits now,' Fidelma sighed. She turned to the young brother. 'Sinsear, would you mind handing Abbess Ballgel the phial of holy blood from your *marsupium*? The abbess has been fretful about it ever since she realised that it was missing.'

Brother Sinsear started, his face white. As if in a dream he opened his waist purse and handed it over.

'I found it on the ground . . . I meant to give it to you before . . .'

Fidelma shook her head sadly.

'One of the most terrible passions is love turned to hatred because of rejection. A lover who sees the object of their love with a rival can sometimes be transformed into a fiend incarnate.'

Brother Cano looked astounded.

'Cessair did not reject me,' he exclaimed. 'I tell you again, I did not kill her. We planned to go away together.'

'It is Sinsear to whom I refer,' replied Fidelma. 'It was Sinsear whose love had turned to a rage that wanted to hurt and mutilate her.'

Sinsear was staring at her open-mouthed.

'Sinsear here had been in love with Cessair for a long time. Being young and unable to articulate his love, he worshipped her from afar, dreaming of the day when he could summon up courage to declare himself. Then Cano arrived. At first the two were good friends. Then Sinsear introduced Cano to his love. Horror! Cano and Cessair fell truly in love. Day by day, Sinsear found himself watching their passion, and his jealousy grew to such a peak at what he saw as Cessair's rejection of him, that his mind broke with the anguish. He would revenge himself on Cessair with such a vengeance that hell did not possess.'

Sinsear's face was drained of all emotion now.

'He suggested to Cano that he invite Cessair to a rendez-vous in the hut and gave him the pretext of discussing a means of leaving the abbeys. Then he left Fosse in plenty of time to climb the old oak, hiding among the low hanging branches, to await the arrival of Cessair and her companion. That was why Sister Della did not hear anyone approach them from behind. He jumped down. I saw the indentation of where he landed. He landed just behind Della and felled her with a blow before she knew it. Am I right?'

Sinsear did not respond.

'Perhaps then he revealed his twisted love to Cessair? Perhaps he begged her to go with him. Did she react in horror, did she laugh? How did she treat this frenzied would-be lover? We only know how it resulted. He struck her several blows on the head and then, in a gruesome ritual, which serves to demonstrate his immaturity, he decided to punish her beauty by which she had beguiled him by mutilating her face with a knife. Whether he tied her first to the tree or not, we do not know unless he tells us. But I have no doubt that she was dead by then.

'Something made him pick up the phial of holy blood and his religious training took the better of him, for instead of leaving it in Cessair's purse, he put it in his own for safe-keeping. Knowing the missing phial was irrelevant, I could not account for its disappearance before.

'Perhaps then he heard Sister Della coming to. He turned and raced on to Nivelles to raise the alarm. He believed that Sister Della would probably go to Fosse to raise the alarm which is why he chose Nivelles.'

Abbot Heribert was staring at Sinsear, seeing the truth of Fidelma's accusation confirmed in his cold features.

'How did you first suspect him?' he asked.

'Many reasons can be mentioned if you think back over the events. But, according to his story, Sinsear went along the path in search of Cessair and Della. He found Cessair dead and tied to the tree. He claimed that he had reached the point after Della had disappeared. But how could he have seen the body tied to the tree when it was on the far side of the tree to the path he was travelling?

'Even allowing for the fact that he somehow might have spotted something that made him suspicious, that he was so distraught that he did not think to cut her down and see if he could revive her, why did he run on to Nivelles?'

'For help. He wished to raise the alarm and, as he pointed out when you asked, Nivelles was closer than Fosse to the place. It is logical.'

'There was an even closer place to seek help,' Fidelma pointed out. 'Why not go there? He knew that Brother Cano was waiting in the woodsman's hut just a few hundred metres away. Had he been innocent, he would have rushed to seek Cano and get immediate help.'

The scream made them freeze.

Sinsear had drawn a knife and made a thrust at Brother Cano. He was babbling incoherently.

Cano reacted by striking out in self-defence, felling the young monk with a blow to the jaw.

'Now you can punish him by whatever laws apply here,' Fidelma told Abbot Heribert. She turned to the abbess. 'And we, Ballgel, shall escort poor Sister Della back to Nivelles. We have much to talk about . . .' She paused and glanced sadly at Brother Cano who was now sitting quietly, his head in his hands.

'Even the ancients were acutely aware of the role of emotions causing the symptoms of mental illness. *Aegra amans* – the lover's disease – can make people lose all reason. Even the most mature people can go mad, and to the young and immature love can destroy the soul as well as the mind.'

Our Lady of Death

❧

The awesome moaning of the wind blended chillingly with the howling of wolves. They were nearby, these fearsome night hunters. Sister Fidelma knew it but could not see them because of the cold, driving snow against her face. It came at her in clouds; clouds of whirling, ice-cold, tiny pellicles. It obliterated the landscape and she could scarcely see beyond her arm's length in front of her.

Had it not been for the urgency of reaching Cashel, the seat of the kings of Muman, she would not have been attempting the journey northwards through these great, forbidding peaks of Sléibhte an Comeraigh. She bent forward in the saddle of her horse, which only her rank as a *dálaigh* of the law courts of the five kings of Ireland entitled her to have. A simple religieuse would not be able to lay claim to such a means of transportation. But then Fidelma was no ordinary religieuse. She was a daughter of a former king of Cashel, an advocate of the law of the *Fenechus* and qualified to the level of *Anruth*, one degree below the highest qualification in Ireland. The wind drove the snow continuously against her. It plastered the strands of red hair that spilled from her *cubhal*, or head-dress, against her pale forehead. She wished the wind's direction would change, even for a moment or two, for it would have been more comfortable to have had the wind at her back. But it was constantly raging from the north.

The threatening howl of the wolves seemed close. Was it her imagination or had it been gradually getting closer as she rode the isolated mountain track? She shivered and once more wished that she had stopped for the night at the last *bruidhen* or hostel in order to await more clement weather. But the snow storm had set in and it would be several days before conditions improved. Sooner or later she would have to tackle the journey. The message from her brother, Colgú, had said her presence was needed urgently for their mother lay dying. Only that fact brought Fidelma traversing the forbidding tracks through the snowbound mountains in such intemperate conditions.

Her face was frozen and so were her hands as she confronted the fierce wind-driven snow. In spite of her heavy woollen cloak, she found her teeth chattering. A dark shape loomed abruptly out of the snow nearby. Her heart caught in her mouth as her horse shied and skittered on the trail for a moment. Then she was able to relax and steady the beast with a sigh of relief, as the regal shape of a great stag stared momentarily at her from a distance of a few yards before recklessly turning and bounding away into the cover of the white curtain that blocked out the landscape.

Continuing on, she reached what she felt must be the crest of a rise and found the wind so fierce here that it threatened to sweep her from her horse. Even the beast put its head down to the ground and seemed to stagger at the icy onslaught. Masses of loose powdery snow drifted this way and that in the howling and shrieking of the tempest.

Fidelma blinked at the indistinct blur of the landscape beyond.

She felt sure she had seen a light. Or was it her imagination? She blinked again and urged her horse onwards, straining to keep her eyes focused. She automatically pulled her cloak higher up around her neck.

Yes! She had seen it. A light, surely!

She halted her horse and slipped off, making sure she had

the reins looped securely around her arm. The snow came up to her knees, making walking almost impossible, but she could not urge her mount through the drifting snow without making sure it was safe enough first. After a moment or two she came to a wooden pole. She peered upwards. Barely discernible in the flurries above her head hung a dancing storm lantern.

She stared around in surprise. The swirling snow revealed nothing. But she was sure that the lantern was the traditional sign of a *bruidhen*, an inn, for it was the law that all inns had to keep a lantern burning to indicate their presence at night or in severe weather conditions.

She gazed back at the pole with its lantern, and chose a direction, moving awkwardly forward in the deep, clinging snow. Suddenly the wind momentarily dropped and she caught sight of the large, dark shadow of a building. Then the blizzard resumed its course and she staggered, head down, in the direction of the building. More by good luck than any other form of guidance, she came to a horse's hitching rail and tethered her beast there, before feeling her way along the cold stone walls towards the door.

There was a sign fixed there but she could not decipher it. She also saw, to her curiosity, a ring of herbs hanging from the door, almost obliterated in their coating of snow.

She found the iron handle, twisted it and pushed. The door remained shut. She frowned in annoyance. It was the law that a *brugh-fer*, an innkeeper, had to keep the door of his inn open at all times, day and night and in all weathers. She tried again.

The wind was easing a little now and its petulant crying had died away to a soft whispering moan.

Irritated, Fidelma raised a clenched fist and hammered at the door.

Did she hear a cry of alarm or was it simply the wailing wind?

There was no other answer.

She hammered, angrily this time.

Then she did hear a noise. A footstep and a harsh male cry.

'God and his saints stand between us and all that is evil! Begone foul spirit!'

Fidelma was thunderstruck for a moment. Then she thrust out her jaw.

'Open, innkeeper; open to a *dálaigh* of the courts; open to a Sister of the Abbey of Kildare! In the name of charity, open to a refugee from the storm!'

There was a moment's silence. Then she thought she heard voices raised in argument. She hammered again.

There came the sound of bolts being drawn and the door swung inwards. A blast of warm air enveloped Fidelma and she pushed hurriedly into the room beyond, shaking the snow from her woollen cloak.

'What manner of hostel is this that ignores the laws of the Brehons?' she demanded, turning to the figure that was now closing the wooden door behind her.

The man was tall and thin; a gaunt, pallid figure of middle-age, his temples greying. He was poorly attired and his height was offset by a permanent stoop. But it was not that which caused Fidelma's eyes to widen a fraction. It was the horror on the man's face; not a momentary expression of horror but a graven expression that was set deep and permanently into his cadaverous features. Tragedy and grief stalked across the lines of his face.

'I have a horse tethered outside. The poor beast will freeze to death if not attended,' Fidelma snapped, when the man did not answer her question but simply stood staring at her.

'Who are you?' demanded a shrill woman's voice behind her.

Fidelma swung round. The woman who stood there had once been handsome. Now age was causing her features to run with surplus flesh, and lines marked her face. Her eyes stared, black and apparently without pupils, at Fidelma. She had the feeling that here was a woman whom, at some awesome moment in her life, the pulsating blood of life had frozen and never regained its regular ebb and flow. What surprised her more was that the woman held before her a tall ornate crucifix. She held it as if it were some protective icon against the terror that afflicted her.

She and the man were well matched.

'Speak! What manner of person are you?'

Fidelma sniffed in annoyance.

'If you are the keepers of this inn, all you should know is that I am a weary traveller in these mountains, driven to seek refuge from the blizzard.'

The woman was not cowed by her haughty tone.

'It is not all we need to know,' she corrected just as firmly. 'Tell us whether you mean us harm or not.'

Fidelma was surprised.

'I came here to shelter from the storm, that is all. I am Fidelma of Kildare,' replied the religieuse in annoyance. 'Moreover, I am a *dálaigh* of the courts, qualified to the level of *Anruth* and sister to Colgú, *tánaiste* of this kingdom.'

The grandiloquence of her reply was an indication of the annoyance Fidelma felt, for normally she was not one given to stating more than was ever necessary. She had never felt the need to mention that her brother, Colgú, was heir-apparent to the kingdom of Cashel before. However, she felt that she needed to stir these people out of their curious mood.

As she spoke she swung off her cloak, displaying her habit, and she noticed that the woman's eyes fell upon the ornately worked crucifix which hung from her neck. Did she see some expression of reassurance in those cold unfeeling eyes?

The woman put down her cross and gave a bob of her head.

'Forgive us, Sister. I am Monchae, wife to Belach, the innkeeper.'

Belach seemed to be hesitating at the door.

'Shall I see to the horse?' he asked hesitantly.

'Unless you want it to freeze to death,' snapped Fidelma, making her way to a large open fire in which sods of turf were singing as they caused a warmth to envelop the room. From the corner of her eyes she saw Belach hesitate a moment longer and then, swinging a cloak around his shoulders, he took from behind the door a sword and went out into the blizzard.

Fidelma was astonished. She had never seen an ostler take a sword to assist him in putting a horse to stable before.

Monchae was pushing the iron handle on which hung a cauldron across the glowing turf fire.

'What place is this?' demanded Fidelma as she chose a chair to stretch out in front of the warmth of the fire. The room was low beamed and comfortable but devoid of decorations apart from a tall statuette of the Madonna and Child, executed in some form of painted plaster; a gaudy, alabaster figurine. It dominated as the centre display at the end of a large table where, presumably, guests dined.

'This is Brugh-na-Bhelach. You have just come off the shoulder of the mountain known as Fionn's Seat. The River Tua is but a mile to the north of here. We do not have many travellers this way in winter. Which direction are you heading?'

'North to Cashel,' replied Fidelma.

Monchae ladled a cup of steaming liquid from the cauldron over the fire and handed it to her. Although the liquid must have been warming the vessel, Fidelma could not feel it as she cupped her frozen hands around it and let the steaming vapour assail her nostrils. It smelled good. She sipped slowly, her sense of taste confirming what her sense of smell had told her.

She glanced up at the woman.

'Tell me, Monchae, why was the door of this hostel barred? Why did I have to beg to be admitted? Do you and your husband, Belach, know the law of hostelkeepers?'

Monchae pressed her lips together.

'Will you report us to the *bó-aire* of the territory?'

The *bó-aire* was the local magistrate.

'I am more concerned at hearing your reasons,' replied Fidelma. 'Someone might have perished from the cold before you and your husband, Belach, opened your door.'

The woman looked agitated, chewing her lip as if she would draw blood from it.

The door opened abruptly, with a wild gust of cold air, sending snowflakes swirling across the room and a stream of icy wind enveloping them.

Belach stood poised a moment in its frame, a ghastly look upon his pale features, and then, with a sound which resembled a soft moan, he entered and barred the door behind him. He still carried the sword as a weapon.

Fidelma watched him throw the bolts with curiosity.

Monchae stood, both hands raised to her cheeks.

Belach turned from the door and his lips were trembling.

'I heard it!' he muttered, his eyes darting from his wife to Fidelma, as though he did not want her to hear. 'I heard it!'

'Oh Mary, mother of God, save us!' cried the woman, swaying as if she would faint.

'What does this mean?' Fidelma demanded as sternly as she could.

Belach turned, pleading to her.

'I was in the barn, bedding down your horse, Sister, and I heard it.'

'But what?' cried Fidelma, trying to keep her patience.

'The spirit of Mugrán,' wailed Monchae suddenly, giving way to a fit of sobbing. 'Save us, Sister. For the pity of Christ! Save us!'

Fidelma rose and went to the woman, taking her gently but firmly by the arm and leading her to the fire. She could see that her husband, Belach, was too nervous to attend to the wants of his wife and so she went to a jug, assessed its contents as *corma*, a spirit distilled from barley, and poured a little into a cup. She handed it to the woman and told her to drink.

'Now what is all this about? I cannot help you unless you tell me.'

Monchae looked at Belach, as if seeking permission, and he nodded slowly in response.

'Tell her from the beginning,' he muttered.

Fidelma smiled encouragingly at the woman. 'A good place to start,' she joked lightly. But there was no humorous response on the features of the innkeeper's wife.

Fidelma seated herself before Monchae and faced her expectantly.

Monchae paused a moment and then began to speak, hesitantly at first and then more quickly as she gained confidence in the story.

'I was a young girl when I came to this place. I came as a young bride to the *brugh-fer*, the innkeeper, who was then a man named Mugrán. You see,' she added hurriedly, 'Belach is my second husband.'

She paused, but when Fidelma made no comment, she went on.

'Mugrán was a good man. But often given to wild fantasies. He was a good man for the music, an excellent piper. Often he entertained here in this very room and people would come far and wide to hear him. But he was a restless soul. I found that I was doing all the work of running the inn while he pursued his dreams. Mugrán's younger brother, Cano, used to help me but he was much influenced by his brother.

'Six years ago our local chieftain lit the *crois-tara*, the fiery cross, and sent his rider from village to village, raising the clans to send a band of fighting men to fight Guaire of Connacht in the service of Cathal Cú cen Máthair of Cashel. One morning Mugrán announced that he and young Cano were leaving to join that band of warriors. When I protested, he said that I should not fear for my security. He had placed in the inn an inheritance which would keep me from want. If anything happened to him then I would not be lacking for anything. With that, he and Cano just rose and left.'

Even now her voice was full of indignation.

'Time passed. Seasons came and went and I struggled to keep the inn going. Then, when the snows of winter were clearing, a messenger came to me who said a great battle had been fought on the shores of Loch Derg and my man had been slain in it. They brought me his bloodstained tunic as token. Cano, it seemed, had been killed at his side, and they brought me a bloodstained cloak as proof.'

She paused and sniffed.

'It is no use saying that I grieved for him. Not for my man, Mugrán. We had hardly been together for he was always searching out new, wild schemes to occupy his fancy. I could no more have tethered his heart than I could train the inn's cat to come and go at my will. Still, the inn was now mine, and mine by right as well as inheritance, for had I not worked to keep it while he pursued his fantasies? After the news came, and the *bó-aire* confirmed that the inn was mine since my man was dead by the shores of the far-off loch, I continued to work to run the inn. But life was hard, it was a struggle. Visitors along these isolated tracks are few and come seldom.'

'But what of the inheritance Mugrán had left in the inn that would keep you from want?' asked Fidelma, intrigued and caught up in the story.

The woman gave a harsh bark of laughter.

'I searched and searched and found nothing. It was just one of Mugrán's dreams again. One of his silly fantasies. He probably said it to keep me from complaining when he left.'

'Then what?' Fidelma pressed, when she paused.

'A year passed and I met Belach.' She nodded to her husband. 'Belach and I loved one another from the start. Ah, not the love of a dog for the sheep, you understand, but the love of a salmon for the stream. We married and have worked together since. And I insisted that we re-named this inn Brugh-na-Bhelach. Life has been difficult for us, but we have worked and made a living here.'

Belach had moved forward and caught Monchae's hand in his. The symbolism assured Fidelma that Monchae and Belach were still in love after the years that they had shared together.

'We've had five years of happiness,' Belach told Fidelma. 'And if the evil spirits claim us now, they will not steal those five years from us.'

'Evil spirits?' frowned Fidelma.

'Seven days ago it started,' Monchae said heavily. 'I was out feeding the pigs when I thought I heard the sounds of music from up on the mountain. I listened. Sure enough, I heard the sound of pipe music, high up in the air. I felt suddenly cold for it was a tune, as I well remember, that Mugrán was fond of playing.

'I came into the inn and sought out Belach. But he had not heard the music. We went out and listened but could hear nothing more than the gathering winds across the mountains that betokened the storms to come.

'The next day, at the noon hour, I heard a thud on the door of the inn. Thinking it a traveller who could not lift the latch. I opened the door. There was no one there . . . or so I thought until I glanced down. At the foot of the door was . . .' Monchae genuflected hastily. 'At the foot of the door was a dead raven. There was no sign of how it met its death. It seemed to have flown into the door and killed itself.'

Fidelma sat back with pursed lips.

She could see which way the story was going. The sound of music, a dead raven lying at the door. These were all the portents of death among the rural folk of the five kingdoms. She found herself shivering slightly in spite of her rational faith.

'We have heard the music several times since,' interrupted Belach for the first time. 'I have heard it.'

'And whereabouts does this music come from?'

Belach spread one hand, as if gesturing towards the mountains outside.

'High up, high up in the air. All around us.'

'It is the lamentation of the dead,' moaned Monchae. 'There is a curse on us.'

Fidelma sniffed.

'There is no curse unless God wills it.'

'Help us, Sister,' whispered Monchae. 'I fear it is Mugrán come to claim our souls, a vengeance for my love for Belach and not for him.'

Fidelma gazed in quiet amusement at the woman.

'How did you reckon this?'

'Because I have heard him. I have heard his voice, moaning to me from the Otherworld, crying to me. "I am alone! I am alone!" he called. "Join me, Monchae!" Ah, how many times have I heard that ghostly wail?'

Fidelma saw that the woman was serious.

'You heard this? When and where?'

'It was three days ago in the barn. I was tending the goats that we have there, milking them to prepare cheese when I heard the whisper of Mugrán's voice. I swear it was his voice. It sounded all around me.'

'Did you search?' Fidelma asked.

'Search? For a spirit?' Monchae sounded shocked. 'I ran into the inn and took up my crucifix.'

'I searched,' intervened Belach more rationally. 'I searched, for, like you Sister, I look for answers in this world before I seek out the Otherworld. But there was no one in the barn, nor the inn, who could have made that sound. But, again like you Sister, I continued to have my doubts. I took our ass and rode down into the valley to the *bóthan* of Dallán, the chieftain who had been with Mugrán on the shores of Loch Derg. He took oath that Mugrán was dead these last six years and that he had personally seen the body. What could I do further?'

Fidelma nodded slowly.

'So only you, Monchae, have heard Mugrán's voice?'

'No!' Belach interrupted again and surprised her. 'By the apostles of Patrick, I have heard the voice as well.'

'And what did this voice say?'

'It said: "Beware, Belach. You walk in a dead man's shoes without the blessing of his spirit." That is what it said.'

'And where did you hear this?'

'Like Monchae, I heard the voice speak to me within the barn.'

'Very well. You have seen a dead raven, heard pipe music from far off and heard a voice which you think is that of the spirit of Mugrán. There can still be a logical explanation for such phenomena.'

'Explanation?' Monchae's voice was harsh. 'Then explain this to me, Sister. Last night, I heard the music again. It awoke me. The snow storm had died down and the sky was clear with the moon shining down, reflecting on the snow, making it as bright as day. I heard the music playing again.

'I took my courage in my hands and went to the window and unfixed the shutter. There is a tiny knoll no more than one hundred yards away, a small snowy knoll. There was a figure of a man standing upon it, and in his hands were a set of pipes on which he was playing a lament. Then he paused and looked straight at me. "I am alone, Monchae!" he called. "Soon I will come for you. For you and Belach." He turned and . . .'

She gave a sudden sob and collapsed into Belach's embrace.

Fidelma gazed thoughtfully at her.

'Was this figure corporeal? Was it of flesh and blood?'

Monchae raised her fearful gaze to Fidelma.

'That is just it. The body shimmered.'

'Shimmered?'

'It had a strange luminescence about it, as if it shone

with some spectral fire. It was clearly a demon from the Otherworld.'

Fidelma turned to Belach.

'And did you see this vision?' she asked, half expecting him to confirm it.

'No. I heard Monchae scream in terror; it was her scream which awoke me. When she told me what had passed, I went out into the night to the knoll. I had hoped that I would find tracks there. Signs that a human being had stood there. But there were none.'

'No signs of the snow being disturbed?' pressed Fidelma.

'There were no human tracks, I tell you,' Belach said irritably. 'The snow was smooth. But there was one thing . . .'

'Tell me.'

'The snow seemed to shine with a curious luminosity, sparkling in an uncanny light.'

'But you saw no footprints nor signs of anyone?'

'No.'

The woman was sobbing now.

'It is true, it is true, Sister. The ghost of Mugrán will soon come for us. Our remaining time on earth is short.'

Fidelma sat back and closed her eyes a moment in deep thought.

'Only the Living God can decide what is your allotted span of life,' she said in almost absent-minded reproof.

Monchae and Belach stood watching her uncertainly as Fidelma stretched before the fire.

'Well,' she said at last, 'while I am here, I shall need a meal and a bed for the night.'

Belach inclined his head.

'That you may have, Sister, and most welcome. But if you will say a prayer to our Lady . . .? Let this haunting cease. She needs not the deaths of Monchae and myself to prove that she is the blessed mother of Christ.'

Fidelma sniffed in irritation.

'I would not readily blame the ills of the world on the Holy Family,' she said stiffly. But, seeing their frightened faces, she relented in her theology. 'I will say a prayer to Our Lady. Now bring me some food.'

Something awoke Fidelma. She lay with her heart beating fast, her body tense. The sound had seemed part of her dream. The dropping of a heavy object. Now she lay trying to identify it. The storm had apparently abated, since she had fallen asleep in the small chamber to which Monchae had shown her after her meal. There was a silence beyond the shuttered windows. An eerie stillness. She did not make a further move but lay, listening intently.

There came to her ears a creaking sound. The inn was full of the moans of its ageing timbers. Perhaps it had been a dream? She was about to turn over when she heard a noise. She frowned, not being able to identify it. Ah, there it was again. A soft thump.

She eased herself out of her warm bed, shivering in the cold night. It must be well after midnight. Reaching for her heavy robe, she draped it over her shoulders and moved stealthily towards the door, opening it as quietly as she could and pausing to listen.

The sound had come from downstairs.

She knew that she was alone in the inn with Monchae and Belach and they had retired when she had, their room being at the top of the stairs. She glanced towards it and saw the door firmly shut.

She walked with quiet, padding feet, imitating the soft walk of a cat, along the wooden boards to the head of the stairs and peered down into the darkness.

The sound made her freeze a moment. It was a curious sound, like something soft but weighty being dragged over the bare boards.

She paused, staring down the well of the stairs into the main room of the inn where the eerie red glow of the dying

450

embers of the fire cast shadows which chased one another in the gloom. Fidelma bit her lip and shivered. She wished that she had a candle to light her way. Slowly, she began to descend the stairs.

She was halfway down when her bare foot came into contact with a board that was loose. It gave forth a heavy creak which sounded like a thunderclap in the night.

Fidelma froze.

A split second later she heard a scuffling noise in the darkness of the room below and then she was hastening down the rest of the stairs into the gloom.

'If anyone is here, identify yourself in the name of Christ!' she called, making her voice as stern as she could, and trying to ignore the wild beating of her heart.

There was a distant thud and then silence.

She peered around the deserted room of the inn, her eyes darting here and there as the red shadows danced across the walls. She could see nothing.

Then . . . there was a sound behind her.

She whirled round.

Belach stood on the bottom stair, his wife, Monchae, peering fearfully over his shoulder.

'You heard it, too?' he whispered nervously.

'I heard it,' confirmed Fidelma.

'God look down on us,' sighed the man.

Fidelma made an impatient gesture.

'Light a candle, Belach, and we will search this place.'

The innkeeper shrugged.

'There is no purpose, Sister. We have heard such noises before and made a search. Nothing is ever found.'

'Indeed,' echoed his wife, 'why search for temporal signs from a spectre?'

Fidelma set her jaw grimly.

'Why would a spectre make noises?' she replied. 'Only something with a corporeal existence makes a noise. Now give me a light.'

Reluctantly, Belach lit a lamp. The innkeeper and his wife stood by the bottom of the stairs as Fidelma began a careful search of the inn. She had barely begun when Monchae gave a sudden shriek and fell forward onto the floor.

Fidelma hurried quickly to her side. Belach was patting her hands in a feeble attempt to revive her senses.

'She's fainted,' muttered the man unnecessarily.

'Get some water,' instructed Fidelma, and when the water had been splashed against the woman's forehead and some of it nursed between her lips, Monchae blinked and opened her eyes.

'What was it?' snapped Fidelma. 'What made you faint?'

Monchae stared at her a moment or two, her face pale, her teeth chattering.

'The pipes!' she stammered. 'The pipes!'

'I heard no pipes,' Fidelma replied.

'No. Mugrán's pipes . . . on the table!'

Leaving Belach to help Monchae to her feet, Fidelma turned, holding her candle high, and beheld a set of pipes lying on the table. There was nothing remarkable about them. Fidelma had seen many of better quality and workmanship.

'What are you telling me?' she asked, as Monchae was led forward by Belach, still trembling.

'These are Mugrán's pipes. The pipes he took away with him to war. It must be true. His ghost has returned. Oh, saints protect us!'

She clung desperately to her husband.

Fidelma reached forward to examine the pipes.

They seemed entirely of this world. They were of the variety called *cetharchóire*, meaning four-tuned, with a chanter, two shorter reed-drones and a long drone. A simple pipe to be found in almost any household in Ireland. She pressed her lips tightly, realising that when they had all retired for the night there had been no sign of any pipes on the table.

'How are you sure that these are the pipes of Mugrán?' she asked.

'I know them!' The woman was vehement. 'How do you know what garment belongs to you, or what knife? You know its weave, its stains, its markings . . .'

She began to sob hysterically.

Fidelma ordered Belach to take the woman back to her bed.

'Have a care, Sister,' the man muttered, as he led his wife away. 'We are surely dealing with evil powers here.'

Fidelma smiled thinly.

'I am a representative of the greater power, Belach. Everything that happens can only occur when under His will.'

After they had gone, she stood staring at the pipes for a while and finally gave up the conundrum with a sigh. She left them on the table and climbed the stairs back to her own bed, thankful it was still warm for she realised, for the first time, that her feet and legs were freezing. The night was truly chill.

She lay for a while thinking about the mystery which she had found here in this desolate mountain spot and wondering if there was some supernatural solution to it. Fidelma acknowledged that there were powers of darkness. Indeed, one would be a fool to believe in God and to refuse to believe in the Devil. If there was good, then there was, undoubtedly, evil. But, in her experience, evil tended to be a human condition.

She had fallen asleep. It could not have been for long. It was still dark when she started awake again.

It took a moment or two for her to realise what it was which had aroused her for the second time that night.

Far off she could hear pipes playing. It was a sweet, gentle sound. The sound of the sleep-producing *súan-traige*, the beautiful, sorrowing lullaby.

'*Codail re suanán saine . . .*'

'Sleep with pleasant slumber . . .'

Fidelma knew the tune well, for many a time had she been lulled into drowsiness as a child by its sweet melody.

She sat up abruptly and swung out of bed. The music was real. It was outside the inn. She went to the shuttered window and cautiously eased it open a crack.

Outside the snow lay like a crisp white carpet across the surrounding hills and mountains. The sky was still shrouded with heavy grey-white snow clouds. Even so, the nightscape was light, in spite of the fact that the moon was only a soft glow hung with ice crystals that produced a halo around its orb. One could see for miles. The atmosphere was icy chill and still. Vapour from her breath made bursts of short-lived clouds in the air before her.

It was then that her heart began to hammer as if a mad drummer was beating a warning to wake the dead.

She stood shock still.

About a hundred yards from the inn was a small round knoll. On the knoll stood the figure of a lonely piper and he was playing the sweet lullaby that woke her. But the thing that caused her to feel dizzy with awe and apprehension was the fact that the figure shimmered as if a curious light emanated from him, sparkling like little stars against the brightness of the reflecting snow.

She stood still, watching. Then the melody trailed off and the figure turned its head in the direction of the inn. It gave vent to an awesome, pitiful cry.

'I am alone! I am alone, Monchae! Why did you desert me? I am alone! I will come for you soon!'

Perhaps it was the cry that stirred Fidelma into action.

She turned, grabbed her leather shoes and seized her cloak, and hurried down the stairs into the gloomy interior of the main room of the inn. She heard Belach's cry on the stair behind her.

'Don't go out, Sister! It is evil! It is the shade of Mugrán!'

She paid no heed. She threw open the bolts of the door

and went plunging into the icy stillness of the night. She ran through the deep snow, feeling its coldness against her bare legs, up towards the knoll. But long before she got there, she realised that the figure had disappeared.

She reached the knoll and paused. There was no one in sight. The nocturnal piper had vanished. She drew her cloak closer around her shoulders and shivered. But it was the night chill rather than the idea of the spectre that caused her to tremble.

Catching her breath against the icy air, she looked down. There were no footprints. But the snow, on careful inspection, had not lain in pristine condition across the knoll. Its surface was rough, ruffled as if a wind had blown across it. It was then she noticed the curious reflective quality of it. She bent forward and scooped a handful of snow in her palm and examined it. It seemed to twinkle and reflect as she held it.

Fidelma gave a long, deep sigh. She turned and retraced her steps back to the inn.

Belach was waiting anxiously by the door. She noticed that he now held the sword in his hand.

She grinned mischievously.

'If it were a spirit, that would be of little assistance,' she observed dryly.

Belach said nothing, but he locked and bolted the door behind Fidelma as she came into the room. He replaced the sword without comment as she went to the fire to warm herself after her exertion into the night.

Monchae was standing on the bottom step, her arms folded across her breast, moaning a little.

Fidelma went in search of the jug of *corma* and poured out some of the spirit. She swallowed and then took a wooden cup to Monchae and told her to drink it.

'You heard it? You saw it?' The wife of the innkeeper wailed.

Fidelma nodded.

Belach bit his lip.

'It is the ghost of Mugrán. We are doomed.'

'Nonsense!' snapped Fidelma.

'Then explain that!' replied Belach, pointing to the table. There was nothing on the table. It was then Fidelma realised what was missing. She had left the pipes on the table when she had returned to bed.

'It is two hours or so until sunrise,' Fidelma said slowly. 'I want you two to return to bed. There is something here which I must deal with. Whatever occurs, I do not wish either of you to stir from your room unless I specifically call you.'

Belach stared at her with white, taut features.

'You mean that you will do battle with this evil force?'

Fidelma smiled thinly.

'That is what I mean,' she said emphatically.

Reluctantly, Belach helped Monchae back up the stairs, leaving Fidelma standing in the darkness. She stood still, thinking for a while. She had an instinct that whatever was happening in this troubled, isolated inn, it was building up towards its climax. Perhaps that climax would come before sunrise. There was no logic to the idea but Fidelma had long come to the belief that one should not ignore one's instincts.

She turned and made her way towards a darkened alcove at the far end of the room in which only a deep wooden bench was situated. She tightened her cloak against the chill, seated herself and prepared to wait. Wait for what, she did not know. But she believed that she would not have to wait for long before some other manifestation occurred.

It was only a short time before she heard the sounds of the pipe once more.

The sweet, melodious lullaby was gone. The pipes were now wild keening. It was the hair-raising lament of the *gol-traige*, full of pain, sorrow and longing.

Fidelma held her head to one side.

The music was no longer outside the old inn but seeming to echo from within, seeping up under the floorboards, through the walls and down from the rafters.

She shivered but made no move to go in search of the sound, praying all the while that neither Monchae nor Belach would disobey her instructions and leave their room.

She waited until the tune came to an end.

There was silence in the old building.

Then she heard the sound, the sound she had heard on her first waking. It was a soft, dragging noise. Her body tensed as she bent forward in the alcove, her eyes narrowed as she tried to focus into the darkness.

A figure seemed to be rising from the floor, upwards, slowly upwards on the far side of the room.

Fidelma held her breath.

The figure, reaching its full height, appeared to be clutching a set of pipes beneath its arm. It moved towards the table in a curious limping gait.

Fidelma noticed that, now and again, as the light of the glowing embers in the hearth caught it, the figure's cloak sparkled and danced with a myriad pinpricks of fire.

Fidelma rose to her feet.

'The charade is over!' she cried harshly.

The figure dropped the pipes and wheeled around, seeking to identify the speaker. Then it seemed to catch its breath.

'Is that you, Monchae?' came a sibilant, mocking whisper.

Then, before Fidelma could prepare herself, the figure seemed to fly across the room at her. She caught sight of light flashing on an upraised blade and instinct made her react by grasping at the descending arm with both hands, twisting her body to take the weight of the impact.

The figure grunted angrily as the surprise of the attack failed.

The collision of their bodies threw Fidelma back into the alcove, slamming her against the wooden seat. She grunted in pain. The figure had shaken her grip loose and once more the knife hand was descending.

'You should have fled while you had the chance, Monchae,' came the masculine growl. 'I had no wish to harm you or the old man. I just wanted to get you out of this inn. Now, you must die!'

Fidelma sprang aside once more, feverishly searching for some weapon, some means of defence.

Her flaying hand caught against something. She dimly recognised it as the alabaster figure of the Madonna and Child. Automatically, her fingers closed on it and she swung it up like a club. She struck the figure where she thought the side of the head would be.

She was surprised at the shock of the impact. The alabaster seemed to shatter into pieces, as she would have expected from a plaster statuette, but its impact seemed firm and weighty, causing a vibration in her hand and arm. The sound was like a sickening smack of flesh meeting a hard substance.

The figure grunted, a curious sound as the air was sharply expelled from his lungs. Then he dropped to the floor. She heard the sound of metal ringing on the floor planks as the knife dropped and bounced.

Fidelma stood for a moment or two, shoulders heaving as she sought to recover her breath and control her pounding emotions.

Slowly she walked to the foot of the stairs and called up in a firm voice.

'You can come down now. I have laid your ghost!'

She turned, stumbling a little in the darkness, until she found a candle and lit it. Then she went back to the figure of her erstwhile assailant. He lay on his side, hands outstretched. He was a young man. She gave a soft intake of breath when she saw the ugly wound on his temple. She reached forward and felt for a pulse. There was none.

She looked round curiously. The impact of a plaster statuette could not have caused such a death blow.

Fragments and powdered plaster were scattered in a large area. But there, lying in the debris was a long cylindrical tube of sacking. It was no more than a foot high and perhaps one inch in diameter. Fidelma bent and picked it up. It was heavy. She sighed and replaced it where she had found it.

Monchae and Belach were creeping down the stairs now.

'Belach, have you a lantern?' asked Fidelma, as she stood up.

'Yes. What is it?' demanded the innkeeper.

'Light it, if you please. I think we have solved your haunting.'

As she spoke she turned and walked across the floor to the spot where she had seen the figure rise, as if from the floor. There was a trap-door and beneath it some steps which led into a tunnel.

Belach had lit the lamp.

'What has happened?' he demanded.

'Your ghost was simply a man,' Fidelma explained.

Monchae let out a moan.

'You mean it is Mugrán? He was not killed at Loch Derg?'

Fidelma perched herself on the edge of the table and shook her head. She stooped to pick up the pipes where the figure had dropped them on the table.

'No; it was someone who looked and sounded a little like Mugrán as you knew him. Take a look at his face, Monchae. I think you will recognise Cano, Mugrán's younger brother.'

A gasp of astonishment from the woman confirmed Fidelma's identification.

'But why, what . . .?'

'A sad but simple tale. Cano was not killed as reported at Loch Derg. He was probably badly wounded and returned to this land with a limp. I presume that he did not have a limp when he went away?'

'He did not,' Monchae confirmed.

'Mugrán was dead. He took Mugrán's pipes. Why he took so long to get back here, we shall never know. Perhaps he did not need money until now, or perhaps the idea never occurred to him . . .'

'I don't understand,' Monchae said, collapsing into a chair by the table.

'Cano remembered that Mugrán had some money. A lot of money he had saved. Mugrán told you that if he lost his life, then there was money in the inn and you would never want for anything. Isn't that right?'

Monchae made an affirmative gesture. 'But as I told you, it was just Mugrán's fantasy. We searched the inn everywhere and could find no sign of any money. Anyway, my man, Belach, and I are content with things as they are.'

Fidelma smiled softly.

'Perhaps it was when Cano realised that you had not found his brother's hoard that he made up his mind to find it himself.'

'But it isn't here,' protested Belach, coming to the support of his wife.

'But it *was*,' insisted Fidelma. 'Cano knew it. But he didn't know where. He needed time to search. How could he get you away from the inn sufficiently long to search? That was when he conceived a convoluted idea to drive you out by pretending to be the ghost of his brother. He had his brother's pipes and could play the same tunes as his brother had played. His appearance and his voice made him pass for the person you once knew, Monchae, but, of course, only at a distance with muffled voice. He began to haunt you.'

'What of the shimmering effect?' demanded Belach. 'How could he produce such an effect?'

'I have seen a yellow clay-like substance that gives off that curious luminosity,' Fidelma assured them. 'It can be scooped from the walls of the caves west of here. It is called *mearnáil*, a phosphorus, a substance that glows in the gloom. If you examine Cano's cloak you will see that he has smeared it in this yellowing clay.'

'But he left no footprints,' protested Belach. 'He left no footprints in the snow.'

'But he did leave some tell-tale sign,' Fidelma pointed out. 'You see, he took the branch of a bush and, as he walked backwards away from the knoll, he swept away his footprints. But while it does disguise the footprints, one can still see the ruffled surface of the snow where the bush has swept over its top layer. It is an old trick, taught to warriors, to hide their tracks from their enemies.'

'But surely he could not survive in the cold outside all these nights?' Monchae said. It was the sort of aspect which would strike a woman's precise and practical logic.

'He did not. He slept in the inn, or at least in the stable. Once or twice he tried to search the inn while you lay asleep. Hence the bumps and sounds that sometimes awakened you. But he knew, however, that he could only search properly if he could move you out.'

'He was here with us in the inn?' Belach was aghast.

Fidelma nodded to the open trap-door in the floor.

'It seemed that he knew more of the secret passages of the inn than either of you. After all, Cano was brought up here.'

There was a silence.

Monchae gave a low sigh.

'All that and there was no treasure. Poor Cano. He was not really evil. Did you have to kill him, Sister?'

Fidelma compressed her lips for a moment.

'Everything is in God's hands,' she said in resignation. 'In my struggle, I seized the statuette of Our Lady and struck out at Cano. It caught him on the temple and fragmented.'

'But it was only alabaster. It would not have killed him, surely?'

'It was what was inside that killed him. The very thing he was looking for. It lies there on the floor.'

'What is it?' whispered Monchae, when Belach reached down to pick up the cylindrical object in sackcloth.

'It is a roll of coins. It is Mugrán's treasure. It acted as a bar of metal to the head of Cano and killed him. Our Lady had been protecting the treasure all these years and, in the final analysis, Our Lady meted out death to him that was not rightful heir to that treasure.'

Fidelma suddenly saw the light creeping in through the shutters of the inn.

'And now day is breaking. I need to break my fast and be on my way to Cashel. I'll leave a note for your *bó-aire* explaining matters. But I have urgent business in Cashel. If he wants me, I shall be there.'

Monchae stood regarding the shattered pieces of the statuette.

'I will have a new statuette of Our Lady made,' she said softly.

'You can afford it now,' replied Fidelma solemnly.

Acknowledgements

'Hemlock at Vespers' – originally appeared in *Midwinter Mysteries 3*, edited by Hilary Hale (UK: Little, Brown 1993); first USA publication in *Murder Most Irish*, edited by Ed Gorman, Larry Segriff and Martin H. Greenberg (Barnes & Noble, 1996)

'The High King's Sword' – originally published in *The Mammoth Book of Historical Whodunnits*, edited by Mike Ashley (UK: Robinson, 1993; USA: Carroll & Graf, 1993)

'Murder in Repose' – originally published in *Great Irish Detective Stories*, edited by Peter Haining (UK: Souvenir Press, 1993)

'Murder by Miracle' – originally published in *Constable New Crimes 2*, edited by Maxim Jakubowski (UK: Constable, 1993); first USA publication in *The Year's Best Mystery & Suspense Stories*, edited by Edward D. Hoch (Walker & Co., 1994)

'A Canticle for Wulfstan' – originally published in *Midwinter Mysteries 4*, edited by Hilary Hale (UK: Little, Brown, 1994); first USA publication in *Ellery Queen's Mystery Magazine* (May, 1994)

'Abbey Sinister' – originally published in *The Mammoth Book of Historical Detectives*, edited by Mike Ashley (UK: Robinson, 1995; USA: Carroll & Graf, 1995)

'The Poisoned Chalice' – originally published in *Classical*

Whodunnits, edited by Mike Ashley (UK: Robinson, 1996; USA; Carroll & Graf 1996)

'Tarnished Halo' – originally published in *Midwinter Mysteries 5*, edited by Hilary Hale (UK: Little, Brown, 1995)

'The Horse that Died for Shame' – originally published in *Murder at the Races*, edited by Peter Haining (UK: Orion, 1995)

'At the Tent of Holofernes' – originally published in *Ellery Queen's Mystery Magazine* (USA: December, 1998)

'A Scream from the Sepulchre' – originally published in *Ellery Queen's Mystery Magazine* (USA: May, 1998)

'Invitation to a Poisoning' – originally published in *Past Poisons*, edited by Maxim Jakubowski (UK: Headline, 1998)

'Those that Trespass' – originally published in *Chronicles of Crime*, edited by Maxim Jakubowski (UK: Headline, 1999)

'Holy Blood' – originally published in *Great Irish Stories of Murder and Mystery*, edited by Peter Haining (UK: Souvenir Press, 1999)

'Our Lady of Death' – originally published in *Dark Detectives*, edited by Steve Jones (USA: Fedogan & Bremer, 1999)

If you enjoyed this book here is a selection of other bestselling titles from Headline

THE DEMON ARCHER	Paul Doherty	£5.99 ☐
JANE AND THE GENIUS OF THE PLACE	Stephanie Barron	£5.99 ☐
PAST POISONS	Ed. Maxim Jakubowski	£5.99 ☐
SQUIRE THROWLEIGH'S HEIR	Michael Jecks	£5.99 ☐
THE COMPLAINT OF THE DOVE	Hannah March	£5.99 ☐
THE FOXES OF WARWICK	Edward Marston	£5.99 ☐
BEDFORD SQUARE	Anne Perry	£5.99 ☐
THE GERMANICUS MOSAIC	Rosemary Rowe	£5.99 ☐
THE CONCUBINE'S TATTOO	Laura Joh Rowland	£5.99 ☐
THE WEAVER'S INHERITANCE	Kate Sedley	£5.99 ☐
SEARCH THE DARK	Charles Todd	£5.99 ☐
THE MONK WHO VANISHED	Peter Tremayne	£5.99 ☐

Headline books are available at your local bookshop or newsagent. Alternatively, books can be ordered direct from the publisher. Just tick the titles you want and fill in the form below. Prices and availability subject to change without notice.

Buy four books from the selection above and get free postage and packaging and delivery within 48 hours. Just send a cheque or postal order made payable to Bookpoint Ltd to the value of the total cover price of the four books. Alternatively, if you wish to buy fewer than four books the following postage and packaging applies:

UK and BFPO £4.30 for one book; £6.30 for two books; £8.30 for three books.

Overseas and Eire: £4.80 for one book; £7.10 for 2 or 3 books (surface mail).

Please enclose a cheque or postal order made payable to *Bookpoint Limited*, and send to: Headline Publishing Ltd, 39 Milton Park, Abingdon, OXON OX14 4TD, UK.
Email Address: orders@bookpoint.co.uk

If you would prefer to pay by credit card, our call team would be delighted to take your order by telephone. Our direct line is 01235 400 414 (lines open 9.00 am–6.00 pm Monday to Saturday 24 hour message answering service). Alternatively you can send a fax on 01235 400 454.

Name ....

Address ....

....

....

If you would prefer to pay by credit card, please complete:
Please debit my Visa/Access/Diner's Card/American Express (delete as applicable) card number:

															.		

Signature .... Expiry Date ....